"Five thousand pounds?"

"So you would steal from me and then overcharge me to recover my own goods?"

She looked him right in the eye. "Once again, I did not steal anything from you, or from anyone else. Make me a counteroffer, or bid me good day and leave."

Incredulous, he shook his head. "This is ridiculous." He grabbed her hand, pulling her up against him. "You're not frightened of me, are you?" he murmured.

"Is this your intent? I'd heard you were a fearsome opponent, but you seem to be harping on one point of contention, which does neither of us any good. Make me a counteroffer, my lord."

He lowered his head and kissed her upturned mouth. Sensation flooded through him. He didn't know how to describe what she tasted like—sunshine, warm summer breezes, heat, desire.

When she began to kiss him back, he forced himself to lift his face away again.

"How was that?" he drawled.

Sarala cleared her throat, belatedly recovering her hand and backing away.

"Fair. But hardly worth five thousand pounds."

By Suzanne Enoch

SOMETHING SINFUL
DON'T LOOK DOWN
AN INVITATION TO SIN
FLIRTING WITH DANGER
SIN AND SENSIBILITY
ENGLAND'S PERFECT HERO
LONDON'S PERFECT SCOUNDREL
THE RAKE
A MATTER OF SCANDAL
MEET ME AT MIDNIGHT
REFORMING A RAKE
TAMING RAFE
BY LOVE UNDONE
STOLEN KISSES
LADY ROGUE

Coming in November 2006
The Exciting Contemporary Romance

BILLIONAIRES PREFER BLONDES

Suzanne Enoch

Something Sinful

AVON BOOKS
An Imprint of HarperCollins*Publishers*

AVON BOOKS
An Imprint of HarperCollins *Publishers*
10 East 53rd Street
New York, New York 10022-5299

ISBN-13: 978-0-7394-7408-2

Printed in the U.S.A.

To my sister, Nancy, for spending two weeks in England with me and not minding that I had to go into every bookstore between Salisbury and London.

And to our Blue Badge guide, Bryan Gorin, who knows the coolest stuff and *drives a London taxi—even if he does take it on the wrong side of the street.*

Chapter 1

"Caine, where the devil are my boots?" Charlemagne Griffin bent to look beneath his bed, flinging up the blankets and groping into the murkiness. His fingers touched a lone book, but no boots.

"They're on their way up, my lord," the valet returned in his light Irish lilt, his expression horrified as he gazed at his master rooting about the bedchamber. "We had some difficulty getting that mud off them after your trip to Tattersall's."

Charlemagne straightened, dusting off his pantaloons. He flipped over the book he'd found to look at the cover. *A Hundred Days in Rome.* So that was where he'd left the damned thing. "Go encourage them to hurry," he said absently, settling on the corner of the bed and flipping the book open. "I refuse to be teased for being unable to dress faster than a female."

Caine stooped in a bow, backing out the door as he did so. "Right away, m'lord."

A knock came at his bedchamber door just as Charlemagne had begun reacquainting himself with day thirty-seven in an adventurer's exploration of Rome. "Enter," he said, looking up from the book.

His younger brother, Zachary, strolled into the room. "You can't go to a party in your stockings, Shay."

"My thanks. I'd be a social pariah without you."

Zach nodded. "Glad you realized that." He wandered closer. "Rumor has it that you were busy today."

"Is that your way of saying that you heard I purchased Dooley's bay hunter?"

"Aha. As soon as I came across Dooley in White's, and he was practically in tears over letting the horse go at such an abysmal price, I *knew* it had to be you who bought it."

Charlemagne smiled. "It *was* a good price, if I say so myself."

"So tell me your secret. Do you use witchcraft to put spells on your opponents? I can't think of any other reason that otherwise sensible men would sell you the entire moon for a stick and a broken wheel."

"I wouldn't have much use for the moon."

The valet scratched at the door and pushed it open. "Your boots, my lord. Good as new."

Looking over Caine's head as the valet knelt to shove on the Hobys, Charlemagne chuckled. "Since you asked, Zach, the secret is patience. Patience and observation. A hunter at any price, for instance, is no good to a man who can't afford to pay his household wages."

"That sounds a bit coldhearted."

"That's why we call it business, and not pleasure." Charlemagne stood, stomping into his left boot. "Besides, Dooley's hunter wasn't my only target for the day. I—"

"For God's sake," Zachary cut in, leading the way out to the stairs, "we're going to a party. I don't want to have to look at all the other guests and secretly know how many of them you've ground into dust during the course of the day."

"Fine," Charlemagne returned with a half scowl, somewhat amazed that, with Zachary's aversion to the harsh realities of business, his younger brother had managed to survive long enough to marry. "I don't expect you to be able to grasp the nuances of a business deal."

"Good. Tell someone smarter than I am."

"That hardly narrows it down."

From the noise at the foot of the stairs, the rest of the Griffin clan had arrived. Over the past year their family had expanded by two—Eleanor's husband, Valentine Corbett, Marquis of Deverill; and Zachary's wife, Caroline. Happy as he was for his siblings, at times Charlemagne could do without the resulting chaos.

"There you are, Shay," Eleanor said, sweeping forward to kiss him on the cheek.

"You look lovely, Nell, as do you, Caroline." His gaze found Sebastian, the Duke of Melbourne. Their eldest sibling, Seb was the only other Griffin who shared his own affection for business. The duke stood in his office doorway with Valentine. Charlemagne joined them. "How was your meeting with Liverpool?" he asked.

"Promising," the duke returned. "I think he's finally beginning to realize that pride is no reason to keep from doing business with the Colonies."

"Pride might not be a reason, but lack of imagination is even more difficult to overcome," Charlemagne put in.

"You won't hear me arguing with that. How did your own venture go today?"

Zachary came up behind Shay and clapped him on the shoulder. "He made Dooley cry. I saw it myself."

Satisfying as it had been to acquire a prime hunter for a great deal less than it was worth, his second trip out had been far more interesting, and with far more possibilities. Charlemagne stifled a frown. "Dooley didn't have to accept my offer. As for my conversation with Cap—"

"Did Valentine tell you his news?" Melbourne broke in.

"The news is hardly the sole property of Valentine," Eleanor said, moving forward to take her husband's arm.

Zachary whooped, pounding Valentine on the back. "You old dog. And to think that a year ago the idea of marriage made you shriek like a chit."

"And now I seem to be procreating. It's been an odd twelve months," the marquis agreed, lowering his head to kiss Eleanor. "Glad I didn't miss it."

"Mm, so am I," she returned, chuckling.

Charlemagne took a step back as the congratulations circled around and around. Another member of the family. The babe wouldn't bear the Griffin name, but it would carry on the Griffin bloodline, just as Melbourne's seven-year-old daughter Penelope did. And from Caroline's expression, whatever she'd said about not having room in her life to be domestic, the thought was beginning to cross *her* mind, as well. Good. The more the merrier, he supposed.

The talk turned to baby names, for which Valentine was apparently willing to accept bribes, and Charlemagne backed to the front door. "I'm supposed to meet with Shipley in twenty minutes," he said in a low voice to the butler as Stanton handed him his hat and gloves. "I won't disturb their fun, but if anyone should miss me, tell them I went on ahead to the party."

Stanton nodded. "Very good, my lord."

The quiet and cool evening breeze of the front portico felt welcome, and Charlemagne paused on the shallow granite steps to take a deep breath. Three coaches stood awaiting passengers, and he walked to the one at the fore. "Let's go," he said, climbing in.

To himself he could admit he felt a bit irked that Melbourne had cut off his description of this afternoon's business dealings, especially after his brother had been the one to ask about them in the first place. Ah, well. At eight-and-twenty he hardly needed anyone's approval or affirmation of his skills—though a little appreciation would have been nice. Babies did trump just about everything but a Derby victory, though. Charlemagne smiled as he pulled a cigar from his pocket and lit it on the coach lantern. Just about everything. He preferred a good negotiation, himself.

The Brinston butler announced him as he entered the ballroom, and Charlemagne found himself engulfed by the crowd. When he finally emerged at the refreshment table on the far side of the room, he'd put his name on three chits' dance cards, delayed Lord Shipley and Lord Polk until luncheon tomorrow, and given the prime minister, Liverpool, a pair of his best American cigars. That might help the man see Melbourne's point of view about trade and tariffs.

He glanced toward the door as he signaled for a glass of claret, but the remainder of the extended Griffin clan hadn't yet arrived. Sebastian would probably be annoyed that one of the group had fled the house, but as far as Charlemagne was concerned, a bachelor was only supposed to be able to stand so much domestically oriented news.

Someone gripped his elbow, and he nearly spilled the claret. His older brother had a reputation for being something of a mind reader, but he could hardly simply materialize. Probably not, anyway. As Charlemagne turned around he smiled, his curiosity turning to vexation. This was much worse than facing an annoyed Sebastian. "Harkley," he said, reaching over to shake the hand of the portly gentleman before him. "I thought you still in Madrid."

The viscount made a face, jowls wobbling. "Too damned much talk about Bonaparte. Came back for a bloody taste of civilization."

"I'm afraid that you'll find much of the talk here is about Bonaparte, as well," Charlemagne returned.

"Your brother about?"

"Melbourne? He hasn't arrived yet." Hm. Liverpool detested Harkley, and at the moment Sebastian needed the prime minister's cooperation. Thinking quickly, Charlemagne gave a pained smile. "When he does appear, you may want to avoid him. He's been a bit sour-faced the last few days. Tariff disagreements, a new war with the Colonies. Mostly annoyances, but there is all that possible bloodshed and loss of life."

Harkley toasted him with his own glass of spirits. "My thanks for the warning. I certainly don't want His Grace snarling at me before I can even say hello."

"Glad I could be of help. You . . ."

A splash of color flickered in front of the refreshment table, drawing his gaze. Whatever he'd been about to say, he forgot. A goddess stood taking a delicate bite of candied orange peel. No, not a goddess, Charlemagne amended after a moment. Definitely a female of flesh and blood. Lightning shot from the back of his skull to his groin. Good God.

"—who can afford that without a partner to invest some additional blunt?" Harkley was saying.

Charlemagne handed him the half-empty glass of claret. "Excuse me."

In a few steps he stood across the table from her. Hair black as midnight coiled about her head and ended in a tail banded by a long, narrow shaft of gold running down along the small of her back. Gold sparkled on her eyelids, the soft glitter taken up by beading throughout the length of her deep red gown. Eyes as green and bottomless as pools of emeralds flicked past him and then returned.

Down, lad, he ordered himself, and inclined his head to her.

She'd never been to a London Society gathering before. He knew that, because he attended most of them. If she'd shown her face anywhere, he would have seen her. And if he'd seen her, he would have remembered.

"You're staring," she said, a slight, exotic upturn of an accent buried beneath her proper English tones.

"Yes, I seem to be," he returned. Not just her voice, but the whole of her felt almost tangibly exotic, foreign, and enticing. Epithets like "goddess" or "Aphrodite" or "Venus" flew through his mind, but he just as swiftly disregarded them. She'd probably been endlessly bombarded by poetry and flattery, and that wasn't his style, anyway. Getting what he wanted—and taking whatever steps were necessary to accomplish that goal—*that* was his style. "I'm Charlemagne Griffin."

She lifted a glittering eyebrow. " 'Charlemagne'?"

He liked the way she said his name. Suppressing another faint shudder of his muscles, he circled the table to stand directly in front of her, speaking as he did so. "My mother's idea. Father named my oldest brother after himself and his own father, and so she decided that if I couldn't have the family name, I should have a famous one. My friends call me Shay." He took a slow step closer, reaching out for her hand and brushing her knuckles softly with his lips. "And who might you be?"

At that she blinked and glanced about as though she'd just realized she was forgetting something. Was she spoken for? Had some lord imported her from somewhere without the rest of them getting so much as a look at her? Nonterritorial about females as he generally considered himself, the idea frustrated and annoyed him. He waited silently, though, for her to make the next step. If she was spoken for, he was fully prepared to detest her betrothed, but he didn't poach. Not ever.

She faced him again. "Shouldn't a mutual acquaintance be introducing us?"

At least she hadn't thrown a fiancé in his face. Charlemagne shrugged, adamantly opposed to the idea of adding *any* third person to their conversation. "In the grand scheme of things, I doubt it will matter that we've done it ourselves. Pray tell me your name."

She bit her lower lip, then seemed to think better of that. "My mother warned me about men like you, very forward and sure of themselves and uncaring of a lady's reputation."

Now she seemed to be baiting him. "Tell me your mother's name," he returned. "Then I would at least have a clue as to your identity."

"Very well," she said with a smile that could have melted a stone statue. "My mother is Helen Carlisle, Marchioness of Hanover."

This time Charlemagne frowned. He knew England's peers; with his family's connections, he doubted there were any nobles he *didn't* know. "The Marquis of Hanover died a bachelor, just over a year ago."

The temptress nodded. "My father, Howard, was his younger brother."

Now things were beginning to make sense. "Your father lived in India."

"As did my mother and I. We've only been in London for ten days."

He'd been right about her *being* exotic rather than merely *looking* that way. Unable to resist, he brushed a finger along the beading at the shoulder of her gown. He could swear he scented cinnamon in the air around her. "Have you, now? Ten days only?"

Her dark-lined eyes met his. "Ten days. We've only just opened the house, and I have to admit that I'm acquainted with barely a soul."

Good. All the more for him. "I would call us acquainted if you'd only tell me your name," he suggested in a low voice.

She looked up at him through dark, curling lashes. "Very well. Sarala. Sarala Anne Carlisle."

Charlemagne drew a slow breath, absorbing the information. " 'Sarala'?"

"My father's idea. Mother thought it was too native, but we never expected to leave Delhi."

"Sarala," he said again, savoring the way it rolled along his tongue. Just the sound of it conjured images of brightly colored saris and spicy curry and naked, sultry nights. "Lady Sarala. It suits you."

"Hm. As I'm beginning to believe Charlemagne suits you. You're very sure of yourself, aren't you?"

Shay lifted an eyebrow. Obviously she didn't have the least idea who he was. "I'm not certain that's a compliment, though some members of my family might appreciate it." He chuckled. "My older brother, especially."

"The one with the family's traditional Christian name. Who might he be? I've told you my family history. It's only fair that you divulge yours."

He hesitated. Charlemagne had no objection at all to being the second son and heir-presumptive to the Melbourne title. But if Lady Sarala Carlisle knew his heritage, she might not speak to him with the same refreshing freedom.

"Come now. Don't tell me you're a tailor masquerading as a nobleman," Lady Sarala cajoled.

"Hardly." The orchestra began a waltz, and he took her hand again, placing it over the dark blue sleeve of his superfine jacket. "I'll tell you while we dance."

"That's very forward of you. What if I've given this dance to someone else?"

He looked down at her. "You haven't."

"And you know this because . . ."

"Because you barely know a soul in London. You just said so." So she wasn't the sharpest knife on the rack. Something about her conjured images of warm nights and soft silk sheets.

"I'm not at all certain this is proper."

"It is," he returned, drawing her closer. Whatever odd sensation had overcome him this evening, he intended to enjoy it. Charlemagne slid his hand around her slender waist—and stopped as a hand clamped down on his shoulder.

"I'm occu—" he began as he looked behind him. "Oh, it's you."

Sebastian glanced from him to Lady Sarala and back again. "What's amiss?"

Charlemagne tried to set aside his own mental debate over whether Melbourne had fantastical or abysmal timing.

"Nothing's amiss. I told Shipley I'd speak with him at nine o'clock, and you were naming offspring."

"I believe you were going to tell me about that silk sh—"

"Later," Charlemagne interrupted, flashing an unfelt grin at his brother. "As I said, I'm occupied."

With a lifted eyebrow and one of his unreadable looks, Sebastian backed off. *Ha.* Shay didn't need to be placated like an infant. And if Melbourne genuinely wanted to know about the silks, he could wait until after the waltz. Charlemagne swept Lady Sarala into the dance.

"Who was that?" Lady Sarala asked, looking from him to Sebastian.

"My brother, Melbourne."

Her green eyes widened a little. "Melbourne, as in Sebastian Griffin, the Duke of Melbourne?"

So the foreign princess *did* know something of London Society. "I told you I wasn't a tailor."

"Yes, but I didn't realize you were one of *those* Griffins. You're famous. Your brother married a painter last year."

"Not *that* brother," Charlemagne returned, indicating Melbourne, "but yes. Zachary did."

Her gaze went to Sebastian again. "He doesn't look very pleased with you. It's not because we're dancing, is it?"

"I daresay I may dance with whomever I please," he noted, sinking back into the humming, expectant energy between them. Damn Melbourne, anyway. At three-and-thirty Sebastian looked precisely like what he was—the very wealthy head of a powerful and well-favored family, and obviously a distracting personage to a naive and exotic foreign beauty. "He's only annoyed because tomorrow I'm going to make a very lucrative business deal that he doesn't know the least detail about. He hates being kept in the dark."

Green eyes gazed at him luminously. "How exciting," she

breathed, her chest rising and falling with her quick breath. "Is this deal a secret, then?"

So now she found him more interesting than Melbourne again. *Good.* "No," he answered, considering. "Not really."

Her lips formed a slight, disappointed pout. "Oh."

Damnation. "I mean in a sense, I suppose it is a secret," he amended hastily. Zachary was right; sometimes he could be very obtuse about women and their flighty imaginations. He hardly considered it to be his fault, however, that most females found business far beyond their ability to comprehend or appreciate. In this one instance he could decorate the canvas a little, he supposed. "If the wrong people should hear about it, the price of the shipment would treble."

" 'Shipment'?" she repeated in a low voice. "Is it from America?"

"No, from China."

"Oh, I've always longed to visit China," she exclaimed, though she kept her voice low.

She was taking this "secret" silliness seriously. Charlemagne smiled at her. "Just between you and me, then, the ship *Wayward* docked at Blackfriar's this afternoon. Her cargo is five hundred bolts of the very finest Chinese silk I've ever set eyes on. The captain's sold cargo to me before, so I'm the only one he contacted." He lowered his voice still further, though with the noise from the orchestra and the guests around them, he doubted anyone could overhear even if they wanted to. It sounded very conspiratorial, at any rate, and it gave him an excuse to hold her a little closer in his arms.

"Blink," he continued, "bought the bolts outright rather—"

"Blink?" she broke in at a whisper.

"Peter Blink. The *Wayward*'s captain. He bought the shipment outright rather than taking a percentage for the transportation of the cargo . . ." Charlemagne trailed off, realizing that he was getting carried away again. She probably had no idea about the intricacies of business, and even less interest in them. She wanted to hear about intrigue and secrets. Little as he liked pointless flights of fancy, tonight he definitely felt in the mood to indulge this particular Indian princess.

He drew a breath. "So our captain is very eager to sell and recoup his expenses so he can pay his crew before they mutiny."

"A mutiny?"

"Oh, definitely, if he can't pay them. But since I am very eager to take possession of the silks, I doubt anyone will be gulleted."

Lady Sarala clutched his fingers. "And when is this duel to prevent a gulleting to take place?"

"At ten o'clock tomorrow, which is why I won't make an appearance until three-quarters past."

"Goodness," she breathed. "And that will make Captain Blink even more anxious and cause him to lower his price further."

"That's the idea," he responded. Women might not have an interest in business, but they did appreciate power and confidence. Lady Sarala obviously realized that he had those qualities in spades.

"That's brilliant." She smiled again, her teeth white against skin tanned by the Indian sun. "And you do this sort of thing all the time?"

Charlemagne nodded. "All the time," he murmured.

"Your brother the duke must rely on you for so much."

And now back to Sebastian, damn it all. "He does rely on me, but these silks are my affair. I have my own business in addition to shares in the family enterprise." In fact, this wasn't part of the general Griffin family business. It was his own venture, his own risk, with his own blunt.

She continued to gaze at him admiringly. "Your mother did name you well, Lord Charlemagne."

If he'd been a female, he would have blushed. For the briefest of moments, though, Charlemagne wished the Indian princess had more to contribute to the conversation than compliments and a pleasantly heaving bosom. True, he didn't expect much of most women—his sister Eleanor and Zach's Caroline being exceptions to the rule of the prettier the face, the emptier the head—but that was exactly the reason his affairs tended to be brief and of secondary importance to the rest of his life. She would look very fine spread on his bedsheets, but if she could actually have comprehended his plan in more than the broad terms he'd laid out for her, this one would have been difficult to set aside.

The waltz ended, and at her request he escorted her to the refreshments table. Whatever doubts he had about her mental acuity, he still couldn't seem to make himself bid her good evening. "Are you residing at Carlisle House, then?" he asked.

"We are."

"Perhaps you wouldn't object if I called on you there."

She lowered glittering lids. "Perhaps I wouldn't."

Charlemagne's partner for the country dance cleared her throat from a few feet away, and he blinked. "Then perhaps I shall see you soon, Lady Sarala," he murmured, kissing her knuckles again before he reluctantly released her.

As he moved through the country dance he noted that his princess remained unpartnered by the sweetmeats. It made sense; as she'd said she'd hardly had the time to become acquainted with anyone. And her appearance, while definitely . . . stimulating, could be a bit off-putting to some of the younger bucks. He definitely wouldn't classify her as demure. Electrifying, perhaps, but not demure.

When he'd discharged his obligation for the next two dances, Charlemagne went out to the balcony for a breath of air. All evening long he could swear the scent of cinnamon clung to him, and it continued to leave him distinctly and uncharacteristically distracted.

"I'm not going to resort to dancing with you to get an answer," Sebastian said, joining him at the balcony railing.

"Good God, I should hope not," Charlemagne retorted.

"If you'd stayed home for another five minutes, I would have gotten to you, you know. A child for Eleanor is somewhat significant to her—and to all of us."

"I'm aware of that." He gave the duke a sideways look. "And I hope I haven't given the impression that I require your approval before I venture any of my own blunt."

"You never have before," Sebastian conceded. "You're a fine businessman, Shay, as if you needed the reassurance." He sighed uncharacteristically. "Honestly, with the way Zachary's been cornering me about his cattle breeding program, and now Nell with baby names, or ponies from Peep—well, my daughter comes first, of course—or *your* exploits, it's not much of a contest."

Charlemagne grinned. "So I may tell Zach and Nell that other than Peep, I'm your favorite?"

"Very amusing. At times you are the only one with any sense. I'll grant you that. So tell me about the silks."

"Not much to tell yet," Charlemagne returned, shrugging, "except that I should be the proud owner of five hundred bolts by eleven o'clock tomorrow morning." He glanced at his older brother. "And I did have to meet with Shipley. I put him off until luncheon tomorrow. I wasn't sulking."

"I didn't think you were, but your disappearance did

surprise me a little." The duke put an arm around his shoulder. "Let's find some port to toast your success-to-be then, shall we?"

"By all means."

And if Lady Sarala's "perhaps" meant what he thought it did, they might very well be toasting his private success-to-be, as well. At any rate, he intended to have cinnamon in his tea in the morning.

Chapter 2

"What do you mean, you already sold the silks?"

Captain Peter Blink sat back in his chair, his suntanned face growing pale. "Well, uh, the other gentleman said you, uh, weren't coming, so . . . so naturally when he offered to purchase the—"

"*What* other gentleman?" Charlemagne demanded, his voice clipped as he struggled not to strike the *Wayward*'s captain.

"The one—he was just here. Surely you passed him on your way in. I didn't know—well, he said you—"

Snarling an expletive, Charlemagne strode out of Blink's ramshackle warehouse office and back outside into the bright morning sun. Narrowing his eyes, he cast about for the man he'd barely given a first thought, much less a second. Tall, wearing dark, not terribly well-tailored clothes, a satchel—

There he was. Clenching his jaw, Shay started after him. This damned interloper and Blink had both just earned themselves a very large problem with a very angry Griffin.

A half-dozen sailors and dockworkers had begun loading bolts of silk—*his* silk—into a pair of wagons. Just in front of them, the tall man leaned into the window of a closed coach and handed over some papers to the occupant. Charlemagne slowed his approach to watch. Angry or not, he wasn't a fool; the more he knew about the circumstances, the better his position would be. And damned Blink was the one who had blundered and sold the shipment out from under him; this fellow and whomever he worked for had merely taken advantage of that fact.

After a short conversation and a nod, the tall man pulled open the coach door and climbed in. Shay moved closer, dodging the workers who carried away his bolts of silk. He was rarely outmaneuvered, and he had a perverse desire to have a word with the fellow who had accomplished that feat today.

The coach began to rumble off, and he quickened his pace to a half run. "You there!" he shouted. "Stop that coach!" With a look back at him the driver pulled the team in, and Charlemagne drew even with the door. "Look here, there's been some sort of mis—"

He stopped dead as all three of the coach's occupants looked up at him. The tall man, a female clearly dressed as a maid, and the third one. *Her.* The Indian princess. The subject of the rather heated dream he'd had last night.

"You?" he stammered.

"Good morning, my lord," she said coolly, and rapped on the window with gloved knuckles. "Driver, carry on."

"Just a damned minute, Sarala," Charlemagne returned, striding after the coach. "You are not—"

She leaned out the window. “Oh, and thank you for the very helpful information, my lord,” she called, and disappeared inside again.

Several distinct and unpleasant thoughts roiled through his mind. So the chit thought she could best him—and taunt him. Charlemagne began to curse again. Moving fast and barely refraining from shoving people out of his way, he returned to where he’d left his horse Jaunty and his secretary Roberts, along with the men he’d hired to transport the silks.

“That was very quickly done, my lo—”

“Wait here,” he snapped at his secretary, swinging into the saddle. Not even the profanity spewing from beneath his breath could cool his temper. Sarala Carlisle hadn’t just thought to—she actually *had* bested him. And his first impulse was to ride down her damned coach and break her bloody neck.

Before he’d ridden beyond the end of the warehouse, though, Charlemagne slowed Jaunty to a halt. Angry—no, furious—as he was, first and foremost he was a Griffin. And Griffins didn’t kill people over business. Not unless they truly deserved it. And technically this was his fault. He’d discussed business with a lovely, simple chit only to discover that while she was indeed beautiful, he’d apparently erred in his assessment of her intelligence.

He pulled out his pocket watch. *Damnation.* He had a perplexed secretary and several laborers waiting for him, and a luncheon appointment with two commerce ministers. Slowly he turned the chestnut around and walked back to where Roberts waited. After luncheon, however, he had every intention of tracking down that blasted woman and getting his bloody shipment back.

* * *

Lady Sarala couldn't help looking down the street as a footman opened the coach's door and helped her to the ground. "Is my father in, Blankman?" she called to the butler who stood at the top of the steps.

"Lord Hanover is in his office, my lady," the large, gray-liveried butler intoned, gesturing the coach around to the stables at the back of the house.

She glanced over her shoulder once more as she slipped through the front door and into the house's cold, dim interior. In the weeks since they'd left India she'd given up the hope of ever being truly warm again, but she couldn't help wishing for just one day of true heat here in London. And this was summer; even the idea of winter filled her with foreboding.

And so did her last sight of Lord Charlemagne Griffin. Obviously he hadn't expected to see her at Blackfriar's pier. But for heaven's sake, business was business, and he should have known better than to tell a stranger all the details of a lucrative transaction he'd barely begun, much less completed.

She had no idea what he would have done if she hadn't told the driver to leave. He'd looked angry enough to reach through the window to strangle her. The memory of his expression made her shiver. And even that was nothing close to the shivers he'd given her last night when he'd told her his plans to nab the silk—or when he'd kissed her knuckles.

"There you are, child," her mother said from the depths of the morning room. "Where on earth have you been?"

With a sigh Sarala backtracked down the hall and stopped in the morning room doorway. "I had a little business to attend to. Is Pita still in his office?"

" 'Papa,' you mean," Helen Carlisle, Lady Hanover, corrected, lowering her embroidery to frown. "Or 'Father.' "

"I like 'Papa' better," Sarala returned with a pained smile. For heaven's sake, she'd just forgotten for a moment. She'd called her father Pita for twenty-two years, after all.

"Then use 'Papa,'" her mother said unsympathetically. "And what do you mean, you had business? Ladies don't conduct business."

"I helped Pi— Papa with affairs in Delhi all the time. You know that."

"What I know is that we're not in Delhi any longer. We're in London, and thank goodness for that. Another year or two in India and I daresay you would have forgotten how to speak English altogether."

"Yes, *Mama*," Sarala intoned, declining to note that since the majority of her father's business had been with Indians, it had been a solid business decision for the two of them to learn to speak Hindi. "Is *Father* in his office?"

"He's back early from Parliament, so I imagine that he is. Don't keep him long. He's reviewing our finances."

"I won't." Pushing away from the doorframe, Sarala turned down the hallway again.

"Sarala."

Closing her eyes for just a moment as she felt the remains of her brief satisfaction of the morning ebbing, she returned to the morning room. "Yes, Mama?"

"This business to which you attended. Please tell me you didn't go alone."

"I met Mr. Warrick. He actually conducted the business. I waited in the coach with my maid." *And hated every blasted minute of that nonsense.*

"Good. Go see your father, then." The marchioness sighed, lifting her embroidery again. "You two are as alike as peas in a pod, anyway. I don't know how I manage."

Pretending she couldn't hear her mama's muttering,

Sarala hurried to the marquis's small office at the back of the house. "Pita," she whispered, rapping on the door and opening it a crack, "I'm back."

"Sarala, my *ladakii,*" Howard Carlisle, the new Marquis of Hanover, said, rising from behind his mahogany desk to kiss her cheek as she entered the room. "How did we do?"

Sarala handed him the leather binder she'd clutched all the way home, half convinced Lord Charlemagne would appear, wrench open the coach door, and take it from her. "You are now the proud owner of five hundred bolts of very fine Chinese silk. Warrick is putting it into storage as we speak."

"Ha, ha! Excellent." Seating himself again, he opened the binder to pull out the contents. "One guinea apiece. Not bad at all, *ladakii.*"

Sarala grinned, appeased again. "I had to send Warrick back to the table twice to get that price. He would have settled at a guinea, ten shillings."

"I don't doubt it. He knows numbers, but he hasn't much of a backbone."

"And I should warn you not to call me *ladakii* any longer," Sarala continued. "I've already been reprimanded for referring to you as Pita."

"So I suppose that henceforth I should settle for calling you 'daughter.' Ah, well. Your mama's only trying to help us fit in. We should be more appreciative."

"But I don't want to fit in. All I've heard since we left the ship is what proper English ladies *don't* do. And they apparently don't do anything except shop and gossip. It's ridiculous."

"It's the way things are, Sarala." He glanced at the open ledger books before him. "And I'm afraid we're here to stay. We'll have to adapt, you and I." The marquis cleared his throat. "Any difficulties at all? What about that fellow who told you about the shipment?"

Sarala shrugged, keeping her expression carefully bland. "He arrived late to the table. His loss. Our gain." She doubted the Duke of Melbourne's brother would describe the venture that way, but if he was half the businessman rumor made him out to be, he would realize that he'd erred and would give up his claim on the silks. Her last glimpse of his expression made her secretly doubt that, but if he didn't appear, then she wasn't going to say anything about it.

An hour and a half with the commerce ministry usually left Charlemagne happy as a cat with a bowl of cream. Not today, though. He'd barely managed to keep up his corner of the conversation, and he knew neither Polk nor Shipley had been keen on his views of the tariff conflicts with the United States, or whatever the Colonies were calling themselves these days.

He hadn't expected them to like his suggestions, but generally he went to the effort of charming them around to seeing his point of view. Today he'd spent the entire meeting doing nothing but imagining his hands around Sarala Carlisle's slender neck, or his mouth hard on hers, their naked bodies entwined in a hot, heaving p—

"How was luncheon?"

Starting, he looked up from tearing off his gloves and throwing them into the hat that Stanton the butler held silently for him. "What?"

"I asked how your meeting went," Sebastian said from the top of the Griffin House stairs. "Not well, I presume, judging from your expression."

"I thought you had Parliament."

"I did. We adjourned early. How did you think Polk and

Shipley managed to meet with you if we hadn't recessed?"

"Some people skip sessions."

"I don't." The duke waved a hand at Stanton, who instantly vanished down the hallway. "I know the idiots disagree with our stand that negotiations would serve us better than war, but that's hardly a surprise to you."

"Ha. Shipley still thinks America will return to the fold, the halfwit. He's worse than Liverpool, calling the Yanks traitors."

"What has your hackles up, then?"

"Nothing." Charlemagne started up the stairs, only refraining from taking them two at a time because Melbourne was watching him. "I'm only here to change my jacket. I've another appointment."

"With whom?"

With a damned Indian princess who owed him five hundred bolts of fine Chinese silk. "No one you know."

"I doubt that. I know everyone. You took care of your silk shipment this morning, so . . ." The duke gave him an intent look and paused.

Damn it, Sebastian couldn't read minds, and Charlemagne wasn't about to inform his older brother voluntarily about *anything* that had transpired this morning. "So?" he prompted.

"So I'm assuming your appointment is of a more personal nature. Whoever she is, Shay, if she makes you this angry I suggest you look elsewhere."

"It's business, not pleasure," Shay grunted, passing his brother and heading for his bedchamber. "And I'm not angry. I'm . . . focused."

"Ah," the duke said from behind him. "I see."

Actually he was feeling extremely unfocused. It was all

so damned odd, and he didn't appreciate the sensation or the circumstances one bloody little bit.

By the time he reached Carlisle House his brain had begun to sort things out rationally, and he was able to resist the urge to pound on the door and smash the pots of ferns on the front portico. The chit obviously ran wild, so he wouldn't deal with her. Business was business, and business was for men.

A large, gray-clothed man opened the door. "Yes?"

"Charlemagne Griffin, here to see Lord Hanover."

The butler blinked. Someone in the household knew him by name, at least. He stepped back, gesturing Charlemagne to follow him inside. "If you'll wait in the morning room, I shall fetch him."

The morning room was small, tasteful, and, unless he was mistaken, smelled of cinnamon. The scent forcibly reminded him of the chit who'd bested him. And considering what she'd been doing with him in his dreams, it almost felt like a double loss on his part. And he didn't like to lose.

Before the butler could finish closing him into the room, he heard a rush of footsteps and a hurried, muttered conversation. A second later the door swung open again, and the lady herself practically skidded into the room. She wore a frilled dressing gown, one sleeve hanging to reveal a tantalizing view of smooth collarbone and shoulder. That black hair was everywhere, half up and tumbled down, caressing her cheek and sagging into an unfinished knot at the back.

The angry comment Charlemagne had been about to make vanished back into his throat, making him cough a little. Glory.

Belatedly she tugged up her sleeve. "Lord Charlemagne."

Mentally he shook himself. *Business, man. Business.* "You stole my silks."

"I did no such thing. You informed me of a potentially lucrative business opportunity, and I acted on that information."

He narrowed his eyes. "I discussed my business with you because I was under the impression that you were an admirer—not a rival."

She snorted. "Then you made two mistakes."

Charlemagne took a step closer. "Where's your father? I came to speak with him, to discuss the return of my property in a rational manner."

Lady Sarala gave what might have been a brief frown, then lifted her chin. "This is *my* affair, and you will discuss it with me, or not at all."

Good God, she had some nerve. And her sleeve had sagged again, so that he could see the pulse at her throat and the quick lift of her breast. "Then return my property," he said, returning his gaze to her soft mouth.

"It's not your property. But for a price, I will let you have every stitch."

He knew he shouldn't ask, but he couldn't stop himself. "What price, then?"

"Five thousand pounds."

His jaw fell open, then clamped shut. "*Five thousand pounds?* So you would steal from me and then overcharge me to recover my own goods?"

She looked him right in the eye. "Once again, I did not steal anything from you, or from anyone else. Make me a counter offer, or bid me good day and leave."

Incredulous, he shook his head. "This is ridiculous. Where's the liquor?"

"Over there." Lady Sarala pointed toward the cabinet beneath the window.

Her fingers shook, and he grabbed her hand, pulling her up against him. "You're not frightened of me, are you?" he murmured.

"Is that your intent? I'd heard you were a fearsome opponent, but you seem to be harping on one point of contention, which does neither of us any good. Make me a counter offer, my lord."

He lowered his head and kissed her upturned mouth. Sensation flooded through him, all the way to his cock. He didn't know how to describe what she tasted like—sunshine, warm summer breezes, heat, desire.

When she began to kiss him back, he forced himself to lift his face away again. "How was that?" he drawled.

Sarala cleared her throat, belatedly recovering her hand and backing away. "Fair. But hardly worth five thousand pounds."

Mm-hm. She knew how to play the game; he could concede that. But no one played it as well as he did. "You have a rare focus, Lady Sarala. I'll give you that. And I'll acknowledge that you are the owner of something which was meant to be mine."

Her eyes widened. "You admit it?"

"I just did. What did you actually pay for them, since we both know it wasn't five thousand pounds?"

"Something less than that. I acquired them, however, in order to make a profit, as I assume you meant to do. I have yet to hear a counter offer."

His gaze lowered to her mouth again. "Very well. Since you won't tell me, I'll assume you managed a fair price, which would be what, a guinea and a half per bolt? That's the exact amount I will compensate you for them."

She hesitated for a heartbeat. If he hadn't been looking for it, he probably wouldn't have seen it. "Where, then, is my profit?" she demanded.

"Your profit is in learning not to cross a man simply because he deigns to dance with you."

"Ah. I wouldn't say you deigned as much as begged to dance with me over my objections," she countered. "Five thousand pounds."

Charlemagne took a slow breath. This afternoon had gone nothing like he'd imagined. And at the moment he wouldn't describe that as a bad thing. "No."

"Then I believe we are finished here. Good day, my lord."

He caught her arm again as she began to turn away. "I have contacts who would appreciate the quality of these silks and pay me what they're worth. You've been in London for eleven days now, according to what you told me last night. I would assume, given that fact, that your plan is to sell the bolts off one by one to dress shops and seamstresses."

Lady Sarala delayed a moment before removing her arm from his loose grip. "What I plan for the silks is my own business, and certainly none of yours. And since I don't believe you've offered me anything I want," she returned in the same low voice, "I'll tell you good day once again. But do keep in mind that any negotiations are to be conducted with me—not my father. Unless you can't match wits with a female." She went to the door, and the butler practically fell into the room as she opened it.

It wasn't wits he wanted to match with her, but something much more physical and intimate. "Very well." Charlemagne shoved away his more heated thoughts in favor of a few that might leave him some dignity, and went into the hallway to collect his hat and gloves. "I hope you don't think this is over, Lady Sarala," he said, facing her again as the butler opened the front door. "I want my silks back." Unable to resist, he lowered his gaze once more to her sensuous mouth. "But I do have something you may want in return. We'll merely have to discover what that something might be."

Before she could reply, he left to collect Jaunty. This was one negotiation he had no intention of losing.

Selfish, arrogant man. A day later, and her mind still refused to let go of her conversation with Charlemagne Griffin. If any mistakes or errors had been made, they were his. All that nonsense about the silks being his was just that—nonsense. Thank goodness she'd seen him ride up the drive after luncheon yesterday and had intercepted Blankman before the butler could tell her father that someone had come calling. That would have been a true disaster, especially with a half-dozen gossiping ladies of her mother's acquaintance eating sandwiches in the drawing room, as they were again today. And thank goodness they hadn't seen her running through the house in her dressing gown before she'd made it back to her bedchamber.

"My lady?"

Sarala shook herself. "I think I'll wear that one tonight," she said to her maid, indicating the deep blue gown her maid held in her left hand. "With the silver barrettes."

"But my lady, the marchioness told me specifically that you was only to wear the gowns made since you've been in London. She said the others were too outdated, and some of 'em not even in the English style. All those was to go to the rag and bone man."

Sarala took a deep breath. Perhaps she'd encouraged the seamstresses in Delhi to stray a bit toward the native style, but she'd been raised to appreciate it, after all. Perhaps the blue gown had a snugger waist and lower neckline than the gowns she'd acquired in London, but there was nothing wrong with it. And it was not outdated. The red one she'd worn night before last had been of a similar style, and *that man* had seemed to appreciate it.

Of course that particular gentleman would probably never speak to her again. All she could hope for at this juncture was that he was too much of a gentleman to cut her in public. Just the idea that he could ruin her for besting him in a business venture was patently unfair; that he would actually do so, unthinkable.

Still, best be a little cautious tonight, just in case. With a grimace she flicked her fingers toward the pale peach gown her mother had particularly liked. "The blue one goes back in the wardrobe—not to the rag and bone man."

Jenny curtsied. "Yes, my lady. And you'll be splendid in the peach. I'll go press it."

Splendid and perfectly, properly British. Yes, she'd also been raised British, but the most fun she'd had in India had been when she'd managed to steal away from home for an outing with some of her native friends. Her mother made sense, insisting that she fit in here now, but Sarala didn't particularly like being in this wretched, rainy place to begin with. If she needed an example to prove it, the thing she most looked forward to was another encounter with Lord Charlemagne Griffin, and that couldn't possibly come out well.

He'd kissed her yesterday, and she'd let him. She never did anything like that during a business negotiation. Business was business. Of course it didn't hurt that her opponent in this instance had high cheekbones, a sensuous, expressive mouth, and dark hair that brushed his collar—or that he had shoulders which filled out his coat, thighs which looked as though he spent as much time on horseback as on foot, and not an ounce of fat on his lean, muscular frame.

Sarala scowled. Yes, he was devilishly handsome, and powerful, and he knew it. He was arrogant enough to tell other people of his pending business dealings and then expect that they would do nothing about it. Well, yesterday he'd been taught a lesson. And she had acquired a fortune in silk—which, if nothing else, would help her father get out from under some of the debts Uncle Roger had left behind.

She sat in one of the overstuffed chairs beneath her window, picked up her discarded book on Roman history, and glanced outside. Thankfully her mother's daily set of luncheon guests had begun departing—in another quarter of an hour the house would be free of the gossip brigade. That everyone had missed Lord Charlemagne's visit yesterday had been a tremendous stroke of luck, but even the strategy she and her father had begun planning afterward for reselling the silks to a selection of high-class dress shops hadn't distracted her from realizing how close a call she'd had. A lady didn't conduct business, and she could only continue to do so if she, her father, and Charlemagne were the only ones who knew about it. India had been so much easier.

Sarala lifted the skirt of her dressing gown to her knee. On her left ankle the dainty henna tattoo her friend Nahi had given her as a farewell gift from India still showed, though it had begun to fade a little. Sarala smiled, lowering her skirt again. If her mother ever found out that she'd been tattooed, temporarily or not, she would have the devil to pay.

Jenny scratched at the door and opened it again. "My lady, the marchioness has asked to see you in the drawing room."

Sarala nodded, unhappy if unsurprised, and reached for a green muslin day gown. Most of her mother's friends were old acquaintances from more than two decades ago before she'd left London for India. The majority of them seemed to be hapless busybodies moaning over the current state of things and trying to marry off their daughters or sons to one another's children. They were probably the reason Charlemagne had acquired such a low opinion of women and thought they had no head for business.

She certainly had no objection to marrying, but she wasn't going to be bandied about and matched hither and thither to fit some mama's matrimonial puzzle. She'd been a marquis's daughter for less than a year, and she didn't consider that the fact had increased or decreased her value. Other people did. Of course with the way the lot of them frowned at her hair and her tanned skin and what they whispered was her foreign accent, they probably wouldn't want her joining their family, anyway.

Her mother sat before the fire in the large drawing room; despite her stated delight at being back in civilization, as she called it, the marchioness seemed to be having her own problems adjusting to the cooler weather. Sarala could already almost recite the coming conversation; a lecture on behavior or etiquette inevitably followed one of her mama's luncheons. What surprised her, though, was the presence of her father, leaning against the mantel and looking distinctly as though he wished to be elsewhere.

"Yes, Mama?"

"My dear, your father and I have been discussing the way you've adapted to the family's new position and residence."

"What have I done wrong now?" Sarala asked flatly.

"Nothing. It's more . . . something we've done to you."

Sarala frowned. "Beg pardon?"

The marchioness cleared her throat, then motioned at her husband. “Your father has something to tell you.”

Howard Carlisle shook his head. “This is not my idea. I’m here under protest.”

“Howar— Fine. Fine.” Sending a scowl at her husband, the marchioness sat forward. “You know that your father and I settled in India with the idea of staying there, and that his position with the East India Company . . . benefited from his ability to gain the trust of the local citizenry.”

“I know all that,” Sarala replied. “I certainly have no regrets about growing up in Delhi, if that’s what’s troubling you.”

“It is. *I*—we—have regrets about the way we raised you in Delhi. As I was saying, we never expected to return to England, and so when your father insisted that we give you a native name, I didn’t object too strongly. Now, however, we *are* here, and you are an English marquis’s daughter. It’s not Indians whose trust and cooperation we need to cultivate any longer.”

Deep worry burrowed into Sarala’s chest. This sounded more serious than the what-to-wear talk, or the how-to-be-demure lecture. “Yes?” she prompted after a moment.

“We—that is, your father and I—have decided that in order to ease your path into proper London Society, you should be known by and referred to as Sarah, rather than Sarala.”

Sarala’s jaw dropped. “I beg your pardon?” she stammered, while her father pretended to be elsewhere.

“Sarah is an English name. It will serve you well, and you’ll have an easier time making friends and meeting eligible young gentlem—”

“You’re changing my *name*?”

“As I said, it’s better for y—”

"This was the idea of those gossiping friends of yours, wasn't it?"

The marchioness put out a hand. "Please do not insult my friends. Think of it as everyone else does, Sarah. What's the f—"

"Sarala," Sarala broke in.

"Sarah," her mother countered in an equally firm voice. "What's the first thing everyone says when you've been introduced?"

"Here? They comment on what a pretty and unusual name I have."

The marchioness gazed at her. "And then what? Why have you only danced a half-dozen times since we arrived here? Why haven't you been invited out to tea or to go walking? Why don't you have any friends in London?"

"Mama, that's not fair. We've been here less than a fortnight. Both you and Papa have friends from before you left London. I don't."

"And you won't, if the first impression everyone has of you is that you're odd. It's bad enough that your skin is so dark—I always said you should wear a bonnet and carry a parasol, and you never listened to me."

Obviously her mother had made up *her* mind. Sarala turned to her father. "Papa, you can't be seriously considering this. It's absurd. You named me Sarala."

The marquis shifted. "Consider that we're only shortening your name. Sarah can be your pet name, except that it's how everyone will know you. I know it's a difficult thing, but in this instance I do think your mother has the right of it."

Sarala backed to the doorway, feeling as though someone had drugged her and spun her into some outlandish nightmare. "I like my name. I've had it for two-and-twenty years. I'm not giving it back."

"You're going to have to, Sarah. We haven't made this decision lightly. You will have to, unless you want to be miserable here in England. And there must be other changes, as well. I've already discussed your wardrobe with your maid, and don't think your father and I didn't notice that paint on your face night before last."

"It's fashionable in Delhi."

"For the last time, Sarah, we are not in Delhi any longer! And we never will be again, unless you marry some peer who wants to make his living there. When you return, then you may change your name back, but not until then."

"I cannot believe you would do this." Growling, Sarala stormed out of the drawing room and back up to her bedchamber. Her parents could call her whatever they liked; she certainly couldn't stop them. As for herself, she'd grown up as Sarala, and that was who she would remain.

If she went by Sarah in her own mind and in her own heart, the next thing she knew, she would become one of those English ladies who didn't conduct business. A blink after that, she would be selling the blasted silks to Charlemagne Griffin for a shilling. And that was *not* going to happen. Ever.

Chapter 3

"I'm merely pointing out the fact that tariffs don't concern my business. I raise English cows on English grass and sell English butter and cream to proper English households." Smothering a grin behind a mouthful of roast pheasant, Lord Zachary Griffin lifted both eyebrows.

"That's the stupidest, most short-sighted economic argument I've ever heard," Charlemagne retorted. "Pass the salt."

"It's not an economic argument. Those give me a headache. It's a statement about how much I don't care about whatever it is you and Melbourne are arguing over."

"Twit."

Melbourne's daughter, Penelope, lowered her glass of lemonade. "Papa, Uncle Shay said 'twit.' "

"Yes, I heard him, Peep. Thank you very much. Mind your tongue, Charlemagne."

"That's right," Peep continued. "There are ladies present."

"Oh, I don't mind," Lady Caroline, Zachary's auburn-haired bride, said with a chuckle.

"Me, neither." Eleanor, Lady Deverill, handed the salt down the long table to her brother. "In fact, I'd have to say that I agree with Shay's assessment. You are a twit, Zachary."

"Thank you, Nell," Charlemagne returned, "both for the salt and the agreement."

Pasting an affronted expression on his face, Zachary leaned forward to gaze at their brother-in-law, Deverill, the only one who hadn't contributed to the conversation. "And what do you say, Valentine?"

"You're a twit." The marquis returned to his pudding.

"Oh, thank you very m—"

"Papa, now everybody's saying it!"

"Yes, everyone has appalling manners," the duke agreed. "Desist. Valentine, do you know of anything that might persuade Morgan to change his vote in Parliament tomorrow?"

"I presume you mean blackmail," the Marquis of Deverill replied. "I've heard that he finds ladies' night rails very comfortable."

Peep giggled, wide-eyed. "He wears ladies' clothes?"

The marquis lifted an eyebrow. "Only at night."

Melbourne cleared his throat. "I was actually asking about political activities. But given our audience," he continued, with a pointed glance at his seven-year-old daughter, "we can continue this later."

Valentine nodded. "You started it. I'm perfectly happy to stay out of the Griffin dynastic struggle. I have your sister, and that is all I require."

"God, you sound domestic," Zachary chortled.

"At least I'm not obsessed with cows."

Generally Charlemagne enjoyed these evenings, when the

extended Griffin clan came together for dinner before a soiree or an evening at the theater. Tonight, however, his thoughts were already on the ball at Lady Mantz-Dillings', and more specifically, on who else might be attending. He hadn't seen the devious chit in a day, and only the devil knew what she might have done with his silks in that time.

"Yes, Shay, we do get first pick of your silks, don't we?" his sister, Eleanor, was saying.

He shook himself. "Certainly. As soon as I get them sorted out, Nell, you and Caroline may select a bolt each."

"Is the quality as fine as you'd hoped?"

Lady Caroline Griffin, the newest member of the family, thankfully had a wit and intelligence that more than equaled her husband Zachary's, but she still showed a bit of reserve in Melbourne's presence. Charlemagne couldn't blame her for that; her claim to nobility lay in her great-grandfather, and she was a professional portraitist, of all things. And she knew that Melbourne had initially disliked the match. To his credit the duke had softened considerably, and that was probably in part because Caroline could definitely hold her own when push came to shove.

"They are the finest I've ever seen," he returned. "I should make a tidy profit." If he could wrest them back from a certain clever, stubborn, exotic chit. After a moment he realized that everyone still gazed at him. "What?"

"And you tease me over my obsession with cattle." Zachary grinned at him. "I only asked if you were going to sell the lot of it up in Milford, or piecemeal here in London."

"I'm not certain yet." And if some of the silk began appearing in local dress shops, he wanted an excuse for it.

Melbourne eyed him. "I thought you had Tannen chomping at the bit for the entire lot."

Damn. This was the last time he would count his chickens or his eggs before he had the ownership papers in hand. Neither, though, was he going to admit to having been outmaneuvered by a chit just off the boat from India. "I'm reassessing," he improvised.

"They *must* be good quality, then."

"You have no idea, Seb."

As soon as he could manage it without appearing to be rushing, Charlemagne got everyone away from the dinner table and out to their waiting coaches. There. At least he'd been fairly smooth about it, and now he could determine whether Lady Sarala Carlisle was brave enough to face him on neutral ground, or whether she would only stand up to him in the safety of her own home.

"Why the hurry?" Zachary asked as he settled into the coach beside his wife.

Charlemagne opposite him, conjured a frown. "What hurry?"

"It's barely half past nine, and Cook made strawberry cakes."

"If we waited for you to finish eating, we'd never leave," Charlemagne retorted.

Zachary looked thoughtful. "Can't argue with that, I suppose." He reached over and took his wife's hand, twining his fingers with hers. "Did Caroline tell you that Prinny wants to sit for her next month? The finished portrait's to go up in the main gallery at Carlton House."

"If His Majesty approves of it," his wife added, shaking her head at him.

"I'm not surprised," Charlemagne said. "In fact, the only thing about you that continues to astonish me, Caroline, is that you agreed to marry Zachary."

She snorted delicately, looking sideways at her husband. "He's very persuasive, and much more artistically inclined than you give him credit for."

For the moment Charlemagne settled for nodding. He liked Caroline, and he was glad that Zachary had been able to persuade her to marry him. They obviously loved each other—and while he wasn't jealous, he certainly recognized the rarity of the phenomenon. "The rest of us give him credit. We just don't like to let him know it. Swelled head and all that."

"Why, thank you, Shay."

Charlemagne shrugged. "Melbourne and I aren't completely unobservant."

"Neither am I. Who was the chit you were dancing with the other night?"

With some effort Charlemagne managed a puzzled look. "Eloisa Harding? You know her."

"Not her. The glittering one with the black hair."

"Oh, her. She's Hanover's niece. The new marquis's daughter."

"They've just come from India or something, haven't they?"

"I believe so."

"Hm. From her coloring and choice of wardrobe, apparently the chit's gone native."

"Apparently." Charlemagne shifted. The less conversation about Sarala Carlisle, the better. At least until he'd reacquired his silks.

"Do you believe Valentine about Morgan?" Zach continued, thankfully changing the subject without having to be prompted to do so.

"He has a tendency to know odd things about people. It's rather like having a professional spy in the family."

"As long as he's not gathering information about us."

And amen to that. It would be bad enough if Melbourne was to discover how he'd managed to bungle what he'd boasted to be an easy deal; if London at large found out he'd been bested by a chit, he'd never live it down. And in the business circles he frequented, that could be fatal—to his reputation, anyway. The situation, therefore, needed to be corrected, and as quickly as possible.

"Couldn't you smile at him?" Lady Hanover murmured from behind her fan.

"Which one?" Sarala returned, her gaze on the doorway rather than on the crowd already filling the Mantz-Dilling ballroom. Lord Charlemagne had clearly sent her a challenge with his parting words, though the more she thought about them, the more they'd sounded . . . personal rather than professional. She'd stayed in last night, but hadn't been able to come up with an excuse to do so for two nights in a row. Had he looked for her? Low heat ran through her belly.

"Him, over there. Lord Purdey."

Reluctantly Sarala looked in the direction her mother indicated. "The one in the scarlet vest? Oh, Mama, he's hideous and ridiculous."

"Hush, before he hears you. Mrs. Westerley says he has four thousand a year, and a grand estate in Suffolk."

"His eyes are crossed, and he's drooling on his own boots. Besides, I daresay you know nothing about him but the state of his finances."

"What else is there to know? He's unmarried, and wealthy."

"Does he read? Does he like the theater? Is he able to carry on an intelligent conversation? Between bouts of drooling, of course."

Lady Hanover eyed her. "You certainly have an odd idea of courting."

"You can't even settle on one name for me—how am I supposed to be able to settle on a potential husband?"

"Enough of that nonsense. Go over to the dessert table and smile, or you'll end up with no one on your dance card again."

Swallowing a sudden surge of nerves, Sarala smiled and attempted to stroll nonchalantly to the crowded food tables. Wearing the perfectly tasteful peach and gold gown her mother had recommended, her hair in a stylish upswept bun and a trace of rouge on her cheeks, she suited her new perfectly ordinary, perfectly English name. The rich, deep palette of colors she'd grown up around made everything she saw now seem pale and flat and plain in comparison. Apparently that was the way in which the proper young ladies of Society wished to be seen.

And apparently now she'd become one of the dull multitudes. No one but she had even batted an eye when the Mantz-Dilling butler had announced her as Lady Sarah Carlisle. Her mother seemed assured that not standing out would gain her the interest of every single gentleman in the room, but she had her doubts.

"I've brought you something," a low, masculine voice said.

Her heart jumped as she turned around. "Five thousand pounds?" she suggested, looking up into the gray eyes of Charlemagne Griffin.

"Hardly." For a moment he gazed at her. Then, taking her hand, he brought it to his lips. As he released her, he slipped a small velvet bag into her fingers. "Put it in your reticule," he instructed in a low voice, "and look at it later."

She closed her fingers around it. "I won't be bribed, you know."

The twinkle in his eyes matched the glitter of the onyx pin stuck through his starched white cravat. "How do you know it's a bribe? Perhaps it's a threat. A dead toad, or a piece of coal or something."

Her lips curved upward despite her best efforts. "So many wondrous possibilities."

"I suppose I could tell you what it is. The curiosity of females is rather notorious."

"Don't you mean the curiosity of felines? I believe it was a cat that curiosity killed. I'm of a different persuasion, and if it suits your strategy for me to look, then I won't do so."

She couldn't read the quick expression that passed behind his eyes, but she thought it might have been appreciation. "Are you certain you're not curious?" he pursued, handing her a glass of Madeira and taking one for himself.

"Let's say I'm equal parts curious and cautious." Setting down the glass for a moment, she slipped the small bundle into her reticule. Very well, so she *was* curious—excessively so—but she had no intention of letting him know he'd surprised her. In business it was always very bad form to show surprise.

"Shay!"

With a slight start he turned his head to view a small cluster of gentlemen at the far end of the table. "Damned Willits," he muttered, and faced her again. "I need to speak with him. Will you forgive me?"

"Unless he's terribly evil or a spy, I don't believe you have anything to apologize for. I—"

"Give me your dance card," he interrupted, holding out his hand.

"You might ask me, rather than demanding."

He smiled, the expression doing remarkably handsome things to his face and some more complicated ones to her insides. "If I asked, you might refuse. Your dance card, my lady."

With what she hoped looked like an exasperated frown, Sarala handed the thing over. "There. I thought we were business rivals. Not dancing partners."

"Perhaps we're both." His brows lowered. "This says 'Sarah.' "

She flushed. "My parents' idea. It doesn't signify."

"They altered your name?"

Sarala gave an irritated sigh. "Not that it's any of your affair, but they thought I would have an easier time being accepted into English Society if I had a more English name."

He gazed at her speculatively. "Now that you mention it, tonight you do look almost . . . English."

It probably wasn't meant to be an insult, but it almost felt like one. "I *am* English," she stated, because her mother would expect her to, "whatever my name is. Why should I not appear to be so?"

"Shay!"

"In a moment," he barked back, then took a step closer to her. "So between you and me, do I call you Sarah, or Sarala?"

"Sarala," she answered, refusing to be moved by his intimate tone. Gifts, a kiss, private conversations—whatever he might claim, every move he made was designed to take him closer to his goal of getting the silks.

He found a pencil and wrote his name on her card. "Very good then, Sarala," he murmured, handing it back to her. "And try the raspberry tarts here. I think they'll suit you."

As he left her for the group of noblemen, Sarala turned

over the card. He'd selected the evening's only waltz. And apparently if raspberry tarts suited her, she had a sour interior and a sweet outside. She took one and bit into it, sweet and tart mingling in her mouth. Delicious.

Someone tugged on her sleeve. She started, nearly dropping both the Madeira and the sweet tart. "Yes?"

The man in front of her was actually an inch or so shorter than she was, so that she had a splendid view of his round, balding pate. He sketched a deep bow, bringing into her sight the thinning hair on the back of his head, as well.

"Francis Henning," he said as he straightened. "You're the girl from India. Lady Sarah."

So someone *had* noticed her name tonight. "I am," she answered, watching as he bobbed his head again.

"Grand. I saw Lord Shay taking a dance from you, and thought I might do so as well."

"Oh. That's very generous of you, Mr. Henning, but not necess—"

"Perfectly fine," he continued, snatching the card from where she'd partially tucked it into her reticule and scribbling on it. "Good enough for a Griffin, can't be higher or mightier than that."

"Uh . . . Thank you," she said, gingerly retrieving the card and just managing not to spill anything.

After that, the men present seemed either to assume that she had Lord Charlemagne's approval, or that if she would dance with Mr. Henning she would dance with anyone. At any rate, within five minutes her dance card was full, and for the first time since she'd left India she had a partner for every soiree. In part the developments pleased her, because she did love to dance, but on the other hand her mother would now claim that the evening had turned out so well because of her name change.

She'd sort it out later. At the moment her attention stayed on the only waltz of the evening and on one sneaky, arrogant business rival who apparently thought she could be seduced into selling to him.

"Tradition or not," Melbourne said, gesturing for a glass of wine, "horses and wagons have their limitations."

"So you think we should carve up the countryside with more canals and turn all horses into hog feed?"

Charlemagne at his brother's elbow took a large swallow of Madeira and silently counted to five. "That's a bit drastic, wouldn't you say?" he drawled. "Nothing beats a horse and wagon for short trips, but a boat on a canal can carry five times the load over longer distances. The population of London keeps growing, and if we can't keep the citizens supplied, *they'll* be eating our horses." He forced a grin he didn't feel. "And I'm rather fond of my horse."

Willits chuckled. "I've learned never to count Melbourne wrong, but this all seems too progressive to me."

"I think it's a question of whether you'd rather be considered ahead of your time or be left behind." In the guise of gesturing for another drink, Charlemagne stole a glance over his shoulder at Lady Sarala. She'd stood up for every dance so far this evening, a far cry from her exotic solitude of two nights before. Apparently the gentlemen of London found her more acceptable tonight, though whatever she chose to wear or whatever her name, she couldn't disguise the warm glow of her skin, the quiet grace of her movement, or the cinnamon scent of her hair. All that and a damned sharp wit, too. Hell, she'd outwitted him, and that *never* happened.

"—multitude of investors?"

Charlemagne blinked, not having the faintest idea what

Willits was talking about. "Beg pardon?" he asked, glancing at Melbourne for a hint. His brother sent him a faint frown.

"We're never adverse to partnerships," the duke said smoothly, "but I think we have a bit more research to do on the project first. What's important at this early point is the support of Parliament."

Of course Willits wanted to invest; Griffin projects rarely ended up being less than profitable. And no wonder Melbourne appeared somewhat annoyed. The "more research" speech generally came from Charlemagne.

"Apologies," Charlemagne muttered, as Sebastian made their excuses and gestured him toward the gaming rooms.

"No matter." The duke took a slow breath. "Are you feeling well?"

"Me? Of course." Charlemagne stopped in the doorway. He usually enjoyed a game or two of wits and billiards, but tonight he found himself reluctant to leave the ballroom. "Why do you ask?"

"You seem . . . distracted."

"My mind did drift a bit for a moment." Charlemagne pasted a carefree expression on his face. "Maybe I was hoping that by now damned Willits could have carried on that entire conversation by himself."

With a rare smile, Sebastian clapped him on the shoulder. "That will never happen. However, I suppose hope does spring eternal, etcetera, etcetera."

"I suppose so." As the duke vanished into the smoky gaming room, Charlemagne finished off his second drink of the evening. As usual, his older brother knew what he was talking about. Aside from money, one thing they'd never lacked for was hangers-on.

And Melbourne was right about something else, too. He

had been distracted earlier, and it hadn't been merely for a moment. In his defense, it did have to do with business—seven hundred and fifty guineas' worth, or five thousand pounds if he listened to the painfully overwrought price named by Sarala Carlisle.

Lines began to form for a country dance, and once more the Indian princess took to the dance floor. Every gentleman with whom she danced could be a potential silk buyer, or worse, someone to whom she could brag about the way she'd outfoxed one of the Griffins. Straightening, Charlemagne strolled over to the gaggle of hopeful debutantes who blocked the path to the best desserts.

"Miss Allen?" he said, matching a face with a vague memory of an introduction.

A narrow-faced blonde with a shy, engaging smile curtsied almost in half. "Yes, my Lord Charlemagne?"

"If you're not spoken for, may I have this dance?"

"It would be my pleasure, my lord."

He took the chit's hand and guided her to their place in line. Two couples down, Zachary lifted an eyebrow at him. Charlemagne ignored his brother. Perhaps he didn't dance very often, but he did take the floor on occasion, after all.

As the music began, the facing lines of couples bowed and curtsied to one another, and then alternate numbers stepped forward to weave around the neighboring dancers. Charlemagne moved with the others, waiting until he touched Lady Sarala's hand and stepped around behind her. "You haven't peeked, have you?" he whispered.

She circled him. "Peeked at what?"

Charlemagne hid his frown. "The bag in your reticule." They moved away from each other, and he had to wait until the dance drew them together again. "Well?"

"I'd nearly forgotten it was there." Circle, turn, dip. "So no, I haven't peeked."

"You didn't forget anything," he returned softly.

A blush crept along her cheekbones, but she swirled away before she could answer—if she intended to answer. He knew she was curious, though, whatever she might claim. He wished there was a way to see her face when she opened it, but a Griffin couldn't give a gift to an unattached young lady without causing a scandal—even if their connection was purely business. And however much he wanted the silks back, he wouldn't ruin her to accomplish that. Quite simply, it would be cheating.

The dance ended, and he returned Miss Allen to her friends, who immediately surrounded her with giggles and whispers. He could pick another one for the next dance, he assumed, but it was a quadrille and he didn't see the point.

"Miss Allen?" Zachary muttered, throwing an arm across Charlemagne's shoulders.

"I thought it was nice," Caroline put in, taking Shay's free arm. "I don't imagine she gets much opportunity to dance. You've rendered her the chance now. So don't tease him, Zachary."

"Hm. I remain unscathed," Charlemagne returned, lifting a glass of wine from the tray of a passing footman. He wouldn't drink it—two glasses was his limit at most soirees—but it gave him a moment. "It is good to see that you've finally found someone who's willing to tolerate your rhythmless plodding, Zach." He looked over at his brother's wife. "That's why he married you, I'm afraid. Because you don't mind getting your feet tromped on."

"Fine, I'll leave you be," his younger brother conceded,

releasing him. "Just don't enlighten Caro about any more of my faults she hasn't already discovered."

Caroline chuckled. "I know them all, Zachary."

Her husband moved around to kiss her lightly on the lips. "Such great skill with a brush, and such poor taste in men."

"Oh, I don't know about that," she whispered back, smiling.

"Good God, go home and stop subjecting me to such unfiltered sweetness." With a grin Charlemagne shifted Caroline's hand from his arm to Zachary's.

"That, Shay, is a very good idea. Give our good nights to Melbourne, will you?"

"Anything. Just go."

Whispering to each other, his brother and sister-in-law slipped out of the ballroom. For a brief moment he allowed himself to envy their happiness and contentment, then squared his shoulders and dove back into the mass of political and social intrigue. The younger two Griffin siblings had married, and they were welcome to it, but he felt no need to enter into matrimony. Melbourne needed a strong right arm to see to the multitude of businesses owned by the family, and almost from the moment Shay had entered Oxford, he'd fallen into that role. He relished it, the nuances and complexities, the reading of opponents and matching tactics to character.

That was his present problem with Sarala Carlisle. He hadn't quite figured out her character, yet. He'd tried several strategies, up to and including that very . . . pleasurable kiss, but she still hadn't lowered her idiotic price a whit. Hence his gift. Her reaction to it should give him the additional information and insight he required.

By the time the waltz came about, Charlemagne had regained his usual practical equilibrium. It had been quite a couple of days of surprises, after all, not the least of which being that he had a very attractive opponent for what was supposed to have been a quick, simple transaction. But for God's sake, he'd charmed females out of their clothes; charming this one out of a stack of Chinese silks would have to be easier than that.

Lady Sarala stood beside an older woman who wore a stylish gown of the latest style. They had similar features, and Charlemagne assumed this to be Lady Hanover, Sarala's mother. Odd that the mother could look so English while the daughter, wearing clothes of the same fashion, looked so exotic.

"Lady Sarala," he said, reaching her side and perfectly aware that the marchioness was the one trying to change Sarala's name.

The daughter curtsied, a slight upturn of her lips the only clue that she'd noted his choice of address. Who in their right mind could assign her the name Sarah after she'd grown up as Sarala? Ridiculous. Criminal, almost. Like calling a peacock a pigeon. Everyone knew the quality of the bird, regardless of the name.

"My lord," she said, straightening again. "Have you met my mother, Lady Hanover? Mama, Lord Charlemagne Griffin."

The marchioness curtsied, as well. "My lord. Thank you for dancing with our *Sarah* evening before last."

So her mother, at least, didn't know he'd stopped by Carlisle House yesterday. If she did, she would have considered that more significant than a dance. "No need to thank me, my lady. Dancing with Lady *Sarala* is a pleasure I mean to repeat—at this very moment, in fact."

Lady Hanover fluffed one of her daughter's peach-colored

lace sleeves. "*Sarah* has danced every dance tonight. So many interested gentlemen."

"Mama," Sarala said in a low voice.

"How could any gentleman not be interested in such a charming young thing as Lady *Sarala*?" Charlemagne broke in, beginning to worry that they would miss the dance. "With your permission, Lady Hanover?"

"Oh, of course, my lord. Go on, *Sarah*."

Charlemagne took Sarala's hand, leading the way across the crowded dance floor. Last time he'd danced with her, he'd thought her attractive and naive. Tonight, his heart beat faster. Tonight wasn't going to be about him boasting and her making admiring comments. And she couldn't make some dismissive comment and send him away—not without making a spectacle of herself.

"While I appreciate your support of my name, you shouldn't have said that other," Sarala commented as she placed a hand on his shoulder.

"Said what other?"

"Said that any gentleman would be interested in me. Now my mother will think you mean to court me."

He smiled into her eyes. "Who's to say I don't mean to court you?"

"We both know that the only thing you're courting is my five hundred bolts of silk."

True, but at the same time he'd never conducted a business negotiation remotely like this in his life. And he'd told Zachary that business was one thing, and pleasure another. Apparently he hadn't learned everything. "Why don't you return the silks to me, and we'll see if I ask you to dance again?" Charlemagne pulled her a little closer. "Because I can almost guarantee you that I will."

"We are speaking of silks. Nothing else. And I have offered to sell them to you."

"For an outrageous price."

"Considering that I have no obligation to sell you anything, you can accept my price, make me a reasonable counter offer, or walk away." She looked at him from beneath her long, dark lashes. "And admit defeat, of course."

"I do love a challenge," he murmured back at her. "And considering that this negotiation is far from finished, I have no reason to admit defeat."

"Call it what you will, then, but I am not going to hold on to the shipment indefinitely while you play at claiming it. I am going to sell it to whoever is willing to meet my price—whether that is you or someone else."

"Oh, you'll sell to me," Charlemagne returned, for the first time wondering if perhaps she did have another buyer dangling on the line. Did she speak to this mystery opponent in the same sharp, amusing way? He had more than a hunch that was not the case. "I suggest we meet at eleven o'clock tomorrow morning at the eastern end of Rotten Row in Hyde Park. Do you know where that is?"

"Yes, I do. I hardly think it's the place for business, however." Her green gaze met his speculatively.

"You'd be surprised where business takes place in London. And pleasure, for that matter."

For a moment she waltzed silently in his arms, lithe and light as moonlight. "Why tomorrow, then? Why not conclude our negotiations tonight?"

Because the negotiations he wanted to engage in with her tonight had nothing to do with the price of a bolt of silk. "Because if we are seen chatting after a waltz, people *will* think I'm in pursuit of you, rather than a shipment of silks."

He grinned, every muscle in his body feeling electric and alive. "Besides, when we meet tomorrow you'll be able to tell me what you think of your surprise."

"Unless the surprise is five thousand pounds, it won't make the least bit of difference."

Perhaps it wouldn't, but Charlemagne still wanted to know what she would think of it. And as for its worth, he would leave it to her to guess. This wasn't about money; this was about winning—the bolts of cloth, of course.

She might think herself a chess player, but placing the pieces on the board and moving them were two very different things. And he felt in the mood to deliver a few lessons.

Chapter 4

Sarala sat back to look over the letter she'd just finished. Madame Costanza's Dress Shop had a reputation for catering to more expensive and exotic tastes, and Madame Costanza had one for being a shrewd businesswoman. Obviously she couldn't rely on Charlemagne Griffin to offer a price she could live with, and neither had she ever subscribed to the axiom of putting all her eggs in one basket, as it were.

Five hundred bolts was far too much silk for one shop to be able to afford, but there were more than five hundred dress shops in London and the south of England. And a great many of them advertised in newspapers and fashion pages. At this point it wouldn't be economical to visit them all, but some judicious letter writing should show her who might be most interested in purchasing some fine Chinese silk for a reasonable price.

A dozen letters later she put away the stack of newspapers,

flexed her fingers, bundled up the missives, and took them downstairs for Blankman to send out by post in the morning. Counted with the ones she'd written last evening, she had a fair number of prospects. That done, she went back up to her bedchamber to face the more troublesome aspect of the evening.

She placed her reticule in the center of her small mahogany reading table, then sat to face it. With Jenny's help she'd shed her silk gown and donned her night rail, gone through the ritual of having her bed turned down and her hair brushed out. She'd danced every dance at the ball, and weariness pulled at her. Humming below that, though, was curiosity—though probably not for the reasons Lord Charlemagne would have expected. She loved a puzzle, and he'd presented her with a good one.

He'd made her an offer for the silks; one that would earn her two hundred and fifty guineas. A fair sum, yes, but she knew the silks were worth far more than that. He knew it, as well.

What had he given her, then? A note, a letter, something explaining how dearly he'd wanted those silks and imploring her to give them up at some ridiculously low price? She didn't see how a letter could be more persuasive than his kiss, and *that* hadn't swayed her one jot.

A gift, then. "Ah, that's the rub," she murmured, circling the table. Because under the circumstances it wasn't a gift; it was a bribe. Whatever it was, obviously it was meant to better his negotiation position, likely by softening hers. Therefore, she knew full well that she would best be served by not opening anything and instead returning it to Lord Charlemagne at the appointed time tomorrow.

Squaring her shoulders, Sarala turned her back on the table and its contents and climbed into bed. That would show Lord Charlemagne, Shay to his friends; whatever he meant to accomplish by this, she would be unaffected. And her stance regarding the silks wouldn't have changed, either. Her price remained five thousand pounds, unless he countered with something less insulting than a guinea and a half per bolt.

"There. Curiosity and females, ha." Perhaps next time he would consider his position before he insulted every member of her sex.

The idea of maintaining a blissful ignorance lasted for nearly five minutes, until she realized that he would base their next conversation, his next argument, on the assumption that she knew what she'd been given. Pretending ignorance could therefore very well be to her advantage, but actual ignorance wouldn't serve any purpose at all.

"We can't have that," she murmured, and climbed out of bed again. Firmly reminding herself that this was about business and not about curiosity, Sarala returned to the reading table and pulled open her reticule. Inside, the small velvet pouch lay wedged between her coin purse and a small tortoiseshell mirror.

Interesting as it was trying to guess what Charlemagne thought would be an effective bribe, *knowing* would serve her better. She pulled the fine braided strings and opened the pouch.

She turned it over, and a silver chain spilled onto her palm. Attached to it by a small loop was an intricate, delicate silver setting surrounding a small, multifaceted stone. Sarala held it up to the candlelight. Blood red. A ruby.

She couldn't help her slow intake of breath. It was lovely, after all. And no doubt an Indian ruby, since given her past firstly it wouldn't make sense for it to be from somewhere else, and secondly he was a Griffin and could easily afford such a thing.

So he'd given her a gift worth probably more than the five hundred bolts of silk. Sarala liked to consider herself a logical female, and logically a keen businessman wouldn't bestow a bribe worth more than the property he was trying to acquire. Therefore, this bribe wasn't about acquiring property; it was about acquiring *her.* Heat began low inside her, though she tried to set that sensation aside.

Well, he had some nerve, turning what would have been an interesting, invigorating negotiation into what was clearly his idea of a seduction. Yes, he was attractive and intelligent, but for heaven's sake, she'd just arrived in England. She had no intention of succumbing to the suave maneuverings of the first man who looked in her direction, simply because he expected her to do so.

No, he did not have the reins of these proceedings. She did. And she had silks to dispose of. If he thought she could be bought with a ruby because it came from India, as though that meant he knew every ounce of her character, he had a surprise coming.

As far as she was concerned, this was *still* about the silks. He'd just demonstrated how easily he could afford the price she asked, and so as of this moment she would accept no offer lower than six thousand pounds from him. Ha. And as for acquiring *her* . . . it would take far more than a kiss, a ruby, and some admittedly invigorating arguments.

Whatever he thought, they were still opponents. He expected her to meet him in Hyde Park in the morning. She would do so, but she didn't think he would like the conversation very much.

* * *

"I'm afraid it's rather overcast today, my lady," Jenny said as she pulled open the bedchamber curtains. "It smells like rain, if I do say so myself."

"More rain?" Sarala stretched and climbed out from under the covers. "I thought this was summer."

"Oh, it is. Honestly it's been colder than it ought this year. I imagine you won't want to go shopping today after all."

"Shopping, no. But I've heard that Hyde Park is lovely, and I'd like to take a walk. Please put out a warm cloak for me."

"But you said you'd never go out when the air was cold like this, my lady."

"I changed my mind. Mama does keep saying I'll have to get used to it, after all."

The maid smiled. "That's the spirit, Lady Sarala." Her face fell. "Oh, I meant Lady Sarah! I do beg your pardon, my lady. Blankman told us, and I forgot. Please don't—"

"No worries, Jenny." For heaven's sake, she had no intention of sacking anyone for not succumbing to her mother's silliness. "For everyone's sake, though, I suppose we'd best try to stay with Sarah." At least in her mother's hearing, and for her maid's sake.

As she descended the front stairs, her father stood in the foyer accepting his hat and gloves from the butler. "Sar . . . ah, I'm glad to see you this morning."

So she was truly on her own in the quest to keep her real name. "Good morning, Papa." She gave him a peck on the cheek as Blankman pulled open the front door. "Have you eaten?"

"Yes. Just on my way to Parliament. The one consistency throughout the territories of England seems to be that powerful men need to argue about things which the rest of the population figured out the answer to long ago."

She laughed. "Well, if they couldn't argue, they'd probably

occupy themselves with actually *doing* things, and that would cause all kinds of trouble."

"Indeed, it would." The marquis chuckled. "By the by, I haven't had a chance to ask about for buyers of silk. Have you?"

"I sent out a dozen inquiries more this morning," she returned, "and I have several parties already interested in bidding." *Well, one, anyway.* "I know we can't waste five hundred guineas stacked away in a warehouse."

Her father kissed her on the forehead. "Your uncle did leave us some debts. Your skills at negotiating will be greatly appreciated. I have Warrick making a few inquiries, as well."

She nodded, though after his performance in purchasing the silks, she didn't have much faith left that her father's accountant could sell them at any kind of profit. "I'm seeing a party about an offer this morning. I'll do my best."

"Good. Take Warrick along, then. You know your mother doesn't approve of your engaging in business dealings. And certainly not unattended."

"Yes, I know. I shall be the very soul of discretion, Papa. Don't worry."

Sarala watched him out the door and into his coach. She'd managed not to agree to include Mr. Warrick, but she preferred to avoid lying, even by omission, to her father. But she certainly wasn't going to pit the accountant against Shay Griffin. What a disaster that would be.

No, this project was all hers from now on, and neither her mother, her altering name, nor pretty rubies would sway her from her task.

As she and Jenny arrived at the east end of Rotten Row half an hour later, Sarala fairly vibrated with eagerness to begin the morning's negotiations. She barely kept from smiling as Lord Charlemagne's barouche came into view standing amid a small crowd of other vehicles. Apparently he was as popular out-of-doors as he was beneath ballroom chandelier lights. Today the majority of the moths attracted to his flame seemed to be female—but then the titled men would be in Parliament.

"Wonderful," she muttered, pulling her cloak closer around her shoulders. In the middle of a gathering like that, she certainly couldn't simply walk up to him. Nor could she mention anything about his so-called gift and what he could do with it.

"My lady," Jenny said, "you're shivering. We should go back to the house before you catch a chill."

Given their surroundings and the number of witnesses, they probably should. Now that she considered it, Charlemagne had probably chosen the setting just so she *wouldn't* dare return the ruby. On the other hand, she'd wasted a good portion of the morning walking out to the park. And besides, she wasn't so easily thwarted.

She would watch him interacting with his admirers, and she would observe. Everyone had a weakness, and he'd probably used the ruby to look for hers. She needed to find his before time and her family's need to repay debts wore her down to his insulting price. "We'll go in a few minutes," she returned, seeing the maid eyeing her.

Jenny looked from her to the center of the crowd of vehicles. "Begging your pardon, but ain't that the gentleman who tried to jump into the coach the other day? The one you sent away from the house before your parents should see him? Lord Champagne?"

"Charlemagne," she corrected. "Named after the famous

king of most of Western Europe. And he certainly behaves like royalty, doesn't he?"

"Well, I'd say he's handsome as anything. But you said he was mad."

She'd actually meant mad as in angry yesterday, but the other fit today. "He may well be." She looked at him again, more closely this time. Yes, he *was* handsome; previously she'd been so concerned with his information and then his offers that she hadn't just . . . seen him.

They stood watching at the edge of the trees for several minutes. Lord Charlemagne had an engaging smile, even when he wasn't using it to try to gain an advantage in negotiations. He did seem to have a gift that she lacked for being endlessly charming in the face of silliness, but then he would have had more occasion to use it and more reason to practice it than she did.

After five minutes or so she turned her attention to the females—and the far smaller number of men—who surrounded her eleven o'clock appointment. Pretty, twittery young things in well-appointed carriages—posies seeking money or a title through matrimony, she supposed. The men as a whole and with the notable exception of Charlemagne appeared somewhat shabbier, but then they most likely hoped to improve their circumstances by association, or at worst by marrying one of Charlemagne's cast-offs.

When she looked back at the reason for all the chaos, she found gray eyes gazing squarely at her. *Damnation.* Now she couldn't leave without looking as though she were intimidated or jealous, and she still couldn't approach without appearing to be one of the hopeful female throng.

At that moment, however, he said something she couldn't hear. Almost immediately the mass of horses and vehicles parted before his carriage and then began to disperse. In another second or two his barouche pulled up beside her.

"Lady Sarala. Good morning," he said with that charming smile of his, and tipped his hat.

"Lord Moses. And I thought the parting of the Red Sea was an allegory."

He lifted an eyebrow, then glanced back over his shoulder. "Oh, that. They aren't as persistent as the Egyptian army, though considerably more deadly to my ability to remain awake."

Sarala chuckled. "I shall attempt to do better." Perhaps laughing wasn't strictly professional, but he was wittier than she'd expected from their first meeting. Three days ago—heavens, had it been only three days?—she'd thought him arrogant, thick-headed, and boastful. He'd shown at least the middle of those to be untrue. No, he was a far worthier opponent—both over the silks and now apparently over her person—than she'd expected, and she'd best never forget that.

"I doubt that being interesting will be much of a challenge for you."

"Why, thank you, my lord."

"Might I offer you a tour of London? Or at least of the part surrounding Hyde Park?"

And thus the black knight moved his first chess piece of the day, a flanking maneuver undoubtedly meant to distract her from his frontal assault on the silks. "You don't expect me to climb into your barouche with you," she said, scowling.

"Your maid will join us, naturally." He gestured at the seat opposite his. "And I do have several very nice lap blankets, and a pan of coals beneath that seat."

It was a blatantly unfair use of his knowledge of her

warm, Indian past, she decided. He'd probably consulted an almanac and realized the weather would be chill before he'd suggested the time and location for their meeting today.

"Well?" he prompted. "I'd be just as happy to remain here and you there. I only thought you'd enjoy seeing some of the local sights. If I'm—"

"Open the door, if you please," she interrupted. As long as she knew what his rook was up to, she wouldn't be in danger of being mated. Sarala coughed to cover her abrupt amusement at the analogy.

He opened the door as she requested, and even stood to offer a hand to Jenny and her. At least he hadn't gloated about his first victory. And she had several moves he wouldn't see coming.

On the path just north of Rotten Row another barouche, this one with the Deverill crest on the door panel, came to a stop. "Who is she, I wonder?" Eleanor, Lady Deverill, asked as she looked toward her older brother's carriage.

"I saw him dancing with her last night," her companion and sister-in-law, Lady Caroline Griffin, answered. "Zachary even asked Shay a question about her, and he pretended disinterest. She's the one just here from India. Lady Sarah or something. There's some confusion about what her name actually is, I believe."

Eleanor kept her gaze on her brother, though her heart jumped. "He *pretended* disinterest? You're certain it wasn't actual disinterest?"

"It could have been, I suppose. You know him much better than I do."

Eleanor turned back to face her companion and newfound friend. "You don't need to pretend ignorance to make me feel better. I know Zach's told you all about the Griffin clan. And I also know you're rather observant."

"Well, Zachary's assessments aren't always very helpful. The first time I asked him about Shay's character he said, and I quote, 'Shay? He's got bloody numbers running through his head all day and all night, and he likes it that way. He's mad, in other words.'" Her cheeks reddened. "And excuse my language."

Eleanor smiled. "No need. I grew up with the lot of them, if you'll remember." She watched as Shay's carriage turned west along the Rotten Row riding path. "Considering that he literally said there was nothing special about Lady Sarah last night, *and* that I saw him dancing with her a night or two before, *and* that today he's taking her riding in Melbourne's barouche, *and* that he hates riding in barouches, *and* that he broke an engagement to take Peep to the museum today to be here at all, I would say his disinterest was most definitely feigned."

"And so what do we do?"

Nell's smile deepened into a heartfelt grin. "What we do, dear Caroline," she answered, "is continue to observe. I know it's not proper for a sister to speak of her brother's mistresses, but Shay has had a few over the years, and they've tended to be . . . ordinary. Nothing to upend his schedule or take any part of his stupendously large mind away from things that actually interest him."

Her sister-in-law frowned. "But this Sarah is a marquis's daughter, and new to London. Making her his mistress could ruin her, couldn't it? That doesn't seem like something Shay would—"

"No, it isn't." Eleanor chuckled. "This is going to be *very* interesting." She signaled for Dawson to head the team toward home before the rain could begin. "And we are not going to tell Sebastian anything. Melbourne will want to step in, one way or the other, and for once I'd like to see what happens when he doesn't meddle."

"You think he won't find out?"

"I think if anyone can keep him from doing so, it will be Shay."

"Oh, dear," Caroline sighed, her eyes dancing with amusement, "this *is* going to be interesting, isn't it?"

"I should hope so."

Charlemagne directed his driver to head around the boundary of the park, while he pointed out various sites of historical or political interest along the way. Thank God he'd grown up in London, because whatever power Sarala had initially possessed to distract him had increased tenfold. Despite his best efforts to remain focused on a strategy to acquire the silks, he continually found himself simply . . . gazing at her. If he'd ever been this diligent in studying an opponent before, he couldn't remember it. Of course he'd never given a business rival a ruby necklace, either.

She leaned forward, tapping his left knee with elegant fingers. "What is that?"

He blinked, looking in the direction she gestured. "Kensington Palace. The royal family used it as their main residence until about fifty or so years ago."

"It's stunning. Who lives there now?"

He smiled. "That depends on the time of year. At the moment it's the Duchess of Kent and her daughter, Princess Victoria. Would you care for a tour?"

"Heavens, no. I wouldn't intrude." She eyed him. "You could do that? You know them?"

Only someone who'd never lived in London would ask

that question. "We're third cousins, or some such thing." He turned from the familiar sight of the palace to Sarala. He needed to make a move; it was time he wasn't the only one searching for footing. "Your mother hasn't seen you yet today, has she?"

Green eyes narrowed. "Why do you say that? Do you think I need her approval to engage in business?"

Covering his smile, Charlemagne reached out and touched her dangling left ear bob with his forefinger. "I was referring to these," he said, brushing his fingers against her cheek as he withdrew again. Soft as summer.

She covered the jewelry with both hands. "We are not here to discuss my jewelry. What's wrong with them, anyway?"

"Not a thing. They're lovely. And they suit you. Amethyst peacocks. I had just assumed that since your mother's changed your name, she's attempting to . . . minimize any appearance of foreign influences about your person."

"You're very forward to make that assumption."

He lifted an eyebrow. "Am I wrong?"

"Very well, no. You're correct. My mother probably wouldn't approve of my wearing them. They were a gift from a friend, however." Sarala drew a breath. "And speaking of gifts, I cannot accept one from you."

He'd wondered how he would bring up the topic of the ruby necklace. She'd beaten him to it. "Why can't you accept it?"

"Because whatever it is, we are barely acquainted, and besides, we—"

" 'Whatever it is?' " he interrupted, frowning. Surely she'd been curious enough to at least take a peek. "You didn't look at it?"

Sarala shifted slightly away from her maid, as if that

would prevent the girl from hearing every word of the conversation. "As I was saying, we are business rivals. Would you give a male rival a . . . whatever this is?" She produced the velvet bag from her reticule.

Charlemagne hesitated, honesty warring with the instinct to maintain a position of strength. "Probably not that particular item, but a token of respect wouldn't be out of the question, no."

Her gaze lowered to the bag, then returned to him again. "A token of respect? Is that what it is?"

If it would induce her to keep it, she could call it whatever she liked. "Yes. I merely thought you might appreciate it."

"So it has nothing to do with our negotiations, then."

"Not a thing."

"I see." She lifted her hand and held the pouch out over the road. "Then I could discard it, and nothing would change."

"Dis—" He cleared his throat, setting aside the thought that he'd spent two bloody hours picking it out. "Yes, I suppose so. It would be a shame to see it trampled by horses, though, if I may point that out."

Abruptly she lowered the pouch to her lap and sat forward to glare at him. "How can you give me a gift that's worth more than the entire shipment of silks, tell me it has nothing to do with our negotiations, and when I threaten to drop it, merely point out that horses might trample it? It's ridiculous!" She threw it at his chest. "And it's a bribe of some sort. I won't accept it."

His momentary satisfaction over the fact that she *had* opened the pouch twisted into consternation as he reflexively caught the bundle. "Don't you like it?"

"Of course I like it. But I can't wear it without someone

wondering who gave it to me, and I won't wear it if you think it obligates me to sell you the silks. Especially not if you think it constitutes payment for them."

"I actually didn't think much beyond the fact that it would look well on you," he answered, inwardly swearing at himself. He'd wanted to know how she would view the gift, if it would flatter her and soften her resistance to his maneuverings, business and personal. He had his answer; she'd looked at it from every angle, just as he had, and obviously she hadn't been so much as tempted to keep it, whether it was worth twice what the silks were, or not. Damnation. He'd underestimated her. Again. "You said you like it, so keep it."

"No. Not even if you swear to me that my keeping it won't alter our business rivalry, or the fact that you, being wealthy enough to purchase a ruby on a whim, must pay me six thousand pounds if you want those silks."

"What? *Six* thousand pounds? I told you that it wasn't a bribe."

"So your intentions are matrimonial?"

He actually had to work not to blush. "And why the devil do you assume that?"

"Because when I tell my parents where it came from, that is exactly what *they'll* assume. And so will everyone else."

"No one will know where it came from. I purchased it from a small shop in Greenwich, told the fellow it was for my niece." He hadn't completely lost his mind, after all.

"*I* will know where it came from, Lord Charlemagne. I had hoped that we could conduct this negotiation in a professional manner, but obviously you have a different idea. For your information, I have sent out several inquiries regarding the silks, and expect to hear offers as soon as this afternoon."

"Sarala, I—"

"You may let us out here, my lord."

For a heartbeat he glared at her. "Tollins, here."

"Yes, my lord." The barouche rolled smoothly to a stop.

Charlemagne stood to open the door, then stepped down to help Sarala and her maid to the ground. "I beg your pardon if I've offended your sensibilities," he said stiffly, "and I hope my offer of a gift hasn't removed me from the competition."

He hoped he sounded contrite; he meant to. In his defense, he was unused to both apologies and to making excuses. Hell, on the rare occasions he gave women gifts, they generally just said thank you and then fell on him with their clothes off. Obviously Sarala Carlisle wasn't a typical female.

"Business is business, my lord," she returned succinctly. "I will still consider a reasonable—and I stress *reasonable*—offer from you. Good day."

She was *not* going to dismiss him from two private conversations in a row. "Tollins, drive home," Charlemagne instructed, and strode after her.

"What are you doing?" she blurted as he caught up. "Go away. You're obviously devious, and we should only meet in very public, very crowded locations."

"Certainly, if you feel you're not a match for me otherwise," he drawled, taking her hand and placing it over his sleeve. "But I'd hardly abandon a female in the middle of London."

"We are five streets from Carlisle House, my lord. Perhaps we should negotiate by letter, if my being a female distresses you."

They angled toward the more secluded walking path as a light drizzle began. She seemed to be ignoring it, so he did the same. "Your being a female does not distress me," he stated. "I'd negotiate with a three-legged goat, if it had my silks."

"But you wouldn't buy it a ruby."

"A goat would only eat it."

She snorted, then coughed, obviously trying to cover her amusement. "You are now one of several interested parties, my lord. You will have to offer me something that I want. And what I want is a fair price, not rubies."

"Is it?" he returned. Charlemagne tugged her around to face him, leaned down, and kissed her.

Chapter 5

Charlemagne's mouth molded against Sarala's. He felt her surprise and then her arms wrapping around his shoulders. Soft, warm lips met his with even more heat than before, and lightning swept down his spine.

Something smacked him hard across the back of the head. Startled, he released Sarala and whipped around. "What the—"

Sarala's maid swung the parasol at him again, wielding it like a club. "You take your hands off her!" the girl sputtered, dancing just out of his reach.

"My hands are off her. Desist."

"Jenny, it's all right," Sarala broke in, moving past him as though to shelter him from the petite servant's onslaught.

"It's not all right, my lady. I'm here to chaperone you, and I can't have any tomcat who wanders by accosting your virtue."

Charlemagne frowned. "'Tomcat'?" he repeated carefully. As if he would go about rutting with every female in the park. Not bloody likely. Hell, he hadn't had time for a mistress in nearly three months. He didn't want one now. He wanted Sarala. Shay blinked, trying to focus again and blaming his confusion on being bashed on the head.

Sarala continued forward and took the parasol from her maid's hand. "Lord Charlemagne isn't a tomcat, and he wasn't attempting to assault my virtue, Jenny. He's losing the negotiation, so he's attempting either to startle me into making a mistake, or to seduce the silk shipment away from me." Calmly she faced him, one eyebrow lifted and only the twinkle in her eyes giving away her glee at his being beaten with a parasol. "So which was it, my lord? Startlement or seduction?"

Charlemagne backed away a step. All he needed was for her to begin clobbering him, too. He hadn't meant to kiss her at all, either time. Her wit, her intelligence, her confidence, the way she had a logical counter for his every approach—she simply drew him. But if she knew or realized how spiderwebbed his brain had become, he would never get those silks. "If you were a man," he improvised, using every ounce of skill to keep his tone light and edged with humor, "I would play cards or billiards with you to test your mettle."

"Would that be 'test,' or 'taste'?" she queried.

That was when he heard the tremor in her voice. She'd felt it, too—the pull between them. As he realized he hadn't lost ground, Charlemagne smiled. "I'll let you come to your own conclusions, Sarala." He turned on his heel, heading for the closer southern border of the park. "And I shall call on you at noon tomorrow. I'll bring a picnic luncheon."

"I'm not available," she called after him.

Charlemagne didn't slow. "Yes, you are," he returned, his

smile deepening now that she couldn't see his face. Being something of an expert, he could say with a fair amount of assurance that that had been one hell of a kiss. And this negotiation was far from over.

"My lady," Jenny said, "we need to get you out of the rain."

Sarala shook herself, finally realizing that they were indeed being rained upon. "Yes, I suppose so." She handed the parasol back to the maid. The flimsy thing could barely fend off a light morning dew, and now the handle was broken, but it might serve to keep her dress from complete ruin. "Let's go home."

Jenny opened the parasol and held it up over Sarala's head as they walked. "I hope I didn't do wrong, my lady, but for him—a lord—to kiss you like that in public, well, I couldn't—"

"Jenny, you didn't do anything wrong. Thank you very much for looking after me." Slowing, Sarala faced the maid. "I would appreciate, however, if you kept it between us."

"Of course, my lady." She hesitated. "You're all right, then?"

"Yes, I'm perfectly fine. Just a little startled."

The kiss *had* startled her, but not because of the act itself. She'd been anticipating another one for what felt like weeks. And it proved that she hadn't imagined it the first time—the kiss had felt exactly as she'd remembered—warm, and confident, and intimate. Surreptitiously she ran one finger along her lips.

In the course of various business dealings she'd managed on her father's behalf, men had attempted seduction before. Apparently if they couldn't overwhelm her mind, their next and only remaining strategy was to attempt to bed her—as if that would miraculously turn her witless. They had been the idiots.

Charlemagne's kisses, though, then and now, hadn't felt like those of a man trying to exert his dominance or authority. He'd said he admired her. Nothing in his embrace contradicted his words. And that troubled her a little, because he kissed very well. Very well, indeed.

Once they reached the outer boundary of Hyde Park, she took control of the damaged parasol while Jenny hailed a hack. The drizzle continued soft and gray, and with the sun gone and the light east breeze, Sarala longed to sit in front of a warm fire. The blankets and warm coals of Lord Shay's barouche had been heavenly.

She imagined that Shay would be soaked to the bone by the time he reached Griffin House, for he'd had no parasol or hooded coat, but it served him right. Perhaps she was enjoying this very unusual negotiation, but a straightforward exchange of numbers and a handshake would have been much easier on her nerves. Well, not her nerves, precisely, though she did feel . . . jittery whenever she caught sight of Charlemagne Griffin. And she certainly hadn't been the least bit bored over the past few days, thanks to those silks—and to her opponent.

"Lady Sarah," the butler said, as he accepted her wet cloak, "your mother is awaiting you in the drawing room."

Blast it, she was going to freeze to death before she ever made it back to her bedchamber to find dry clothes. "Thank you, Blankman."

"I'll bring you some hot tea, my lady," Jenny put in, helping to remove her bonnet and gloves.

"Thank you, Jenny."

Taking a deep breath in an attempt to clear her mind of

warm kisses and other things at which Lord Charlemagne was undoubtedly equally skilled, Sarala climbed the stairs to the drawing room. She rapped softly on the closed door, then pushed it open. "Mama, you wanted to . . . see me?"

Half a dozen matrons turned to face her. Blast it all. No wonder Blankman had given her such a sympathetic look. Mama had undoubtedly forbidden him to warn her that visitors were present.

"Sarah. Come here, darling."

Pasting a smile on her face, Sarala crossed the room. Belatedly she tucked a strand of wet hair away behind her left ear, and then with a jolt realized she still wore the peacock ear bobs. Damn, damn, damn.

The marchioness, seated on the couch beside Lady Allendale, took Sarala's hands and pulled her forward so they could kiss cheeks. "Take those things off at once," her mother whispered.

Sarala hurriedly removed the ear bobs and tucked them into her pelisse pocket. Inside, her fingers felt another shape—the ruby pendant. *That devious devil.*

"I believe you know everyone, don't you, my dear?"

"Yes, Mama." Sarala made a curtsy to the room in general. "If you'll pardon me, I'll go change."

"Nonsense, my dear," Mrs. Wendon said, brandishing a gingerbread biscuit. "You look charming. Doesn't she, Mary?"

Lady Mary Doorley nodded. "Indeed. Just the thing, I'm certain."

Sarala hid a frown. "Just the thing for what?"

"Oh, yes, and her accent is charming, as well."

"Just the thing for what?" Sarala repeated. It had taken her only a day to figure out her mother's old gaggle of friends. They were all matchmakers to the core. And if she was charming, then they were thinking of setting her after some man. She began to feel as if she'd been surrounded by a pack of hungry, laughing hyenas. "Excuse me, but what are you talking about?"

The marchioness reached out to take her daughter's hand again. "We've all been speculating, Sarah," she said expansively, her voice shaking with barely suppressed excitement, "about which gentleman might be the best match for you. I personally favor the Duke of Melbourne, but Lady A—"

"The Duke of—Lord Charlemagne's brother?"

Just inside the doorway a tea tray crashed to the floor. Sarala jumped.

"Apologies, my lady," Jenny squeaked, sending Sarala a miserable look as she knelt to pick up the scattered teapot and accessories and replace them on the silver tray.

"It's no matter, Jenny," Sarala put in before her mother could criticize the maid. "We have tea already. I only hope you haven't caught a cold with me keeping you out in the rain like that."

"Oh, thank you, Lady Sarah," the maid whispered, curtsying and backing the jumbled tea set out of the room.

Sarala was actually the grateful one. The accident at least gave her a moment to compose herself. Her mother actually thought she would suit the Duke of Melbourne? Ridiculous, and even more so in light of the fact that she was practically at war with the man's brother—despite the kisses.

"I still think she would better suit Lord John Tundle," Lady Allendale said, rubbing her hands together with obvious relish. "He served in India several years ago."

"I beg your pardon, Lady Allendale," Sarala said carefully, trying to pull her thoughts together, "but do you not have a granddaughter just making her debut this Season? Why would you promote my interest over hers?"

Mrs. Wendon burst out laughing. "Because she already tried to set Millicent on half the gentlemen of the *ton*, and the poor girl has succumbed to the vapors each and every time. One of them told Lady A that her granddaughter seemed in need of a curative."

"The girl's too delicate for her own good," Lady Allendale said unsympathetically.

"You can't ignore that she and Lord Epping would look very well together, with his fair features and her dark ones." Mrs. Wendon sipped at her tea.

The ladies began a long, loud debate over whether Melbourne should be the target and who would attend the Franfield recital that evening, and whether Sarala would show better on the stage or in the audience. Considering her barely adequate skill with the pianoforte, Sarala knew where she would prefer to be, but obviously none of this was her decision.

"You mustn't mind them, you know," a quiet voice came from behind her.

She looked up to see Augusta, Lady Gerard, standing at the back of the couch. As she reviewed the conversation, Lady Gerard did seem to be the only one who hadn't offered a suggestion to alter her marital status. "They seem very enthusiastic," Sarala offered diplomatically.

The elderly woman gestured for her to shift over, and then sat down on the sofa beside her. "They've all mostly married off their own children, and everyone knows grandchildren can't be managed, so they've decided to loan you all of their matchmaking expertise."

"So I see."

Pale blue eyes met hers. "You may speak your mind with me, Sarala. Or should I call you Sarah?"

Sarala took a deep breath. It would be so nice to be able

to speak frankly with another woman. She'd missed that more than anything else in the weeks since she'd left India and her friends behind. That to her was far more important than being tossed into matrimony. At the same time, she had no intention of saying the wrong thing to the wrong person.

"My mother wishes me to go by Sarah," she answered, meeting the baroness's cool gaze.

"Mujhe ap pareshan lage," Lady Gerard murmured. "You seem worried to me."

"You speak Hindi?"

"Not as well as I used to. My husband was stationed in Delhi for fifteen years, though well before your time, I'm afraid. India is a lovely country, and very different from England."

"*Very* different," Sarala agreed vehemently. "Were you sorry to leave?"

"I was sorry to leave friends, and happy to reacquaint myself with others back in England. I don't imagine you have anyone with whom to renew old friendships here though, do you? You were born in India."

"You know a great deal about me, my lady."

"I know a great deal about a great many people. That's why I'm always invited to parties. For instance, I know that the Duke of Melbourne would never offer for you."

Sarala lifted an eyebrow. "And why is that?"

Lady Gerard chuckled. "Don't be offended, my dear. It has little to do with you. Melbourne is a singularly uncooperative sort of single gentleman: a widower who loved his wife. And aside from that, Melbourne . . . is England. The Griffins have been landowners and nobles here since they came from Rome eighteen hundred years ago. And no Griffin has ever married outside of England since then." She chuckled again. "He's literally more English than Prinny and the rest of the royal family."

No Griffin has ever married outside of England. "That seems a bit stuffy of them," Sarala returned lightly, smoothing her skirt and throttling the urge to touch her lips again. As she'd suspected, Charlemagne's kiss had been a strategic maneuver. Lady Gerard's comments confirmed it. "I suppose, though, that with the best of England's females to choose from, they've never needed to look elsewhere."

"You don't seem disappointed to hear your poor prospects of marrying the duke," the baroness noted.

"I've only seen him twice, and have certainly never spoken to him." She smiled, warming even further to the elderly woman in the dark green muslin gown. "Actually, I've barely spoken to anyone Mama's friends have mentioned. At least all the chaos should afford me the opportunity to meet more people."

"You are a practical lass, aren't you?"

"I attempt to be. I've learned to lead with my mind rather than my heart, at any rate."

Lady Gerard took a sip of tea, eyeing her from over the rim of the cup. "How old are you?"

"Two-and-twenty."

"That's a hard lesson to be learned by one as young as you are."

Sarala forced a laugh. As if she had *any* intention of telling anyone how she'd learned that particular lesson. But it was another reason she'd never marry anyone as well known as the Duke of Melbourne. "It's something that makes sense," she offered instead. "After all, I've been in London for less than a fortnight, and already my name's been changed and my mother's trying to marry me to a granite figurehead to whom I've never even been introduced. If I were a silly girl, I could well be overset by now."

The baroness burst into laughter, drawing the attention of the other ladies in the room. "What's so amusing over there?" Lady Allendale asked, furrowing her thin, straight brows. "You must include us in your jests."

"That would overset *her,*" Lady Gerard whispered. "Oh, it was nothing," she continued in a louder voice. "Merely an agreement on the sad weather we're having this year."

"It is sad, indeed." Lady Allendale took Lady Hanover's hand. "You weren't here, but this past winter the Thames nearly froze over. All the young people made a huge game of the weather, but I thought it was dreadful. Dreadful and cold."

"Please, ladies, we must keep our eyes on the target," Mrs. Wendon broke in. "Namely on how Lady Sarah is to attract Epping's attention."

"You mean Lord John Tundle."

"I most certainly meant Epping."

"This is exciting," Sarala's mother chortled. "Do you think it could actually work? And I haven't ruled out Melbourne, yet."

"Our task is to make it work. Now, as I was saying . . ."

"Is anyone home?" Charlemagne asked, handing over his sopping wet greatcoat to Stanton.

The butler managed to look stoic and dismayed all at the same time as he took the garment with two fingers. "His Grace is away at a meeting, and Lady Penelope is upstairs protesting the necessity of learning French. And you have a note sent over from Gaston House."

Charlemagne frowned, accepting the folded missive from

his personal London residence and trying not to get it wet. "It's from Oswald." He glanced at Stanton's carefully blank face. "I'll be in the billiards room. I'd appreciate if you'd have Cook send up some hot soup. Chicken, preferably."

"Very good, my lord." The butler turned for the servants' hall, then hesitated. "Do you wish me to send Caine up to tend you? If I may be so bold, you appear to be rather . . . damp."

"Soaked to the skin, actually. Yes, have Caine meet me in my bedchamber."

"I'll see to it at once, my lord."

Still dripping from his hair and boots, Charlemagne climbed the Griffin House stairs to his trio of private rooms at the back of the house. Stanton's litany of the location of family members used to take much longer, but now with first Eleanor and then Zachary married and living elsewhere, the butler's task had become a little easier.

His own hadn't, however. And that was why he should never have kissed Sarala once, much less twice. Flirtations and the occasional lover were one thing, but whatever it was about Sarala that had confounded him so, didn't feel casual or something to be pursued on slow evenings. And she tasted like cinnamon, though that might have been his imagination.

Shaking out his hair and attempting to clear his waterlogged brain at the same time, Shay set aside the Gaston House butler's note and shed his jacket and cravat. Business and the Griffin family and ancient artifacts and writings. Those were his interests, though not necessarily in that order. Playing about at getting those silks back wasn't precisely good business, but at least he could honestly declare that it was somewhat business-related.

Kissing Sarala, though—he couldn't categorize, justify, or clarify anything about it. She could claim he'd done it to coerce her, and at least that explanation made some sort of sense. Otherwise he would just have to admit he'd been seized by an odd and hopefully temporary madness.

Caine scratched at the door, thankfully rousing him from his pointless reverie. "Enter," he called, going to work on the buttons of his waistcoat.

"Stanton said you were caught in the rain, m'lord," the valet said, his Irish accent deepening in obvious amusement.

"Yes. My own fault—I decided to walk home."

"No worries, m'lord. I've already sent for the coach, and we'll have you to White's in good time."

Charlemagne frowned. "White's?"

Nodding, Caine pulled a folded paper from his pocket as a brief look of concern crossed his narrow face. "I always make a note of all your appointments, since I admit to my shame that my memory's not as solid as yours." He unfolded the paper and glanced at the numerous chicken scratches. "Yes. Last week you said you'd moved your monthly meeting with your brother the duke to—"

"—to one o'clock today at White's," Shay finished. "Damnation. I forgot."

"It's no matter, m'lord. You'll be there on time."

"Thank you, Caine. And please tell Cook I won't be needing the soup."

"Of course, m'lord."

As Charlemagne dried himself off and dressed in a dark brown jacket with light gray waistcoat and dark gray trousers, his frown deepened. He knew better than anyone how unusual it was for him to forget an appointment. Even worse, he and Sebastian met for luncheon monthly—their chance to discuss business and family without siblings or nieces or distractions other than fellow diners who felt they had to stop by and say hello.

What the devil was wrong with him? He and Melbourne had made their monthly meetings a five-year-long tradition. Charlemagne checked the knot of his cravat, nodded at Caine, then at the last minute remembered Oswald's note and crammed it into his pocket to read in the coach as he went downstairs. Stanton had found a dry greatcoat for him, and with another nod he headed outside to the coach. In a moment he was rumbling down the street on the way to White's.

"Good afternoon, Lord Charlemagne," the maitre d' at White's greeted him as he shed his poor weather gear.

"Peabody."

"His Grace just arrived a moment ago, and is at your usual table."

"My thanks. Send some rum by, if you please. I need to warm my bones a little."

"Very good, my lord."

Sebastian looked up from a small stack of papers as Charlemagne approached. "I told you not to take the barouche this morning."

Charlemagne seated himself. "I made it worse by walking home. Apologies for being late." A silent footman delivered the rum. "I think Caine was devastated at the carnage to my wardrobe, but he hid it well."

"Mm-hm. As long as you didn't drip water all over the new Persian carpet in the billiards room."

"So you made the purchase. You have a certain sideways sensibility about you, you know."

"Because I inquired about the carpet before I asked about your health?" Sebastian sliced off a section of table cheese and bit into it. "My thanks for noticing."

"You're welcome. And your carpet and I are both fine."

He pulled the Gaston House note from his pocket and nudged it in Sebastian's direction. "It's from Oswald."

"Your butler?"

Charlemagne nodded. "Apparently someone tried to break into Gaston House last night. Oswald and a pair of footmen heard the noise and drove them off, but a window was broken."

"That's odd," the duke commented, reading the note before he handed it back over. "I would think most of London would know not to break into a house owned by one of the Griffins."

"Yes, well, apparently I'm not as terror-inspiring as you are." Gaston House had been their maternal grandmother's, and though technically it was his London residence, he barely spent more than a fortnight there each year—and that was mostly when he had negotiations to straighten out and couldn't do it in noisy Griffin House. Not that Griffin House was nearly as noisy as it used to be.

"Considering that your butler could break an elephant in half, hopefully the culprits are terrified now. By the by, I ordered the lamb and kidney for you. And I may have some good news."

Charlemagne looked from the papers at his brother's elbow to Melbourne. "Prinny and Liverpool liked the canal expansion idea?"

"They did, but that's not what I was talking about. Do you remember Reginald Burney-Smythe?"

"Viscount Dannon's brother? He's a banker, isn't he?"

"Investor, these days. He has some connections in Madrid. One, in particular, who's expressed an interest in acquiring fine quality silk. Apparently he's willing to buy at up to six quid per bolt."

His mind already working on a suitable response, Charlemagne reminded himself that despite his younger siblings' claims, Melbourne could not read anyone's thoughts. "I'll keep that in mind," he said, "but at the moment I have a lead on an even better deal."

"You should let Burney-Smythe know, then. He could be a good source of information."

"If you have the address, I'll send him a note."

"Good." Melbourne gazed at him for a moment. "How many possible buyers do you have, Shay? I have to admit, all this interest has made me a bit curious to see the finest silk ever to come out of China."

"I'll conduct a tour of the warehouse when Nell and Caroline come to choose their dress material."

"You're not using any of our warehouses to store them."

Of course Sebastian would know that; he kept detailed records of what was where, and when. With the amount of commerce the Griffins conducted, that in itself was a daunting task. "I have my own storage facilities. Why so curious?"

"No reason." The duke gave a rare smile. "Since you're obviously cooking up something secretive and highly profitable, I'll change the subject. Peep apparently broke into your study yesterday morning."

Charlemagne nodded, unconcerned, as two plates of lamb and kidney appeared before them. "I told her I'd already bought her birthday present. She was probably looking for it."

"I think she found it."

"I doubt it. I didn't hide it in my rooms. I hid it in hers." Grinning, Charlemagne dug into his luncheon. "She won't get the best of me this year."

"She wore a necklace into the breakfast room. A ruby

pendant. I told her to put it back so she wouldn't spoil your surprise."

Damnation. "Oh, that," he returned, keeping the smile on his face. "That was a bit of a token for someone else."

"A very nice-quality token. Anyone in particular?"

"Not any longer. A change of plans, you might say." And since Sarala had already given him several reasons that she wouldn't wear it even though he'd made every effort to ensure that she could, his little attempt at bribery or whatever it was that had possessed him wouldn't go any farther than the two of them. It didn't need to go beyond that, since she was the one whose attention he'd been trying to get and whose mettle he'd been trying to gauge.

Melbourne finally segued to the burgeoning cotton and tobacco trade with America and the resistance they were still finding from the older and more conservative members of the House of Lords. Shay only half listened, though, as he tried to find a logical reason why he hadn't told his brother that he'd lost the silk to another bidder. At this point and with the lies he'd already told, he didn't know what to say.

Was it pride, embarrassment at being outmaneuvered by a barely English chit? Probably—or it had been three days ago, anyway. Now he'd piled all sorts of nonsense on top of his initial blunder, for which he had no one to blame but himself. And he'd kissed his competition, which made no sense at all.

In addition, he hadn't done much bargaining. She'd stated her outrageously high price, he'd countered with his insultingly low one, and then they'd danced around other topics, literally and figuratively. Obviously now he needed to resolve this before the family got wind of his blundering.

"—when Zachary and Valentine killed a pair of traveling jugglers."

Charlemagne blinked. "What?"

"So you've returned," Melbourne said dryly, sipping his wine.

"I was just contemplating," Shay replied, trying not to sound defensive.

"Contemplating what?"

"Nothing, really. You were talking about a possible blockade against the British in the United States."

"Actually I was talking about how far we can afford to antagonize the Americans by shanghaiing and conscripting their sailors, but I suppose it's roughly the same problem."

"Right." *Pay attention, Shay.* "I've spoken with Admiral Tr—"

"I rely on your counsel, you know," the duke interrupted in a low voice. "I don't just come to these luncheons to hear myself talk."

"I know that, Seb." Charlemagne stirred the fork across his plate. "I apologize. It's . . . I just have several things on my mind."

Melbourne gazed at him. "Anything you would care to discuss?"

"No." He sat forward. "I'll talk with the admiral again. Maybe I can convince him to see reason."

Dark gray eyes continued studying him with an intensity that had reputedly caused several cabinet ministers to excuse themselves from meetings. Finally Sebastian nodded. "Do your best, though the damage has probably already been done. And Shay?"

"Yes?"

"We don't have to restrict our luncheon conversations to business. I am your brother, after all. And your friend. If something is troubling you, I hope you know you can tell me."

Wonderful. Now he had Melbourne worried. For a moment Shay debated simply confessing his stupidity. It had been only three days though. If he could salvage the negotiations with Sarala, conduct them professionally and with his usual, typical acumen, in another day or two everything would be back as it should and he would have nothing to confess. "Perhaps I'm just a bit unsettled," he lied, "with the idea of Nell and Valentine having a child. Aside from the fact that I remember quite clearly when Nell was an infant herself, the idea of Valentine reproducing frankly frightens me."

The duke chuckled, his shoulders lowering a little as he relaxed. "I've been having nightmares about that, myself. But I've never seen Eleanor as happy, so I suppose we'll simply have to hope the child takes after its mother rather than its father."

"Amen to that." Charlemagne toasted him and took a generous swallow of rum.

Chapter 6

"Papa, surely we can find something more useful to do than attend a recital for a group of people we don't even know."

Sarala's mother, bedecked in glorious yellow and probably a bit overdecorated for a recital, swept into the foyer. "Once you attend the recital, you will know them, and they will be grateful for your presence. Then before you know it, you will have made friends."

In truth, Sarala had had much the same thought. If no one in her family had any other agenda, she would have looked forward to the event. "It all sounds well and good," she returned, clutching her cloak closer around her shoulders as the three of them left the house for the coach, "but I know your true reason for wanting us to attend."

"And what might that be?" her father asked as he settled into the coach beside his wife.

"Mama's friends have decided to marry me off to either

Lord Epping or Lord John Tundle, and Mama's set on the Duke of Melbourne." Sarala grinned; the more she thought about it, the sillier it seemed. "Only the poor men don't know it."

"There is nothing remotely poor about the Duke of Melbourne. Keep *that* in mind, Sarah."

The marquis cleared his throat. "I thought you danced the other night with the duke's brother."

Sarala nodded at her father. "Lord Charlemagne. He's quite . . . arrogant. I imagine his brother must be ten times worse."

"Howard, you've met His Grace, haven't you? You could perform the introductions."

The marquis took his wife's hand and squeezed it. "I've exchanged a word or two with him. He's a bright young man with far better things to do than speak with someone just getting his Town bearings again."

"If he knew you, he would speak with you, Papa," Sarala declared. "You are very interesting."

He leaned forward and tweaked her cheek. "And you are very kind to say that, my dear, and I admit that at least I have hunted tigers from the back of an elephant. I doubt His Grace has ever performed that particular feat."

"I doubt very many Englishmen at all have done that."

"Will you two stop it?" Lady Hanover asked, her tone equal parts amusement and exasperation. "This is not a competition. Well, it is, but not the shooting tigers sort. Can you make the introductions, Howard?"

Her husband sighed. "Yes, I can manage it. If he's attending tonight."

"Lady Allendale knows the duke's aunt, Lady Tremaine, and she thinks the whole family may attend. They're old friends of the Franfields."

A shiver ran through Sarala—not at the idea of being introduced to someone who wouldn't marry her, but at the thought she might see Lord Shay for the second time that day.

When they arrived at Franfield House the ballroom was full of chairs, all of them facing a pretty pianoforte and a harp. Thank goodness her mother had declared her playing too poor to show well, and she didn't have to perform tonight. She knew all the notes, but she always became so concerned with precision and the right rhythm that her tutors said she played without feeling. Ha. She had a good deal of feeling. It just so happened that most of that feeling centered around terror.

"Dash it, we're early," her mother said. "I'd hoped we could make a grander entrance."

"Well, it's too late for that now," Lord Hanover commented. "We can't very well leave again and then return later. Shall we find seats?"

"No, we should mingle. Do you see any sign of the Griffins?"

"Not yet, my love. Apparently they are better at making entrances than we are."

"None of your sarcasm now, Howard."

Considering that the only person there at the moment with whom Sarala was acquainted happened to be Mr. Francis Henning, mingling seemed a terribly dull and useless idea. After taking one look at her mother's determinedly happy countenance, however, she reconsidered.

"Good evening, Mr. Henning," she said, accepting a glass of punch from a footman.

"Oh, I say, Lady Sarala." He bobbed his head, jowls shaking. "Or did I hear you was Sarah, now? You ain't having a laugh at all us young bucks, are you?"

She gritted her teeth. "Certainly not, Mr. Henning. I . . . go by both names. Call me what you will."

"That's—" He stiffened as he glanced beyond her shoulder. "Drat. My grandmama's here. Excuse me. I have to go fetch her some punch." He sprinted off.

Sarala turned around to see a stout woman with a shock of snow white hair scowling as she jabbed a walking stick in Mr. Henning's chest. As she watched, the cane swung in her direction and back again.

Hm. It probably meant nothing. She was, after all, something of a curiosity—no matter how conservative her dress, she couldn't hide her tanned skin, and most people seemed to think she had an accent. On the other hand, she also remembered what Lady Gerard had said about the Griffin family's standards of marriage. Perhaps Melbourne and his kin weren't the only ones to prefer England-born English.

"You're not mingling, dear," Lady Hanover said from behind her.

"I'm trying to. All of the participants playing in the recital must be elsewhere."

"You know, several of the Society ladies host luncheons. Normally I wouldn't attend because most of them seem to be havens for gossip and rumor spreading, but I see now that you and I will simply have to grin and bear it. It's the best way for you to meet other young ladies of your station."

"I would like that." She would also like for any new friends she met to know her as Sarala, but even Mr. Henning had now heard of her name change. And since tradition and custom made it impossible for her to join her father for a business luncheon at one of his clubs, she supposed tea and gossip would have to do.

Lady Hanover kissed her cheek. "That's the spirit." The marchioness looked up as more guests appeared in the doorway. "Ah, look, Mrs. Wendon and Lady Allendale have come to show their support."

More likely they'd come to see whom they could send swooping after Sarala first: Lord John Tundle or Lord Epping. She had no idea whether either gentleman would be in attendance, but she had enough to think about with Charlemagne keeping her on her toes and her mother setting her on Melbourne.

Twenty minutes later at the sound of a familiar male laugh she spun around—and knocked into the arm of a man standing behind her. "Excuse me," she said, rising on her toes to make out Shay Griffin standing with his brother and sister-in-law. He'd come. A thrill of anticipation ran down her spine.

The man she'd bumped into put a hand on her wrist. "No, please excuse me," he returned in a low, cultured drawl. "I don't believe we've been introduced. I'm Melbourne."

The breath froze in Sarala's throat as her gaze jolted to his face. She belatedly dipped a curtsy. "Your Grace. I am—"

"You're Lady Sarah Carlisle," he finished.

His dark gray eyes weren't on her face. For a single, disconcerting moment she thought he was gazing at her bosom—until she remembered the necklace. Shay had said no one would know where it came from. It had best not be a Griffin family heirloom, or someone was going to get their eye blackened. "I am, Your Grace. I'm pleased to make your acquaintance."

Oh, heavens. Out of all possible outcomes, she hadn't expected the duke to be the one to notice the ruby. After all her trepidation, her mother hadn't even asked her about the jewel. In India she had had several ardent suitors, so perhaps her parents thought it had been a gift from one of them. Good.

She needed only one person to react to the necklace, and that was Shay Griffin. She couldn't imagine what he would say when he realized she'd accepted his "gift" and still meant to demand six thousand pounds for the silks. He was the one who'd said one had nothing to do with the other, after all. But if his brother knew something about it, that changed everything.

"You and your parents are newly arrived from India, I believe," Melbourne continued.

He hadn't mentioned anything about the necklace. Perhaps he only admired fine jewelry, for the ruby definitely qualified as that. His gray gaze, a shade or two darker than that of his younger brother, met hers squarely.

"Yes, we are. We arrived in London just a fortnight ago."

He stirred just a trace. "Then your acquaintance with your fellows must be limited. You and your parents must come sit with my family."

What? "I—That's very generous of you, Your Grace, but I can't speak for my parents."

The duke nodded. "Where is your father?"

Thankful that her hand remained steady, she pointed. With another half nod the Duke of Melbourne turned on his heel and left her standing there. "Oh, for heaven's sake," she breathed.

A pair of hands clutched her shoulders. Sarala jumped, squeaking.

"What did he say?" her mother whispered. "And stop that silly squawking at once."

"You startled me," Sarala returned, trying to settle her heartbeat as she faced the marchioness. "He only asked when we'd arrived in London. And—"

"My dears," her father broke in, joining them, "this will rattle your nerves a bit, I'm afraid. The Duke of Melbourne just approached me and asked if we'd care to sit with him tonight."

This time it was her mother who squeaked. "Heaven be praised," she said vehemently. "You must have made an impression on him, Sarah. This is wonderful news."

Sarala wasn't quite so certain about that, but she kept her mouth shut. Perhaps Charlemagne had asked his brother to intervene and bargain for the silks. The duke, of course, wouldn't want to deal with her, so he'd requested that her father join them. That made sense, though if Melbourne thought he could use his name and high station to force down the price, she would have to step in. Her family couldn't afford to take a loss simply to assuage some man's overlarge share of pride.

How cowardly of Charlemagne to arrange for reinforcements, though as their hostess appeared and urged everyone to take their seats, she had to admit that it didn't seem quite his style to hand over control of his business dealings to anyone else—even a brother.

"Fix your sleeve, Sarah," Lady Hanover whispered.

"My sleeve is fine, Mama. You need to stop worrying."

"I'm not worrying. I only want to be certain that you'll make a good impression. This is your best chance, my darling. How many people do you think are ever invited to join the Griffin family?"

They hadn't been asked to join the Griffin family; they'd been asked to sit with them, which was an entirely different box of cats. Disputing semantics at the moment, though, wouldn't do anything but spoil her mother's buoyant mood.

Sarala took the moments as they made their way through the settling crowd to revise the approach she'd planned. With his family about, she couldn't be as direct with Charlemagne as she wanted, nor as she'd intended. In fact, she should probably remove the necklace and save it for his silly picnic luncheon tomorrow.

Before she could do so, her father stopped just in front of her to shake the duke's hand. "Your Grace, may I present my wife, Lady Hanover? And I believe you've met our daughter, Lady Sarah."

Lady Hanover curtsied deeply, nearly pulling Sarala to the floor beside her. "Your Grace. Thank you for the great honor you do us."

"My pleasure. Have you met my family?"

Sarala smiled as Melbourne introduced each member of the Griffin clan. When her gaze found Charlemagne, he was already looking at her and ignoring her parents. Her mouth went dry. Slowly his gaze trailed down her face to her throat, and almost imperceptibly his eyes widened. Abruptly she was glad she hadn't had the chance to remove the ruby.

Aha. With a wily smile, the white queen moved onto the chessboard. *Check.*

There was no mistaking the faint smile on Sarala's face as the two families seated themselves. She'd worn the necklace, and she knew she'd surprised him. Blast it all. Had Melbourne seen it? For God's sake, Charlemagne hoped not. This negotiation was complicated enough without him having to explain his strategy to his brother.

Did this mean she would accept his offer of seven hundred and fifty guineas for the shipment? Hm. He needed to find out. "I'll fetch everyone a punch," he said. "Lady Sarala, might I impose on you to lend a hand?"

Zachary started to say something, probably gentlemanly, about offering his assistance, and Shay trod on his toe. As he gazed at Sarala pointedly, she nodded. "With pleasure."

"I'll save you a seat right here, Sarah," the girl's mother

said, patting a seat between herself and Melbourne. "Do hurry back."

"We won't be a moment," Charlemagne put in, taking Sarala's hand and putting it across his arm.

"You seem to have dried off," Sarala whispered as they pushed to the edge of the settling crowd and Lady Franfield appeared to announce the evening's players and their selections.

Her quiet voice sent a warm tremor down his spine. "As did you," he returned in the same tone, coming to a halt beside the refreshment table at the back of the room. "And you found my gift."

"Yes. Since you ignored my wishes and my warnings and pressed it on me, I thought to at least make some use of it."

The first player, the Franfields' daughter Hattie, took her place at the pianoforte. Using the cover of the polite applause and then the Haydn concerto, Charlemagne moved closer to Sarala, handing her a pair of glasses as he did so. "I'm glad you did. It looks splendid on you."

"I hope you still think so when I tell you that the price of the silks remains at six thousand pounds, Lord Charlemagne."

His mouth quirked. If she'd been a man, he would have been complimenting the size of her balls. "Call me Shay," he said instead. "We are friendly adversaries, are we not?" The wording didn't seem adequate, but he didn't think words existed that could accurately describe their odd relationship.

"Shay, then," she said softly.

Abruptly he wanted to kiss her again. Some sort of physical contact became absolutely necessary. He glanced about, to see that everyone but the footman in charge of the refreshments table had their backs turned to watch the Haydn performance. With a shallow breath he reached out to cup her cheek, brushing the strands of hair at her ear with the tips of his fingers. For the briefest of moments her eyes closed.

Just as swiftly they flew open again. "Desist as once," she hissed, taking a step back.

"You had an eyelash. On your cheek."

"Oh. Thank you, then."

The queen she'd put into play earlier seemed distracted, and so he moved his knight in. "And I have no intention of paying six thousand pounds for anything. Give me back the necklace if you're going to punish me for making it a gift."

"I will not." She gave an exaggerated sigh. "Very well, then. I'll lower my price to five thousand pounds."

"Don't expect me to be grateful." God, he wanted her. "Why don't you accompany me into the morning room, and I'll check for eyelashes again?"

"You mean you'll kiss me again," she whispered. "You really must cease doing that. It's very bad business."

"But I enjoy kissing you." Eleanor took that moment to glance over her shoulder at them, and he made a show of handing Sarala another glass—which had the added benefit of filling both her hands. "Do you know what I think?"

"*I* think you are never going to make me a reasonable counter offer," she said even more quietly, through slightly parted lips.

"I didn't ask what *you* thought," he countered, the grin touching his mouth again. "What *I* think is that you are as sensual as you are brilliant."

"I'm not brilliant. I'm merely smarter than you."

"And you're blushing," he returned, ignoring her sarcasm and using every ounce of willpower to keep from caressing her soft skin again.

"I am not. I am flushed with the frustration of waiting for

you to say something meaningful. Now if we don't rejoin our party, people will begin to talk."

"But has it occurred to you, Sarala, that if I make you a reasonable offer, you won't have an excuse to insult me any longer?"

She took a breath, her green gaze meeting his. "If that has occurred to you, I wonder that you haven't taken steps to stop me from insulting you."

Why hadn't he taken steps? Because she'd never attended a London recital before in her life, never been presented at court, obviously never learned that while tanned skin might be exotic, it was also very improper in an English-bred chit. Because while they both might be English nobility, he was a Griffin, and she was the foreign-born daughter of a second son promoted to the peerage only by an accidental death. "I like being insulted by you," he said instead. "I like bantering with you. And if you can tell me truthfully that you don't enjoy it as well, then we'll reconvene in your father's office, which is where this negotiation should have begun in the first place."

Sarala took a step closer, lifting her chin. "Don't you dare threaten with pulling this affair away from me. If you do so, I will call you a coward and a cheat."

Cinnamon crept softly across his senses. Charlemagne swallowed. "Then we're in agreement, and we can resume our business tomorrow during our picnic—which you have to agree is the only place we can continue to meet under any circumstances."

For a moment she stayed silent, while he concentrated on accounts that didn't balance, tariffs that prevented fair trade, anything that kept his body from reacting to her as it badly wanted to.

"Very well," she finally conceded. "Business will wait

until tomorrow." She maneuvered a fourth glass into her nimble fingers and started to turn around.

She had better control of herself than he did. As that dawned on him, he put a hand on her shoulder, turning her back to face him again. "Since business is put aside, we will have to be social. Tell me of a typical day for you in India."

That seemed to surprise her. "We have to get back to the others."

"They haven't even noticed that we're gone," he decided. "Tell me."

"Why?"

"I'm interested."

She took a slow breath, her bosom rising and falling deliciously. Shay hadn't been lying about his interest, nor was he trying to cajole her into liking or trusting him. Her life, what had made her who she had become, did genuinely fascinate him. Hm. If his younger brother had overheard, he would be laughing; Charlemagne couldn't count the number of times Zach had teased him about his disdain for small talk and his lack of interest in what most women had to say.

"During the summer," she began, her exquisite accent deepening as she spoke, "the only time to go walking was early in the morning. My friend Nahi and I would stroll along the street between the Red Fort palace and the Jama Masjid mosque—two of the most beautiful buildings in the world—on our way into old Delhi to visit the street markets."

"Just the two of you?"

"We usually had carrying boys with us to help manage our purchases, and when Colonel White saw us he would send along a pair of soldiers to keep us company."

"I should hope so."

She smiled softly. "They weren't necessary. I wasn't

afraid. Nahi is Indian, and I speak Hindi as well as anyone. Papa's position with the East India Company was negotiating with the local growers, and I grew up as his assistant." Her smile faded, replaced by that lonely look he'd seen when he first caught sight of her.

"Tell me about the market."

"It was wondrous, half pirate romance and half fairy tale." She shifted, moving a breath closer to him. "Vendors selling chickens or goats, pottery or hashish right next to stalls offering vegetables and rainbows of saris and beads. I can still smell the dust and spice in the air, and feel the warm breeze on my face."

Charlemagne swallowed again as she tilted her face up to the imaginary breeze. *Say something before you kiss her again, you idiot.* "The chickens and goats surprise me. I thought Hindus didn't eat meat."

"Most of them don't. Some eat eggs and drink goats' milk, and a great many of the shoppers were English or worked for English families."

"Did you ever wear a sari?"

She chuckled, covering her mouth as her mother turned around and gestured fiercely at her to return. "Once, that my mother knows about," she whispered, starting back along the row of chairs. "She was furious, but it was for Nahi's wedding and I was in the ceremony. When she saw my bare feet she nearly fainted."

"Once that your mother knows about," Shay repeated, wishing for the fourth or fifth time that night that they had the room to themselves. "How many other times that she didn't know about?"

"Hundreds."

They reached the families, and with a smile Sarala handed glasses of punch to her mother, Eleanor, and Caroline. Shay passed over the rest, and took the remaining seat beside his sister as Sarala's mother in the row in front of him yanked Sarala down between herself and Melbourne.

He scarcely noted the change of performers and music as the evening wore on. After Sarala's story, he felt transported. The yellow sun, the bird songs, the taste of saffron seemed in his eyes and mouth as if he were standing there in the Delhi market beside her. It had been almost painful to hear how clearly and dearly she loved where she'd come from, and how lost she felt to be elsewhere and probably never to return.

As the last piece ended he shook himself, joining in the applause. He stood as Sarala did, stepping forward to stand directly behind her, only her chair between them. "You make me wish to be in India," he whispered.

Sarala turned around to look into his eyes. "You aren't quite what I expected."

More pleased than he would ever admit aloud, Charlemagne inclined his head. "I hope you were pleasantly surprised, then."

"I was. I am. Thus far."

"Perhaps tomorrow I'll find a few encouraging things to tell you about Engl—"

"Oh, Your Grace," Lady Hanover interrupted, "thank you so much for taking us under your wing tonight."

Melbourne gave one of his charming smiles that didn't touch his eyes. "My pleasure, Lady Hanover. And I hope you enjoyed the Franfields' party, Lady Sarah."

"I did indeed," Sarala returned. "It was delightful to make the acquaintance of you and your family."

"And?" her mother prompted, nudging her forward.

Sarala's smile could have blinded. "And I would love to continue the acquaintance," she said, all teeth and unsmiling eyes.

The duke inclined his head. "Thank you again." With his usual charm, Sebastian then separated the Griffin brood from the Carlisles, and Charlemagne helped Zachary collect hats and cloaks and canes as they made their way outside. "Hattie's playing is much improved this year," Eleanor said, kissing each of her brothers and Caroline on the cheek, and then Valentine on the lips. "Thank you for coming tonight."

"Yes, supporting friends is all well and good, but next time I say we go someplace where we can play cards and get a decent glass of sherry," Deverill commented, lifting an eyebrow when Nell glared at him.

"You are so uncivilized," she returned with a grin and an exaggerated sigh.

"And that is why you find me so irresistible."

Melbourne put an arm around his closest friend. "Mm-hm. I know that's why I do."

"This is too sweet for me." Zachary shook Melbourne's free hand. Charlemagne offered his, but at the last moment Zach dodged it and leaned in to plant a kiss on his left ear instead.

"Oh, good God. My apologies, Caroline, for having to put up with him," Shay said feelingly, rubbing his ear.

"Are you riding with us or with Zachary?" Deverill asked, signaling for his coach to approach, Zachary and Caroline's following behind it.

"Not Zachary, obviously." Melbourne took Caroline's arm to help her into her coach.

Charlemagne looked from the coach to the cloudy night sky. "You know, since it's stopped raining, I think I'll walk home."

"I'll join you, then," Melbourne said promptly, turning around again.

"Nonsense. The moon's nearly out, and I may detour to the Society Club. I haven't decided yet."

He knew Sebastian would want to return home in time to read Peep a bedtime story. Besides, he needed to clear his head and decide on a strategy for tomorrow, and he couldn't do it with his nearly omniscient brother accompanying him. India still seemed to surround him, and if he ever wanted to get to sleep, he needed to distance himself a little from it—and from the Indian princess who intrigued and aggravated him more with each passing moment. Yes, a brisk walk would be just the thing.

Sebastian watched Shay disappear down the street. His younger brother's odd distraction troubled him—even more now that he might have found the cause. "Let's call it an evening, shall we?"

Eleanor put a hand on his arm. "That was nice of you, to invite Hanover and his family to join us."

He nodded. "It seemed prudent to gain their acquaintance."

His sister's hand remained. "And why is that?"

So Nell knew something about Shay's interactions with the daughter. "Why are you asking?"

She withdrew her hand. "No reason."

"I have the same nonreason."

"Don't interfere, Sebastian. For goodness' sake."

Zachary stepped in. "What the devil's going on?"

Caroline cleared her throat. "We think Shay may have an interest in Lady Sarah."

"Shay, interested in a chit?" Zachary's surprise folded into a frown. "Then we're not interfering, are we? If you do step in, Melbourne, I'll inform Shay about it."

"I didn't say anything about anything," Sebastian put in, mindful that both siblings present had accused him of meddling in their affairs—which he had. "Gaining knowledge is not interfering."

"That's right," Eleanor put in thoughtfully. "And so inviting Lady Sarah to my luncheon at the end of the week wouldn't be interfering, either." She turned back to Melbourne. "Not that I'll tell you a whit about what we might discuss."

"Do as you will," Sebastian said, lifting his hands in mock surrender. And so without taking any steps at all, he'd gotten the rest of his family to meddle for him. Not a bad night's work.

Chapter 7

"Yes, I'll just walk home and die from an inflamation of the lungs. Brilliant, Shay."

The problem, Charlemagne reflected, was that he was used to making a decision based on circumstance, knowledge, and logical hypothesis, and then acting. Over the past few days, however, and tonight especially, he found himself delving deeper into himself, toward thoughtfulness. Being thoughtful meant . . . musing, seeking information beyond what he required for a successful endeavor. It was a detriment to decision making, but splendid for making him insane.

Charlemagne pulled his greatcoat closer around his shoulders and turned up Pall Mall Street. No, walking tonight hadn't been his most brilliant decision, but in his defense he damned well didn't want to listen yet to Melbourne commenting about his impression of the Carlisles.

He knew precisely what his brother would say about

Hanover and family: that Lord Hanover seemed jovial enough, Lady Hanover practically rabid about joining the Griffin social circle, and Sarala—well, she'd changed her name in order to appear more English. Too tanned and too forward, she might at least have kept her own name, foreign or not, though neither choice spoke particularly well for her. All in all they were acceptable, but hardly worth overlooking the oddities and detriments in exchange for the friendship.

Why had Melbourne invited them over in the first place? People generally sought him out—not the other way around. It was odd, and considering his own dealings with Sarala, troubling. This negotiation didn't need his brother's interference.

A dark figure slipped along a brick wall and into an alley in front of him.

Charlemagne slowed, listening. *Bloody hell.* He hadn't brought his pistol to the recital. His only weapon was his walking cane, though thankfully that wasn't as useless as it might appear. Surreptitiously he loosened the neck with his fingers, ready to drop the hollow sheath and expose the razor-sharp rapier inside.

Aware and wary, he continued along his path. Equal to his reputation for wit and sense was his rare and short temper. And despite Sarala's actions, neither she nor anyone else had roused his anger in some time. His heart rate sped—not from fear, but from anticipation. Being wealthy didn't make him helpless, for Lucifer's sake. Not even close.

At this time of night the streets were generally still fairly busy with people leaving the theater, gentlemen arriving at or leaving clubs, or ladies who did their best work by lamplight. Tonight with the cold and damp, he could have been in London alone.

He continued on to the next street, but nothing else caught his attention. No sound but the distant clattering of hooves on cobblestone, no movement but the light, chill breeze that bent the ends of the grass growing at the foot of the wall. And still every muscle and sinew told him that someone watched him.

The sensation followed him the remaining five streets to Griffin House. A night at the club and a brandy might be exactly what he needed, but he also knew the wisdom of a safe port and reinforcements. Those lay ahead of him. And whether this was all in his imagination or not, he didn't take risks. Not of that sort, anyway.

Stanton pulled open the door as he reached it. "You've beaten the rain, my lord," the butler intoned, stepping aside to let him pass.

"Close the door," Charlemagne murmured, still facing the interior of the house.

The door clicked shut. "Is something amiss, my l—"

"Is Melbourne home?"

"Yes. I beg your—"

Charlemagne bolted the door. "Keep an eye out," he said over his shoulder, and strode up the stairs. The billiards room lay at the front of the house, and he hurried to the window. Standing to one side of the curtains, he surveyed up and down the street. Nothing. "Damn," he muttered.

"Shay?"

Without looking, he knew that Sebastian stood in the darkened doorway behind him. "Just an odd feeling," he said, his gaze still on the dark outside.

"What sort of odd feeling?" Quietly Sebastian joined him at the far side of the window.

"I kept thinking someone was watching me." Charlemagne turned from the view. His brother was studying him, his expression cool and alert despite the late hour. "It . . . Looking at it now, it must have been my imagination."

The duke nodded. "You being so prone to flights of fancy and hysterics. What did you see?"

Charlemagne shrugged. "A shadow. Probably an owl or a stray cloud. I'll tell Stanton to go to bed. Apologies for the disruption."

"Don't apologize, Shay. And I'll see to Stanton." Slowly Sebastian pulled the curtains closed, shutting the night out for both of them.

With a sigh Charlemagne led the way out of the room. Melbourne at least had the compassion not to make fun, but he might as well not have troubled with the restraint. "Which is worse?" he asked, "being wrong about being followed or having a herd of ruffians attacking the house?"

The duke clapped him on the shoulder. "The ruffians," he answered. "Though anyone would have to be insane to attempt a siege on this house."

And yet this morning someone had attempted to break into Gaston House. A coincidence? Logically, yes, but obviously it had been enough to make him uneasy. "It was an owl, Seb. Or a shadow." As if on cue the rain began again outside, tapping quiet fingers against the windows. "Or perhaps I'm just getting old and forgetful."

"You can't be, because I'm five years older than you are, and I'm still young and vigorous. I'll see you in the morning."

"Good night."

Caine waited in his private rooms, but Charlemagne sent him off to bed. Unsettled as he felt this evening, he didn't want a valet hovering over him.

He shed most of his clothes and blew out the bedside

candle, then took a seat by the window. With the curtains partially pulled he had a view of the carriage drive at the side of the house and not much more. If he had a mind to sneak into Griffin House, however, the narrow drive offered the best way to the back of the mansion.

For a long time he sat unmoving, watching through the dark mist of rain. Whatever he'd told Sebastian, the shadow hadn't felt like an owl. And for other than that brief moment of passing shade, he or it had been stealthy enough to completely avoid his detection.

When an hour had passed with no further shadows or even a damp, prowling cat, he rose, pulled on a dressing robe, and made his way quietly downstairs. No harm in making a quick check of the windows in case any of them might be open to the rain. Or he could tell himself that was the reason, though why he bothered with the self-deception, he didn't know. Something had made him uneasy, and he simply wasn't quite ready, yet, to ignore the prickling sensation along the back of his skull.

Charlemagne moved silently into the morning room. Just as he paused, he heard it—a swift, quiet intake of breath.

He ducked as a form launched at him from the corner. Twisting at the same moment, he shoved upward. With a yelp his opponent launched into the air and over the back of the couch. Growling, his blood up, Charlemagne charged after him. How dare anyone launch an attack against this house—his brother lived here. His seven-year-old niece lived here.

"Have at you, you bastard," he snarled, coiling his fist around the man's collar and yanking him upright. A table crashed over, dumping a vase of roses and one of his history of Greece books onto the floor.

Another figure galloped into the darkness. "Hold there,

you scoundrel!" Stanton's strident voice came, followed by the distinct sound of a pistol cocking.

"Thank God, Stanton! Help!" the other man yelped before Charlemagne could say anything.

Charlemagne jerked his attacker closer even as what the man had said began to sink in. The fellow knew the butler's name. And further, Stanton was advancing on *him,* the pistol aimed in the general direction of his head.

"What the devil is going on?" he rumbled.

The butler froze. "Lord Charlemagne?"

"Get some damned light in here, Stanton!"

As if on cue, Sebastian thundered down the stairs and into the morning room. He held a lantern in one hand, and a pistol in the other. "Stanton, what—" His gaze locked on Charlemagne's for a heartbeat, then the pistol lowered. "Oh."

"Ah, my lord?" a half-strangled voice came from just beyond his fist. "If you don't mind, I—"

Charlemagne loosened his grip and Tom the footman staggered backward. "Apologies," he said stiffly, his gaze still on his older brother. "A word with you, Melbourne?"

Sebastian nodded. "As you were, Stanton."

"Very good, Your Grace. Tom, get yourself a cup of tea and return to your post."

With his older brother on his heels, Charlemagne returned to the hallway beneath the stairs. "You set guards."

"I asked Stanton to have a few servants keep an eye on the house." With a half smile the duke brushed by him and returned upstairs. "Try not to kill any of them."

"I told you that I must have seen an owl."

"Someone broke into your home. As you know, we have enemies. I'm not going to ignore the possibility that one of them might be desperate enough to attempt to directly do any of us harm." Sebastian paused on the landing. "And even without all that, to paraphrase Hamlet, I believe you can tell a hawk from a handsaw."

"Only when the wind is north by northwest, apparently."

"Well, it's blowing tonight. Go to bed, Shay. The house is secure."

Slowly Charlemagne followed his brother upstairs to the first floor. The house might be secure, but he wasn't so certain about his own mind.

Lady Hanover swished into the breakfast room. "My maid tells me you have a picnic with Lord Charlemagne Griffin today."

Sarala glanced up, then returned to buttering her toasted bread. "Yes, at noon," she returned, making as little of it as possible. Today was business. She didn't want her mother trying to turn her meeting with Shay into something more than it was. "I believe he's taking me for a drive. To show me London." Calling it a picnic sounded good as an excuse, anyway. In reality, he'd probably forget about it. He wanted silk, and she wanted a good price for it. The end.

"A picnic and a drive. That's splendid. Do you think his brother might join you?"

She didn't bother to ask which brother she might be referring to. "I hardly think the Duke of Melbourne would go on a picnic with his brother, me, or anyone else. And besides, everyone but you seems resigned to the idea that Melbourne will never remarry."

"One never knows, my love. Wear your green muslin, just in case. And that pearl necklace of yours."

"Mama, I am not wearing pearls on a picnic. I thought you wanted me to fit in, not become the female at whom everyone points and laughs."

The marchioness sighed. "Very well. All I can do is try."

She breezed out of the room again, and Sarala glanced at the clock sitting on the mantel. He would be by in just over two hours. A small flutter of nerves ran through her. Oh, she did enjoy a good negotiation.

Of course he would have to view this seriously and stop flirting with her before she could actually call it a negotiation. At the moment she wasn't certain what this little meeting would mean, though she had to admit that the whole episode was rather fun. And different. And the most interesting thing she'd encountered since the family had left India.

Her mother didn't reappear for breakfast, and her father had asked for eggs and ham to be delivered to his office. That couldn't be good. Her late Uncle Roger's debts were causing a continuing slow leak of the family coffers, and she knew the situation increasingly worried the new Marquis of Hanover. Doing well as a merchant and doing well enough to support three estates, a London house, and a London life, were completely different animals.

That was why despite her nerves this morning she'd volunteered to run an errand for her father. Luckily Uncle Roger had several rather valuable if hideous antiques she'd been authorized to dispose of.

The butler appeared in the doorway. "My lady, you have a caller."

Immediately her heart began to pound. But Shay had said noon; of that she was certain. "Who is it, Blankman?"

The butler produced a salver. A calling card with a pretty embossed silver border of vines and roses lay in the middle of the silver tray. Ornate lettering spelled out the name of Eleanor, Lady Deverill. In the upper left corner a small, regal griffin perched. Interesting that the marchioness chose to keep part of her family's ancient coat of arms, whatever her married name and status might be. And they were certainly nothing to sneeze at.

But why would Lady Deverill want to see her, and at half past nine in the morning? "Where do you have her waiting?" she asked, wiping butter from her fingertips and standing.

"In the morning room, my lady," Blankman returned, his tone indicating that she should have known that. She supposed all the good guests were stashed in the morning room; where the inferior ones went, she had no idea. The cellar, perhaps.

"Very good. Please have some tea brought in for us."

Sarala hurried down the hallway, made a quick check of her appearance in the mirror there, and strolled through the open morning room door. With perfect brunette hair, perfectly coiffed, and an elegant blue morning gown beneath a darker blue pelisse studded with what looked like sapphires, Eleanor Griffin-cum-Corbett looked like precisely what she was: one of the wealthiest, loveliest, and most influential young ladies in England.

"Good morning, my lady." As the marchioness faced her, Sarala made a shallow curtsy.

"Lady Sarah," the marchioness returned in her smooth, cultured voice. "I apologize for calling on you so early in the day."

"Not at all. I was about to step out to see Mr. Pooley."

"The antiques dealer?"

"Yes," Sarala returned, covering her surprise. How would a wealthy marchioness know of a minor antiques buyer? Whatever the answer, Lady Deverill certainly didn't need to know that the Carlisle family was selling heirlooms—even ugly, disliked ones.

For a brief moment Eleanor Corbett looked as though she expected an invitation to join the expedition, but she recovered her expression so quickly that Sarala might have imagined it. Instead the marchioness smiled.

"I enjoyed meeting you last night," she said. "I thought since you've had such a short time to become acquainted with anyone, that I would invite you to join me for luncheon the day after tomorrow. Some of my friends and I meet once a week. I think you would like them, and they, you."

Again Sarala was surprised, and deeply pleased. The circle of ladies whom Lady Deverill called friend was the most selective, well-respected, and sought-after in London. They certainly didn't need an unknown almost-foreigner joining them, but she'd missed female friendship, and she had liked what she knew of the lady standing before her. Still, her negotiator's instincts told her that she mustn't appear too eager. "That's very kind of you, my lady, but I—"

"Eleanor, please. And say you'll come, at least once."

So the marchioness was apparently sincere. That was some good news. Sarala nodded. "I believe I am free on Friday."

The marchioness smiled. "Wonderful. I'll send a coach for you at half past twelve."

Sarala couldn't help her return smile. Lady Deverill continued to seem genuinely pleased by her answer. "I'll see you then, my la— Eleanor."

For several minutes after the marchioness left, Sarala sat alone in the morning room. That had been odd, if opportune. In light of that, perhaps she should just be thankful and accept the gift of friendship offered her.

"Sarala? Oh, there you are." Her father leaned into the room, glanced about the interior, and entered.

"Has my name reverted, then?" she asked, facing him. "Thank goodness."

"Oops. No. You're still Sarah. It was my mistake." He

cocked his head as she met his answer with a dour expression. "You're not still upset about the moniker alteration, are you? It's harmless, really."

"Honestly, I still don't see the point. If the plan was to Anglify me, it should have been done before we arrived here. At this point it merely seems to be causing confusion among those whose acquaintance I made during the first ten days of our residence here." At least Charlemagne hadn't yet bowed to her parents' belated attempts to make her more . . . bland.

The marquis gave a half smile. "I don't want to see *you* changed, you know. Not the important bits, anyway."

"My thanks. Have you sent for Mr. Warrick yet? I want to get that old clock to Mr. Pooley before anyone else ventures into the streets to see what we're doing." Though if Lady Deverill was already making calls, the rest of Mayfair might very well be, too.

"That's why I came looking for you. There's no need to go see Pooley this morning, after all."

"No? Did you find money buried beneath the stairs?"

"If only. No, the Duke of Melbourne's youngest brother, Lord Zachary—do you remember him from last night?—sent over a note asking if I'd be willing to rent him that pasture land we inherited outside of Bath. He's breeding cattle there, you know."

Sarala stifled her quick frown. "Yes, I'd heard something about that."

"What a coup that a Griffin wants to do business with us. We—or you—must have made quite an impression last night."

She'd barely spoken with anyone but Shay last night. Apparently *someone* had been impressed, however, because in one morning she'd gone from a rivalry with one Griffin to entanglements with two additional members of the family.

What were the odds of it all being coincidence? "Can't we get rid of the clock anyway, Pati?" she asked, because he would expect her to say something. "It's covered with all those very well-endowed hunting dogs."

Her father snorted. "I'll see if I can relegate it to the attic collection. We may need it again, eventually." He pulled out his pocket watch and snapped it open. "I have to go and meet Lord Zachary. This rental money won't save us, but it should stave off the wolves for another few weeks. Which reminds me—do you have good news for me yet about those silks?"

She nodded. "Three merchants so far have expressed an interest. I'd like to wait another few days to see what else comes in before I set a price. And I still have that offer for seven hundred and fifty guineas, though I wouldn't dream of selling for that price."

The marquis chuckled again. "So you have that worm still dangling on your hook? I wish I had time to sit in on the negotiations. You are an artist, my dear. If you decide to deal, just don't take every guinea he owns."

"I promise, Papa." She only wished she would have that chance. *That* would be something to see.

"Good, my love. I'll see you for dinner, yes?"

"And the theater. Remember, the new production of *The Tempest* premieres tonight at Drury Lane."

"How could I forget?" He smiled again. "You see, there is something about London you appreciate."

Sarala sighed. "Yes, one something."

"It's a starting point, though." He kissed her on the cheek. "I'll see you at dinner."

After her father left, Sarala returned to her bedchamber to work some figures. Once again she wished for her own office, but she knew as well as anyone that that would never happen. As she'd expected, Madame Costanza had made an offer for ten bolts, at two guineas apiece. The other two shops had offered a bit less and were in for only two bolts of silk each. It was a poor way to dispose of such a large shipment, but unless she could hook a large distributor, it seemed the most practical way to go. Unless of course Charlemagne decided to be reasonable.

She tucked the letters into her reticule in case he needed proof that she wasn't simply sitting about waiting to play with him. The minimum price she would accept for the entire shipment was twelve hundred guineas. Charlemagne Griffin could easily afford that, but would he pay it? He'd scoffed at her price of five thousand pounds, but in all truth she'd expected him to. Today, though, she meant to be serious; fun as the bantering was, her father needed the money.

With that new determination in mind, she summoned Jenny again. "Will you please fetch my brown and yellow muslin?" she asked as soon as the maid arrived.

"Your mama said you were to wear the new green one today, my lady." It had already been laid out for her, in fact; a low-cut, slim-waisted creation perfect for attracting a man's attentions. Of course the man her mother had in mind was the Duke of Melbourne, and she wasn't likely to see him today—and even if that weren't the case, she knew as well as anyone that if he did ever mean to remarry, his eyes would be raised toward a much loftier prize than she represented. As for his brother, after those surprising kisses and considering her family's need, she meant to make it very clear that she had nothing on her mind but business.

Frowning at the green confection, Sarala picked up her embroidery scissors and walked to the bed. Ignoring Jenny's gasp, she cut the seam along the front six inches of the dress's hem. "There. I can't wear it like that, and you can't be blamed for not carrying out my mother's instructions."

"Oh, dear," the maid muttered.

"We'll say I was putting it on and accidentally stepped on the hem. The brown and yellow dress, if you please."

"Very well, my lady."

Despite the simple and conservative look of the gown she'd chosen, it took her an inordinately long time to dress. Thank goodness she hadn't had to go to Pooley's, or she never would have been ready in time. She turned this way and that, checking to see that from every conceivable angle she looked like a serious business woman—competent, confident, and not to be trifled with. No more of that kissing, for heaven's sake. Besides being contrary to the practices of fair negotiations, it had nearly accomplished what Lord Charlemagne had intended—to leave her befuddled and confused and far too amenable to any offer he might make.

"Are you certain you won't at least wear the gold comb in your hair, my lady?" Jenny pleaded. "Please forgive me for saying it, but this attire looks quite . . . plain."

"Plain is my aim," Sarala said firmly. "And I shan't need a comb, because I will be wearing my brown bonnet."

"Your brown . . . Yes, my lady."

Even she couldn't claim to be particularly fond of the brown oversized monstrosity of a hat, but it had been a gift from Nahi's grandmother. At the moment she was glad she'd kept it, despite her private assessment that it could be used as a dwelling for a small family.

There. Hair pulled back into a tight knot, any loose strands around her face both minimized and hidden by her plain brown bonnet, and a simple, high-necked brown and yellow muslin covered by an equally plain brown pelisse, all up to her throat and down nearly to her fingers. Clearly she wouldn't welcome or tolerate any nonsense. And in her private opinion, she'd never looked more English.

With a last turn in front of the full-length mirror, she went downstairs to await Lord Charlemagne and pretend that she was as composed on the inside as she looked on the outside. No fluttering nerves for her. She wondered which strategy he would attempt today: whether he meant to flatter and seduce, or bully, or actually be logical and fair-minded. She felt ready for anything her rather sneaky opponent might attempt.

"Sarah, what in heaven's name are you wearing?" her mother demanded from the morning room doorway.

"My brown muslin."

"I can see that! Don't be impertinent."

Sarala grimaced. "I apologize, Mama. I only—"

"You were to wear your green dress. The one with the pretty lace at the neck."

"I stepped on the hem while I was putting it on."

"Very likely. Have Jenny mend it at once. Thankfully you still have time to look attractive."

"Forgive me, but I thought my first priority was to look English. Doesn't this dress better suit that purpose?"

"Only if you wish to become a vicar's wife. Go and change at—"

"My lady," Blankman said importantly from behind the marchioness, "Lady Sarah has a caller."

A tremor ran through Sarala. He'd arrived twelve minutes early. Did that signal his impatience to acquire the silks? If so, all the better for her. Sarala stood. "I'm sorry, Mama, but there's no time. I can't very well keep a Griffin waiting while my maid mends a gown."

"Of course you can't." Lady Hanover grabbed one of her

daughter's history books, hurried to the nearest chair, and seated herself. "Show him in, Blankman."

"Very good, my lady."

Her mother absolutely could not be present for any negotiations. "But Mama—" Before Sarala could more than begin her protest, the butler vanished back down the length of the hallway.

"Sit down, Sarah."

She complied just as Blankman returned, Lord Charlemagne on his heels. "Lord Charlemagne Griffin," the butler intoned, and backed out the door to allow their guest entry.

Shay bowed, while Sarala scrambled back to her feet to duplicate her mother's curtsy. "My lord," they said in broken unison.

"Lady Hanover, Lady Sarala," he drawled, his gray gaze flicking toward her mother as he said the latter name.

Sarala couldn't help a small spark of satisfaction. At least someone still preferred her real name.

"Good morning, my lord. Do come and sit with us before you make off with our Sarah." Lady Hanover made a grand gesture toward the sofa where Sarala had perched herself.

To her surprise he dropped onto the sofa beside her. "Yes, thank you for allowing me to escort Lady Sarala about London," he said, shaking his head as a maid appeared with an offer of tea. "It's not often I get the chance to show the Town to someone for the first time."

Oh, he was in fine form today. In addition, he looked very dashing. Where she'd chosen to appear conservative and perhaps a bit severe—all to good purpose, of course—Lord Charlemagne stood as the definition of the word "dashing" in buckskin breeches and tasseled Hessian boots together with a tan coat, black waistcoat, and a wonderfully tied cravat.

"We're delighted you've taken such an interest in *Sarah*,

for that is what we call her," her mother said expansively. "You are too kind."

"Not at all," he returned just as graciously, shifting to face Sarala. "And escorting *Sarala* is entirely my pleasure, I assure you."

For a moment Sarala's mother looked nonplussed. She didn't often encounter anyone who simply countermanded her wishes, and politely at that.

"Shouldn't we be going?" Sarala asked, trying to arrange an exit before anything unpleasant should happen.

"How is your brother this morning?" Lady Hanover went on, the force of her cheerfulness a bit unnerving even to her daughter. "I only ask because he was so gracious in asking us to sit with him last evening."

For the briefest of moments Sarala saw what might have been annoyance speed across Charlemagne's handsome face, but it was gone before she could be sure. "He was in good spirits when I last saw him." He pulled out his etched silver pocket watch and opened it. "If you'll excuse us, Lady Hanover, Lady *Sarala* and I should take our leave."

Her mother stood, tittering. "By all means! Don't let me keep you and *Sarah* from your amusements."

Chapter 8

"Is your new strategy to earn my gratitude by becoming a mortal enemy of my mother?" Sarala asked. Moments ago, Shay had handed her up into his phaeton, then had taken the reins of his team of bays. Now they were tooling along toward St. James's Park.

"I equate it to my family suddenly deciding I'd be better served if they called me John. Charlemagne has its difficulties, I admit, but it's part of who and what I am."

"Well. Then thank you."

Shay nodded. "You're welcome. But more importantly, what the devil are you wearing?"

One slender hand went to the brim of her enormous brown bonnet. "I don't know what you mean," she said, all innocence. "I am dressed in the current fashion, am I not?"

"You look nearly like a nun. And that hat could shade all of Wiltshire."

She faced him, having to turn well sideways to look around the edge of her bonnet. "I'm sorry you don't approve of my wardrobe, but my appearance is irrelevant to our negotiations."

Charlemagne couldn't stop the shout of laughter that broke from his chest. "So this attire of yours is so I'll look upon you as a rival rather than as a chit?"

"Precisely. And what's so amusing about that?"

"You could wear a sack, Sarala, and you'd still be as lovely as autumn roses."

Since he was looking for it, he caught the hesitation of her fingers, the unconscious smoothing of her ridiculously prim skirts while she conjured an appropriate response. Ha. He did affect her. Thank God his attraction wasn't completely one-sided, since she was halfway to driving him mad as it was. And conservative as her gown happened to be, on her he found it enchanting—like a princess trying to hide her beauty by dressing in burlap. Warm arousal ran through his veins. And that hat . . .

"Might we return to Hyde Park today?" she asked, hesitating again with that affecting combination of innocence and the exotic.

They were headed in the opposite direction, but he immediately turned north along Regent Street. "Certainly. May I ask why?"

"I wanted to see the Serpentine. My maid told me a queen had it built there in the park."

One more turn, west on Piccadilly Street, and they were on their way to Hyde Park. "You truly are a stranger to London, aren't you?" He forgot at times that she knew so little of what had surrounded him for his entire life. She seemed so capable and sure of herself that he couldn't imagine her unsure of her footing anywhere. "Yes, the Serpentine is in the middle of Hyde Park. Queen Caroline, George II's wife, had the Westbourne dammed to create a lake and add to the overall beauty of the park."

"England is a very strange place, making lakes to add to the scenery." She grinned. "But if you wish to use your knowledge of geography and architecture to overwhelm me, please know that I'm completely aware of your strategy."

Except that at the moment his only strategy had been to entertain the Indian princess. "You're the one who wanted to see the Serpentine. But thank you for thinking I'm a genius of subterfuge."

"You're also a genius of feigned innocence, my lord."

"You called me Shay the other day."

She looked up at him. "Shay," she repeated softly.

He pulled the horses up so sharply that the tiger nearly fell off the back of the phaeton. "Now who's using their wiles?"

Her eyes sparkled emerald. "I have no idea what you're talking about. I only uttered one word."

"It's the way you said it. Do it again, so I can listen more carefully this time." And so he could better cover the shiver of his muscles.

"You, sir, are entirely too frivolous," she retorted with a chuckle.

"Good God, I don't think anyone's ever called me frivolous before." In fact, he was certain of it. He clucked to start the team off again.

"Hm. Does this mean I've judged you incorrectly, or that you're only frivolous in my presence?"

"I have no intention of responding to that, on the grounds that it would be impossible for me to come through in anything but a shambles." Actually, he seemed to be several things in her presence that he couldn't be bothered with at any other time or with any other person. Certainly not with a female; if it had been anyone else, he would have complained that she was wasting his time. Here, with her, he couldn't imagine anything more interesting. Not while they were clothed, at any rate. "If you're not going to say my name again, we may as well discuss something else."

"Silks?" she suggested dryly. "I was hoping we could get to that. I've been doing some calculations," Sarala continued, folding her hands together on her lap. "I think a figure of three thousand five hundred pounds would be fair to both sides. What do you say to that?"

"I say that if you're willing to lower your price by fifteen hundred pounds before we've barely begun, there's probably something wrong with what you're trying to sell me." That wasn't quite true; the price *was* a fair one. He simply wasn't ready to pay it yet.

"That is not true, and you know it! *You're* the one who told *me* about the silks, if you'll recall. I have begun to receive other offers. If you continue to offer me nothing, don't think I shall refrain from engaging in business with another party."

Charlemagne lowered his gaze for a moment. "Sarala, I think you know as well as I do that this is not . . . typical. And neither do I think you would want me to use every means I possess to regain that shipment."

When he looked up, his eyes met hers. "So I'm to tolerate your flirtations and compliments and insultingly low offers for as long as you wish to entertain yourself with my presence?"

If he'd thought that she meant a word of that, he would have settled the negotiations right then. "You keep agreeing to meet with me, princess, when you know how each previous encounter has gone. And yes, you have the silks, and yes, you could sell them to anyone you choose. And I *do* believe you have other offers, because I believe you to be a competent businesswoman. But the point is, you haven't sold yet. So don't claim that I've invited you here under false pretenses, when I think you enjoy my company as much as I enjoy yours."

"You're very sure of yourself," she returned immediately, as they stopped beneath a beech tree. "How do you know I'm not working my wiles on you, ensnaring you to the point where you would give me any price I ask?"

Charlemagne laughed. "How do you know I'm not doing the same thing?" He hopped to the ground as his tiger moved to the head of the team. "You shouldn't give away your strategy, at any rate. It'll weaken your position."

"I hardly need business lessons from you."

Still chuckling as he circled the back of the phaeton to reach her side, he held his hands out to her. "Don't be so quick to rebuff my offer of instruction, either. For all you know, there might be several very interesting things I could teach you."

She met his gaze squarely. "I don't suppose you'd care to name them, Shay? It is the only way we could both be certain what's being offered and how interested I might be."

Good God. Sarala wrapped her fingers around his, and heat ran beneath his skin at the touch. A goose honked from somewhere close by, and he jumped. The feeling of being watched hadn't returned this morning, but he continued to remain vigilant—or he tried to—nonetheless. Obviously, his mind and his body had other ideas where Sarala Carlisle was concerned. She continued to watch him closely as he helped her to the ground. "Between you and me, Sarala," he said in a low voice, his hands on her hips as he drew her slowly closer, "a statement like the one you just made would not serve a proper chit well in London."

Color darkened her cheeks. "You began it," she protested. "I only responded in kind."

"So I did. I apologize." For a moment they stood inches apart, gazing at each other while he tried to remember why he couldn't just kiss her again. *The park. They were in the middle of damned Hyde Park.* Charlemagne abruptly released her, clearing his throat as he did so. "I hope you have an appetite, because Cook was extremely generous with the portions in our basket."

Feeling unaccountably awkward, like a schoolboy on his first outing with a member of the opposite sex, he pulled the blanket from the top of the picnic basket and spread it in the shade of a nearby tree. Whatever he'd said to get her here, he knew full well that this looked like a courtship—and that anyone passing by would likely think so as well. The fact that the word had even occurred to him, much less that he'd applied it to one particular woman, should have stunned him, but everything surrounding every encounter with Sarala seemed both dreamlike and intensely clear.

He gave it all up as madness, and had simply begun for the first time to let things play out as they would—no strategy, no planning required except for making certain that he spent as much time as possible with her. The most dismaying thought was that perhaps she *did* consider all of this a strategy, and that for the second time she was well on the way to outwitting him.

Hauling the heavy basket over to the blanket, he set it down and offered a hand to the momentarily silent Sarala. He shouldn't have spoken as he had, but she certainly hadn't seemed offended. Figuring her out was a devil of an effort—and one he was enjoying mightily.

Rather than take his hand, Sarala sank onto the blanket on her own. "The last time I sat on a blanket," she said abruptly, "it was to learn how to charm a cobra."

He grinned, not entirely surprised. "I hope you're not comparing me with the snake."

Sarala pursed her lips. "No, but the techniques of business negotiation and snake charming are very similar."

"How so?"

"Well," she began, at the same time reaching down to pull off her shoes, "it's mostly distraction and redirection." She paused, her eyes on her task. "Is it working?" she finally continued.

One by one the brown walking shoes landed on the blanket beside her, leaving him with a tantalizing glimpse of ankle. Had that been a henna tattoo? Sweet Lucifer.

Absolutely it was working. "Just how bold are you?" he asked.

"This bold." Leaning forward onto her hands, she stretched out to kiss him softly on the mouth, her bonnet enveloping both of them.

Lightning speared straight down his spine to his crotch. He kissed her back hard and hot, her soft lips molding to his. For Christ's sake, he should have chosen a more secluded spot for luncheon. The parked phaeton offered some protection from curious eyes, but not nearly enough. Peeling her out of that ridiculous goose-necked gown, freeing her hair from the confines of that enormous bonnet . . . Just the thought left him hard and aching.

Keenly aware of where they were and just how fleeting their privacy was likely to be, Charlemagne reluctantly retreated an inch. "Someone might see us, Saral—"

She turned her head so swiftly to look that she nearly took his nose off with the brim of her bonnet. "I only wanted to see if a third kiss would be as distracting as the first and second."

He stifled his purely male, prideful smile. "And was it?"

"I meant for you."

This time he scowled. "Very amusing."

"Oh, don't get me wrong—you kiss quite well. As a weapon, though, it can cut both ways."

Charlemagne eyed her. "So according to you, I kissed you previously solely to strengthen my bargaining position."

"Yes," she answered succinctly.

"And so you kissed me today to demonstrate that my so-called tactics aren't working?"

"To demonstrate that I'm perfectly aware of them." She folded her hands over her lap. "Shall we eat?"

"Twenty-five hundred pounds," he ground out. *He* would not be the one to look like a besotted fool. And if she wanted a negotiation, he would give her one.

She blinked. "Those silks are worth far more than that. And if you won't open the picnic basket, I will." So saying, she tugged it toward her and flipped open the lid.

If not for the color lingering in her cheeks and the slight tremor in her hands, he would have thought her kiss had been exactly what she claimed—a lesson in turnabout as fair play. No one, however, kissed that hungrily simply to demonstrate a point. One thing he hadn't anticipated, though, was that she had had lessons in snake charming. He blew out his breath. *Enjoy the moment, idiot.*

"Ham and currants?" she asked, handing him a cloth-wrapped sandwich.

He made certain his fingers brushed hers as he took it. "Hand me the Madeira and I'll pour us some."

"Certainly." She complied, handing him the bottle and two glasses. "May I ask you a question?"

"You don't need my permission, but of course."

"How many of your other business rivals have you taken on picnics?"

Charlemagne laughed at the sly sparkle in her eyes. "None. And if you're about to ask how many of them I've kissed, the answer is the same." He handed her a glass of ruby red Madeira.

"Very well, I'll be more broad. How many of your opponents have been females?"

"I got into a bidding war with Lady Adulsen over a nearly two-thousand-year-old marble bust of Caesar, but that's the only one I recall."

"And who won?"

Charlemagne grinned. "I'll invite you to Griffin House for dinner and show it to you. It's in the billiards room."

Sarala drank a large gulp of Madeira. "If you can afford to relegate such a treasure to your billiards room, you can afford to pay thirty-five hundred pounds for those silks."

"Yes, but what I can afford and what I'm willing to pay are two entirely different entities."

"I see." She drew a breath and turned to gaze out over the Serpentine. "So you own a Roman bust of Caesar. Have you acquired anything else as ancient?"

It wasn't just idle conversation; he could hear the genuine curiosity in her voice. Sarala liked antiques. Another oddity for a young, barely English chit. "I've been collecting since I was sixteen," he returned. "On my Grand Tour I returned with so many 'lumps of stone,' as Zach called them, that I was forced to open my own house in London to display them."

"But you live at your brother's house."

Charlemagne hesitated. One didn't share Griffin secrets with anyone not a Griffin. "Melbourne and I work together a great deal. And with his young daughter there, it just made sense for me to stay in residence." That, and Sebastian had asked all of his siblings to return to Griffin House after his wife had died. Occasionally Charlemagne wondered what Seb would have done, left to his own devices with only a crying three-year-old daughter for company. The answer still kept him awake at night sometimes. And that was the other reason that while Eleanor and Zachary had married and moved to other houses in London, he remained.

"I have to admit," Sarala said, thankfully lifting him away from the memory of those months after Charlotte had died, "my interest while I was growing up was always English history and its connection to Rome."

"Truly, or are you just saying that to impress me?" he asked with another smile, digging into the basket for the peaches and grapes Cook had packed.

"I don't need to impress you," she retorted, from her haughty tone as amused as he was. "I own the silks."

"In that case, after luncheon there's somewhere I would like to take you."

"And where would that be?"

"Inside the old Tower grounds at the center of Town. You can see the remains of the Roman walls that surrounded the old city of Londinium."

"Oh, my goodness. I would very much enjoy seeing that."

"And I would very much enjoy showing them to you, Sarala." And he *was* impressed, each day more, by the black-haired princess seated barefoot beside him. And that troubled him as much as it excited him.

Chapter 9

The Duke of Melbourne found his youngest brother sitting at a table in the front window of the Society Club. "Isn't there somewhere less conspicuous?" he asked, eyeing both the crowded room and the thick knot of passersby and gawkers outside.

"No. I already asked." Zachary gestured at the head waiter, who immediately began toward them from across the room. "I'm sure Martins would de-chair someone if *you* inquired, though. Lord Talmidge and his nephews, perhaps?"

With an annoyed glance at Zachary, Sebastian settled into his waiting seat. "And then I'd have to support the nephews after Talmidge's subsequent apoplexy and death. Thank you, no."

"Your Grace, we are honored by your presence," Martins

exclaimed in his permanently hushed voice, bowing practically to his knees. "What might I do for you?"

"A bottle of your best white wine and a plate of your best snapper."

"Orange duck for me, Martins."

"At once, Your Grace, my lord."

Once the waiter had rushed away, Sebastian returned his attention to his brother. "All right, I'm here. What did you want to discuss?"

Zachary leaned forward. "First I want a promise that you won't kill the messenger."

"Very well."

His brother lifted an eyebrow. "You're not going to ask what the message is *before* you promise not to flay me alive?"

Another footman appeared with their wine, and Sebastian gestured for Zachary to do the tasting and voicing of approval. He'd learned from experience that the most expensive bottles in an establishment tended to equal the oldest, and that *that* didn't always equate with the best-tasting. Zachary didn't turn any unusual colors, though, so Sebastian allowed his own glass to be filled.

"Firstly, Zach," he said, taking a swallow of the wine, "I'm not likely to flay any family members in public, which we both know. Secondly, since Shay's not here and you asked specifically that we meet away from the house, I presume this is about him. Thirdly, since I *am* here, I deduce that you need something you can't get on your own. So proceed."

"St. George's buttonholes, but you're frightening. No wonder Nell says you can read minds."

"I can, but it's rude," Sebastian said mildly. "Indulge me and speak aloud."

"Very well. It's not precisely about Shay, but it *is* about the Carlisles."

As he'd suspected. "And?"

"And I invited them to share your box tonight at Drury Lane Theater."

That, he hadn't anticipated. "The same box I refused to give over to you and Eleanor because Shay and I wanted to attend in peace and quiet?"

"That very one."

"So you—"

"You said we should take steps to become better acquainted with the Carlisle family."

"All I said was that gaining knowledge is not interfering." For the sake of his relationship with all his siblings, he wanted that to remain very clear.

"Yes, well, with that in mind, what better strategy could there be but asking them to share the best box in the house for a premiere when by their late arrival in London they'd been forced to take terrible seats in the back corner of the lower level?"

"And you know this because?"

"I had a meeting with Hanover this morning. He's renting me some prime grazing pasture just east of Bath."

"Did he complain about his seats?" The question might sound innocent, but the answer could be significant—dissatisfaction, ambition, it all meant something.

"Not a bit. It came up in passing conversation about the glut of social events this Season. He seemed happy to have acquired tickets at all. Apparently *The Tempest* is his daughter's favorite play."

Hm. It was also Shay's favorite play. Sebastian wondered whether his erudite brother had mentioned that fact to the chit. Most husband-hunting females named *Romeo and Juliet* as their favorite. *Twelfth Night* or *Much Ado About Nothing* came a close second, but he'd never heard of *The Tempest* even making the list.

"Am I to send a coach for the Carlisles, then?"

"No. They'll meet you in the lobby." Zachary started to say something more, but subsided as their luncheon arrived. His brother obviously had some sort of chemical imbalance that enabled him to eat almost constantly without any ill effects, but prevented him from thinking while doing so.

"When I tell Shay about our guests, whose idea is it supposed to be?" Sebastian prompted after a few minutes. "I certainly don't want to tangle anyone's machinations."

Zachary swallowed a huge mouthful of roast duck. "Oh. It was your suggestion that they might want to join you, since you knew how difficult seats would be to acquire."

"Of course I did. Have I done anything else I need to know about?"

"Not yet. I'll let you know."

"Thank you. And Zachary?"

Belatedly his brother looked up from his plate. "Yes?"

"In the future I will expect you to inform me of my actions *before* I've taken them."

This time Zachary's swallow didn't go down his gullet nearly as smoothly. "Of course, Seb. This was a . . . a singular event."

Sebastian smiled. "Glad to hear it."

Sarala hummed an Indian lullaby as Jenny pulled her hair up into an artistic tangle. If she kept a diary, today would have been peppered with underlines and exclamation marks. Being in the company of Lord Shay Griffin definitely had its advantages. With him making the requests, not only had they gained access to every bit of Roman wall within the confines of the old Tower of London grounds, they'd been provided with a guide who knew things about London's history she'd never even imagined.

The entire day . . . glittered. She couldn't think of a better way to describe it. And if Shay had an odd way of negotiating that made her skin tingle and her heart beat faster, at the moment she could think of nothing wrong with that at all. For the first time since she'd left India she'd been able to discuss antiques, business practices, and politics with someone other than her father.

Even in Delhi the conversations hadn't been as exciting. Shay wasn't an old, company-starved former governor of India or a condescending officer or even an amused, ambitious young nobleman looking for income opportunities. For a moment she frowned, wishing she hadn't conjured that particular image. No, no, no—she'd been thinking about Charlemagne.

He was aggravating, yes, but he was also confident and very intelligent and handsome. And somewhere in the last few days any condescension he might have expressed toward her had vanished. And fine a negotiator as he was, he kissed as sinfully as the devil, himself.

If only he would agree to her very reasonable offer—though she had to admit that she hadn't been pushing as hard or as well as she knew she could do. If he did agree to her price, he would no longer have a reason to pretend to pursue her, or to show her that there were some rather remarkable things to see in England. Given her usual loyalty to her father and her admittedly well-developed liking for business, the choice between spending time with Shay and having guineas in the family's coffer was surprisingly difficult. Yet despite all that, she couldn't help humming.

And now tonight she would see *The Tempest.* Her father had told her how inferior their seats were likely to be, and her mother had protested going at all because they would be so far from the "right" people that no one but bankers and solicitors and possibly grocers would even know they were there.

Sarala, however, didn't care if they had to stand in the hallway. Not only was *The Tempest* her favorite Shakespeare play, but she would see the famous Edmund Kean as Prospero.

"You're in a good mood, my lady," Jenny noted, as she shifted from hair to necklace and ear bobs.

"Yes, I suppose I am."

"Then your picnic with Lord Charlemagne must have gone well."

"It did. And he took me sightseeing afterward."

"Did your gown prevent any more of that kissing from him?"

"Jenny!"

The maid bobbed her head. "Mayhap I'm too bold, but Lady Sarah, your mother Lady Hanover hired me to help look after you. And you don't know London as well as most. I grew up here. And lords kissing ladies they ain't married to, it ain't a good thing."

"Which is why we won't say anything more about it to anyone." Sarala forced a smile. "For heaven's sake, Jenny, it's only one of Lord Shay's negotiation tactics, anyway."

"That's some very strange negotiating, Lady Sarah."

"Yes, and very unsuccessful, too. I'll leave it to him to realize that in his own time, though, because he does kiss quite well."

The maid flushed crimson. "Goodness."

Goodness had little to do with any of this, Sarala was

certain. But it was blasted fun, nevertheless. "So promise me that this will remain between us, Jenny."

"Oh, I prom—"

The bedchamber door flew open, rattling the perfume bottles on her dressing table. "I have the best news ever!" Lady Hanover exclaimed, doing an actual pirouette.

"What in the world is it, Mama?" Sarala asked, grinning at her mother's obvious enthusiasm.

"Your dear father just informed me that he's given up our theater seats."

"What?" Sarala shot to her feet, one ear bob hitting the floor. "How is that good news? What a terrible thing to say! You know how much I've been looking forward to seeing *The Tem—*"

"Let me finish! He's given up our seats because the Duke of Melbourne has invited us to share his box!"

Sarala blinked. "Melbourne's box?"

"Yes! Now you see why I'm so enraptured." Lady Hanover stopped in mid-twirl. "I only hope that brother of his doesn't attend. I don't know how much more strongly I can suggest that he call you Sarah."

"Mama, Lord Charlemagne was introduced to me as Sarala," Sarala explained, declining to admit that they'd introduced themselves and refusing to question why she wanted her mother to like her chief business rival. "That's the only—"

"You cannot wear that dress now."

Sarala stopped to glance down at her attire. "You asked me to wear the yellow silk, Mama." Oh, for heaven's sake. Not only could she not dress as she wished, but now even wearing what she'd been told was wrong.

"That was before we knew we would be sitting in Drury

Lane Theater's prime box. Now you must wear the new lavender and white silk gown with the beading."

"Mama, that one still needs the lace panel put in at the neck."

"No, it doesn't. It's perfect as it is. You'll look charming. Fetch it at once, Jenny."

The maid curtsied and hurried to the wardrobe. "Right away, my lady."

"And I'll stay right here while you dress, Sarah, just to make certain you don't step on any hems."

As Jenny returned, Sarala silently lifted her arms over her head. In a second the yellow gown was gone and she was wearing the very low-cut lavender one.

"Splendid. Where's that ruby you wore last night?"

For a second Sarala's heart skipped, then she realized it was a general question and not an accusatory one. "That one?" she said flippantly. "But all the Griffins saw me wear it last night." And if Shay saw her wearing it after their picnic, he would think she'd become smitten with him or something, and she would have to sell off the silks piecemeal because she'd never get a decent price from him.

"That's true. Very good thinking, darling. The silver one with the pearl drop, then. And the matching ear bobs."

Jenny was still fastening the necklace around Sarala's neck as her mother hurried them downstairs to dinner. Her father arrived a moment later, and the footmen immediately began serving.

"Why the hurry, my dear?" the marquis asked. "The play doesn't begin for two hours."

"Because you said we're to meet His Grace inside the theater, and I want to be certain we have time to be seen chatting with him."

"Are any other of the Griffins attending, Papa?" Sarala asked.

"Not that middle son, I hope. Do you know that he refused to call Sarah by her name, and insisted on referring to our daughter by that—that other name?"

Sarala sighed. "You can't even say it to demonstrate a point? I did own it for two-and-twenty years." And she still owned it, as far as she was concerned.

"I don't know who might join us," her father returned, ignoring his wife's outburst. "Zachary only said that Melbourne wished us to join him. The—"

" 'Him,' you said," her mother broke in. " 'To join him.' It must be Melbourne alone. This is so wonderful I can barely breathe."

"Shall I fetch some smelling salts?" Sarala suggested, not certain she could make herself return to the dining room once she'd escaped.

"Nonsense. Eat your venison. I want us to be there at least half an hour early. An hour would be better."

Sarala and her father exchanged looks. "Yes, Mama," she said. At least this way her mother wasn't complaining about having to go to the theater any longer, though she continued to put in barbs about Shay. Sarala hoped Melbourne had a few drinks to ease his nerves before he arrived to meet them.

But why had the duke made the invitation in the first place? They'd joined him just last night, after all. Certainly he had enough family and friends and hangers-on that he had no need to demonstrate his kindness—or charity—to the same people two nights in a row.

Unless her mother was correct, and she'd somehow caught the duke's eye. But that was so silly a notion she couldn't even conjure a chill about it. Still, her instincts told her something was afoot. A luncheon invitation from Lady Deverill, business with Lord Zachary, and now two successive evenings in the Duke of Melbourne's company—it was very odd. The only Griffin with whom she had a reason to interact was Shay, and neither of her parents knew about that. Nor, she suspected, did his family.

The only thing to do, she supposed, was to go and see *The Tempest*. And to pay close attention to anything the duke might say. Her mother was certain to read everything as a declaration of marriage. That could never happen. Someone therefore needed to keep a logical eye and ear on events.

Sarala honestly thought she and her parents would be left standing in the Drury Lane Theater lobby, trying to pretend they weren't being ignored by most of the other well-acquainted members of the *haute ton*. She was wrong. In fact, the only people who didn't appear to be present and attempting to chat with them were the members of the Griffin family.

"Good evening, Hanover," a tall man with powerful shoulders and a shock of gray hair said, shaking her father's hand.

"Your Grace. A pleasure to see you here. May I present my wife and daughter? Lady Hanover, Lady Sarah, the Duke of Monmouth."

The duke sketched an abrupt bow. "Ladies. I hope we'll all be enjoying the performance tonight."

Sarala smiled. "I'm looking forward to it."

The Duke of Monmouth. And he was only one of several dozen who'd seemed to make a point of coming over and inquiring after the Carlisle family's health or how they were enjoying London. Abruptly her family had gone from being barely noticed to being the don't-miss family of the evening.

And as the crowd stirred near the theater entrance, Sarala realized why. The Duke of Melbourne strolled into the lobby, Charlemagne at his side. As soon as she could force her eyes from the lean, black-clad Shay, she glanced about the lobby. The noise in the room didn't diminish, but its cadence changed. Everyone knew who'd just arrived, and everyone would watch their actions—with whom they conversed, who they seemed to avoid—all evening.

Heavens. If she hadn't snatched the shipment of silks out from under Shay's nose, their one waltz at the Brinston soiree probably would have been both the beginning and the end of their acquaintance. But now for some reason *all* the Griffins seemed to be going out of their way to welcome the Carlisles to London. Of *course* the rest of Society would notice.

"Hanover," the duke said, offering his hand as he reached them. "Zachary said you'd agreed to join us."

"Thank you for the invitation. Our Sarah's been in raptures about seeing *The Tempest* for days."

Gray eyes, cool and assessing, shifted to her. "Have you now?"

She nodded, heat rising in her veins as she felt rather than saw Charlemagne stop at her elbow. "I've dragged Papa to every performance in Delhi since I was eight, but I'm afraid they were few and far between."

At her side, Shay stirred. "We've arrived a bit late. Perhaps we should take our seats."

If they didn't, Sarala doubted anyone at all would leave the lobby for fear of missing something. As the duke nodded, Charlemagne offered his arm to her. Since she had no idea where they were going, she wrapped her fingers around his warm sleeve. In a moment they were several steps ahead of the rest of their party.

"Why didn't you tell me you wished to see *The Tempest*?" he asked in a low voice.

"It didn't occur to me to say anything." She glanced up at his strong profile. "Why did your brother invite us to his box?"

"You'd have to ask Melbourne."

"You didn't suggest that he invite us?"

"I would have, if I'd known of your interest, but he's the one who informed me that you'd be joining us."

Sarala swallowed. "So it was all His Grace's idea?"

"It would seem so." He smiled, the expression lighting his gray eyes. "Not that I have any objection to seeing you again today."

"Ah. If the invitation had been from you, I would have said that you're still attempting to convince me to lower my price by offering interesting bribes, but since this was none of your idea, I don't feel the slightest need to budge."

Shay chuckled. "If you were a man, I think you would make a very fine prime minister. You certainly twist events to your advantage like one."

She drew a slow breath. "If I were a man, I think this negotiation would have been finished by now."

"Perhaps." He guided her around a curving wall and through a curtained doorway, pulling her closer to him as he did so. "Very well, definitely. You are breathtaking this evening," he murmured, his gray gaze lowering briefly to her half-naked bosom before raising to her face again.

Her skin heated, but he'd looked at her the same way when she'd worn the brown gown that came up practically to her chin. "Now who's being bold?" she whispered.

"You have no idea how much restraint I am currently showing," he returned in the same tone, his lips brushing her ear in the near darkness as he shifted out of the doorway to make room for her parents and the duke.

Heavens. She'd worn low-cut gowns before, but this was the first made in the current English style. Despite her protest to her mother, she actually liked it. It was the *reason* for the gown that troubled her.

Melbourne gestured for her and her parents to take the three seats at the front of the box, but her father shook his head. "You young people brave the foreground; Helen and I may doze with fewer people noticing in the rear."

"As you wish. Lady Sarah?" The duke handed her into the middle chair, while he sat to her right and Shay to her left.

Very aware of the crowd below and determined not to give them anything to talk about, Sarala deliberately turned her attention to the stage on their left. It seemed practically close enough to touch, if she just stretched out her fingers far enough.

"My lady," Melbourne's quiet, cultured voice came, pulling her out of her reverie, "may I ask why you favor *The Tempest* above the rest of Shakespeare's works?"

She smiled as she faced him. "I suppose because in an odd way it feels like the India of myth. Magicians, strange creatures, timely storms, and true love. It's familiar and faraway at the same time, if that makes any sense."

"I suppose it does. Is that how you're finding London? Familiar and yet faraway?"

"More faraway than familiar, I'm afraid. There are so many things to remember that seem so arbitrary."

"Arbitrary to you, perhaps, without the background of a native. I believe *we* refer to those things as traditions, which enables them to be meaningless and yet significant."

Sarala carefully stifled her frown. Had the Duke of Melbourne just rebuked her? His tone had been polite, and his words so mild, that she couldn't be sure. At any rate, he certainly didn't sound as though he was the least bit enamored of her. Just the opposite. Thank goodness for that. Relieved as she felt, though, it didn't explain why she and her family remained in the best box in the theater.

And everyone continued to stare. As countless eyes watched her from the dimness, Sarala abruptly felt . . . terrified. Terrified and vulnerable. She'd gone from being barely noticed to standing at the center of Society's whirlwind. If she moved the wrong way, said the wrong thing in the wrong tone of voice, frowned or smiled too broadly in the face of Melbourne's conversation, she could ruin both herself and her family.

And plainly the duke knew that; in his own way, he'd pointed it out to her. Her mother had wanted her to be popular. Now she was, at least for tonight. Had the marchioness realized what the consequences could be? Of course she hadn't. Lady Hanover saw only the lofty heights; she didn't see how far the fall could be for the imperfect, the ones found lacking. Sarala knew herself to be imperfect, and she knew how very high she happened to be sitting. It was too much. Too much.

Shaking, she reached over to tap Shay on the arm. He immediately faced her. "I think you'll like Kean's portrayal of Prospero," he whispered, smiling. "For once there's a reason for a reputation."

She tried to smile back, but she was having so much trouble breathing that it probably came out as a sickly grimace. "Shay, I—"

His brows lowered. "Good God. What's wrong?"

"I—"

"Never mind." Charlemagne stood, practically hauling her to her feet beside him. "Lady Sarala needs some water," he said to the box in general. "We'll be right back."

He managed to keep what looked like a conventional grip on her arm as they left the box. Once they reached the thankfully empty hallway she closed her eyes and sagged against the wall. "Oh, dear."

When she looked again, Charlemagne was nowhere to be seen. Wonderful. He'd probably gone back inside to watch the beginning of the play. She could hear applause emanating from the auditorium behind her.

"Here." Shay reappeared, shoving a glass into her hand. "It's water. I brought whiskey, too, if you prefer that." He showed her the other glass he carried.

"Water is fine." Gratefully she clutched the glass and gulped it down.

"Not too quickly, or you'll drown yourself," Shay chastised, bodily pulling the glass from her lips.

"I *am* drowning." Finally she could breathe again, though her heart pounded hard enough to burst right through her chest.

"What the devil happened?" Shay gave her a warning glare as he returned the water to her. "Sips."

Obediently she took a dainty swallow. "I don't know. It just occurred to me that half of London was watching me up there, waiting for me to do something . . . un-English."

"Did Melbourne say something to you?" he asked very quietly, his expression serious.

"Heavens, no," she returned hastily. He hadn't, really. "He hardly needed to. All I required was my eyes and ears."

"Well, considering that you *are* English, I don't see how you could do anything un-English."

"Oh, please. I could take my shoes off, or say something

unflattering about snake charmers to those old peers who spent ten minutes earlier talking to my bosom." She looked up into his amused gaze. "How do you do it? Be at ease while the world watches your every move?"

Shay shrugged. "Mostly they're watching Melbourne's every move, but I suppose the trick is to think of something else."

"Something else? Since you won't negotiate, I don't know what I'm supposed to think ab—"

"Negotiate?" he repeated in a soft voice.

Her gaze lowered to his mouth. "Yes. You know, numbers, prices . . ."

"Quantities of goods or services . . ."

"Yes," she whispered. "A battle of wits and n—"

He leaned in and kissed her. He moved slowly, molding his mouth against hers, stealing her breath again and sending her heart racing to an entirely different rhythm than fear. The water glass slipped from her fingers to the thankfully carpeted floor as she slid her arms around his shoulders.

Charlemagne pressed her back against the wall, holding her body against his lean, muscled one. She could taste his hunger, feel his interest, and both aroused her.

"I like negotiating with you," he murmured, kissing her again.

"You are a challenging opponent," she returned, her mouth muffled against his.

"Mm." Finally he lifted his face from hers. "Think about that," he said softly.

Well, how could she possibly think of anything else, now? Heavens, she'd nearly melted. Still, this *was* a part of his negotiation, and she'd best remember that. "That might distract me for a minute or two," she managed a little shakily, "but what shall I do after that?"

He ran his thumb along her lip. "Think about two thousand eight hundred pounds," he suggested, "and your subsequent reasonable acceptance of said offer."

Her breath caught. "I wouldn't call accepting that to be reasonable."

The corners of his mouth curved upward. "Ready to go back to our seats?"

She felt far from ready, but not for any of the reasons that had sent her fleeing before. Kisses and silks and gold coins all tangled in her mind. He'd certainly managed to distract her, all right. Sarala smiled back at him. "Thank you. You may lead on, Prospero."

As he pulled the curtain open and helped her back to her seat, his mouth brushed her ear once more. "Thank you for casting me as the hero," he whispered, releasing her to her chair.

The hero? She wasn't entirely certain what his ultimate role would be, but she'd never enjoyed a business rivalry so much in her life.

Chapter 10

Charlemagne made his way downstairs to the smell of fresh-baked bread. Stanton had informed him that Sebastian was still in the breakfast room—Parliament had an afternoon session today, and with a half-dozen meetings following that, his brother had no doubt taken the rare opportunity to rise late.

"Good morning," he said, strolling in to select his breakfast from the sideboard.

"Good morning," his brother returned. "Have you seen Peep yet?"

"I heard her singing, which I assume means she's awake."

Sebastian sighed. "Yes, she informed me yesterday that she means to take the stage when she's old enough."

Charlemagne grinned. "Last week she favored piracy. I wouldn't worry too much."

"Ah, but it's my job to worry."

"You need to think more like Prospero." He cleared his throat. "Ahem.

'These our actors
(As I foretold you) were all spirits, and
Are melted into air, into thin air,
And like the baseless fabric of this vision,
The cloud-capp'd tow'rs, the gorgeous palaces,
The solemn temples, the great globe itself
Yes, all which it inherit, shall dissolve,
And like this insubstantial pageant faded
Leave not a track behind. We are such stuff
As dreams are made on; and our little life
Is rounded with a sleep.'"

The duke eyed him. "And that's supposed to make me feel better? Please don't ever try to depress me."

Laughing, Charlemagne took the seat opposite his brother. "It's a good play. You're actually rather Prospero-like yourself, don't you think? Magically manipulating events to follow the track you think they should?"

"Yes, but that's supposed to be a secret." The duke unfolded the morning edition of the *Times* and nudged it at Charlemagne. "Have you seen this?"

"What?" Taking a bite of toast, Charlemagne turned the paper to face him—and nearly choked.

"You didn't know, then."

"How was I supposed to know?" He read the headline and the caption beneath it again, thinking he must have misinterpreted. "'Ship's Captain Missing; Foul Play Is Feared in the Disappearance of Peter Blink, Captain of the *Wayward*.' Christ."

"He was the one from whom you purchased the silk, wasn't he?"

He *would* have bought the silks from Blink, if Sarala hadn't beaten him to it. But very few people knew he'd been outmaneuvered. Like Melbourne, most thought him the owner of the shipment. *Good God.* Ice crept into his chest. It couldn't be connected to the silks. He was overreacting. "Yes, that was Blink," he answered when he realized Melbourne was still gazing at him.

"Could he have gone on a drunk? He is a sea captain. It's not all that uncommon for his ilk, I believe."

"I suppose so," Charlemagne returned, glancing through the article. "Does this say who reported him missing?"

"His first mate. Apparently they were supposed to set sail for the Mediterranean on Monday, but he never appeared to supervise the resupply or pay the port fees."

That wasn't like Blink. The man had a definite eye for opportunity, but he wasn't careless. "I wonder," he said slowly.

"Wonder what?"

"Well, it's just so odd, and it puts me in mind of the attempted break-in at my house, and that feeling I had the other night, about—"

"Good morning, Papa." Penelope pranced into the breakfast room. "Good morning, Uncle Shay. What feeling did you have?"

Charlemagne hid a scowl as he leaned over to kiss his niece's cheek. "A feeling of cold wet trickling down my back because I got caught in the rain."

She made a face. "Yuck. It's not going to rain today, is it?"

"I don't believe so, Peep. Why do you ask?"

She filled a plate to overflowing with grapes and set it down beside her father. "Because I am going to give you another chance to take me to the museum today. Amelia Harper said that one of the mummies looked at her. I think she's silly, but I need evidence."

He needed to do a little investigating, himself—mainly to make certain that nothing . . . odd had occurred around Sarala. Thin as the connection between a missing sea captain and an attack on the house of his last known client might be, he'd made more than one deal based on even thinner leads. That silk was supposed to be his, and if any of this was connected, he wanted to know about it. "May I take you this afternoon?" he suggested.

"Yes, you may."

Charlemagne took a few quick bites of toast and then pushed away from the table. "If you'll excuse me, I have a few errands to run."

"A moment, Shay." Sebastian stood, as well. "Penelope, don't let Stanton clear my plate."

"I'll guard it, Papa."

Charlemagne followed his brother into the morning room next door. "What is it?"

"Your feeling. You think this Blink's disappearance is connected to your silk purchase, don't you?"

"I'm not certain. I've just had an odd feeling about this entire business." A feeling that had become irrevocably wrapped into visions of India and a black-haired princess with moss green eyes.

"Then you need to sell them. Now."

Technically, he was still trying to obtain them in the first place. "No one's ever intimidated me into anything," he returned. "And at the moment all I have is a very loose chain of coincidence."

"I don't like it, Shay."

"I don't, either." If this had somehow put Sarala in danger . . . He needed to find out. "I'll let you know."

"Make it fast."

"Don't worry, Seb. It's probably nothing."

His brother nodded. "It's the 'probably' part that has me concerned."

Shay had Jaunty saddled and then rode to Carlisle House. A note would probably have worked just as well, and alarmed her less, but damn it, he wanted to see her. There. Might as well admit it, because denial certainly wasn't helping anything.

When he arrived, though, the butler refused him admittance. "Apologies, my lord," the fellow said stiffly, "but no one's to home."

"Where might I find Lady Sarala, then?"

"Lady *Sarah* has gone to breakfast with Lady Hanover and several others."

The degree of disappointment he felt at missing her startled Shay. For something he hadn't even planned, its importance seemed both ridiculous and very . . . illogical. He cleared his throat as the butler continued to gaze at him. "Perhaps you might answer a question for me, then," he went on.

"I shall endeavor."

"Has anything . . . odd occurred here over the past few days?"

"Odd, my lord?"

"Broken windows, strangers calling, anything like that?"

"Not to my knowledge."

Shay nodded, backing away from the door. "Very good, then. There's, ah, been a rash of burglaries. I just wanted to be sure that the Carlisles remained secure."

"I'd like to see someone try to break in here, m'lord," the butler returned, his Cockney accent creeping into his speech. "I'd show 'em what for."

"Glad to hear it. Thank you."

That was something, he supposed, though it didn't say much for him if he was now racing about Town in a panic because a sea captain had gone on a drunk somewhere. Yes, he'd clearly lost his mind.

When he returned to Griffin House, Sebastian had left for Parliament, and Peep waited on the bottommost stair step for him. "I'm going to make some drawings," she announced, hefting a large sketch pad. "I borrowed this from Aunt Caroline."

"That's a good idea, Peep," he returned, ushering her out the front door as Tollins brought the curricle around. "You can document the position of the suspicious mummy."

"Exactly. Amelia Harper is feather-headed, and I am going to prove it. Mummies can't move."

Inside the British Museum, Penelope led the way directly to the Egyptian rooms, Charlemagne in her wake. There were several new pieces to the exhibit, and he was rather grateful for the distraction.

"Uncle Shay, may I borrow your walking cane?"

He started to hand it over, then stopped. "Why, may I ask?"

"I would like to poke that mummy."

Charlemagne swallowed his grin as best he could. "I don't think that would be appropriate, Peep. If it helps, I can give you my personal assurance that the fellow is deceased."

"I know that," she said impatiently, circling the sarcophagus. "I want to see if his head moves."

At that moment one of the curators strolled into the room.

"Ah. Perhaps we might ask an authority," Charlemagne suggested.

Peep held up her small hand to stop him from moving. "I will do it. This is my investigation. You wait here."

"Of course, my lady."

The museum employee was clearly thrilled to be of service to a member of the Griffin family, even a seven-year-old one.

Once Peep and the curator were deep in conversation, Charlemagne smiled again and strolled over to read the wall plaque halfway down the length of the room. Someone had collected part of the inner wall of a tomb and turned it over to the museum. For a long moment he stood looking at the yellow and red and black hieroglyphics. "Amazing," he muttered, leaning in to look more closely. He had a tablet of similar writing himself, displayed in the drawing room of Gaston House. The colors of this one, though, were exceptional.

A shadow slipped across the edge of his vision and behind a huge granite bust of Amenhotep. Charlemagne took a quick glance to see Peep leaning over the rim of the sarcophagus while the curator pointed something out to her. The museum wasn't terribly crowded, but there were a handful of other people roaming the catacomb of rooms and hallways. This, though, felt different.

Obviously he couldn't leave Penelope behind in the room, and he didn't want to begin some sort of crazed shadow chase through the museum with her in tow. Taking a breath and testing his grip on his cane, he turned and made directly for the statue.

Nothing. Slowly he circled its considerable girth, just to be certain. Only a dozen other visitors were in the room, none of them viewing the likeness of Amenhotep with him at the moment. "Damnation," he muttered. "You're going mad, you know."

He turned back—and then he saw the shadow.

The man stood at the far end of the hall, watching him. Medium height, lean build, and long black hair braided into a tail over one shoulder, he was as clearly a warrior as if he wore armor rather than a loose shirt and pants, clearly designed with ease of movement in mind. The fellow was foreign—Chinese, unless Charlemagne was greatly mistaken—and after a long moment spent looking at each other the man bowed and then vanished around the corner.

Charlemagne's first instinct was to go after him. In the next second he realized that it was probably a trap, either for him or to separate him from his niece. Which meant first that he couldn't follow, and second that he and Peep needed to get out of the museum before anyone attempted something more serious than lures.

"Peep," he called, making a show of pulling out his pocket watch.

"I haven't drawn anything yet," she returned from her seat on the bench against the wall.

He returned to her side. "Did the curator explain the lack of movement of mummies to your satisfaction?"

"Yes, he did. I would still like some illustrations, though, so I can show them to Amelia Harper when I prove that she's dim-witted."

"I would suggest a bit more diplomacy than that," he said, taking her sketch pad under his arm and her hand in his. "I have a very well-illustrated book on mummies. You may have it, if you wish."

"May I cut out the pictures?"

Inwardly gritting his teeth, he nodded. "It's for a good

cause." And it would get her out of what had become a considerably less friendly place.

On the way back to Griffin House he took the time to run through several possible scenarios. A Chinese warrior and Blink's disappearance—if they were related, then one more piece instantly fell into that equation: the Chinese silks. And the Chinaman had apparently followed him, and intentionally. That meant that at least someone thought *he* had the silks, which was good. It meant Sarala was safe and out of this particular arithmetic problem, at least for now. Apparently he wasn't the only one to think that women didn't engage in business.

One thing was for certain, though; the next time he saw a shadow, he was going to hunt it down.

"You look like you've been dragged behind a mule," Sebastian said calmly the next day, handing his hat to Stanton as Charlemagne exited the library.

"I've been doing some research," Shay said, blowing out his breath. "What time is it?"

"Half past noon," the duke answered without checking. "Friday, in case you've lost track of that, as well."

He felt like he had. Since the return from the museum yesterday he'd been going nonstop—tracking down everyone he knew who'd done business with Blink, reading up on his histories of China, pulling in favors from the government to learn which foreign diplomats were currently in London, and trying to determine once and for all whether any of this nonsense was connected or not.

"I'm sorry I wasn't home last evening," Sebastian continued, motioning him toward the stairs. "What did you find out about Blink?"

"Not much." Shay stopped at the foot of the stairs,

declining to follow his brother up. "I need to go see someone." He hadn't seen Sarala in longer than he'd seen Sebastian, and she needed to know that something odd seemed to be going on. Aside from that, he hadn't had a good argument in nearly two days. He missed her.

"Anyone in particular?"

"No."

"You're courting her, aren't you?"

Charlemagne nearly fell on his face. "What? Who?" he sputtered, facing Melbourne.

"Don't dissemble, Shay. You think we don't all know? Why do you think we've been making the effort of becoming acquainted with the family?"

"*What?*" Abruptly several things made sense. God, he'd been an idiot. A distracted, soft-headed, idiot. "For God's sake, she—she's not—I'm not—" He drew a breath, trying to chart a course clear of this mess without looking like a complete muggins. "Sarala . . . she bought the silks from Blink, right out from under me. I've been trying to acquire them back from her."

Melbourne opened and closed his mouth several times. Charlemagne realized he'd never really seen his brother truly surprised—until this moment. "You're doing business with her," Sebastian said flatly.

"I've been attempting to. She's a good negotiator."

The duke shook his head. "This does not make any sense. I've been open-minded, stayed out of matters, and you—"

"Now just a minute. What matters have you been staying out of, Seb? What's going—"

The front window shattered.

Sebastian on his heels, Charlemagne thundered into the blue room, grabbing one of the old Griffin family swords off the wall as he went. Nothing.

No, not nothing, he amended a heartbeat later, taking in the small bundle resting against the leg of a chair. "There," he said, moving forward to grab it while his brother barked some order that had Tom the footman standing at the open front door with a musket in his hands.

"What is it?" Melbourne asked, moving to his side.

Shay hefted it. "A rock. It's wrapped in . . . silk." A very fine quality silk. The cold that had been burrowing into his chest since he'd read the newspaper yesterday stopped his heart. "Christ. I have to go."

"Go where?" Sebastian demanded as Charlemagne thrust the rock at him and headed out the door.

"To see Sarala."

"You are not going out alone."

"I can take care of myself. And I need to finalize my purchase before someone realizes that it's not me who owns the silks."

"Shay! If it's just business, then why—"

He could finish the question himself, Charlemagne realized, as he ran toward the stable. Why put himself in danger over a business deal when it had been yanked out from under him in the first place? And he knew the answer, as well. Sarala wasn't simply a business rival. He wasn't quite certain what she was, but he had no intention of allowing her to remain in a position that could potentially be very dangerous.

The wrapped rock message needed to be answered, as well, but before he could deal with that, he needed to put himself in the position of being the one they would have to deal with, and he needed to minimize the danger to Sarala and his family. He could stay at Gaston House until they settled matters.

His mind continued to race as a groom brought Jaunty up. He swung into the saddle and goaded the chestnut down the front drive. Out of the corner of his eye he saw Melbourne come out to the front portico, but he otherwise ignored his brother. Whatever mess he'd caused between the Griffins and the Carlisles, it would have to wait.

The streets of Mayfair thronged with vendors and pedestrians and servants collecting vegetables and milk for the day. With a scowl at the congestion he turned Jaunty into an alleyway—and stopped as for the second time the shadow materialized in front of him.

This time the Chinese warrior carried a long, curved, and very sharp-looking saber in his hands.

Charlemagne quickly dismounted. In the same motion he pulled his pistol from his greatcoat pocket and cocked it. "I don't doubt your proficiency with your weapon," he said coolly, shifting toward the nearest wall so no one could come up behind him, "and I suggest you accept my proficiency with mine."

"Then perhaps we will talk," the swordsman said in excellent, if heavily accented, English.

"You're not the one I saw yesterday at the museum."

"No. That was him." He gestured toward the rooftop opposite Charlemagne. Another man, dressed and armed as the first, crouched in the shadow of a brick chimney and watched them.

Wonderful. Outmaneuvered and outnumbered, but at least if they were here then they weren't assaulting Sarala yet. "You're the reason Captain Blink disappeared as well, I presume? And which of you followed me the other night?"

"Yes, and all of us." A third swordsman appeared from the alley entranceway as the first one spoke again.

"Might I ask why?" Charlemagne considered the major flaw of his character to be his lamentably short temper. He'd worked at curbing it and improving his patience, but there were occasions when an eager willingness to pummel someone could be helpful. After the rather blatant clue of the silk-covered rock, he considered this to be one of those occasions.

"You stole from us. From China."

"I've stolen nothing."

"Emperor Jiaqing says differently. His Eminence wants his property returned and the insult avenged."

"Avenged? Against Blink?"

"He stole property. Property then purchased by you. *You* have insulted the emperor."

"You're talking about the silks."

The first swordsman inclined his head. "They were commissioned specifically for the birthday celebration of Emperor Jiaqing. They must be back in China by that time. You will return His Eminence's stolen property, and you will present yourself to him to be dealt with according to his wisdom. As will your captain."

"He's not *my* captain." They were starting to shift toward him, and he aimed the pistol squarely at the one blocking his path. "If you want the silks back, you will deal with me, gentleman to gentleman. I will meet you tomorrow at noon, at the museum. The same place I saw you yesterday."

It wasn't much of a plan, but it would gain him a day, and a meeting in a public place.

The swordsman gave an elegant, one-shouldered shrug. "Do not lose your courage, as your captain did. If you do, we will hunt you down as we did him."

"My courage is my own concern," Charlemagne said flatly. "But I will be there tomorrow. Will you?" The one on the roof would have to make it past Jaunty below. The shot would have to be to the first swordsman, then the butt of the pistol against the one behind him. It was a longshot, but he was willing.

The first one bowed. "We will be there." He said something in Chinese and abruptly all three of them vanished back into the shadows again.

Charlemagne took a deep breath, slowly released the pistol's hammer, and returned the weapon to his pocket. Jaunty stood nervously on the opposite side of the alley, and he spent a moment calming the chestnut before he swung back into the saddle. Sarala. He needed to reach Sarala.

Chapter 11

"Did *you* invite all these ladies?" Lady Deverill whispered to her sister-in-law.

Lady Caroline Griffin shook her head. "I don't even know who half of them are."

Sarala stood a few feet behind them, a smile pasted on her face and hands held together behind her back so no one would see them shaking. Apparently the "friends" luncheon to which Eleanor had invited her had grown to proportions unimagined. With a breath she took a step forward. "Is there anything I can do?" she asked.

Both women faced her. "No, no, my dear," the marchioness said after a moment. "The unexpected is always expected in this household."

Sarala supposed that Eleanor meant the Deverill household, since that was where the mass of females stood chatting and snacking on biscuits while footmen scurried about to place more tables and chairs in the back garden. The two hostesses might claim to have no idea why half the young ladies of London had arrived uninvited and unannounced, but as Sarala watched them troop by in groups of two or three, she had a fair grasp on what was happening. *She* had become the latest attraction in London. The Griffins were feting her family, inviting them to exclusive events, including her in their intimate gatherings, and everyone wanted to know *why*.

So did she, as a matter of fact, but since Eleanor and Caroline were the only two people with whom she had even the remotest acquaintance, now didn't seem the time to make a straightforward demand for answers. She probably wouldn't like hearing what they had to say, anyway.

After another few moments of whispered discussion, Caroline separated from her sister-in-law and took Sarala's arm. "So, Lady Sarah, what do you think of London so far?" she asked, strolling with her in the direction of the garden. "I was rather overwhelmed by it when I first arrived. It's very different from Witfeld House in Shropshire, even with the crowd we had living there."

"It's very different from Delhi, as well," Sarala answered, "but I'm learning to enjoy it."

"I'm glad to hear that," Lady Caroline returned with a warm smile.

"You're a portraitist aren't you?" Sarala asked, moving the subject away from herself. She'd learned long ago that the best way to get information was by simply getting the other party to talk.

"I am. Do you paint?"

"A little dabbling when I was younger. I had some interest, but not much skill, I'm afraid. How do—"

"What do you enjoy doing, then?"

Drat. For once it seemed it would be rude *not* to talk about herself. Everyone was so blasted interested, where before she'd barely been able to conjure up a dance partner at a soiree. "I read, histories mostly, and occasionally assist my father with his business. Not as much now as in India, of course."

She added that last part in deference to her mother's warning, and those of the marchioness's matchmaking cronies, about women and business. Caroline's expression didn't change, but Sarala couldn't help wondering what Lord Zachary's wife must be thinking. They would have to know that she was somehow responsible for the crowd—or rather that the Griffins' show of interest was somehow responsible. If Sarala—Sarah—turned out to be a hopeless eccentric, it could reflect as badly on them as it did on her.

"May I ask you a question?" Sarala ventured.

"Of course."

"Why am I here?"

Caroline's gaze darted swiftly toward Lady Deverill, then back again. "I'm certain Eleanor explained that we enjoyed your company the other night, and thought you might enjoy ours."

"Yes, she did. But what I find confusing is why the Duke of Melbourne decided to 'notice' my family in the first place. He must have myriad other friends with whom he'd rather attend recitals and the theater."

"I wouldn't presume to try to explain what the Duke of Melbourne might be thinking," Caroline finally answered. "He's rather inscrutable."

And a little rude as well, Sarala added silently. "He's not attempting to woo me, is he?"

As soon as the words came out she regretted them, her

mind flashing to Shay's admonition about propriety and her mother's about showing more reserve. Caroline's face paled, then darkened into a fine blush.

"I . . . I beg your pardon?" she stammered.

"I was only joking," Sarala said hastily, forcing a chuckle.

"Um, well, I don't believe His Grace is courting anyone. Is that—he, I mean—where your interests lie?"

"Heavens, no. He's far too . . . British for my taste."

" 'British.' "

"I mean to say, he seems very . . . unyielding. Rigid."

The volume of twittering beside the doorway at the far end of the room increased, and a heartbeat later Charlemagne strode into the room. Sarala's first feeling was one of relief. A friendly face, one with whom she didn't need to dissemble, or even to watch what she said. Then she saw the look in his eyes as he spotted his sister and made his way over to Eleanor.

"Why didn't you tell me you were having Sarala over for luncheon?" he asked in a low voice, which she nevertheless managed to overhear.

"Hush, Shay. I may invite whomever I wish to dine with me."

"I didn't say you couldn't. I asked why you didn't tell me."

"I—"

"This is part of Melbourne's nonsense, isn't it?"

"I have no idea what—"

"Never mind. Where is she?"

"Shay, this is hardly the place—"

He turned and saw Sarala. "There you are," he said, striding directly up to her. "I need to speak with you."

So much for blending in as simply one of the girls. She'd be lucky if anyone wanted to converse with her at all after this. Or rather, she doubted now that she'd ever be able to have another decent conversation without absurd expectations or being plied with a thousand questions about the Griffins to which she didn't know the answers. "Now?"

"Yes, now. I went to Carlisle House, but your butler said you were here."

Sarala frowned. "Why are you following me about London, Shay?"

"For God's sake, Sarala," he whispered, "if you'll come with me into the other room, I will tell you."

Charlemagne looked annoyed and exasperated, but there was more to his expression than that, even. Something bothered him. Something worried him. Sarala nodded. "Very well."

He took her arm and, without even a backward glance at their rapt audience, led her into a neighboring study and closed the door. Ill-versed as she might have been in propriety, she knew *that* wasn't usual.

"Open the door, Shay."

Shay looked at her for a bare moment, then swept forward and captured her in a hard, deep kiss. Immediately everything—the nervousness, the uncertainty of her place in Society, the worry at having to make polite conversation with people who would rather talk about her than to her—all of it faded into nothing. She kissed him back, flinging her arms around his shoulders and not caring what in the world had made his seeing her so imperative. Heavens, if he would always kiss her like that, she might just *give* him the silks.

He broke the kiss first, looking down into her eyes for a long moment. "I want those silks, Sarala. And I want them now."

She lifted her eyebrows, wondering for a moment if he was truly that devious. "Is that why you kissed me?"

Charlemagne frowned. "No. I kissed you because I can't *not* kiss you. Sell me the silks, Sarala."

If he'd said something that nice to her at any other time, it would have meant considerably more. *Concentrate, Sarala.* "Why do you want them now? You drag your feet about making me a decent offer for almost a week, and now you interrupt my first Society luncheon so you can make demands?"

"Four thousand pounds, Sarala. Sign them over and tell me where they are." He pulled a piece of paper from his pocket and unfolded it. "Sign this and I'll be out of your way."

Four thousand pounds? "I'm not signing anything. You've found a buyer, haven't you? Someone who'll buy for much more than four thousand."

"No . . ." He took a slow step back, running restless fingers through his dark hair. It was the first time she'd seen him show anything like uncertainty. "No, I haven't found a buyer. I'm tired of this silliness, and I want to take them off your hands. Four thousand."

" 'Silliness'? If by silliness you mean your inability to carry out your half of a simple negotiation, then I agree."

He circled her, and she could swear that he leaned in to smell her hair as he passed behind her. An involuntary tremor ran down her spine.

"I just offered you four thousand pounds," he said. "I'd call that straightforward and reasonable."

"The price is now eight thousand."

An elegant eyebrow lowered. "What? You offered them to me for thirty-five hundred just the day before yesterday."

"And you offered me more than that just now. You're the one who said not to appear too eager. You've weakened your own position." Her gaze focused on his mouth; why was it that the more heated the bargaining, the more she wanted to kiss him? "Obviously you want them, so now you shall pay for them."

"You are—" A low curse rumbled from his chest as he stalked up to her again. Taking her chin in his fingers, he leaned in for another plundering kiss. "Fine," he grumbled, clearing his throat. "Eight thousand. Will a note do? I don't carry that much currency on me." He pulled another piece of paper from his jacket pocket.

"What is going on, Shay?" she demanded with as much clarity as she could, her senses still reeling. "I want some answers."

"Nothing is going on. Eight thousand. Made out to you, or to your father?" he asked, squatting down at a writing desk and grabbing a quill to scrawl out something.

"No. It's twelve thousand now."

"Twelve—" He slammed down the paper and rounded on her so fast that she took a step backward. "I may not be able to stop . . . touching you," he growled, "but this is not a game."

"Certainly it is," she retorted, lifting her chin. He would not intimidate her with his snarls and his large frame. He'd already confessed that he desired her. "You've treated it as one from the beginning."

"No, I haven't. Don't confuse my magnanimity with lack of seriousness. That shipment is mine, and we both know it. I'm doing you the courtesy of offering you fair compensation for it." He took a step closer. "Eight thousand pounds. Sign the paper."

"Not until you tell me which fly you've lured into your web."

He took a harsh breath. "You won't believe me, but the silks belong to the emperor of China, and he wants them back."

Laughter burst from her chest. "You're selling them back to China? That's amazing! I stand in awe of your abilit—"

Charlemagne grabbed her by the shoulders, yanking her up against him. "For the last bloody time, I am not joking. Sign them over to me right this damned minute, Sarala. If you don't—"

"If I don't, then what?" she asked defiantly.

He lowered his mouth over hers once more. Anger and heat and frustration washed over her stronger than before, a wave of aroused yearning. She clutched his lapels, pulling herself against his hard, muscled chest. The paper crushed in his fist as he slid his hands down her back to her hips. A vase rolled off the table behind her and broke on the wood floor. She scarcely noted it.

Good heavens. She'd been wrong. Business and pleasure, at least where Shay was concerned, went together quite well. His tongue teased at her lips, and she opened to him hungrily. They shifted, his hands pulling at her hips as he pushed her toward the couch. Her heel caught on the carpet and they both nearly went down. Sarala didn't care. She moaned, grabbing at him harder.

"Shay."

At the low hiss, Charlemagne lifted his head, his arms still encircling her—thankfully, since her legs felt like water. The Duke of Melbourne stood in the doorway, his face absolutely expressionless. Sarala's heart froze.

"Shit," Shay muttered.

Eleanor pushed past the duke, a half-dozen ladies crowding into the doorway behind her. "Shay, you're keeping my guest from lun . . ." She trailed off, her face going white.

Sarala saw it all unfold as if in a slow, leisurely dream. The curious faces behind the Griffin siblings, the growing feminine roar of gossip and speculation filling both rooms, the way Shay stepped back from her but still kept a hand on her arm. If she needed any confirmation that he was a true gentleman, that small gesture provided it. At least she didn't have to stand alone while she was ruined.

After sending both of them another hard look, Melbourne moved into the middle of the room to join them. "You might have waited until we had the Carlisles over for breakfast tomorrow," he said succinctly, a cool smile on his lean face. "But now I suppose all I can do is be the first to offer the two of you my very warm congratulations." Finally he faced the growing crowd. "I hope all of you ladies will join me in wishing my brother and his wife-to-be well. I do assume you've accepted his offer, Sarah."

What? Oh no, no, no. Amid the suddenly enthusiastic congratulations practically commanded by Melbourne, Sarala opened her mouth to protest. This was a nightmare! In the next second Charlemagne's supporting grip became iron-hard.

"Don't say anything except to express your happiness," he murmured, brushing a strand of hair from her temple with his free hand, making the gesture look and feel like a caress despite the circumstances. "We'll straighten things out later."

" 'Straighten things out?' " she hissed back through a tight smile. "Are you mad? Your brother just said that we're to be married!"

"I know. I was here, too." He took a deep, shaking breath she could feel through his hand on her arm. "Thank you, Sebastian," he continued in a normal tone.

His brother clapped him on the shoulder, none too gently. "You are a careless idiot," the duke muttered darkly.

Sarala wanted to hit someone. At the same time, she felt like fainting. This was far worse than having an audience looking at her in the theater. Oh, goodness.

Someone else's hand took her free arm, and she looked around to see Lady Deverill. "Come, my dear," she said with a smile, drawing Sarala away from Shay.

Charlemagne tightened his grip again, looking between the two women. "This was my fault, Nell."

"I know, you big oaf. Let me take her to get a breath of air."

"Keep her here, send someone for her parents, and get rid of your guests," the duke said quietly, briefly catching his sister's free arm.

Eleanor nodded. "It's being taken care of."

Numbly Sarala allowed herself to be led into the empty library. Shay's own siblings had just called him an idiot and an oaf. She could only imagine what they must think of her. Or what she would think of herself as soon as her mind regained a grasp on some sanity. And then it would only get worse.

"I always thought Zachary was the brainless one," Melbourne roared from the upstairs billiards room at Corbett House, "but this surpasses anything—*anything*—I could imagine from him. This was about your damned shipment of silks?"

Charlemagne leaned back against the billiards table. Considering what had just happened and the last few tense days, his own calm rather surprised him. He rolled a ball back behind him. "Apparently, yes."

"What do you mean, 'apparently'? You told me days ago that you'd taken possession of those silks! What the devil does mauling the virginal daughter of a marquis have to do with buying back some bolts of material? Please explain it to me, Shay!"

"It began as a game, to see who could out-negotiate whom."

He shrugged. "We got carried away. She's sharp as an arrow point, you know."

"Obviously, if she managed to maneuver you into matrimony."

"She didn't maneuver me into anything, and I think you know that." For the first time since Melbourne had broken in on them, anger rolled down Charlemagne's spine. "And I'm the one who just got leg-shackled, so I would suggest that you step back a little, Sebastian."

"You should have been giving yourself that same advice. You said this was all business. I don't . . . kiss my business rivals."

With effort, Charlemagne kept his stance relaxed. "I should hope not. This would be a first for me, as well."

"This is serious, Charlemagne. I have a dozen armed servants at my home guarding my daughter at the moment, you tell me you don't even own what that Chinese fellow wants, and then you rush off to acquire it and end up ruining Lady Sarah instead. I am not amused."

"I'm attempting to explain, if you would shut up for a minute and listen, Melbourne." Charlemagne took a steadying breath. "The night before I was to meet with Captain Blink, I bragged about my coup to Sarala. The next morning when I arrived at Blackfriar's, she'd made the purchase out from under me."

"So I've come to assume, though why you didn't just say you lost the deal back then, I have no idea."

"Because I don't lose deals," Charlemagne said flatly, "and definitely not to chits. But at the moment, that's not the point. What I didn't know—until this morning, actually—was that apparently Blink stole the silks."

"Stole them? From whom?"

"From Emperor Jiaqing of China."

Melbourne blinked. "*The* emperor of China."

"Yes."

"That's a bit of a stretch, to go from a thrown rock, a missing sea captain, and a Chinese mercenary to an emperor, Shay."

"I didn't just imagine it, if that's what you're implying. On the way to Carlisle House to make certain Sarala was safe, I was . . . confronted by *three* Chinese swordsmen informing me that I needed to return the stolen silks and to deliver myself to Emperor Jiaqing for his justice. I would say they're some sort of soldier or royal guard, not mercenaries."

The duke paled, straightening. "Merely saying 'three Chinese swordsmen' is enough to get my attention. This is the nineteenth century, Shay. They can't actually think a high-ranking British nobleman would hand himself over to the emperor for a beheading because of a misunderstanding."

"Sarala didn't believe me, either. I went to find her because I was worried that Blink might have given her name out, as well, so I pursued her to make sure that *I* was the one in possession of the silks. Apparently I offered too generous a price for them, because it made her suspicious." A half smile touched his mouth. "The kisses, I can't . . . quite explain." Not except to say that they'd become as vital to him over the past few days as talking with Sarala was.

"If you're still so amused by all this, let me ask you a question: How certain are you that these so-called Chinese swordsmen were telling the truth?"

Charlemagne began a quick retort, then snapped his mouth closed again. The ramifications of what his brother had just said stunned him like a blow to the gut. Just as quickly, though, he knew it couldn't be true. "No," he said, shaking his head. "Firstly, Sarala hasn't been in London long enough to arrange such a farce, and secondly, she's . . . honest. I mean, she values her skills at business. She would consider it cheating to attempt something so underhanded."

Melbourne continued to gaze at him. The anger had left his expression, but that didn't necessarily mean anything. Shay knew him well enough to realize that the family couldn't be at all pleased by what had happened. Under the best of conditions Sarala was barely English, barely nobility. And these were not the best of conditions.

"Besides," he continued into the silence, "if this was all for show or to raise the price I would pay for the silks, then why did she refuse to sign them over? She had me up to eight thousand quid."

His brother walked to the window. "My guess would be because while eight thousand pounds is well and good, marrying a much larger fortune is even better."

"No. Aside from the honesty, she didn't kiss me. I kissed her."

"That wouldn't be difficult to arrange."

"Now just a—"

"You're obviously besotted with her, Shay." Melbourne approached him again. "A damned business deal never had you this twisted around before. If you'd given me a bloody minute to sort through things, if you'd taken a bloody minute to let me know what was going on, we could have avoided any nastiness. You were caught in an intimate embrace with the unmarried, virginal daughter of a peer."

Wonderful. Now they were back to the beginning once more. "Seb, I won't be shouted at again. Why don't you tell me what 'matters' you've been staying out of?"

Melbourne narrowed his eyes. "Beg pardon? We're discussing you at the moment."

"You said you had been staying out of matters, because you thought I was courting Sarala. I remember quite clearly."

"Shay, you—"

"You know, I thought it was odd that you'd asked the Carlisles to join us at that recital, and then when you invited them to share your box at Drury Lane, but it coincided with what I wanted, so I didn't delve."

"Neither did I," Melbourne said sharply. "I'm not a fool, unlike some of us in this room. I saw your interest, or what I perceived as your interest, so I took steps to become acquainted with the chit's family. That's all."

"No meddling?" Charlemagne asked, deeply surprised that his brother had confessed to anything at all.

"None." The duke blew out a harsh breath. "Until I saw you with her a few minutes ago, that is. Haven't you grasped what's happened, Shay? You are betrothed. Chinese swordsmen or stolen silks or whatever else you've been mishandling, *you are marrying Sarala Carlisle.* And honestly, if you wanted to marry, you might have chosen better."

"Since I am to be married," Charlemagne interrupted, the fog clearing from his mind as what Melbourne was saying sank in, "I suggest you not continue in that tone when you are referring to my future wife." He pushed upright. "Where did Nell stash her? I want to see her."

"Don't promise her anything else until we've come to an agreement with the parents," Sebastian returned, going to the door and pulling it open. "I imagine this mistake of yours will be a costly one, as it is."

With Melbourne continuing to eye him and the entire afternoon still rattling about in his brain like a loose cannon, he couldn't even be certain which way was up, much less determine whether the . . . satisfaction that kept attempting to burrow its way into his heart was the appropriate reaction or not.

"My 'mistake,' as you call it, won't cost you a pence, Melbourne. I—"

"I didn't mean in terms of money. You're logical. Think about it." His brother gave him a last look, then headed for the door. "I have meetings I need to postpone. I'll be in Valentine's office, waiting for Hanover. Do as you will, Shay. Just remember that your actions will continue to affect the rest of us."

"I know that."

Charlemagne let him leave. He and Sebastian hadn't come to blows since they had been children, but if his brother had made one more disparaging remark about Sarala, the loose tether on his ragged temper would have snapped.

The argument did make one thing clear, however—his ignorance about his sudden bride-to-be. What did he really know about Sarala—other than that she liked to be barefoot and knew how to charm cobras and missed India? And that she enjoyed business and negotiating, of course.

"Time to find out," he said, making for the hall door.

Sarala paced up and down Lady Deverill's garden, while a few feet away her hostess pretended to prune roses. She knew it was a pretense, because every minute or so Eleanor would look toward the house, then glance over at her and smile.

"I didn't mean for this to happen," Sarala finally blurted.

"I know. I blame Shay."

Considering the marchioness's choice of words, Sarala didn't feel very reassured. For heaven's sake, what had happened? She and Shay had been arguing, kissing, and then Melbourne had appeared like the personification of Doom. Everyone began congratulating her, and then it had sunk in—married. She and Charlemagne were betrothed. But she couldn't marry him. He was a Griffin, and she was . . . She didn't know what she was, but she certainly knew that she couldn't marry Shay Griffin.

"Sarala."

She jumped at the sound of his low voice. He stood at the edge of the rose garden, his gaze on her and his expression unreadable.

"Go away, Shay," Eleanor stated, dropping her pruners into a bucket. "You've done enough damage for one afternoon."

"This from the chit who eloped to Scotland," he retorted. "You go away. I want to speak with Sarala."

The butler appeared behind Charlemagne. "Begging your pardon, Lady Deverill, Lord Charlemagne, but Lord and Lady Hanover have arrived. I've placed them in the morning room, as you instructed."

"Thank you, Hobbes," Eleanor said. "Where is Melbourne?"

"His Grace is in the library, awaiting Lord Charlemagne."

Shay nodded. "Nell, you stay here with Sarala. Sebastian and I will see to this."

Sarala blinked. They were going to take care of everything, make it smooth and proper and pleasant, face the sting of her parents' anger while she remained elsewhere. "No," she broke in.

"Beg pardon?"

She strode up to Shay. "I said, no. *I* will speak to my parents first. I do still have some say in all of this."

"Of course you do. But the mistake was mine. You needn't face them—"

" 'Mistake'?" she repeated, a bit shrilly. "The 'mistake' was mutual. And *I* will explain it. When my parents have all the facts, then you may speak with them, if you still wish to."

"Sarala, I misspoke. Don't—"

"Excuse me," she said, and walked past the butler into the house.

Once she'd made her way down the hall, for a long moment she stood outside the closed morning room doors. It was the first time she'd been alone since . . . it . . . the "mistake" had happened, and in truth she still had no idea what to make of it all.

"Stupid, stupid, stupid," she muttered. For all the pride she had in the abilities of her mind and of her intellect, she'd made the most simple and obvious of errors—she'd allowed herself to be discovered alone in a room with a man. A man whom she happened to be kissing. Yes, in that sense, Shay had been correct; they *had* made a mistake. Perhaps that was all he'd meant, but his blasted word choice could have been better.

She groaned, rubbing her temple. What she wanted to do was run and scream and punch something very hard, but that would have been as unacceptable in Delhi as it was in London. What she needed to do was tell her parents before Melbourne and Shay appeared and took over everything; took over her life.

With a deep breath she pushed open the door. Her parents, seated on the couch, immediately stood. Lady Hanover looked a bit frazzled, while her father, merely puzzled.

"What's happened?" her mother said, hurrying forward. "You aren't hurt, are you?"

"No, I'm not injured," Sarala said hastily.

"Thank heavens. That footman appeared on our doorstep and practically demanded that we get into the coach and come to Corbett House. I was in the middle of making up a dinner menu."

"Why are we here?" her father asked in a calmer voice.

Oh, she wished she'd been in the room alone with him. Her father, she understood. He could be reasoned with. But that obviously was not going to happen. *Just say it, Sarala,* she ordered herself. *Don't be such a coward.* "As you know, I came here to attend Lady Deverill's luncheon."

"Yes," her mother returned. "And it was good of her to ask you. But what—"

"I should probably mention something else, first." She faced her father. "Charlemagne Griffin is the one who wanted those silks that I purchased. We've been negotiating."

"You went up against Charlemagne Griffin? I've heard about his success at business. His reputation is earned, I presume?"

"That is not the point," the marchioness interrupted. "You were engaged in business with a man. Shame on you, Sarah. I warned you about such things. Lord Charlemagne? Have you angered the Griffins? Oh, heavens. What are we to do? We'll be pariahs in London, now. No one will—"

"He kissed me," Sarala stated.

Her mother sank into a chair.

"He what?" her father asked very quietly.

She lowered her head, then lifted it again. Calm and logical. It was the way she tried to approach everything. She couldn't change that now. "Actually, we kissed each other."

"For God's sake . . ." Slowly the marquis seated himself, as well. "You haven't . . . He hasn't . . ."

"He came to see me here. He had some story about the silks being stolen, but that's not important. What is important is that we kissed, not for the first time, and the duke saw us. And the rest of the guests saw us."

"Oh, dear Lord." Her mother sank her head into her hands. "You're ruined. We're ruined. What are we to do, Howard?"

"Melbourne announced to everyone that we were betrothed. That we'd been planning it, and simply hadn't been able to contain ourselves."

Her mother's head lifted again. "Just—for clarity's sake, which one are you betrothed to? Melbourne, or Charlemagne?"

"Charlemagne. Apologies. I should have stated that more clearly."

For a moment she stood there, watching the emotions play across the faces of her parents. Her father was angry and disappointed, her mother horrified and then ecstatic. As for herself, she still couldn't quite believe what had happened.

The marchioness stood and threw her arms around Sarala. "Oh, my dear, you're to marry a Griffin! Not *the* Griffin, but still, *a* Griffin! And that's far better than anyone else."

"This is all very strange," her father put in. "Where is Lord Charlemagne? And Melbourne?"

"I insisted on speaking with you first. They're waiting." She cleared her throat. If she didn't speak now, she would have very little recourse later. "I think you should know, though, that I don't want to be engaged."

"You don't want to marry a Griffin?" Her mother released her again. "That's mad."

"Shay and I were negotiating a business deal. Improperly, I admit, but I hardly consider any of this grounds for a marriage."

"Of course it is! Would you see yourself ru—"

"You like him though, don't you, daughter?" Lord Hanover interrupted.

"Yes, of course I like him. He's very intelligent." And handsome, and efficient, and clever, and good-humored. But their betrothal hadn't been for any of those reasons. And that was what mattered.

"If you like him, then I'm not certain what you think we should do about it."

"Nothing," her mother said, stomping one foot. "We will accept Lord Charlemagne's very gracious offer of marriage, and that's that."

"But Shay didn't offer. Melbourne offered Shay."

"That doesn't matter!"

Yes, it did. "I will do whatever you think is best for the family, Pati," Sarala said, concentrating on the more reasonable of her parents. "But I still think there must be something we can do."

Looking older and more frail than she'd ever seen, the marquis sat back in the chair. "We'll wait for the duke to make the next step. I suppose as the head of the Griffin family, ultimately what happens is up to him."

At that moment a strong rap sounded on the morning room door. It opened, and the Duke of Melbourne walked into the room, Charlemagne at his heels. "Excuse us," the duke said in a low, even tone, his gaze passing over Sarala and going to her father. "I assume you know now what's happened?"

"Yes, we do." Belatedly the marquis stood, his glare at Shay. "How dare you, sir. Sarah is my daughter."

"No, Sarala is your daughter," Shay countered, his own attention on her.

"That is not—"

"Obviously tempers are a little high at the moment," the

duke interrupted. "I want to assure you that whatever happened and may happen, Charlemagne will do the gentlemanly thing."

"I should hope so," her mother huffed.

"Shouldn't we be having this conversation with Charlemagne then?" Sarala asked, not entirely certain she'd spoken aloud until Melbourne faced her.

For the briefest of moments his jaw worked. "I am head of the family," he answered slowly, "but you will both have a say in the proceedings."

" 'Proceedings'?"

"Sarah," the marchioness hissed. "Behave."

"I think ten o'clock tomorrow morning at Griffin House will suit us all better. You may bring whomever you wish to see that your best interests are addressed. Is that acceptable, Lord Hanover?"

"Yes, completely," the marquis answered.

"Very good. We shall see you then."

"I still need to discuss something with Sarala," Shay put in.

The duke glanced at his brother. "Tomorrow."

"I am not—"

"Good day." Melbourne bowed to the room in general, turned on his heel, and left the room. For a bare moment Shay hesitated, his gaze still on Sarala, before he followed.

"That was interesting." Lord Hanover took Sarala's hand. "And he's correct. Obviously nothing productive will be said today. Let's go home, and I need to contact Warrick and Mr. Dailey."

The solicitor. Of course. Slowly Sarala followed her parents out of the room, through the foyer, and into the carriage in which they'd rushed to Corbett House. Shay hadn't said much, but what he *had* said had been in her defense. The thought intrigued her. Whatever his brother might say, she couldn't imagine him doing something completely against his wishes, and yet he'd let the situation stand.

She'd begun to think she knew him, but after what had happened, she wasn't willing any longer to wager as much as a shilling that she knew what would happen next.

Chapter 12

As soon as Lady Deverill's coach stopped on the front drive to let them out, Sarala escaped into Carlisle House, up the stairs, and into her bedchamber. With her mother going on and on about how they were to become practically royalty, and her father sitting quietly and looking terribly disappointed in her behavior, she couldn't do anything productive. Up in her room at least she could think.

No doubt her mother had hurried to her writing table to begin correspondence that would inform all her friends that she'd been right, or at least the closest to being right, since Sarala—Sarah—had managed to trap one of the Griffins into a marriage. Not *the* Griffin, of course, but who could reasonably expect that? They'd been in Town only a short time, after all.

Sarala plunked herself down at her dressing table and looked into the mirror. "Idiot," she muttered at the young woman facing her. Kissing Shay Griffin was the most nonsensical thing she'd ever done. Or the second most, rather.

And she thought that she'd learned her lesson where men were concerned. Obviously not.

A knock came at her door. "I'm busy," she said, folding her arms and burying her head into them.

"My lady, a gentleman is here, and your parents request your presence," Jenny's voice came.

She lifted her head again. "A gentleman?" It couldn't be Shay; Jenny knew who he was. And Melbourne had set an appointment for tomorrow, so she couldn't imagine he would stop by to chat.

"I didn't catch a name, my lady, but your father seemed to know him well. Will you come down?"

"I'll be there in a moment." She walked to her window. A curricle waited on the short drive. No coat of arms identified it, and she didn't recognize the horse. It could be anyone, she supposed, since her father's acquaintances through Parliament were innumerably greater than hers. At least her mother couldn't set her after whichever poor fellow it was; she had recently become betrothed.

With a deep breath, trying to gather her scattered thoughts so she could at least carry on a civilized conversation, she went downstairs and pushed open the drawing room door.

"Sarah!" her mother exclaimed from her seat by the window. "Look who's found us in London!"

The light-haired, broad-shouldered man in front of the fireplace turned to face her. "Since I last saw you, everything's changed but your beauty," he drawled in his low, familiar voice, and smiled.

Her mouth gaped open for several heartbeats before she realized and closed her lips again. "Viscount DeLayne," she stammered, in another few seconds recovering herself enough to manage a stiff curtsy.

The marchioness sighed. "He is an old friend, Sarah. Don't act as if you've never seen him before."

"Please excuse her this time, my lady. *Sarah,*" and he emphasized the pronunciation, probably to show that he meant to follow the new convention, "has evidently forgotten we are such old friends that she used to call me John."

"John was just saying he'd been in Sussex and actually read of our presence here in a newspaper," her father supplied, handing their guest a glass of claret.

"Yes. It said you were here and enjoying the best of Society in the company of the illustrious Duke of Melbourne and the Griffin family. So of course I had to come and find you." The viscount smiled again. "I can hardly believe it's been over two years since we all last saw one another."

"You must stay for dinner," Lady Hanover stated, picking up the bell at her elbow and shaking it.

"I couldn't impose."

"Nonsense. You're practically family."

The butler slipped into the room. "You rang, my lady?"

"Yes. Tell Cook there will be one more for dinner."

"Right away, my lady."

"Where are you staying in London?" Sarala asked, wishing her heart would stop beating so hard and let her concentrate. As it was, she was half certain everyone in the room could hear it pounding. Why was he here? And why now? Just when she'd thought matters couldn't become more tangled.

Fellow former resident of Delhi or not, as far as she was concerned, John DeLayne wasn't welcome. She had much more pressing matters to deal with without his old ambitious sycophancy. *She'd* realized the truth of his character, even if her parents hadn't.

Back then, the viscount had outranked her father, though without the burden of estates or her uncle's debts, the Carlisles' financial situation had been considerably better than his. In addition, her father's high position with the East India Company had made gaining his friendship very lucrative.

"My cousin William Adamsen has a house here. He's invited me to stay with him for as long as I like."

"That is good news," her father returned. "Don't you think so, Sarah?"

She shook herself. "Yes. Of course. It will be nice to know there's a familiar face close by," she said, because everyone would expect her to say something. Clearing her throat, she edged toward the door. "I beg your pardon, but I'm not feeling quite the thing this afternoon. Will you excuse me?"

"Nonsense, Sarah. You should tell Lord DeLayne your good news."

"No, Mama," she countered quickly, then forced a smile. "He doesn't want to hear my news, especially when it's not certain, yet."

DeLayne looked from one to the other. "I must say, you've whetted my curiosity."

"Oh, I must tell you," the marchioness said, clapping her hands together. "Sarah is to marry the Duke of Melbourne's brother!"

The viscount lifted an eyebrow, brown eyes assessing her. "Indeed?"

"His name is Charlemagne, and nothing's been decided yet."

Slowly his mouth curved into a smile. "Congratulations, Sarah. Well done."

Sarala suppressed a shudder as she bobbed her head at him again and then escaped up to her bedchamber. Now things couldn't get any worse. She hoped.

* * *

They looked like the bloody Spanish Inquisition, waiting to pounce upon and torture heretics into confessions of misdeeds against the Church. Charlemagne was surprised he didn't see their hands wringing in anticipatory glee. And the Carlisles—or the mother, anyway—looked at least as predatory. *Damned solicitors.*

"Well, to begin, we are of course shocked by Lord Charlemagne's ungentlemanlike treatment of our Sarah," Lady Hanover said from across the dining room table. Beside her, a balding solicitor nodded solemnly and made a note of something. That would add five hundred pounds to the pot, Charlemagne thought cynically.

"Afterward he did without delay offer to marry her," Lord Hanover put in.

And two hundred and fifty quid came back out. Oh, good. They were having their own debate, and he didn't need to participate. He didn't particularly want to participate. What he wanted to do was go around the table, snatch up Sarala, kiss her until she stopped looking so somber, and get those damned silks.

She'd barely looked at him since her party had arrived twenty minutes earlier, a pair of solicitors in tow. In fact, she looked more shaken and upset than anyone else in the room—with the possible exception of Melbourne. Truthfully, though, the duke didn't *look* upset as much as he looked ice cold and expressionless. He'd made it perfectly clear yesterday just what he thought of events, and obviously he hadn't changed his opinion since then.

Their own half-dozen solicitors sat against the wall behind them; Melbourne had no doubt wanted to make clear that he was in charge today. He was always in charge, apparently.

Charlemagne looked at Sarala again, then stood. "If you'll excuse us, Sarala and I obviously aren't necessary to these discussions at the moment." He walked around the table. "Would you care to join me for a stroll in the garden, Sarala?"

"I hardly think that's seemly, after all this," Lady Hanover protested, fanning at her face with a sheet of paper, presumably out of shame for his presumption.

"We've already ended up betrothed, my lady," Charlemagne returned in a harder voice than he intended, as he put a hand on Sarala's shoulder. Her muscles jumped beneath his fingers. He hoped it was from surprise at the gesture rather than from dread or loathing. "Shall we?" he continued, making his tone as light as possible.

"Yes, of course," she said, rising.

He offered his arm, but either she didn't notice or she wanted him to think she hadn't noticed. Moving so quickly out to the hallway that he nearly had to trot to keep up, she led the way to the front door. Stanton pulled it open, and with a whisper of muslin skirts she was out on the front portico.

"Are you going to run all the way home?" he asked, reaching out to pull her to a stop.

"I'm not running," she returned, shrugging free of his grip. "I'm . . . not comfortable in there."

"Neither am I. The garden's around this way."

When they'd reached the relative privacy of the rose garden, Charlemagne took the lead, heading to a wooden bench set beneath the low stone wall terrace, an oak tree arching above and behind them. He sat, patting the seat beside him. After a hesitation, Sarala joined him.

"I'm terribly sorry about this," she blurted, facing him.

"You are? I thought you'd be happy."

Her face folded into a frown. "Why in the world would I be happy?"

"You're not ruined."

"No thanks to you."

And abruptly the Sarala he knew and was becoming increasingly fond of returned to the party. "Excuse me?" he returned, lifting an eyebrow.

"The more I think about it, in fact, the more I'm convinced that *you* owe *me* an apology. In fact, I withdraw mine."

"Me? I owe you an apology? For kissing you, I suppose? You practically dared me to do that, Sar—"

"Not the kiss," she interrupted, her gaze lowering to his mouth. Low heat started in his gut. "That silly story about the Chinese emperor and his swordsmen. It was a tactic unworthy of y—"

"It wasn't a story," Charlemagne stated. "And that circumstance hasn't changed. I want—I need—to get those—"

"Oh, please. What do you take me for, Shay? That was the first—no, the second—time you've treated me like an idiot. I thought we were beyond that."

He'd been set for an argument about who had set whom up for a compromise and subsequent betrothal. The fact that they were back to negotiating both amused and worried him. God, she was as focused as he was.

"I was not lying to you," he said succinctly. "Nor was I attempting to treat you like an idiot." He drew a breath. "The newspaper two days ago reported that Captain Peter Blink has gone missing."

Her tanned cheeks paled. "Captain Blink? Truly?"

He nodded, wishing for a brief moment that Sarala was the sort of chit who fainted or cried at the drop of a hat so he could take charge and comfort her. At the same time, he knew that if that had been her character, he never would have kissed her in the first place—or at least not more than once.

"So," she went on when he didn't, "you immediately interpreted a missing ship's captain to mean that the silks must have been stolen from Emperor Jiaqing and that I must be relieved of them at once for my own safety."

It was his turn to frown. "Now who's treating whom like an idiot?"

"Explain, then."

"I am attempting to. The night after the recital—you remember that?—I walked home. I had the . . . distinct sensation that I was followed. And that same morning, someone attempted to break into my home. *My* home. Gaston House."

"And that—"

She was as bad as he was, insisting on proof, accepting hypotheses only as long as they were logical. He wanted to kiss her again, and clenched his fist into his thigh to keep from grabbing her. There would be time for that later. "And then when my niece Peep and I went to the British Museum," he interrupted, "I *saw* a Chinese soldier watching me. Yesterday morning a rock came through the front window of Griffin House. It had been wrapped in fine silk."

"So you—"

"Let me finish. I decided that Blink and the silks must be connected, and with a mysterious Chinaman thrown into the mix I rode to Carlisle House to make certain you were unhurt. I took a shortcut through an alleyway, where I was confronted by three Chinese men carrying swords."

"You . . ." Her skeptical expression began to fade as she studied his face. "You *are* serious."

"That's what I've been trying to tell you." *Finally.* "They informed me that they were hunting down the silks that Blink had stolen, that they had Blink, and that the person who now had possession of the silks—which they assumed was me—needed to return them at once." He left out the part about facing the emperor's justice—for one thing, it might needlessly frighten her, and for another, he didn't want her holding on to the damned things out of some misplaced sense of honor.

Her sensuous mouth opened and closed again. "This is rather incredible."

"I agree. And whatever else goes on today, I still need you to sign those silks over to me. I have a museum appointment at noon to return them."

"If all this is true, then since I purchased the silks, I should return them."

He'd been right not to tell her about the second demand. "I admire your sense of honor and fair play, Sarala," he said, meaning it, "but at the least I would imagine that I'm a better shot than you are. And I have no intention of risking your safety, regardless."

She hesitated. "If I do sign the silks over to you, if I ask no money in return for giving them to you, will His Grace realize that this was all a misunderstanding? Surely he can find a way to extract us from this . . . nonsense without damaging my family's reputation."

For a long moment Charlemagne looked at her, hearing the sadness and desperation in her voice. The realization of it all hit him full in the face, harsh as a blast of cold north wind. To her, what had happened over the past day was a disaster. As for himself, the events had been surprising, but not horrific. "I agreed to pay you eight thousand pounds for the silks," he said quietly, finding it more comfortable to keep up at least the pretense that this was business. "There's no reason to change that."

"But I'll *give* them to you if you'll help me make this go away," she repeated, tears gathering in her moss green eyes and spilling onto her cheeks. "I'll apologize to the duke, I'll let him put a notice in the paper that you were the one who decided to beg off the marriage. Anything, Shay. I—"

"You don't want to marry me."

She met his gaze. "No, I don't."

Of all the things he hadn't expected, the fact that he had more interest in this match than she did surprised him most of all. She'd put all her pride into their battle over the silks, and now she was willing to crawl just to be rid of them. Of him. Something was seriously wrong. Sarala had no idea how much he truly enjoyed her company, enjoyed talking with her and arguing with her and just looking at her.

"Why don't you want to marry me?"

Sarala lifted a fine eyebrow. "You can't be serious. We were negotiating a business deal. We made a mistake, and kissed when we should have . . . shaken hands."

"Firstly," he muttered, "I don't make mistakes. Secondly, we couldn't have shaken hands, because we hadn't come to an agreement. We *still* haven't, apparently."

"You don't make mistakes? That's rather arrogant, wouldn't you say? Especially when you made the mistake of telling me about the silks in the first place."

The more he thought about it, the more he wondered whether that hadn't been the wisest thing he'd ever done, Chinese swordsmen or not. "I consider that to be a fortunate slip," he said instead. Obviously confessing his undying devotion to her would only make her laugh. He wasn't certain whether that was how he felt or not, anyway. Until a few days ago he'd thought that getting the silks back in a manner that would prove his business acumen keener than hers—and maybe stealing another kiss or two from Sarala—was all that mattered. He cleared his throat. "Sarala, we have several things to deal with," he said, choosing each word carefully. "The first is that I need to return the silks. That is separate from anything else between us. Name your price, and I will pay it."

"But—"

"I swear that I will treat the second matter fairly, regardless of the silks, the Chinese, the emperor, or the Duke of Melbourne."

She drew a deep, shuddering breath. "Thank you so much," she whispered, another tear running down her face. "Very well. You offered a price of four thousand pounds. I find that to be fair and acceptable." Squaring her shoulders, she looked him in the eye and held out her hand.

And this time they did shake hands. From begging out of a marriage and back to business, in the space of one heartbeat. He had a great deal to do if she saw no difference between the two. He hoped the Chinese wouldn't drag him off in chains before he could convince his wife-to-be to want to marry him.

Although Charlemagne had said the marriage mess and the silks were two separate disasters, Sarala made sure she signed over ownership of the shipment and told him where the bolts could be found before she returned with him to the house. As far as she was concerned, they *were* entangled, and the more quickly she could extricate herself from one, the sooner she'd be free of both.

Shay had actually been very understanding about their mutual disaster. Even kind. Of course he hadn't been present yesterday evening to hear her mother's rapturous hysterics at the thought that they would all be joining the Griffin family. Sarala certainly wouldn't find an ally under her own roof. Her father was more sympathetic, but he was trying to establish business and political contacts in a city from which he'd been absent for twenty-three years. Insulting the Griffins would be a good way to destroy all that. And John DeLayne had listened and smiled and offered encouraging comments, just like old times in Delhi. Just as if his presence then and now hadn't and wouldn't change the course of her life—for the worse.

"Are you ready to go back into the lions' den?" Shay asked, stopping at the dining room door.

Inside she could hear arguing; it sounded like the same discussion that had been going on when they left. "Do we tell them now that we won't be going through with a wedding?"

Shay shook his head. "Family first, then the solicitors. And I think if we can establish a friendly groundwork on all sides, our chances will be better overall."

It sounded like a battle strategy. In a sense, that was precisely what it was. At least she had a master strategist on her side. And if she said so herself, with the exception of the colossal blunder yesterday, she was a fair hand at this, as well. "Let's go inside, then."

With a half smile he pulled open the door and escorted her through. Immediately her mother stood up to wrench her away from Charlemagne and give her a constricting hug. "There you are, my Sarah! You have no idea what we've been facing in here! This is—"

"I have one condition," Charlemagne broke in, seating himself beside the duke once more.

His brother eyed him. "One?" he said, sarcasm dripping from his low voice.

"For the moment." Shay leaned forward. "From this point onward, *Sarala* is to be referred to and known by her given name." He looked over, meeting her gaze. "If that is your desire."

Another surprise. She'd thought at the least that he would be offended by her pleas to escape a wedding. Instead he had made the one demand she wished she could enforce herself. "Yes, that would be acceptable."

He smiled. "Good." Turning, he glanced at the clock on the mantel. "Now, if you'll excuse me, I have an appointment."

"Excuse you?" her mother broke in. "Excuse you? This meeting is *because* of you! You've already raced off with my daughter to do who knows what, and now you—"

The Duke of Melbourne stood. "That is enough, madame," he said in his cool, controlled voice. "My brother is correct. We both have an urgent appointment at noon. Rest assured that this marriage will go forward, and that you will find the terms acceptable."

"Is this regarding those silks?" her father asked, also rising. "Sarala's told me something of it, and it seems we own a fair share of the problems, as well."

"No, you don't." Shay pushed away from the table. "Sarala has signed the silks over to me. The responsibility is now mine, as it should have been in the first place."

"What is all this about silks? We need to discuss a marriage settlement," her mother demanded.

"All the same, I'd like to join you, if I may," the marquis continued, as though his wife hadn't spoken.

"I'm going, too," Sarala put in. Fair was fair, whatever else might be going on.

"It could be dangerous. No." Charlemagne sent her an annoyed glance.

"The British Museum at noon, Papa," she said, turning to her father. "I believe we can find that on our own, can't we?"

"We certainly can. Helen, we'll continue this meeting another time. Tomorrow, perhaps?"

"Tomorrow is fine," the duke said. "But as for the rest, the Griffins can manage on their own."

Sarala took a deep breath. Shay had used their momentary engagement to straighten out her name nonsense; there was no reason she couldn't use it, as well. "Excuse me, but I believe I'm soon to become a Griffin, myself. I intend to go, in your company or out of it."

She thought she heard Charlemagne utter a curse, but she couldn't be certain. "Let's get moving, then," he said gruffly. "Unless you'd care to bring along jugglers and acrobats."

"That sounds a bit frivolous," she returned matter-of-factly, and led the way to the door.

"Impossible," she thought she heard him mutter. It made her smile.

While they waited for Melbourne's coach, she and her father escorted her mother out to the street, where he hailed a hack for her. "How could you let Melbourne leave the table?" the marchioness cried. "He could settle all of our debts, Howard! Every one of them!"

"That hardly seems fair, Mama," Sarala said as calmly as she could. "I'm as guilty of being indiscreet as Charlemagne is."

"You haven't mentioned that to him, have you?" Her mother clutched her father's sleeve. "Tell me you haven't, Sarala. He is the man. The largest part of the scandal would fall on you. He should therefore assume the larger part of any responsibility."

"I'm certain the Griffins will do so," her father assured them, stepping forward as a hack pulled to the side of the street. "Anything less would reflect poorly on them. Melbourne, from everything I've heard and seen, would not be put in that position by anyone." He handed the marchioness into the coach and gave the driver directions to Carlisle House.

"You had best be right, Howard," she said, as he closed the door. "And for heaven's sake don't get yourself murdered. This all sounds very underhanded."

"I will be cautious, my love. Don't fear."

They took two coaches to the museum, her father's and Melbourne's. Sarala would rather have ridden with the efficient Griffin brothers, but they obviously had their own matters to discuss.

They weren't precisely sheep ready for fleecing, whatever her mother might hope. Sarala knew as well as anyone that marriage was just another kind of business. In India the bride and groom were frequently the last family members to meet. A traditional wedding would take place only after finances, settlements, and dowries had been discussed and agreed upon by all parties.

England wasn't that different, at least among the aristocracy. Considering her part in this, though, she didn't want to see her wedding turned into another spectacle fit for the mercenary meat market. Even if it would never actually take place. Shay had promised.

As for when she did marry, it would be to someone quiet, out of the public eye, and probably of lower social rank. Someone who would be grateful enough to be elevated that he would accept any and all of her . . . shortcomings. Well, to her they weren't shortcomings, but she knew with extreme clarity what any and everyone else thought and would think of her.

Whatever Charlemagne and the Duke of Melbourne had discussed during the ride to the British Museum, both looked grim as they emerged from their coach. "I'll ask you again to go home," Shay said, meeting them as Sarala stepped to the ground. "I will let you know what happens."

"I won't do anything foolish," she returned, "but I will be there."

He sighed. "I thought so. I did have to try, however."

Shay offered his arm, and she wrapped her fingers around his warm blue coat sleeve. "Have you decided on a strategy?" she asked.

"My strategy is that you will wait at the far end of the Egyptian room," he returned. "If anything should go awry, make for *our* coach. Tollins has orders to get you to safety."

Worry shivered down her spine. "There's something you haven't told me, isn't there?"

"No," Charlemagne lied. He wanted her as safe as possible. "Take your father and go look at the mummies."

That was a sentence he'd never thought to utter, he noted as she sent him an annoyed look and led her father away. Charlemagne and Sebastian went down a parallel hallway to the opposite end of the Egyptian room. At Sebastian's hard expression, Charlemagne slowed.

"I don't think they'll attempt anything in public," he said. "That's why I chose this setting."

"They may not have made any overt threats, Shay, but Captain Blink *is* missing."

"I know. I suppose I'll have to make an attempt to recover him, as well."

"I hope that's your last priority," the duke returned in a low, humorless voice. "He began this mess. Let him reap the results."

"That's a bit callous, don't you think?"

"I have other people I'm more concerned about. And I wish you'd tell me exactly what you're planning."

They stopped by the mummy that Peep had been trying to poke. Had that been only the day before yesterday? "I'm not certain. It depends on what they bring to the table."

His brother took his arm. "This is not just another negotiation, Shay. They want to take you to China."

Charlemagne forced a smile he didn't particularly feel. "I can't go to China; I'm getting married."

"That's not amusing. And I don't want you tempted to leave England just to avoid joining the Carlisle family to ours."

He had no intention of avoiding any such thing. "It *is* just another negotiation, Seb. I have something they want, and before I hand it over to them I'll do my damnedest to get an agreement I can live with. Literally."

"Even so, I have two pistols with me if it doesn't go well."

"And I know the signal. But you're going to have to trust me, Sebastian."

"I do."

"Good."

Charlemagne heard his brother's statement of confidence, but he wasn't entirely certain he believed it. If Sebastian was accustomed to anything, it was to being in command—of the family, of the majority of their business, sometimes of the nation. And now he'd been relegated to a supporting position. If everyone lived through it, his brother might find it an enlightening experience.

Across the room Sarala and her father animatedly examined a row of sarcophagi and their accompanying artifacts. He understood why she wanted to be there; if their positions had been reversed, he would have demanded the same. Her presence, though, had the unfortunate consequence of dividing his attention, and if he'd ever needed to concentrate, it was now.

He turned toward the double doors again, just in time to see two of the swordsmen enter the room. They didn't look to be armed, but he wouldn't wager much money on that supposition. In addition, the third one had to be somewhere about, but the one downside of meeting at the British Museum was that there were places to hide everywhere.

He nodded as the older of the two men, the one who'd spoken to him yesterday, approached. "Where's your other friend?" he asked.

"He is close by. I could not think why you would wish to meet here, unless you are afraid to accept the consequences of your actions."

"Let's just say I want to be certain matters are handled fairly," Charlemagne returned, noting as Sebastian shifted a little to one side halfway down the length of the room.

"An interesting choice of words for a thief."

"Would you do me the honor of telling me your name?"

"I am Yun. And I already know your name, English thief. English coward."

Though he'd never done business directly with a Chinese native before, he had made half his personal fortune off men who relied on intimidation by virtue of the size of their swords or their holdings rather than their brains. As for himself, he preferred a combination of brains and brawn. Charlemagne smiled. "I've been quite cooperative, I think, since

Captain Blink apparently wronged both of us and you only informed me of the circumstances yesterday. I give you fair warning, however—if you call me a thief again, you and I will have a serious disagreement."

"Where are Emperor Jiaqing's silks, thief?"

Charlemagne hit him. Yun reeled back several steps, reaching for something at the back of his belt as he charged forward again. A knife. Waiting for the move, Shay ducked the slash and smashed his elbow into Yun's chin. In the same motion he grabbed the knife and slipped it into the nearest sarcophagus.

"I did warn you," he said coolly.

Yun staggered upright again. A few other museum patrons stirred, but when no other commotion followed they went back to their perusal of artifacts.

"So you are more than just pretty words," the swordsman said, pulling a silk handkerchief from somewhere and wiping a drop of blood from his lower lip. "I am warned."

"And I did not know those silks were stolen."

"The emperor's honor was slighted, nonetheless. This is not acceptable."

"You have Blink, don't you?" Charlemagne returned. Whatever Sebastian's opinion, he felt as though he owed the captain something. Despicable act or not, at least he hadn't given up Sarala's name to his hunters. "Perhaps he can make payment."

Yun shook his head. "Emperor Jiaqing does not require money. He requires repayment for lost honor."

In other words, Blink's head on a platter. Literally. "When is the emperor's birthday celebration to be held?" he asked, rather than pursue his questions about the captain. One thing at a time.

"Near your Christmas. There must be time for the clothes to be made, the banners to be hung. We do not have much time."

He was gaining a litany of interesting information. On the emperor's behalf they required the silks, of course, but no monetary compensation would do to assuage the insult of the theft. His head would suffice, apparently, though with Yun now speaking to him civilly, he'd begun to think that they believed his innocence in the theft.

"What other than blood might serve to restore Emperor Jiaqing's honor?" he asked, keeping his left hand carefully away from his breast pocket. That would be Melbourne's signal to leap into the fray—a fray that so far he'd been able to avoid for the most part.

"If you are innocent of theft, Griffin, you have nothing to fear."

Ah, he had a name, now. Definitely a positive sign. "I'm not afraid," Charlemagne countered. "I am a citizen of Britain, however, as is Captain Blink. The emperor has sent you to represent him, has he not?"

Yun inclined his head, his expression still alert, but far less belligerent than it had been. "I am a captain of his personal Dragon Guard."

"I also have a ruler's faith," Shay continued, speaking as clearly and simply as he could. Yun spoke far better English than he did Chinese, but they damned well didn't need a misunderstanding right now. "Perhaps between us we can both satisfy the emperor and bring him to a closer friendship with my Regent, so that such thefts won't happen again."

The soldier looked at him for a long moment. "I think perhaps Captain Blink will be lucky that he sold His Eminence's silks to you. They are in your care and well protected, yes?"

"Yes, they are." At least he hoped to God they were. It occurred to him that other than a few samples taken from the ends of bolts by Blink, he'd never actually set eyes on them. They'd been wrapped in protective cloth when Sarala's people had loaded them into wagons.

"I will consult with my companions," Yun said after a moment. "Their authority is equal to mine in this. If you are attempting to mislead me, be aware that we all know of your sister and your brothers, your niece, and your woman." He angled his chin toward the far end of the room.

Charlemagne clenched his jaw. "I'm not misleading you. When shall we meet next?"

"You think to keep the silks?"

"At the moment I'm keeping them only to prolong Blink's life until you and your companions make a decision."

"On Tuesday morning, then, at ten o'clock."

"At eleven o'clock, at the west end of the pond in St. James's Park." It was fairly open there, so he would be able to see anything coming, and there would be enough people about that someone would notice slashing swords if the negotiations went poorly.

"You still do not trust me," Yun said with a slight smile.

"I trust you as much as you trust me. And Yun, if any member of my family receives so much as a scratch, if so much as a pebble is thrown through a window, I will take a torch to the silks and risk the consequences."

"We understand one another, I think."

With a bow Yun turned and left, the second soldier joining him. Where the third man was, Charlemagne had no idea, but the prickle at the back of his neck told him that

Yun hadn't been lying; the fellow was close by somewhere.

"You hit him?" Sebastian grunted, coming up to join him. "That's how you negotiate with an armed kidnapper?"

"I warned him not to call me a thief." Charlemagne shrugged, moving to meet Sarala and her father as they came forward. "I think we came to an understanding, after that."

"It was marvelous to watch," Sarala breathed, taking his arm. "I could see the advantage pass from him to you just by his stance. Incredibly well done. Is it all settled?"

"Not yet, but we're closer." Despite his generally confident and independent nature, his insides warmed at the compliment from someone who knew the rules of the negotiation game nearly as well as he did. The combination of tension and admiration started heat low in his stomach.

"What's the next step?" she asked, still grinning at him.

"Yes, does one of them get to pummel you, now?" Melbourne put in, from his tone still wary. He would have remembered that there were three swordsmen, even if the Carlisles hadn't.

"Yun—that's the fellow's name—is going to discuss with the other two what an appropriate compensation for the insult to Emperor Jiaqing's honor might be. We're to review my options on Tuesday."

"That's all very civilized, though how you became the British ambassador to China, I don't know. I doubt the government will vote to pay out anything to save Blink's head."

"Someone's insulted the emperor, whether that was Blink's intention or not. I would imagine the larger the gesture of apology, the happier Jiaqing will feel," he returned, heading them toward the museum's main doors. "I reckon it will come down to something from Prinny—a nice, official letter and a gift, hopefully." He glanced at his angry, concerned brother. "You could manage that if necessary, couldn't you?"

"I imagine so. If you've turned this into an international squabble, though, you've put more lives than just yours and Blink's at risk, Shay. You do realize that, I hope?"

"I realize it." By putting himself at the forefront he'd also arranged to make himself the main and first target of any conflicts or reprisals. That had been intentional, and both he and Yun—and Melbourne—knew it. And so the game would continue—as if he didn't have enough on his plate simply convincing Sarala that marrying him wouldn't be such an awful thing to have happen.

Chapter 13

"Is everyone dead?" Lady Hanover wailed from the couch in the upstairs sitting room. "Melbourne's been killed, hasn't he? Oh, one of those Chinese savages scalped him, didn't they?"

"The Chinese don't scalp people, dear," the marquis answered. "They cut off hands or heads for theft."

"Oh, heavens! I'm going to faint! Help me, Sarala!"

Sarala exchanged a pained, amused look with her father and knelt to take her mother's hands. At least she had her name back, now. "No one's dead, Mama," she said soothingly.

She'd been surprised to find the marchioness alone in the sitting room; half of London must know by now that a Griffin had become engaged to her daughter. And Lady Hanover had sent correspondence to that same end. The matchmaking mamas must surely be on their way to Carlisle House.

"Thank heavens Melbourne is safe. You gave me such a scare, Howard."

"Apologies, sweetling."

Her mother insisted on remaining obsessed with the duke despite the fact that Sarala was betrothed to his brother. Whatever came of this, Charlemagne did not belong in Melbourne's shadow. "You should have seen it, Mama," she said. "Shay was brilliant, and the negotiations are going quite well."

"Then where are they? The Griffins? We have our own negotiations to conclude. Howard, you mustn't allow them to bully you into accepting anything less than our fair portion."

The marquis pulled the slip of paper Sarala had given him earlier from his coat pocket. "Don't fret, my dear. Everything will be sorted out. In the meantime, I have Lord Charlemagne's note for the silks Sarala sold to him. Four thousand pounds. Not a bit shabby, that. Well done, Sarala."

"Thank you." She hadn't mentioned that she could have gotten twice that, and she never *would* mention it. That had been a private argument, just between Shay and her.

"Four thousand pounds? But from what you said, my husband, those silks belong to the emperor of China. Surely we could have gotten more if we'd sold them directly back to him."

The marquis tucked the note away again. "Thank you, no. That is one business transaction I am pleased only to observe from a safe distance. And your suggestion would have been a bit unscrupulous, wouldn't you say? Selling stolen property back to the rightful owner?"

"I would think the emperor of China wouldn't notice the expense."

Sarala wasn't so certain of that. Unlike her father, she would have preferred to have been close enough at least to overhear all of the negotiation, but at the very next opportunity she meant to have Shay recite the entire conversation for her. The way he'd looked—strong, confident, and very handsome—she'd had to physically hold herself back from kissing him right there in the middle of the Egyptian room at the British Museum.

That would have spelled the doom of their plans to nullify the betrothal. Even so, she still wanted to kiss him, to feel his warm hands on her naked skin, to—

"—even listening to me, Sarala?"

"Apologies, Mama. What were you saying?"

"I said we must have an engagement ball. Do you think Melbourne would host? I don't think there's been a soiree held at Griffin House in over three years. Wouldn't that be a coup if one were to be held there for you?"

"Mama, there hasn't been a soiree held there in that time because the duke's wife died three years ago. I am *not* going to ask them to hold a party on my behalf. The engagement was only to protect my reputation, anyway. For all I know, Charlemagne might change his mind. And I would be glad of it. However much you wanted me to marry a Griffin, this is . . . cheating."

That was the crux of it, she realized; yes, she was attracted to Shay, but even if there hadn't been extenuating circumstances, she had no desire to be married because of an accident. She and Charlemagne both preferred to deal honestly, and under these circumstances she had no idea what his honest feelings were or what he might actually have intended. Certainly he'd kissed other ladies before her—and she didn't want to be known simply as the one who'd been able to trap him. That would be unbearable.

The marchioness pulled her hands free and stood to pace. "You are speaking absolute nonsense, child. And *that* is why we must reach an agreement as soon as possible—so neither of you *can* change your minds."

"That's horrid!"

"It's the way things are." Someone knocked at the front door, and she heard Blankman pull it open. "That will be Lady Allendale," her mother continued. "We need to begin planning the wedding."

Oh, for heaven's sake. "I'll leave you to it, then," Sarala said, standing.

"Sarala, you need to begin showing more enthusiasm, or the Griffins will think you're not appreciative."

Sarala took a deep breath. That was too much. Not that a union with the Griffin family wouldn't on the surface be beneficial to her own family, but this was an ongoing negotiation. Showing humble appreciation at this point would put them in a defensive position. That was pure logic.

"My lady, Lady Allendale and Lady Mary Doorley have arrived, inquiring if you are available to see them," the butler said, approaching from the doorway, a salver and calling cards in one hand.

"Yes, show them in. And send in some tea, Blankman."

"Right away, my lady."

"I have some correspondence," Sarala said, hurrying for the opposite door. Her father trotted directly on her heels.

"Very well, then. Do go," Lady Hanover said with a dismissive wave. "We're only beginning to plan the festivities, and I hardly want you about if you're going to scowl at everything we say."

Not taking the time to answer, Sarala made for the back stairs and her bedchamber beyond. Once inside, she picked up the book she'd been reading on the Roman conquest of Britain. Slowly, though, she lowered the weighty thing to her lap.

She should feel appreciative. Ha. *HA*. What she felt was trapped, cornered into something she hadn't intended because of something she hadn't been able to resist. If only Shay Griffin hadn't danced with her that night.

But he had, and she remembered quite clearly that it had been the first time since she'd left India that she'd enjoyed where she was and what she was doing. Even when she'd misjudged him, thought he was merely arrogant, tricking the information out of him had been delightful. Knowing now how very intelligent he was made the memory of that moment even more satisfying.

Delightful. That was every moment with Shay, even when they were arguing—especially when they were arguing. Arguing meant kisses and desire and heat.

Someone scratched at her door. "My lady?" Jenny's voice came.

"Enter."

Her maid walked into the room, a piece of paper in her hand and a wide smile on her face. "Blankman said this just arrived for you."

Sarala took it. "Thank you. What are you smiling at? You look like the cat who found the cream."

"You and Lord Charlemagne, my lady. Everything was in such an uproar yesterday, but I wanted to wish you well."

"Thank you, Jenny, but it was just a misunderstanding. Shay will explain it to his brother, and then I'll explain it to Mama and Papa, and we'll go on as we did before."

"So you don't wish to marry him?"

"That was not my intention." She unfolded the missive, and a heavy gold coin fell into her palm. Furrowing her brow, she lifted it closer. In surprisingly clear relief the profile of Emperor Hadrian gazed out over his empire. A Roman coin, and one nearly seventeen hundred years old. Only one person would send her such a fine-quality artifact. Her eyes skipped down to the signature line. *Shay.* Her heart gave an unsettled roll. "Would you fetch me some peppermint tea?" she asked. She wanted to be alone as she read the note.

Jenny dipped a curtsy. "Right away, Lady *Sarala.*"

Sarala sank into the chair beneath the window as the maid departed. Charlemagne had a dark, sure hand—he knew what he meant to write, and he didn't hesitate about it. She smoothed the paper along her skirt and lifted it again.

"Dearest Sarala," she read, "I saw this in one of my display cabinets, and thought of you—not that you're ancient, nor do you bear a resemblance to Hadrian."

She snorted, quickly covering her mouth to muffle the sound. Considering how full of events the day had been, it surprised her that he'd thought of her, much less that he'd thought to send her a gift.

"I intend to be lurking in your garden at three o'clock," the note continued. "I would like to see you there, if you're able to slip away. Regards, Shay."

A breath of excitement ran through her at the thought of seeing him, of talking to him again so soon. He'd remembered that she liked Roman history. Sarala grinned, examining the coin again. Remarkable—and she wasn't certain whether she meant the coin, or the gift giver. Nothing could come of this; she wouldn't disgrace her family or his—but perhaps after this mess was finished, she could keep him as a friend.

Friends. Did friends kiss as he'd kissed her? Would their relationship be a romantic one? In the middle of London with such a well-known and powerful personage as Shay, she couldn't imagine they could simply be lovers—not without her reputation being torn into tatters. And once either of them was married to someone else . . .

Sarala shook herself. Putting the cart in front of the horse was one thing, but she didn't even have a cart. What she did have, however, was a secret rendezvous in an hour with a man she very much respected and admired. And wanted. Smiling, she rose to place Hadrian's coin inside the small, glass-topped box where she kept her more interesting treasures. It was a pity she couldn't put Charlemagne in there, to simply take him out when she wanted to chat or feel a man's hands on her bare skin.

Her door opened again. "Here's your tea, my lady," Jenny said. "And Lady Hanover has requested your presence downstairs."

Damnation. "Did she say why?"

"Something about selecting the wedding party, my lady."

The wedding party. Charlemagne needed to convince his brother to risk the stir that calling off the engagement might cause; the longer they let her mother loose upon London planning a wedding, the worse off everyone would be afterward.

"Where are you off to?"

Charlemagne glanced toward the door of his bedchamber as Zachary slipped into the room. With a stifled sigh he finished pulling on his gray jacket. "I'm going for a ride."

"I'll join you."

"I don't want you to join me. I want some peace and quiet. You are the antithesis of both."

Zach leaned one haunch against the dressing table. "You're a bit testy, aren't you?"

"What are you doing here? It's the middle of the afternoon—too late for luncheon, and too early for dinner."

"I came to see my soon-to-be-married brother." Zachary grimaced. "Actually I came to see Melbourne, but he's in a fouler mood than you are. And I thought he was angry when I said I wanted to marry Caroline."

Charlemagne began an insult, but there didn't seem to be much of a point. Instead he sat on the dressing chair. "He was angry because he thought you'd been tricked into doing something unwise."

"That does sound familiar, doesn't it?"

"You mean for me?" Shay returned. "Everyone seems to assume that I made a mistake, and yet no one's asked for my opinion."

"Most likely because you've never hesitated to express it before."

"I'm getting married. That's my opinion."

Zachary looked at him for a minute. "That's not an opinion; correct me if I'm wrong, but I believe it to be a fact. And you can hardly blame us for being concerned. If you're being a gentleman, there are probably ways around this."

"What the devil are you talking about?" Shay asked, though he had a fairly good idea.

"You have to know what Seb thinks—that Sarah overwhelmed you with her talk of being alone and friendless in Lon—"

"Sarala," Charlemagne corrected. "And she didn't overwhelm me with anything." Actually she had, but not with lust or whatever it was that Zachary had been going to suggest. The woman herself overwhelmed him. Her accent, her eyes, her hair, her skin—all that began it, but what finished him off was her intelligence, her borderline cynicism that made him look at his own England through a foreigner's eyes, her sense of humor, the way her mind worked.

"That's what Caro said."

Charlemagne shook himself. "What?"

"Yes, I can see that you're completely unaffected by the

chit," his brother stated dryly. "My wife is of the opinion that you two are so logical and straightforward that once you were caught kissing, you couldn't imagine a way around it."

"How romantic we are."

"You're the one who compromised a chit into marriage. Not me. And you told Seb you were negotiating a business transaction. Forgive me if that talk doesn't make my knees weak."

"Your mind is weak."

"At least I have some romance in my bones. You have pencil lead. And ink for blood."

Charlemagne actually did find Zachary's commentary interesting. Obviously Sarala had seen their kissing as a ploy on his part to gain the advantage in a business negotiation. So did his entire family, apparently. Ink for blood. Did Sarala not see him as he saw her, then? Did she not imagine them, bodies entwined, while she cried out in pleasure?

Standing, he clapped his brother on the back. "Thank you, Zach. You've made several things very clear."

"I have?" Zachary rose, as well. "Of course I have. That's why I came. What are you going to do, then? Tell Melbourne you're begging off? Let the chit escape unscathed?"

"No. I'm going to make her fall in love with me, and then I'm going to marry her."

At fifteen minutes before three o'clock Charlemagne left Jaunty at a friend's stable and walked the last street to Carlisle House. A few weeks ago, before he'd met Sarala, he would have spent the afternoon inspecting the silk shipment and making certain they could be delivered on Tuesday as required. And now, from the moment his actions had forced Sebastian into announcing a wedding he'd been able to think of little but marrying Lady Sarala Anne Carlisle. He wanted to see her again.

Five carriages stood in the house's drive as he approached. With a glance toward the front door, he edged around the side of the house. Several windows opened onto the side garden, and he kept low until he reached a short hedgerow with a stone bench. He'd never been inside the house farther than the morning room, but he guessed he was somewhere outside the library.

His footman had reported his missive delivered to the house, but as for whether Sarala would come out to meet him, he could only guess. However, knowing her natural curiosity as he'd come to over the past days, he would have been willing to wager a considerable amount of money that she would appear.

Behind him someone moved closer to a window. " . . . a Griffin involved, of course the wedding will be at Westminster Abbey," a female voice said from inside.

"Oh, do you think the Regent will attend?" He recognized that voice as Lady Hanover's. So this was the wedding discussion. Interesting.

"I think *everyone* will attend. It will be the event of the entire Season. After all, Lady Deverill eloped to Scotland, and Lord Zachary apparently insisted on a small ceremony in Shropshire. This is the Griffins' last and best opportunity to make a splash, if Melbourne's so uncooperative as to want to remain a widower."

"But wasn't Melbourne married at Westminster?"

He recognized that voice, too, and sat straighter. Sarala. That surprised him, considering her stated reluctance to go through with any of this. Unless she *had* fooled him as Sebastian had suggested—which still didn't make sense to him. Zachary's observations made more sense, but he wasn't going to write anything in stone until he'd satisfied his own curiosity and answered every one of his own questions.

"That was nearly eight years ago, Lady Sarala," another female responded. "Since Melbourne's not likely to marry there again, even if some lady does eventually melt his stony heart, this is their last opportunity until his daughter, Penelope, comes of age."

Oh, good God. Anger swirled under his skin. His family's tragedies had been reduced to this? How could everyone dismiss what they'd been through—that both their parents had died when Sebastian had been seventeen and he twelve, and Charlotte when Peep was only three? Charlemagne felt thankful that Sebastian hadn't heard any of this version of their lives.

"I think selecting the church should be up to both families," Sarala's voice came again. "And I still think you're all speaking far too soon."

"Sarala, that's enough."

"I'm sorry, Mama. I just don't understand why this is a celebration. I erred in my behavior. Shay erred in his. It was nothing serious, there was nothing scandalous or ruinous about it, and I don't think anything will end up coming of it." Skirts rustled. "Now if you'll excuse me, I need a breath of air."

A door closed. "Don't fret, Helen," one of the others said. "She'll become more enthusiastic. Every girl's dream is a fine wedding. And this will be the finest."

Charlemagne stood a moment later as Sarala emerged onto the path. Her head was bare, black hair glinting bronze in the sunlight, her eyes darkening to emeralds as she spotted him.

"Hello," she said, smiling.

"Shh," he murmured, and gestured toward the window beyond the hedge. "This way."

He offered his hand, and after a brief moment she took it, wrapping her fingers around his. Silently he led the way toward the stables, farther from the house. A stack of hay bales rested to one side of the building, and he took a seat there. "Hello," he returned, still holding her hand.

"How long were you outside the library?" she asked, her cheeks darkening.

"Long enough to hear that we are going to have the finest wedding in the history of weddings."

"Oh, dear. That was not my suggestion. I don't even know why Mama wanted me in there. Obviously what we want has nothing to do with the planning."

She'd said "we," at least. "Did you get the coin?"

"Yes. Thank you so much. It's in exquisite condition."

"It came from a meadow outside of Verulamium about eight years ago."

"Did you find it yourself?"

His grin deepened. "I got thrown from a friend's horse and ended up with a mouthful of grass, eye-to-eye with Hadrian under an oak tree."

Sarala chuckled. "You might have said you dug through ancient ruins for hours to find this one treasure, which you then passed on to me."

Charlemagne laughed, as well. "I'll remember that for next time." Their gazes met, and as lightning ran down his spine, he leaned in to kiss her.

Her bones simply melted. Sarala swept her arms up around his shoulders, pulling herself closer against his chest and flat, muscled abdomen. Attraction and heat. He obviously felt it toward her, and she knew she felt it toward him.

Oh, everything was so complicated. And all she had to do

was absolutely nothing, and she would end up married to this remarkable man. But would he be happy with that? If he wasn't, she certainly wouldn't be—and she had no intention of spending her life in a state of bitter misery.

Pulling away from him felt like the most difficult thing she'd ever done. "Shay?"

Gray eyes held hers squarely. "Yes?"

"Have you spoken with your brother?"

"Actually, I spoke with Zachary. He said that we're straightforward and have no imaginations, and saw agreeing to all this as the logical conclusion of events."

"Well, that's not very kind."

"No, it isn't. And it's not true. I didn't kiss you to acquire the silks."

"Then why did you kiss me? That first time."

"Because I couldn't not kiss you."

She realized her hands were still clutching his lapels. Clearing her throat, she smoothed the fine material. His declaration sounded good, but considering that until yesterday she'd owned his silks, *he* could clearly be taken advantage of, even if he hadn't done so to her. "So you can honestly say that when you kissed me yesterday in your sister's morning room, you did so with the intention that we would soon be married."

"No, I couldn't say that. I know I probably would have been sitting here with you today, regardless."

He brushed a strand of her hair behind her ear, and she shivered. "And I'd probably be sitting here with you. You do kiss very well, Shay."

His responding chuckle reverberated through his chest and up through her palms to her heart. "Then what's your complaint, princess?"

Sarala frowned, pulling completely away from him. "Don't call me that."

"Why not? When I first saw you I thought you looked like an Indian princess."

"But I'm not Indian. I'm English. And I'm certainly not a princess."

Shay's brow furrowed. "Perhaps not a literal princess, but what—"

"You are going to talk to the duke, aren't you?"

For a long moment he sat silently beside her. She knew the answer then, before he spoke. Sarala wanted to hear the words from him, though, the way he said them. That would speak as strongly as the actual sounds of the sentences.

"No, I'm not going to ask Sebastian to help us avoid a marriage," he finally said in a quiet voice.

"Why not? You promised me!"

"For two reasons. Firstly, we were caught kissing—not just kissing, but grabbing on to each other and knocking things onto the floor. Whatever I said or Melbourne said or you said, you would be ruined, Sarala."

"I could accept—"

"No. *I* couldn't accept that. It would make me . . . an animal."

"You've kissed women before and haven't married them. I've kissed men before and haven't married them."

She thought for a brief moment that his expression darkened. "There's a difference," he returned, his voice still quiet, but less cool. "Those previous encounters were mutually discreet. None of those women were exposed, none of them were ruined. Everyone knows what happened at Corbett House."

"I don't care!"

"Yes, you do. I've seen women be ruined, Sarala. It's . . . unimaginable that if anyone could prevent it they would allow it to happen."

The anger in his voice wasn't aimed at her, but it gave her pause, nonetheless. This was a man who could buy and sell people, estates, countries, even. And the knowledge of what he'd seen, of what might have happened to her if he or Melbourne hadn't stepped in and done what they considered to be their gentlemanly duty, infuriated him. "So you think we have to get married," she said slowly, her heart pounding so hard and so fast he could most likely hear it.

"Yes, I do. There are much worse things than a forced marriage, Sarala. And scandal is one of them."

"Then what is your second reason? Why did you bother to come up with one? Your first reason was . . . compelling enough, don't you think?" Her voice broke, but she didn't try to cover it, or the tears that she felt gathering in her eyes. He would know how she felt.

"Maybe it was, but it isn't the only reason I didn't talk to Melbourne. And I wanted you to know there was a second reason." He lifted a hand toward her again, then hesitated and lowered it. "You have to let me begin and finish, though, because it doesn't sound very well at the start."

For the first time since she'd read his note an hour ago, a glimmer of amusement touched her. She nodded. "I'll let you finish."

"Very well." Charlemagne looked down for a moment, clearing his throat. "I like you. A great deal. I have met . . . a fair number of women in my life, and none of them . . . tempted me. I mean to say, I have—I'm not—I have experience, but I had a good idea that I would remain unmarried. Melbourne could use the assistance, and my other siblings seemed to enjoy domesticity enough for the rest of us."

Sarala sat and listened to him. He'd said he would begin badly, but the "I like you" had certainly claimed her attention. Whatever followed was obviously meant to ease her mind, but so many thoughts roiled through her skull that she didn't think anything would help.

He cleared his throat again. "At any rate, you interest me more than any woman I've ever met. We are betrothed, but we aren't yet married. And I won't marry you—not until you become as fond of me as I am of you."

Very well, she'd been wrong. That *did* help.

Chapter 14

"So we could be permanently engaged," Sarala said skeptically, standing to pace back and forth in front of him.

Charlemagne nodded. He was sweating; he'd half expected her to slap him for saying that he wouldn't let her out of the engagement, or for implying that he liked her against his better judgment. He had no idea how to explain everything to her, but from the way she continued to listen, he mustn't have done too badly. "I don't intend that we should be, though."

"Ah. You're going to convince me to care for you?"

"Yes, I am."

"First will you answer one question of mine?"

"Of course."

Sarala sat again, taking his left hand between hers. "I've seen how much you enjoy business, and how well you conduct business when you want to."

He furrowed his brow. "Are you suggesting that I didn't want to conduct business well when I was dealing with you and the silks?"

"Come now. It took you a week and a threat from China to convince you to make me a reasonable offer for them. Anyway, let me finish."

"Very well. Dazzle me."

"My question is, is wooing me or whatever you're planning going to be another negotiation, Shay? Am I five hundred bolts of silk, now? I know the difference between business and pleasure. Which one is this going to be?"

Obviously from her confusion about the reason for his kisses, she didn't know everything she thought she did. Even so, there were times, Charlemagne had begun to realize, that conversation with a brilliant woman could be both taxing and a bit dodgy. And her question definitely had merit. He did feel some of that familiar rush through his veins at the prospect of winning her heart—though that wasn't necessarily a bad thing. Still, how to answer without putting himself into a hole?

"Well?" she prompted.

He grinned. "Come here," he murmured, drawing her closer and taking her mouth again. Warm, soft lips, the faint scent of cinnamon—business or pleasure, he wouldn't have traded the sensation of her pressing against him for anything.

Heat pulsed through him, heavy and arousing. He was trying to be patient, sensitive both to her reservations and to her virginity, but however long their betrothal might last, he was not going to wait forever to make love to her. That had not been part of any agreement or negotiation. And when she'd said that she'd kissed other men—his first impulse had been to demand their names, hunt them down, and pummel all of them. The fact that they all probably resided in India didn't lessen his motivation one damned bit.

Finally when neither of them could breathe any longer, he backed off an inch or two, resting his forehead against hers. "Tomorrow night is the Wexton masked ball," he said. "We always dine together before we go. You and your parents should join us."

"We weren't invited to the Wexton masked ball," she returned, her eyes still focused on his mouth.

"You are now. I'll send your father over a note in the morning."

"But I don't have anything to wear. And *you* didn't answer my question."

He grinned, rising and slowly pulling her to her feet beside him. If he'd answered her question about his motives any more thoroughly, they would both be naked. Silently he led her back to the stone bench, the closest he could get to the house without risking being seen from the library. "You'll think of something to wear to the ball. And yes, I did answer your question. Just to clarify, though, this isn't a negotiation, Sarala. It's a seduction."

"Oh," she whispered, and leaned up to kiss him again.

Divided loyalties, possible international scandals, all of it faded away at the sweet, heady taste of her. Disciplined and logic-driven as he considered himself, it took every ounce of self-control to keep from pulling her to the ground and using his body to convince her that they belonged together. If this was an illness, he didn't want to find a cure.

"You'd best go," he finally murmured, kissing her throat.

Sarala visibly drew herself together again. "Yes. It was nice of you to come by and explain your reasoning." She smiled, touching his cheek. "Quite considerate of you."

"I try to be reasonable and considerate." With one last swift kiss he wrenched himself away from her and slipped back out of the garden without looking back. If he had, he would have fallen to quoting *Romeo and Juliet* about the sweet sorrow of parting. Yes, something had definitely happened to him, and while he was in Sarala's company, all he could think was that it was about damned time.

The nearer he came to Griffin House, however, the more the rest of the world returned. That sensation deepened as Stanton pulled open the front door, and he stepped into the foyer to see Sebastian there pulling on his gloves.

"Where the devil were you?" the duke asked, his tone short.

"I went to see Sarala. What's wrong?"

Melbourne snorted. "What's wrong? Just a few minor potholes—you know, Chinese swordsmen who want my brother imprisoned in China, things like that."

The duke remained angry and distant, as he had since he'd barged into Nell's library to see him and Sarala kissing. Charlemagne needed to settle things with Sebastian; obviously they couldn't continue as they were, and yet he had a few other pressing matters on his own plate. "Then where are you off to?" he asked.

"To Carlton House. I thought I'd best inform Prinny and Liverpool about the silk fiasco, to at least prepare them for the idea of making amends or reparations. If you're not too involved with socializing, I thought you might wish to attend."

"Of course I'll attend." He took back his hat from Stanton.

"Uncle Shay?"

He looked up toward the first floor railing. "Yes, Peep?"

She stood on tiptoe looking down at him, dark ringlets of hair framing her face. "I heard a rumor from someone I can't name that you are getting married."

"Yes, I am."

"Why wasn't I directly informed, then?"

"I beg your pardon, Peep. Things have been a bit mad over the past few days."

"Yes, but I haven't even met her."

He forced a smile, very aware of Sebastian's restless stirring at his back. "She and her family will be joining us for dinner tomorrow night, before the Wexton soiree. You will meet her then."

"All right. I have some questions about her, however. When you return, we should have a meeting."

"Out of the mouths of babes," the babe's father murmured.

"When I return then, Peep."

Brushing past his brother, Charlemagne headed for the coach waiting outside and climbed in. A moment later Sebastian joined him, and the coach rumbled off down the drive.

"What did you say to Peep?" he asked after a moment of silence. "I assume you were the source she won't divulge."

The duke shrugged, his gaze out the small window. "She asked me what all the commotion was this morning. I said we were in negotiations over your betrothed."

"That's all you said?"

"That's all I said. Why do you ask?"

"Because if Sarala is going to join this family, which I intend she should do, I don't want Peep already disposed to look down on her or dislike her because you aren't pleased with the circumstances."

"Displeasure doesn't even begin to describe it, Shay."

Charlemagne sat forward. He would have preferred a good night's rest before he confronted an opponent as formidable as his brother, but if the fight was to be now, so be it. "Is your displeasure over Sarala and her family, or is it because I'm marrying at all?"

"You were trapped, Shay. Tricked. Compromised by someone who realized the integrity of this family and figured out how to use it against us."

"I would have asked her to marry me anyway, Seb," Charlemagne returned, doing his damnedest to keep a rein on his temper. He sensed that Melbourne would let loose, and one of them needed to maintain control. "Not quite as soon, but I think I would have asked her. She's remarkable."

"Her mother's an ambitious title hunter."

"Yes, she is. I think they were actually hoping *you* would fall for Sarala. If it makes a difference, she spent yesterday and this morning asking me to speak with you about calling everything off. As far as she was concerned, we were negotiating for the silks. Period. The kissing was my idea, but she thought I was doing it to 'befuddle her' I believe she said. She begged me to convince you to find a way out of this."

Finally Sebastian sat back to look at him. "I don't understand. You . . . haven't been unhappy. I know that."

"I've been perfectly happy. And I'm happier, now." He drew a breath. "If the problem is . . . If for business reasons you'd prefer me to remain at Griffin House, there's no shortage of space even with the addition of Sarala." Unless the duke's opinion of Sarala changed that would be impossible, because Charlemagne simply wouldn't subject her to that, but his brother needed to realize his own part in this equation, as well—and that he wouldn't be abandoned.

"I didn't think to keep the lot of you trapped there forever," Sebastian said flatly. "Don't misinterpret my objections as being because of my personal situation. My first concern is for the Griffin family."

"She's English, and she's a marquis's daughter."

"She's an oddity. I don't know what the devil her father was thinking, to name her Sarala, to let her absorb Indian culture to the point that she finds her own kind strange, but his decisions didn't do her any favors."

"She learned how to charm cobras."

"Shay, you're not helping anyth—"

"My point being, I am perfectly aware of everything you just said. And all of that is part of what makes her so remarkable to me, including her accent and the tan of her skin. So before you begin handing down proclamations of your dissatisfaction with her upbringing, perhaps you should have a conversation with her. She enjoys Roman history and reads Greek. You might even like her, Sebastian. And the snake charming might come in useful for someone in your position with the government."

"Damnation, Shay, you've done this the way you do everything. You assess all the points, make your decision, and then charge in regardless of barricades or common sense."

"It's not I—"

"It concerns me that you never mentioned her," Melbourne interrupted, "much less how you apparently feel about her, before I forced you into it. That doesn't sound like a love match to me."

"Honestly," Shay said, pretending that the word "love" hadn't shaken him a little, "she attracts me, but I *am* occasionally an idiot."

"Do tell."

"I wanted to keep her for myself," he said abruptly, scowling. "It doesn't make sense, I know, but I think in the back of my mind I knew I didn't want to have this conversation with you, and that if you realized what was going on, I wouldn't be able to avoid it." Charlemagne shrugged, trying to hide his reluctance to let a skeptic into his private thoughts when he hadn't entirely sorted them out yet. "Besides, how often am I wrong?"

"It only takes once, brother."

"This isn't that once."

Several emotions passed across his brother's usually impassive face. "If I could find a way for you to end the betrothal without scandalizing anyone, would you take it?"

"No."

"Would she?"

Cold speared through his chest. He'd made definite progress this morning, but Sarala's damned sense of honor and her reluctance at being manipulated could still raise its proud head at any moment. "You know she would," he said slowly, "but I would appreciate if you wouldn't ask her that yet."

"That's not precisely fair to her now, is it?"

Charlemagne narrowed his eyes. "Don't pretend for a second that you're looking out for her best interests. If when I've done my best and she still isn't happy with the idea of marrying me, then . . ." The thought of it left him so heartsick he couldn't even finish the sentence.

"I see." Sebastian flicked an imaginary speck of dust from his sleeve. "Should I plan an engagement ball then, or would you prefer that I wait?"

"Waiting would seem suspicious. But from what I've overheard, her mother's already got us married and living at Windsor Castle or some such thing, so if you'd prefer it, I'll take care of that negotiating."

"God, yes. Please do." Melbourne returned to the window, then sat back once more. "I'll talk with Sarala."

It wasn't much, but at the same time coming from Melbourne, it was a great deal. Charlemagne knew just how far he was pushing things—after all, the Griffin family wasn't just them. It was the Grifanus line dating back to before the time of Hadrian, and all the generations since then. And his brother felt that burden every day, because it was his direct heritage. He was a duke because of those ancestors, and he would never betray them or their memories. "Thank you, Sebastian."

"Yes, well, the Chinese government still might lop your head off, and then I won't have to bother with any of this."

"We'll try to remain optimistic, then."

"Did you see this?" Lady Hanover asked, waving a note in Sarala's direction. "I told you that knowing the right people makes all the difference. Oh, I'm so glad you never married in India."

"That's not what you said at the time," Sarala noted, setting aside her Roman history. She'd had the chance, and despite the present mess, she'd never been more thankful to have avoided it.

"I never did. But don't change the subject."

Considering the griffin on the wax seal that hung from the bottom of the missive, she had a fair idea both who'd sent the note and what it contained. Her mother loved her surprises though, so she set aside her book. "What in the world is it?"

"It is a note from the Duke of Melbourne, inviting us to dine with them tonight, and inquiring whether we would care to join them at the Wexton masked ball afterward! And to think the invitations for that ball went out weeks ago, before we ever arrived in London!"

"That's good, then." A shiver of nervousness went through her. She'd encountered all of the Griffins en masse before, but that had been when they were at the recital. Having their undivided attention focused on her, and knowing now that Shay intended for her to join their ranks—oh, dear.

"Good? It's wonderful! I must find your father and tell him. I think he's playing billiards with Lord DeLayne."

"De— John is here?"

"He arrived a few minutes ago."

Her mother hurried from the morning room and made her way to the stairs. Hurriedly Sarala rose and followed her. "Mama," she hissed.

Her mother stopped on the first landing. "What is it, darling?"

"Are you certain you should tell Papa about the ball while Lord DeLayne is standing there? He probably wasn't invited, either, since he's only just come to London."

"Oh, yes, you're right. I'll hand the note to your father, and let him read it."

Blowing out her breath, Sarala watched her mother vanish up the stairs toward the billiards room. She had been half convinced that Melbourne wouldn't do it. After all, everyone knew that the Wexton party was bound to be the event of the Season. He could just as easily have had them over for dinner any other night. A low buzz of excitement joined the nervous fluttering of her stomach. A masked ball. She knew what she wanted to wear—heavens, she'd known from the moment Shay had mentioned the party to her—but she had two problems: her nerves, and her mother. If either one got the better of her, she'd never be able to go through with it. She shouldn't go through with it.

She heard a knock at the front door. A moment later the butler, armed with a salver and calling cards, appeared in the morning room doorway.

"My lady, Lady Deverill and Lady Caroline Griffin wish to know if you are in."

Sarala stood, another bolt of nerves diving into her stomach. At this rate she might not survive to marry Charlemagne. "Of course I'm in. And bring some tea, if you please."

Both ladies had been very kind to her two days ago when the disaster had occurred, but she'd been so frazzled that she hadn't had any idea what they might actually have thought about everything. If it had been her watching a brother or brother-in-law caught and forced to announce marriage with someone practically a foreigner, she wasn't certain how kind she would be.

"Good morning," Lady Deverill said as she strolled into the room, Lady Caroline behind her.

"Good morning." Sarala went forward to take each lady's hand.

To her surprise, though, Caroline kissed her on the cheek. "How are you?" she asked.

"A bit disconcerted," Sarala admitted. "What may I do for you?"

"We have a favor to ask of you," Eleanor said, sitting in the chair Sarala indicated.

They probably wanted to ask her to return to India. Sarala pushed that thought aside with a forced smile. "Anything."

"Well, as you know, tonight is the Wexton masked ball. Sebastian has invited you to join us, hasn't he?"

She nodded. "We received his note this morning."

"Good." Caroline cleared her throat. "Shall I, Nell, or do you want to?"

"Heavens, what is it?" Sarala broke in, a genuine smile breaking through her nervousness at the realization that she wasn't the only one who felt on uncertain ground. For the sake of their family they would have to be friendly to her, she realized. Whether they meant that friendship or not—that was what she wished to determine. "You don't want me to kill someone, do you?"

"Not yet. We wanted to ask your help with costumes for tonight, actually."

"*My* help?"

"We thought," Eleanor took up, "Caro and I, that is, that it would be fun if the three of us dressed as Indian—Hindu—ladies. But please, if you don't feel comfortable about that, we won't do anything of the sort."

"You know, I honestly thought of dressing that way, myself," Sarala admitted. "But if I may say, I have no intention of doing anything which might . . . further damage your or anyone else's opinion of me."

"Because you're betrothed to Shay?" Eleanor asked. "I know my brother well enough to state that he's never gotten involved in anything he didn't want to. Charlemagne has a remarkable capacity to get things accomplished. So if anything, I would be angry at him for ambushing you, rather than the other way around."

It sounded sincere. She wanted them to be sincere. Assuming, however, wouldn't get her anywhere. "He didn't ambush me. Please don't think that."

"I don't." The marchioness accepted a cup of tea from a footman. "I saw the way you two looked at one another."

Slowly she smiled. "And I invited you to luncheon before I knew either of your . . . feelings for one another."

"I'm not certain *I* know what those are."

Caroline took her hand. "You will, eventually."

"Indeed," Lady Deverill put in. "So what do you think? Should we all dress like princesses from India?"

Shay had said she looked like one. It *would* be fun to dress that way, especially if it was to be for last time. "I did bring several traditional *salwar kadeez* and saris and veils with me. Shall we take a look?"

Caroline clapped again. "I think Zachary may faint," she said, chuckling.

The Marquis of Hanover stepped into the room. "Ladies," he intoned, sketching a shallow bow. "My butler said you were here. I was wondering, would it be possible to bring one more with us tonight? I have a friend also recently arrived from India, and I think he would—"

"Of course," Eleanor broke in. "The more the merrier. I'll let Melbourne know our party will include one more."

"Splendid. I shall leave you to your fun, then." With another nod, Sarala's father left the room again.

Sarala hid her sudden disappointment as she summoned Jenny and led the way to her bedchamber. It made sense that her father would want to include John DeLayne in their party, but she had several reasons to wish otherwise—the largest being that she didn't want Charlemagne Griffin and Lord DeLayne ever to meet. No, it wasn't disappointment she felt. It was dread.

The three women decided to wait until after dinner to don their costumes. For Sarala that was something of a relief; not only had her mother's probable reaction worried her, but this way she would at least have some time to become better acquainted with the Griffin clan in "normal" garb before they experienced her in the clothes of an Indian native.

At just before seven in the evening she and her parents arrived at Griffin House for the second time in her life. A festive feeling filled the air this time, a tremendous improvement over the tense, solicitor-choked atmosphere of the day before. Her mother's complaints over the lack of a settlement continued, but at least they had slowed after the arrival of the duke's invitation.

Viscount DeLayne had returned home to change for the evening, and she imagined he would appear at Griffin House shortly. Invitations to such an auspicious place for something as intimate as a family dinner were far more rare even than tickets to an event as sought after as the Wexton soiree.

She stepped down from the coach with the assistance of a liveried footman and made her way up the shallow marble steps, through the wide double doors, and into the large foyer.

"Hello."

She turned to see Charlemagne standing in a neighboring doorway and gazing at her. "Hello. You look very handsome tonight."

"My sister says I clean up well."

He did, indeed. His long-tailed black coat set off a black and gold waistcoat and black trousers that hugged his muscular thighs. His snow-white cravat was austere and elegant, pierced by a ruby pin—the only ornamentation he wore. An Indian ruby, no doubt. She tried not to read anything into his choice of decoration, but just by noticing it, she supposed that she already had.

"I thought I might take you into the billiards room to show you that bust of Caesar," he continued.

"Am I not supposed to greet the Duke of Melbourne before I begin wandering about his house?"

He lifted an eyebrow. "I live here, too, and you've greeted me. There'll be time enough for Melbourne tonight." He took her fingers, tugging her forward. "Come and see Caesar."

"As long as you're not attempting to get me into more trouble, yes, I would like that." Then at least she wouldn't have to witness the duke greeting her mother.

Shay freed her hand and offered his arm, and she wrapped her fingers around the fine black cloth of his sleeve. She'd been so preoccupied the last time that she couldn't remember much about Griffin House except that it was huge. Tonight she took in the line of fine portraits along the short gallery of the upstairs hallway, the exquisite pieces of china and porcelain and Italian blown glass on the hall tables, and the gold gilding on the upper cornices of the walls.

"How long has your family owned this house?" she asked.

"It actually came to the Griffins from my great-great-great-grandmother, a daughter of the Duke of Cornwall. It became Griffin House in 1648. The rear half of the house burned during the Great Fire, but it was rebuilt in 1667. Various Griffins have modified, modernized, and expanded it since then, of course."

"It seems as though your family has been here since the time of the Romans." She'd heard that from Augusta, Lady Gerard, but if she was to marry into this family, she wanted to know all she could about their ancestry. And even if she wasn't going to marry Charlemagne, she still couldn't help wanting to know about him. Just hearing his voice gave her shivers.

"We have been. There was a Maximus Grifanus, a general under Emperor Trajan. The story is that he fell in love with a local tribal chief's daughter. As a wedding gift the emperor gave him land, and he remained here as a landowner after he retired from the Roman army. His descendants decided they were British more than they were Roman, and after the legions left, they stayed as part of the original aristocracy."

He came to a stop inside the billiards room and indicated a white marble bust between the tall windows opposite. "Zach calls him Uncle Julius, though the chances that we're actually related are rather abysmal."

She went closer to examine the bust. "Even abysmal is somewhat intimidating, don't you think?"

He shrugged. "All families come from somewhere. We simply happen to have kept records."

"I would guess you're actually a bit less cavalier than that about your ancestry," she countered, half her attention still on the statue. She could see why he'd been interested in acquiring it; the quality was extraordinary. It had come from a Roman palace somewhere, and probably one occupied by Caesar, himself. The stone felt cool beneath her fingertips.

A young throat cleared itself in the doorway, and Sarala turned around, surprised. A very petite girl who looked a great deal like Eleanor stood there eyeing her. Hands clasped behind her and rocking back on her heels, in stance she looked more like Melbourne. The duke's daughter, no doubt.

"Uncle Shay, would you be kind enough to introduce me to our guest?" the girl asked.

"Certainly." Charlemagne hid a quick grin. "Peep, Lady Sarala Carlisle. Sarala, my niece, Lady Penelope Griffin."

Sarala curtsied, taking her cue from Charlemagne. "I'm pleased to meet you, Lady Penelope."

The girl curtsied back. "I like your accent," she stated.

Charlemagne stirred, offering a hand to Sarala again.

"She used to live in India, Peep. And she knows how to charm cobras."

"Shay," Sarala began, ready to chastise him for frightening Lady Penelope with talk of snakes. Before she could continue, though, the girl pranced into the room and grabbed her free hand.

"Is it true that the music you play hypnotizes the cobras?" she asked, gray eyes shining with excitement.

"No, it's actually the movement of the instrument that holds its attention, Lady Penelope," Sarala returned, freeing her hands to demonstrate with an imaginary flute.

"You may call me Peep," Penelope said, mimicking the motions. "Like this?"

"That's excellent. Are you certain you've never charmed a cobra before?"

Peep giggled. "Only Uncle Zachary. Which mask are you wearing to the ball tonight?"

Eleanor and Caroline had sworn her to secrecy, but there was no reason she couldn't tell the girl precisely that. She knew how important this meeting was. "I'm afraid it's a secret, but I'll make certain you get to see before we leave the house."

"I would be a pirate," Peep returned, "but Papa says I would frighten all the ladies."

"You frighten me," Shay put in, tugging one of the girl's curls.

"Very amusing. I would like to sit beside Lady Sarala at dinner."

"Sarala, please," she returned, grinning at Charlemagne over his niece's head. "The ladies in your family are all very nice," she said, meaning it.

"They have to compensate for the evil character of the men," he said, lifting her hand and kissing her fingers.

Warmth swirled up her spine in response. For the first time she tried to imagine actually being married to this man. The thought terrified her, but at the same time she felt more . . . excited than she would have believed possible. And the most frightening and exhilarating thought of all was that *he* wanted to marry *her*.

Chapter 15

Peep liked Sarala. Mentioning her cobra-charming abilities had certainly helped, but Charlemagne saw nothing wrong with nudging things in the right direction. And he hadn't made anything up. A large part of Sarala's appeal was her uniqueness, after all.

Tonight she'd dressed well, though obviously not for a masked ball. Once Nell and Caroline arrived, the three women snuck off to a corner to gossip about something, and then after a moment called over a delighted Peep to include her in the secret. Since neither of the other ladies had dressed, either, and since all three had brought their maids with them to Griffin House, Charlemagne assumed they were collectively up to something.

Lady Hanover had dressed in white and gold, a swan mask in her hands, and when Charlemagne saw her start toward where Melbourne spoke with Valentine, he moved to intercept her. She could be the largest problem he faced in working to have Melbourne warm to Sarala. Ambitious mamas, the bane of single men everywhere. He considered his sister-in-law Caroline's mother to be something of a hapless ninny, but at least that woman had spent most of the past year in Shropshire with her six other daughters—or at least the ones who hadn't manage to escape yet via marriage.

"You look very regal this evening, Lady Hanover," he said, stopping between her and the duke.

"Well, thank you, Lord Charlemagne." She smiled. "Or perhaps I may now call you Shay?"

"Please do." He offered his arm to her. "Might I give you a tour of the house? We didn't have time for one the other day."

"Actually, I would like to speak with your brother. There are still some pressing arrangements to be made regarding the settlement and the wedding."

He nodded. "Yes, I know. But Sarala's not marrying Melbourne; she's marrying me. And though I do receive an annual income from the Griffin properties and businesses, I also have my own not-insubstantial means. Sarala will never lack for anything, and I will of course take steps to be certain you and Lord Hanover are able to settle comfortably into your lives here in England."

She looked up at him, olive green eyes speculative. "That was very well said, Shay, with nary an insult to be found."

"Thank y—"

"You didn't once mention, however, your affection for my daughter."

Hm. He reassessed his opinion of the marchioness up a degree or two. "I feel a great deal of affection toward your daughter, my lady, but I think that you either know that already, or it hasn't entered into your consideration at all. Why bring it up now?"

"I don't want it to be forgotten as we muddle our way through all of this. Sarala's lived a very free life—too free, if anyone had asked my opinion—and being forced into something does not make her happy, even if the initial incident was partially her fault. She likes business, as I'm sure you know, but we're not so badly off that we need to sell her away in exchange for settling our debts. If she thinks that's what's happening, she won't tolerate it, either."

"I will keep that in mind, my lady. And we will sit down with you and come to an agreement that satisfies everyone."

She patted his arm. "That, my boy, is all I wanted to hear."

That said, she joined her husband and Zachary, who were no doubt discussing cows and pasture again. For a moment Charlemagne simply stood and watched. If not for the vanished Captain Blink and the Chinese soldiers, he would have considered tonight nearly perfect.

"Your Grace, my lords and ladies," Stanton's stentorian voice came from the doorway, "may I present John, Lord DeLayne."

It was a bit overdramatic for a family dinner, but considering how seldom they entertained at Griffin House, Charlemagne couldn't blame the butler for his enthusiasm. He had no idea who Lord DeLayne was, though Nell's note had named him as a viscount that Lord Hanover knew from India. Obviously he hadn't been back in England for much longer than the Carlisles.

Melbourne, joined by Hanover, strolled over to greet DeLayne as he walked into the drawing room and stopped, looking about somewhat wide-eyed. Charlemagne had thought the viscount would be older, but he couldn't have been more than a year or two senior to Zachary, somewhere in his middle twenties. His face wasn't as tanned as Sarala's; evidently she was an exception among the English living in India. She seemed to be an exception everywhere she went.

He started over to introduce himself, as well, but stopped when a hand closed around his arm. From the sudden rush of his blood he knew who touched him without looking.

"You've finished your plotting then, have you?" he asked with a smile, turning around.

"We weren't plotting," Sarala said grandly. "We were merely conferring." She placed her other hand on his sleeve to join the first.

Charlemagne had to stop himself from leaning down to kiss her upturned mouth. That wouldn't do; engaged or not, the situation remained dodgy. She hadn't even agreed actually to marry him yet. "Whatever you were doing," he managed, mentally shaking himself, "keep an eye on Peep. She'll sell your secrets for a bit of hard candy."

"Ah. Do you have any to buy them with, then?"

He glanced about to be certain no one was close enough to overhear. "You'll have to search my pockets to find out," he murmured.

Sarala's slow smile made his mouth dry. "Perhaps I will."

That wasn't fair. He was trying to be a gentleman, and she was tempting the hell out of him. And she certainly didn't act like the demure, virginal chits who lined up at every soiree looking for a husband. Perhaps, though, she'd learned how to make him insane—she'd had enough practice during their silk negotiations.

"I think you should dress as a siren tonight," he said,

drawing one of her hands up to kiss her palm, mostly because not touching her skin to skin would be physically painful—and not just to his over-patient nether regions. "I feel very tempted to dash myself upon the rocks as it is."

"I'm not giving you any clues about what I'm wearing, though I would prefer that you refrain from suicidal rock bashing."

She glanced over his shoulder before returning her gaze to him, from her expression wishing the two of them could vanish somewhere private, as well. The thought of finally having her made him hard. *Think of something else, Shay,* he ordered silently.

"My Aunt Tremaine will join us at the party tonight," he said, trying mightily to conjure images of clouds and happy little bees—anything that would keep him from ruining the line of his trousers or falling on her. "We invited her for dinner, but she said adding one more to our number would require us to enlist as an army battalion." In truth he thought she'd objected to the idea of the Griffin clan overwhelming Sarala with sheer numbers. His aunt had an uncanny ability to do the right thing at the right moment, and he remained grateful to her.

Sarala laughed. "I look forward to meeting her. Are there any other family members I've missed?"

"No. A few distant cousins, but we don't dig too deeply on purpose. If you go back enough generations, just about every peer is related in one way or another."

"You don't have to do that, you know."

Charlemagne lifted an eyebrow. "Do what?"

"Make light of the status of your family to make me feel more comfortable," she continued quietly. "I *am* the daughter of the Marquis of Hanover, however unfortunately that came to pass. I'm not going to engage in a contest of rank with you, or anyone else."

In his life, contests of rank and power seemed to make up at least a portion of each and every day. "You are a very unusual woman, Sarala."

"My mother just calls me contrary. I prefer your way of putting it." Stanton took that moment to announce dinner, and they joined the exodus to the dining room. "What are you masquerading as tonight?" she continued.

Devil a bit. He usually didn't bother to wear a mask, considering it a rather useless exercise. It made sense, though, damn it all, that if he invited her to join him at a masquerade ball, he needed to participate. If he recalled, Zachary had left several masks behind when he'd moved into his town house. "If you won't tell me your surprise," he improvised, "don't expect me to tell you mine."

Thankfully Peep appeared, commandeering Sarala. Relinquishing her, Charlemagne gestured at Stanton.

"Yes, my lord?"

"Have Caine go through Zachary's old rooms," he whispered, "and find me an appropriate mask for this evening."

"Very good, my lord," the butler whispered back.

When Charlemagne returned to the dining table he found Sarala sandwiched between Peep and the end of the table, with Melbourne at her elbow. Wonderful. He did want Melbourne to chat with Sarala in the hopes that the duke would learn a bit more about her than her accent. Ideally, though, the meeting between Sarala and Melbourne would have taken place *after* he'd managed to convince her to join the family. Charlemagne stifled a curse and took his own seat between Peep and John DeLayne as Stanton and the footmen began serving.

"Lord Charlemagne, yes?" DeLayne said, offering his hand.

"Yes." Charlemagne shook it. "Apologies for not introducing myself to you earlier."

"No worries. I had quite a few people to meet, as it was." The viscount chuckled. "You're the one who proposed to Sarala."

Charlemagne nodded, noting the familiarity with which DeLayne said her name. "I am. Hanover tells me you spent time in India while the Carlisles were there."

"I did indeed. I had some family property there, and went to oversee its sale. I ended up staying for better than two years. Extraordinary place, India."

"And you've just returned?"

"I've been home in Sussex for a little over two years. I had no idea that the Carlisles were in England until I read in the Society page that they had attended a party in the duke's company. We'd become such friends in Delhi that I immediately came to see them."

"I'm sure they're happy to see an old friend."

"Hopefully as happy as I am to see them."

At the head of the table Melbourne had assumed his role of witty, generous host, distributing his attentions equally among family and guests. Charlemagne knew him well enough, though, to see the signs that Sebastian still had serious reservations about all of this. The duke had agreed to not make any judgments until he'd spoken at greater length with Sarala, but Charlemagne remained uneasy nonetheless.

He and Sarala would marry—that was both his preference and his duty as a gentleman. But with Melbourne in the position of being both a brother and a business partner, as well as a friend, the more harmoniously Sarala entered the Griffin family, the better it would be for everyone concerned.

Charlemagne took a generous swallow of wine. As much as he enjoyed the conflicts and intricacies that accompanied any business proceedings, here those same challenges were twisting him up inside. He didn't want to have to choose between Sarala and his family, and he hoped that uncompromisingly rigid as Melbourne was about Griffin honor, the duke would see in her precisely what he himself was beginning to and would come to the same decision.

"... still angry at Uncle Shay for not telling me there were Chinese swordsmen in the museum," Peep was saying to Sarala, "because we could have fought them together. I'm going to be a pirate, after all. Or an actress."

"Penelope," her father chastised, while across the table Zachary choked on his roast pig.

"Begging your pardon," DeLayne put in, "but she is referring to *costumes* of Chinese swordsmen, isn't she?"

"Fighting a wardrobe of costumes would hardly be an adventure for a pirate," Valentine commented dryly.

The viscount lifted both eyebrows. "So there were actual—I mean to say living . . . Chinese—"

"I'm afraid so, John," Lord Hanover began. "It's a long—"

"It's a long and rather dull tale of trade negotiations and a cultural misunderstanding," Charlemagne interrupted. Friend of the Carlisles or not, DeLayne wasn't a business partner, much less family. And unless he was one of the two, he did *not* get to hear about Griffin activities.

"Lord DeLayne," Melbourne took up, "were you stationed in India, or there on business?"

"Business," the viscount replied. "My uncle had been posted there several years ago, and had been granted some land by King George the Third for services rendered. I inherited the land, and went to inspect it."

"He sold it to one of the local *saradara* for a very nice

profit, as I recall," Hanover contributed with a chuckle.

Charlemagne glanced at Sarala, to see her briefly closing her eyes as her father went on about DeLayne's sale. And he'd thought that her mother would be the larger problem where Melbourne was concerned. Interesting that London considered her less English than her parents, and yet she had a better sense of what should be discussed among barely met acquaintances and what shouldn't. At the moment she was embarrassed—and that bothered him.

"Well done, DeLayne," he heard himself say. "What occupies you now that you've returned to England?"

"Oh, you men," Eleanor put in with her usual excellent timing. "Discuss your dull business affairs once we ladies have left the table. I for one want to know how in the world Caroline convinced the Marquis of Wellington to sit for a portrait hatless. I thought that chapeau was permanently attached to his head."

Zachary lifted a glass to toast his wife. "It's because she is brilliant and insightful," he said, grinning.

"And because I've learned that a little judicious flattery works equally well on both sexes," Caroline added.

"And food works very well on Uncle Zachary," Peep said.

Thankfully after that the conversation turned to the merits of painting edible subjects. Charlemagne found it more interesting, though, that DeLayne had traveled to Delhi on business. Had he met the Carlisles through Hanover, or through Sarala?

Once everyone finished dinner the ladies, led by a fiercely giggling Peep and trailed by a flattered—and probably baffled—Lady Hanover, left the dining room to go dress for the ball.

"What do you think they're up to?" Zachary asked, gazing at the closed dining room door through which they'd disappeared.

"They are women," Valentine answered, smiling briefly. "We will never be able to answer that question."

Charlemagne silently agreed with that assessment, though he'd never considered it much of a problem until a few short weeks ago. Until figuring out what a particular woman might be thinking had abruptly become of paramount importance to his heart and to his happiness.

"Do you think they have any idea what we're up to?" Caroline chortled as her maid brushed out her long auburn hair.

"They're men," Eleanor returned, looking at herself in the full-length dressing mirror and making a few last adjustments. "I'm sure they think they know, and I'm sure they'll be very wrong." She grinned at Sarala. "I'm so glad you brought these back to England with you. Valentine may faint alongside Zachary."

"*I* may faint," Sarala's mother said from her seat by the window. "Three ladies wearing trousers—and in public! We'll all be forced to leave the country, I just know it."

Sarala had a few doubts about their reception, herself, but she'd be damned before she would admit that in the face of Eleanor and Caroline's obvious enthusiasm. They were the first friends she'd made since her arrival in London. Whether that friendship would have occurred—or would continue—without Charlemagne's presence in her life, she didn't know, but the relief from loneliness was so marked that she didn't feel up to finding out just yet. It seemed sincere, and for the moment that was all that mattered.

"They're not trousers, Mama, they're *salwar.* And they're very traditional in Delhi. So are the *kadeez* and the saris."

"We are *not* in Delhi!"

"Which are which, Sarala?" Eleanor asked.

"The *kadeez* is the top shirt underneath, and the sari is the wrap that goes around."

"At least tell me you won't be going to the ball in your bare feet," her mother pleaded.

"No. We have matching slippers. Wait, *mojaris*, yes?" Caroline stepped into the red shoes that matched her red sari with its intricate gold thread trim.

Sarala chuckled. "Yes, *mojaris*. Very good."

"Oh, now you're teaching Hindi? This is a disaster."

"Far from it, Lady Hanover. This is extremely fun." Eleanor had chosen the yellow *salwar kadeez* and *sari,* while Sarala's own costume was deep green. She particularly liked the red beading that hung in light tassels from the bottom edge of the delicate combination veil and head covering—it enabled her to wear the ruby Shay had given her.

Finally the maids stepped back, and Sarala joined the other two ladies in front of the dressing mirror. The long *salwar* tapered at the ankle and thankfully concealed the fading henna tattoo on her ankle, though she suspected that Eleanor had seen it while they'd been changing.

"I want to go downstairs first," Peep announced, sporting a spare blue headdress and veil that Sarala had luckily brought along in case of emergency. "I look very good."

"Yes, you do, Peep," Eleanor said, taking her niece's hand. "And I think you should definitely go first. Are we ready?"

Caroline took a deep breath. "As we'll ever be, I suppose."

As they glided down the stairs, young Penelope in front and her mother once again behind, Sarala wondered what Charlemagne would think. If nothing else had truly worked, this would demonstrate once and for all that she was little more than a foreigner. Better that he—and everyone else—understood that before they decided whether the wedding plans should continue.

Penelope marched up to the butler as he stood issuing instructions to a pair of footmen. "Stanton, where is my papa?" she asked.

The butler immediately faced her, his gaze after a bare second going to the rest of the ladies where they stood ranged down the staircase. Sarala didn't know him well at all, but she would have called his expression stunned. "He—they—are in the drawing room, Lady Penelope," he managed shakily.

"Would you open the door for us, Stanton?" Eleanor's cool voice came. Sarala admired her pure courage, but then Eleanor was a Griffin born and bred. There was likely very little she feared, especially when it came to choice of clothing.

The poor butler audibly swallowed. "Ye . . ." He cleared his throat. "Yes, at once, my lady."

Sarala's heart beat as madly as hummingbird wings while they moved into position on the far side of the drawing room door. At a nod from Eleanor, Stanton pushed open the double doors and practically dove out of the way.

"What do you think, Papa?" Peep asked, stopping just inside the doorway and doing her imitation of a snake-charming dance.

The duke turned around. His mouth opened, but no sound came out. After a brief glance at Melbourne, though, Sarala turned her attention to Charlemagne. His expression mirrored that of his older brother. She didn't think he found himself without words often, and she found herself smiling beneath the thin green veil. He'd definitely noticed her, anyway.

"St. George's buttonholes," Zachary rasped, falling backward into a chair.

Lord Deverill set aside his glass of port. "Which one is mine?" he drawled, moving forward as Eleanor waggled her fingers at him.

"That would be me," she breathed.

"Good," he continued, skillfully unhooking one side of the veil and kissing his wife gently on the mouth.

Visibly shaking himself, Charlemagne approached her. "Was this your idea?"

"It was mine," his sister chortled, batting at her husband's hands as he attempted to lift some of the sari's loose wrappings. "Look at Sebastian. He can't even speak."

"I can speak," the duke countered, taking a rather generous swallow from his own glass. Slowly he came forward. "All three of you look lovely," he continued, and stopped beside Shay, directly in front of Sarala. "You will all definitely be the center of everyone's attention tonight. Are you prepared for that?"

"Why shouldn't I be?" Shay answered, before she could. "I'll be the envy of every man in attendance."

She was grateful that Shay had interceded, because from Melbourne's brief glance at his sister, he was less than pleased with their choice of attire. The rest of the men present, though, seemed more of Shay's opinion. Even Sarala's father chuckled, shaking his head as he looked at the three of them.

As they moved into the foyer, the duke did compliment his daughter on her stunning appearance before handing her off to her governess, but as he'd pointed out, young Penelope wouldn't have most of the London aristocracy staring at her all night.

Charlemagne brushed her fingers with his. "You are not

going to be able to keep me away all evening," he whispered, his warm breath caressing her ear.

"Who says I want to keep you away?" Not speaking her mind had gotten her nowhere; being straightforward felt . . . better, anyway.

He curled his hand, grasping hers more strongly. "I'll remember you said that."

"And so you should. Where's your mask?" she asked.

"Blast. Just a moment." He charged up the stairs.

"Now you look like the Sarala I remember from India," John DeLayne said, offering his arm to her.

Sarala made a show of straightening her silver headpiece, pretending she didn't see the gesture. "I don't think you ever saw me dressed like this, my lord," she returned coolly.

"Perhaps not, but you always *felt* like that."

Footsteps thundered back down to the foyer. "Here we are," Shay said, lifting a mask in his fingers.

"The devil?" Sarala said, lifting an eyebrow as they stepped out to the front portico.

"The red matches," he said defensively, gesturing from the half mask to the ruby pin in his cravat.

Zachary pointed at the mask in his brother's hand. "Hey, that's—"

Charlemagne elbowed him in the gut. "Sorry about that, Zach," he muttered with a grin, clearly not sorry about anything.

"You must ride with us," Eleanor said to Sarala, taking her arm.

"Not without me," Shay countered, falling in beside her.

"Lord Hanover, I have a land question for you," Zachary put in, offering his arm to Lady Hanover in the same motion.

For a long moment no one approached John DeLayne,

and Sarala had the bad grace to want to smile. Apparently she wasn't the only one to sense that he was just a bit too happy to join the ranks of the Griffin clan, if only as a hanger-on to almost-relations. The viscount looked from one coach to the other, his smile frozen but beginning to fade just a little.

Behind him Melbourne murmured something to Zachary as he passed by on the way to the Deverill coach. Whatever Zachary said in response didn't look too flattering, but he turned around to collect the viscount. "Ride with us, DeLayne," he said, not offering a pretty excuse for the invitation.

"For an old friend of your family, Lord DeLayne seems to have been somewhat forgotten," Lord Deverill noted, gazing at her as their coach rolled down the drive.

She shrugged, her shoulder brushing Charlemagne's. Once again she'd ended up between Shay and Melbourne, and as surreptitiously as she could, she edged sideways to give the duke a bit more room. "You did us the kindness of inviting us to join you to a very exclusive event. My father shouldn't have asked that you include Lord DeLayne as well."

"So you criticize your father's decision in front of others?" Melbourne asked, his gaze out the window toward the other coach.

"Seb," Charlemagne said, his tone cool.

"I only criticize his overabundance of kindness. I've learned that in Society, kindness seems to take a secondary position to appearance."

The duke made a low sound that might have been a chuckle. "And now you chastise me."

Apparently she'd made a palpable hit. "Only if you saw it as such, Your Grace."

"If anyone thinks there are too many of us," Deverill

drawled, "I'll be happy to take Eleanor home." He ran his fingers along the bottom fringe of her veil. "Very happy."

From Eleanor's expression she wouldn't have minded that, either, but she only patted the marquis on the knee. "I'm afraid, Valentine, that you'll have to dance with me at least once. Be patient."

When they arrived at the large house of Earl and Countess Wexton, half the coaches of London's nobility seemed to be choking the streets in every direction. "There's Hannah Dyson," Eleanor said, peeking out through the curtains. "The poor thing's dressed as a shepherdess again."

"Evidently the chit is very fond of sheep." Deverill stepped down from the coach and offered a hand to his wife.

As they all headed inside, Sarala realized precisely what Melbourne had been talking about. Not only had she, along with Eleanor and Caroline, dressed in highly unusual fashion, but this was her first public outing since the duke had announced her betrothal to Charlemagne.

"I've never seen so many people in one house." Sarala did a slow turn in the foyer. "How do they expect anyone to be able to move?"

Charlemagne chuckled. He'd barely stepped more than a foot away from her since she'd first appeared in her costume. "The trick is to have everyone rotate in the same direction at the same time." He glanced over her shoulder, and his smile deepened. "Aunt Tremaine."

"I'm in costume, lad," a rich female voice returned. "You're not supposed to be able to recognize me."

"What I don't recognize is what you're dressed *as*." Shay leaned down to kiss his aunt's cheek.

"I'm Boadicea, the scourge of Rome." The large woman shifted her substantial breastplate, facing Sarala. "And you must be Lady Sarala. I'm Gladys Tremaine."

Sarala curtsied, immediately liking the older woman. "I'm very pleased to meet you, my lady."

"Oh, please. Call me Aunt Tremaine like all of these silly nieces and nephews of mine. We are to be relations, after all."

"Aunt Tremaine, then," she returned, though she still had some large reservations about the marriage. Larger even than Melbourne's, she would wager. And not for her sake, but for Shay's. He thought he knew all he needed to about her, but she wasn't nearly as certain about that.

Chapter 16

Sarala twirled about the dance floor in a country dance that had lasted for fifteen minutes already. As Shay came around to her again, he blew hair from his eyes. "This is your fault, you know," he muttered, grinning.

And to think, just over a week ago he'd been the only man willing to risk dancing with the oddity she'd been. Now she seemed to be London's oddity, and everyone went out of their way to greet her, to offer to show her about Town, to dance with her.

She and Charlemagne circled each other and grasped hands. "Actually, it's your fault. You've made me interesting."

"All I did was notice your moss green eyes, your . . ." They parted for another circuit of the huge line. ". . . brilliant mind, your . . ." Another quick change of partners. ". . . unique character, and your breathtaking smile before everyone else."

Chuckling and nearly out of air, Sarala took his hand again for their final prance down the middle of the line. "So I'm an odd, plant-colored bluestocking with foul breath."

They slowed as they reached the end of the dance. "Even if you were, I'd still wish to marry you."

Despite his smile, his eyes were serious. Sarala stopped the quip she'd been ready to make. "What if what was wrong with me was something not so obvious?" she asked instead.

His brow furrowed. "Who says that something is wrong with you?"

Across the room she caught sight of John DeLayne, laden with glasses of Madeira and heading in their direction. With a swift breath she took Shay's arm and guided him toward the nearest door. "Come now, Shay. You're a Griffin, and I'm barely English. Compared to half a hundred other young ladies who would love to be married to you, yes, there's something wrong with me."

"I'm not interested in half a hundred other young ladies. Once I set eyes on you, I . . . I've canceled rendezvous with women because I had papers to finish or a meeting to attend. From the moment I met you, though, I've barely thought of anything else." He leaned closer to her as they walked. "I'm not perfect, and I'm not a saint. And you are as tempting to me as sin. Especially tonight, dressed like that."

That settled that. She would have to show him. Telling him only made him wax poetic, and that in turn only made her legs feel as weak as her resolve was becoming. If she couldn't end this farce, then he would have to. And she knew of only one way to convince him.

"What's in here?" she asked, stopping in front of a half-closed door.

"The library."

She pushed open the door and led the way inside. The

fireplace and a few candles provided the only light, but it was enough to see by. "That's a Reynolds portrait, isn't it?" she asked, stopping to view the large painting that hung over the fireplace.

"It is. It's Wexton the year he graduated from Oxford."

"It's extraordinary." He'd left the door open, though it seemed a bit late now to be concerned over her reputation. Her slippers silent on the carpeted floor, she returned to the entryway and swung the door shut.

"Sarala, I don't think this is w—"

"Shh." Returning to the fireplace, she wrapped her hands into his black lapels and leaned up to look him in the eyes. "Are you going to kiss me?" she whispered. "Or should we argue over the price of something first?"

With a slow smile he unfastened one side of her green veil and bent his head to touch his mouth to hers.

She couldn't help her responding moan. Immediately his arms swept around her, pulling her hard against his lean body. She'd wanted him for what seemed like forever, and this time she would make the first step. Their kiss deepened, and she lifted her arms around his shoulders. His mouth became hungrier, teasing at her until she opened to him. Sarala moaned again as his tongue tangled with hers.

He pushed her backward, pressing her between the wall and him. Behind her something clicked, and abruptly a wall panel directly beside them swung open. Shay tore his mouth from hers.

"What the devil?"

Sarala turned to look at the wall where she'd been leaning. A row of raised fleur-de-lis decorated a narrow oak chair rail. Slowly she reached out and pressed one of them. Nothing. The next one, though, pushed inward. "A secret door?"

Shay looked bemused for a moment. "You know, this house used to belong to one of King Henry the Eighth's mistresses. Perhaps this was how he visited her."

Lifting a candle off the mantel, her breathing still hard and her senses reeling, Sarala slipped through the narrow doorway. If she'd been wearing a ball gown rather than the *salwar kadeez,* she never would have been able to get in.

A broad form blocked the light behind her. "Where do you think you're going?" Shay whispered.

"You said you thought this might lead to a bedchamber. I'd like to find out."

"We can reach it by going down the hallway like everyone else."

"Yes, but then everyone will know where we've gone." She looked over her shoulder at him. "Coming?"

"Of course I am." With a low chuckle Charlemagne entered the dark, narrow corridor and pulled the latch to bring the door closed behind them.

He motioned for his unveiled princess to lead the way. Whatever she had in mind, if it was what he was beginning to suspect, he wasn't going to argue with her about it. The passage went on for several yards, and she brushed aside the occasional spider webs like they were nothing. The woman did know how to charm cobras, so spiders wouldn't bother her. Finally the narrow corridor turned sharply to the left and dead-ended. Shay took the candle and lifted it so she could look for the release latch. A moment later another door swung silently open, this time into a large, well-appointed bedchamber.

"Stay here a moment," he said, slipping past her and going to the room's main door. It was closed, but he locked it just in case. Another pair of candles sat in wall sconces, and he lit them with the one he carried.

Sarala emerged from the wall and closed the well-hidden door behind her. "That's really quite ingenious," she said, running her fingers along the door's nearly invisible seam. "If I'd had one of these in Delhi, it would have saved me a great many trips down the trellis outside my bedchamber window."

Charlemagne crossed the room again to stand in front of her. "And who did you go to see on those trips?"

"Not who. What." She lifted a hand to run her fingers along his cheek. "India." Tangling her fingers into his hair, she pulled his face down to kiss him again. The devil mask he'd perched on top of his head fell to the carpeted floor. He'd forgotten he wore it.

Heat spread beneath his skin. "Sarala," he murmured, "I'm attempting to be a gentleman. You're making that rather difficult."

"I want to be with you, Shay," she returned, "and we're in a room with a bed. I think we should make use of it."

Good God. He cleared his throat. "I thought you didn't want to marry me."

"I don't." She frowned even as she pulled his cravat from around his neck and dropped it to the floor. "I can't. But I do like you very much." Her lips touched his throat. "Besides, the bed was good enough for King Henry, you said."

"I think they've changed the mattress since then, but yes, I suppose it was." And the arousal he'd been fighting since he'd seen her in those clothes had him on the outer edge of his control, as it was.

"How much of a gentleman are you?" she asked, unfastening the top button of his waistcoat.

With a growl he lifted her up and set her backward on the bed. "Not that much."

So she'd gone out at night to see India. Seeing her in her

emerald green traditional garb, her dark-lined eyes, and her rich, sun-kissed skin, she *was* India. Silently he knelt before her, cupped both of her cheeks in his hands, and kissed her.

Her silk-draped arms slid down around his shoulders, and she sank into his embrace. Whoever was seducing whom, they both seemed equally eager. And since as far as he was concerned their marriage was already a certainty, he didn't feel as though he was taking advantage.

"The bed, or the floor?" she asked, tugging his coat free.

"Eager, are you?" And very sure of herself. Thank God he wasn't some green youth on his first rendezvous.

"I know what I want."

Alternating his movements with hot, open-mouthed kisses, Charlemagne shed his boots, then turned his attention to removing her green veil and headpiece, then the pins that held her hair in long, braided loops. Once it was free, he tangled the long, black cascade through his hands. With it he gently pulled her head back so he could run his lips and tongue along her throat. Her pulse beat madly against his mouth.

With her eager participation he shed his waistcoat and pulled his shirt from his trousers. "Do you think anyone else knows about those hidden doors?" she asked breathlessly, untying the silk knot at her shoulder.

"I doubt even Lady Wexton knows about them," he returned with a grin, removing her green shoes and setting them on the floor beside him.

He stood, holding a hand down to her so she could rise, as well. While he carefully pulled, she slowly twirled in front of him, yards of green and gold fabric falling away. When the last of the *sari* drifted to the floor, Sarala was left standing in a long, gold-trimmed shirt and loose trousers that narrowed at the ankles.

"Good God, you *are* wearing trousers."

"They're *salwar.* The other part's the *kadeez,* if you were wondering." Her smile deepened. "Are you scandalized?"

In response he slipped his hands under her shirt—*kadeez*—felt the drawstring holding up the trousers, and untied it. "Are you?" he murmured, kneeling to slide the silk material down past her hips, her thighs, and her knees.

"No." Sarala put her hands on his shoulders for balance and lifted her right foot to step out of the *salwar.*

As she shifted and he drew the silk over her left foot, he froze. A delicate brown pattern of diamonds and octagonal flowers and flared arches ringed her ankle. He ran his fingers around it, feeling the bone and flesh and muscle beneath. "Is this what I think it is?" he finally asked, lifting his face to gaze at her.

"It's henna," she returned, her breathing more ragged. "A parting gift from my friend Nahi."

Charlemagne turned her ankle and bent down to kiss the tattoo. She gasped as he trailed his mouth up to her knee and the inside of her thigh. He wanted more, but neither did he want to overwhelm her. Setting her foot down again, he stood, kissing her mouth hungrily. "Do you have any more of those tattoos anywhere?"

She moaned as he dragged her hips forward against his. "Not at the moment." Sarala reached down for the bottom of the *kadeez* and pulled it up, past her belly, her breasts, and over her head. "Touch me, Shay," she breathed, sliding her own hands up under his shirt.

He'd assumed she would be shy about exposing herself to a man, but he wasn't about to complain when she seemed as eager for him as he was for her. Her hands felt warm against his skin. Shifting his kisses to her bare shoulders, he lifted his hands to caress and cup her breasts. Nipples budded beneath his fingers, and she arched her back, gasping again.

Sarala sat back on the bed, grabbing his shoulders and pulling him down over her. He shed his shirt one arm at a time and bent down over her to kiss her again, pressing skin to warm skin. No one else had better know about the secret door.

"You are magnificent, my *premi,*" she said, lying back and pulling him over her.

"What does that mean?"

" 'Lover.' "

"I am that. How do you say 'heaven' in Hindi?" he asked. Breathing her in, near to bursting already, he lowered his mouth to her breasts, gently tugging and licking.

"*Akas'a,*" she returned, knotting her fingers into the back of his hair.

While his mouth was occupied, he reached down to unfasten his breeches, shove them down, and kick them to the floor. Sarala lifted her head, looking at him, watching as he trailed his hand up her thigh and this time slid a finger up into her hot, damp depths. God, she was so ready for him already.

Their eyes met, and she caught hold of his shoulders to pull him up along her again. He paused once more at her soft, perfect breasts, then moved up to take her mouth once more.

She felt like molten fire in his arms, all heat and desire, with not a pinch of hesitation or worry touching her. That, apparently, was all for him to do. Steeling himself for the care and patience he would still have to show, he put a hand beneath one of her knees and lifted, parting her. She moaned again, lifting her hips beneath him, her thigh brushing his hard cock.

"Now, Shay," she pleaded, digging her fingers into his shoulders as he shifted over her.

"Not yet," he murmured, and sank down along her body again. He wanted to taste her, to arouse her and excite her and please her so that after tonight she would never say another word about not wanting to marry him.

With his fingers and his mouth he teased at her until she quivered. "For goodness' sake, Shay, stop that," she gasped, laughing breathlessly. "You'll send me to Bedlam."

"To *akas'a,*" he returned, dipping his fingers into her moist depths once more. "To heaven." He lifted his head to look at her. "This is your last chance, Sarala, if you want to change your mind."

She tugged on his shoulders. "I am not changing my mind. No negotiating."

"No negotiating," he repeated, moving up to kiss her on her soft, swollen lips again.

Breathing hard, he guided himself inside her, pushing forward slowly and carefully, ready for the moment he would meet resistance and have to stop and explain to her that he was about to hurt her for the first and last time. He pressed in further and further, until he was tightly and fully engulfed.

Despite the exquisite sensation, he went rigid with surprise. His body wanted to buck and thrust until he'd emptied himself into her, but he clenched his jaw and held frozen, looking down into her deep green eyes.

"You're not a virgin," he grunted, his self-control poised on a knife blade.

Her mouth parted with her deep, fast breathing, she drew his face down to her again. "Neither are you," she moaned, lifting her hips against his.

"But this—"

"I told you that I couldn't marry you," she said, deep sadness mingling with the desire in her eyes. "But don't leave me yet. Not like this."

"Bloody, bloody hell," he snarled.

She lifted her face to his, kissing him again and again, running her hands down his back to his buttocks and digging in her fingers. "Please," she whispered.

Strong as his will was, the needs of his body were stronger. With a groan, still angry and shocked beyond words, he began moving his hips forward and back, making her his in this moment as deeply and thoroughly as he could. Sarala wrapped her ankles around his thighs, mewling deliciously as his thrusts quickened. Her eyes closed.

"Look at me," he ordered. "I want you to remember who you're with."

Moss green eyes met his again. "I'm with the one I want," she moaned back at him.

She tightened, muffling her mouth against his shoulder as she cried out his name and shattered. His need for delicacy gone, and half swamped by anger, Charlemagne allowed his mind to shut down. He'd wanted her from the first moment he'd set eyes on her, and now in the tight slide of her body around his, he had her. He might not have been her first, but he was damned well going to be her last. Groaning, he pumped his hips harder and faster, again and again, burying his face against her cinnamon-scented neck as with a deep rush he came.

For a long time Sarala just tried to breathe. She held Charlemagne close around his muscular shoulders, not willing or able to let him go. If she did, he might not come back.

Still breathing hard himself, still exquisitely inside her, he lifted his head to look down at her. Gray eyes almost black in the dim candlelight, she thought she could still read his expression. Hurt, and anger.

"Was this all just a ploy so you could marry into the Griffin family?" he finally asked, his voice flat. "Because

Melbourne thought it might be, and I told him that he was being ridiculous."

"What do *you* think?" she asked in return.

He pulled backward, out of her and away from her. The distance physically hurt. "I think I don't like being played for a fool," he said, standing and going after his breeches.

She sat up. "What if I said the same thing? You've obviously been with at least one other woman. More than that, I'd wager. Did you love any of them? *Do* you love any of them? Do you have children?"

"What?" He slammed his clothes back onto the floor, then bent down to pick them up again. "What damned kind of questions are those? I'm a man. I'm supposed to—"

"According to whom?" she returned. Shay liked a good argument. This would simply have to be the best one she'd ever fought. Of course as a Griffin he couldn't—wouldn't—marry her. But being lovers—perhaps for a while they could have that. "And did I not say that I couldn't marry you?"

"Yes, you did say that. And then you practically dragged me in here. Forgive me if I'm somewhat confused."

"I thought this would make matters perfectly clear. Now you can ask Melbourne to extricate both of us from this betrothal."

"So this was a lesson? A demonstration about how ill we suit one another?" He picked up her *kadeez* and threw it at her. "I thought I fit rather well."

Tears stung at the back of her eyes, but she didn't want him to see her cry. "You are only demonstrating that what I said is true. I've been with another man, and therefore I cannot marry a Griffin. I'll find myself a lowly baron or some viscount's nephew who would value my business acumen over my impurity and my sad bloodline."

"That's ridiculous. *You're* ridiculous."

"There is no need to insult me, Shay. I understand the situation quite clearly."

"Be quiet. I'm thinking." He sat on the floor, apparently unwilling to join her on the bed again, and yanked on his breeches.

"Well, we both know I barely have my toe on the line where Society is concerned," she said, unable to keep the sarcasm from her voice.

"You don't toe the line, you mean."

"What?"

"The expression is 'toe the line.' It's from boxing."

"I don't care where it's from." She stood to pull on her *kadeez,* noting that he paused his own dressing for a moment to sweep his eyes along her body. "Just be gentleman enough to help me dress, and then go away."

"No."

Her heart, already bruised, thudded hard. "You won't help me dress?"

"I won't go away."

A tear overflowed her eye and ran down one cheek. "Now you're confusing me."

"I'm still confused, myself," he grumbled. "Who was he?"

"That is none of your business, unless you first care to tell me the names of the women with whom you've been intimate."

"I will do no such thing."

"Then neither will I."

"You," Charlemagne muttered, jabbing a finger at her, "are very vexing, and I would appreciate if you would stop talking for a damned minute so I can think!"

"Why am I vexing to you?" she shot back, putting her hands on her hips and praying no on else could overhear their argument and break the door down. "You've been intimate with other women, so apparently you're now immune to seduction. Why does any of this trouble or confuse you at all?"

"I am not immune to seduction, obviously," he growled, shoving his arms through his waistcoat and buttoning it. He did it wrong, and had to unbutton and begin over again.

"Well, neither am I, idiot. And that's why I led you in h—"

He stopped, facing her again. "What did you call me?"

She flung her arms up, very aware that his gaze had focused on her bare legs. At the moment she wasn't above using anything and everything she had to keep him from leaving the room without at least helping her dress first. "Yes, I've been with a man besides you. *A* man. Once. When I was much younger. I'm not with him now, and I have no wish to be so. I am here, with you, and in case you haven't noticed, I am trying to . . ." Her voice broke, and she cleared her throat, angry. "I am trying to let you know just how much I wanted to be with you, even if I couldn't be so as your wife. If you can't see that I actually did you a favor, then you are an idiot. I - D - I - O -T."

Charlemagne strode up and grabbed her by the arms before she could even gasp. "Who was he?" he demanded again, shaking her.

"That doesn't matter. I thought I loved him, and he was very persuasive. As for tonight, I thought that you would understand . . . wanting to be close to someone. If I was wrong, then I've made another very bad mis—"

He captured her mouth with his. Heat swept down her spine. The kissing, the heat, the desire—this was the easy part. It was the rest of Charlemagne Griffin that aggravated, infuriated, exhilarated, and troubled her. For a moment she gave in, kissing him back hungrily, then pushed away from him.

"You are a confounding woman," he said, running a finger down her bare arm. "And perhaps I am an idiot. I'm not wrong very often, you know."

"I know."

"In the past days, however, you've already caused me to rethink some of my preconceptions about business, and about females. About you, in particular."

She drew a shaky breath. "And?"

"And I would like our betrothal to continue."

"But I'm not . . . pure."

He tilted his head at her. "As you pointed out, neither am I."

Not exactly a definitive declaration of love everlasting, but he'd never used that word with her, anyway. Nor had she said it to him. So it seemed they were back in their previous positions—with one exception. They'd made love, and she'd realized a few things now that she had something to compare her previous experience with. Some things that spoke very favorably about Charlemagne. Tonight, though, didn't seem the time to have that particular discussion.

"What about your family?" she asked slowly.

"This is about us; not them," he countered, grabbing her hand and pulling her toward him again. "But I need a day or two to think. And then we should talk."

"Very well."

As they gazed at each other, she wanted him to kiss her again. She wanted to be in his arms, and hear the passion in his voice. If her stupidity of years past hadn't ruined his opinion of her, did he still want to—could they—actually marry?

Finally Shay cleared his throat. "Let's get you dressed again," he said, "unless you still wish to remain naked."

Relief made her want to sag back onto the bed. "I suppose not," she forced. "The evening's a bit chill."

He snorted, a smile touching his mouth for the first time since he'd peeled her clothes off. "I feel warm enough in your presence, Sarala."

With his somewhat clumsy assistance she managed to get her hair back up, and the *salwar kadeez* on. The sari wrapping was something of a wreck, but she supposed unless an expert in traditional Indian clothing was in attendance, no one else would realize.

His cravat looked little better, but after a few attempts they fluffed it into a tolerable shape. When Shay draped the headpiece and veil over her head, she drew the ends of the fabric across her face and over the hook that held it in place.

"Wait a moment," he said, pulling it loose again. Slowly and gently he kissed her mouth, warm and seductive and full of even more promises she hoped he would keep.

"Is this how you think?" she asked.

"Apparently." He took a step backward, turning to blow out the candles in the wall sconces. "If I still want to marry you, would you still want to marry me?"

He'd asked. He hadn't made a declaration, told her what they needed to do to keep up appearances or avoid a scandal. Warmth flowed into her fingers again. "I don't know," she answered slowly.

Shay nodded. "Then we both have some thinking to do."

Chapter 17

"I've been thinking," Sebastian said, leaning along the billiards table and taking his shot.

"You're always thinking," Charlemagne returned absently from his seat at the card table across the room. "I believe that's why Zach's so frightened of you."

He turned another ledger page, looking for a secure location where he could move the silks and hold them until Emperor Jiaqing's representatives were ready to load them on a ship and return them to China. After all this, he wasn't about to risk the shipment going somewhere else it wasn't supposed to be.

"It's generally the groom's family that holds an engagement ball," the duke continued, moving around the table, cue in hand.

Charlemagne raised his hand. "We talked about this already. And I know how you feel about this business,

Seb. I don't expect you to host a party. I thought I would approach Aunt Tremaine."

"You are not holding your engagement ball at Aunt Tremaine's house. However I feel about the circumstances, you are my brother, and I will do what's proper."

"That's an astonishingly enthusiastic endorsement." With a slight grin he didn't particularly feel, Charlemagne returned to the ledger. Melbourne had a small warehouse just to the south of them. It was a little more than a mile from the Thames and the nearest dock, but it was easily secured and protected.

"We'll need to hold it soon, or it'll look as though we were taken by surprise."

As *he'd* been taken by surprise last night. Charlemagne blew out his breath. He'd encountered the unexpected before, though rarely, but nothing had affected his . . . his heart the way this had. He'd asked for time to think; since then, though, he'd spent most of his time trying to decipher how he'd felt when he'd realized that another man had been with Sarala. And wondering whether he could stand ever feeling that way again. "May I have the use of the warehouse on Half Moon Street for the next fortnight or so?"

The duke faced him. "For the silks? That's a good location."

"Then I'll have Farlow and a half dozen of his people keep a rotating watch. Roberts can coordinate it."

"So now you're all business again? If you've purged yourself of the wish to be married, you need to let me know. Preferably before I host a ball announcing your engagement."

"The *Times* has already run the announcement, thanks to your obsession with propriety."

"Then let's make the soiree a week from Thursday," Melbourne said, otherwise ignoring the sarcasm.

"You might want to consult with Lady Hanover about that."

Melbourne's expression hardened. "I will do no such thing. You're doing that negotiating, as I recall."

"I know for a fact that she has her own ideas about the details of the festivities—and the wedding."

"Mm-hm. And where is that to take place?"

Charlemagne hesitated. It had been an amusing conversation up to this point, but he didn't want to hurt Sebastian. "She mentioned Westminster. I thought St. Paul's would be more appropriate."

"Eleanor married in Gretna Green after an elopement, and Zachary wed in Shropshire to accommodate Caroline's absurdly large family. You should wed at Westminster Abbey."

"I'm a second son."

"You're also my heir presumptive. Westminster Abbey."

"You don't mind, Seb?"

His brother took a breath. "I have nothing but fond memories of my wedding day. I certainly don't wish to tear the church down because Charlotte died four years later."

He was actually talking about it. As far as Charlemagne knew, Sebastian never spoke of Charlotte to anyone but Peep.

"Then Westminster Abbey it is. Thank you."

The duke nodded. "I'll send a letter to that . . . woman and tell her when and where the betrothal ball will be held." He set the cue across the table and walked to the door. "Give me a date sometime before that night, so I can announce it at the party."

Charlemagne frowned. "A date?"

"For the wedding. Unless you intend to get yourself beheaded by foreign swordsmen before then."

"No, I'll try to avoid that." He rose, following his brother into the hallway. "I'm going to inspect the silks and move them from Hanover's warehouse to ours. I thought making certain they're in good condition and protected before I hand them over might be wise."

"Take someone with you. Or I'll go."

"Not necessary. I'll take Timmons and Farlow with his crew and the wagons. And Sarala and her accountant, to make certain I have all the paperwork."

Melbourne hesitated before he vanished into his office. "Is that wise?"

Charlemagne smiled grimly. "You know I'm fairly efficient at taking care of myself. And I'm certainly not going to let anything happen to her." He went to send a note over to Carlisle House, asking if she wished to join him.

"Shay?"

He stopped at the head of the stairs. "Yes?"

"Do you love her? Sarala?"

Heat ran through his chest. "I'm very fond of Sarala. When I come to that moment, you'll be the third person to know."

"Fair enough. Invite her family for luncheon on Wednesday. We'll talk about . . . invitations for the ball." A grimace crossed his face. "And decorations."

Charlemagne chuckled. "Shall I ask Nell over as well?"

"Good God, yes."

A year ago, even a few months ago, he doubted Sebastian would have showed any kind of humor over this at all. Interesting, that. Was Sebastian becoming more human? Or had the onslaught of recent events simply worn him down? Whatever the reason, the change was a welcome one.

"Uncle Shay, I need to talk to you."

He turned around as he sealed the note to Sarala. "I am at your service, Peep."

She strolled into the morning room, brushing at her green muslin skirt as he'd seen Eleanor do on numerous occasions. "I overheard you and Papa upstairs."

Swiftly he ran through the conversation. None of it had been of a particularly intimate or violent nature, thank God. "Yes?"

"I have a disagreement with you."

"Really?" He summoned Stanton to have his note delivered. "About what?" he continued as a servant left the house.

"You can't just decide to be in love, you know."

He frowned, quickly wiping the expression from his face. "I didn't—"

"You told Papa that when you came to the moment when you were in love, you would tell him. That's silly."

"Is it?"

"Yes. You have to *do* some things before you can be in love. It's a proven fact."

"Hm." He moved to the sofa, motioning for her to join him. "Please explain further."

"Very well." She plunked herself down beside him. "When Nell lived here, she and Lady Barbara would sometimes read to one another, and I would go into the room upstairs and listen through the fireplace."

Thank God he'd never brought women to Griffin House. "You shouldn't have done that, Peep."

"How else am I supposed to find out what's going on? Half the time no one tells me anything." She patted his knee. "So you should listen. To be in love, you have to fight a villain, usually with a sword. Sometimes a pistol is acceptable. And then the lady cries, and you beat on your chest or tear your shirt before you sweep her up in your arms." She leaned closer, cupping her hand to his ear. "And then you kiss," she whispered, and straightened again.

"And that's how you fall in love?"

Peep nodded, folding her hands on her lap. "That is how it's done. So you see, you can't just say it. You don't always beat your chest, but since you're the man, you do have to accomplish something heroic. Sometimes, for example, you have to fight a dragon, but I think that might just be a mistake and it's actually a large wolf or a lion or something, because I'm almost positive that dragons are imaginary."

He nodded, clenching his jaw hard to keep from laughing. "Thank you very much. I had no idea."

"I could tell, from what you told Papa. That's why I had to help you."

"So you want me to marry Sarala, then?" he asked, though approval from a seven-year-old seemed a rather pathetic excuse for anything.

"That's why I told you how to be in love." She climbed off the sofa and cobra-charmed her way out of the room.

In a sense, he wished that Peep's litany of requirements for love had been correct. It would certainly be much easier to beat his chest or slay a dragon than to make an intelligent decision—after weighing all the consequences and alternatives—that he was actually in love.

Sarala joined Shay as he walked the perimeter of the new warehouse building. "Tell me again," she asked, "who it is you think might try to take the silks, other than the people to whom you're returning them?"

"I don't know," he said, reaching over to take her hand in his.

She'd noticed that before, that he liked to touch her. Every time he did so now, after what had happened last night, her heart beat faster. "That's not very confidence-inspiring."

"Hm. What I *do* know is that the more people who know about this, the greater the chances are that someone will decide they would enjoy a war with China or an international incident involving my family. All they would need to do is toss a torch onto the roof."

"Hence the dozen armed men lurking about."

"Exactly."

She studied his profile for a moment. Every time she gazed at him warmth rushed through her. After last night, the idea of being married to Charlemagne Phillip Griffin didn't seem so terrible—even with the very high-profile life she would have to live, and the lack of freedom it would entail. Now, though, he was the one who had to decide whether they continued with their betrothal or not. Her behavior had been as unacceptable in Delhi as in London, and of course there would be consequences. Until she knew what the consequences could—would—be, she would have to enjoy this soaring feeling, regardless of whether it was just the result of a very satisfying evening or an anticipation of a life together.

"I'm going with you tomorrow," she stated. "To St. James's Park."

"No, you're not." He gestured at his secretary, Roberts, who hurried over. "Is Farlow clear that no one is to have access to the warehouse without my direct approval?"

"Yes, my lord. He'll have three men here at all times until he hears differently."

"Good."

As soon the secretary left, Sarala pulled her hand free from Shay's. "Do you really think you could stop me?"

"No, but I keep hoping you'll take pity on my overburdened nerves and stay somewhere safe."

She smiled despite her determination not to. "So you're worried about me?"

He took a last look around and started back to the coach with her, holding his hand out to her again. She took it; there didn't seem to be any sense in denying to herself that she craved his touch at least as much as he did hers.

"I'm not so much worried," he answered, "as I am . . . aware. Honestly, when you're anywhere in the vicinity I want to strip your clothes off and make love to you again. It's rather distracting."

"Oh, good heavens." Heat speared down her spine to between her thighs. "Then you've thought about—I mean, you said you wanted a day or two to consider—what you found out—"

"I want to marry you," he said, stopping to face her.

"Is this because you truly want to marry me, or because a Griffin would rather suffer through an unhappy marriage than cause a scandal by calling off a wedding?"

Charlemagne released her hand to summon her coach. She'd annoyed him; she could see that in his still expression. Perhaps she was harping on the same note, but for God's sake, in all her dreams she and her mysterious, unseen husband had been happy. For him the debate might not have signified, but for her it would be a close choice between being ruined and being married miserably.

"Our engagement party is going to be a week from Thursday," he said finally, handing her up into the coach. "Sebastian asked me to set a wedding date before then so he can announce it that night."

"Shay, you can't just ignore this. I want—"

"I told you that I wanted to marry you, Sarala. Take that for what it is: a statement that I would like to spend the rest of my life with you. I don't say such things lightly. In fact, according to my niece I'm taking it too seriously. All I'm supposed to do is fight a dragon and carry you off in my arms."

She lifted an eyebrow. "What?"

"Don't come tomorrow. I'll call on you afterward and let you know how the negotiation went."

He could only do that if he was successful. Sarala grabbed his sleeve. "But what if something happens to you?"

"Then you won't have to worry about my reasons for wanting to marry you," he said, flashing her a grin.

For a moment she scowled at his back, but that obviously wasn't having any effect on his thick head. Blowing out her breath, she sat back in the coach as Jenny and Warrick joined her, the latter informing the coach driver to take them back to Carlisle House.

"What do you think, Mr. Warrick?" she asked him after a moment.

"That Roberts fellow is a bit high in the instep," her father's business manager replied stiffly, "but he seems to have a grasp on events. I could wish that Captain Blink had been more straightforward with me, but considering that those Chinese fellows have threatened to behead him and drag Lord Charlemagne off to China in chains, I think your father will be quite pleased that we extricated ourselves so easily."

Her heart stopped. "What did you just say?"

"I—"

"They want to drag Lord Charlemagne off in chains? He never said anything about that!"

Warrick's cheeks reddened. "Then I apologize. I certainly wouldn't have said anything if—"

"Men," she growled.

Her first instinct was to turn the coach around and confront Shay. She doubted she would get any more information than he'd given her previously, though—she'd learned that much about him, anyway. She could tell herself that she was angry with him for keeping information from her, but beyond that, terror and anxiety pulled at her. If something should happen to him . . .

Sharp worry closed her throat. She'd begun to make friends again because of Shay. She'd begun to find her footing in what was to her a foreign country because of him. Her heart leaped whenever she caught sight of him, and his kisses could curl her toes. She, who'd given up on love before she'd ever turned eighteen, suddenly felt inspired to pursue it again—and that was all because of Charlemagne Griffin. With him, her life would be . . . empty.

"My lady, do we continue?" Jenny asked.

"Yes, we do." She needed to go home and change her gown into something more proper for making a call on someone. And then she needed to go see Eleanor. She hoped the sister would have an insight about how to deal with the brother.

A curricle stood in her front drive, and she frowned as she recognized the bay gelding waiting in the harness. Lord DeLayne seemed to have nothing better to do than pester her father. While Mr. Warrick hurried off to his office, she and Jenny headed for the stairs and her bedchamber. She hoped DeLayne would never know she'd returned home.

"Where did you run off to?" her mother asked, emerging from one of the sitting rooms as Sarala reached the first landing.

"I had to meet Shay about some business," she replied, glossing over the details but pleased that she didn't have to lie about what she'd been doing.

"Well, I have some news for you." The marchioness held up a letter. "Firstly, His Grace the Duke of Melbourne has invited us to luncheon the day after tomorrow to discuss your betrothal soiree and your wedding. Finally that man is seeing reason, and I tell you it's about time. I thought I was going to have to challenge him to a duel to get him to listen to me."

The duke had actually issued an invitation to them? "That's very gentlemanly of him," she offered.

Lady Hanover frowned. "That's all you have to say? As I said before, you have to show more enthusiasm, Sarala. We do not want to appear ungrateful."

"Yes, Mama," she said dutifully, if without much feeling. "I'm very pleased."

"You're impossible. That's what you are. And Lord DeLayne is here to see you. I told him I had no idea where you were or when you would return, but he insisted on waiting. Now *he* is a gentleman. Make certain you invite him to your soiree."

"Yes, Mama. Where is he?"

"Playing whist with your father in the library."

"Thank you, Mama. I'll go see to him." She continued up the stairs.

"And ask him to stay for dinner," the marchioness called after her.

"Yes, Mama."

Both men looked up as she rapped on the open library door. "*Beti*," her father said, smiling. "Is everything in place for tomorrow?"

She just barely refrained from glancing at DeLayne. "Yes, I believe so."

"Splendid. I've been telling John about our adventures."

"Yes," the viscount agreed. "Chinese swordsmen and stolen imperial silk. It's almost too incredible to believe."

Damnation. She'd never expected that her father would be

such an indiscriminate gossip. "The tale is more exciting than the actual event, I'm afraid," she lied, remembering what Shay had said about the dangers of the story spreading.

DeLayne pushed to his feet. "Oh, I don't know about that. But don't worry; no one will hear about any of this from me."

Sarala inclined her head, not feeling particularly relieved. "I'm glad we can count on your discretion."

"Of course. I came to see you this afternoon because I had a letter from Captain Amunford," he continued. "I wondered if I might share it with you."

She liked Charles Amunford, one of the unit commanders stationed in Delhi. "Yes, please."

He gestured her out the door and fell in behind her. "How about the garden? It's a very nice afternoon."

Downstairs Blankman pulled open the front door, and they walked around to the side of the house. "May I see the letter?" Sarala asked.

He cleared his throat. "There isn't one, actually."

She folded her arms, utterly unsurprised. "I didn't think so. Good day, Lord DeLayne." Sarala turned back to the house.

"I wanted an excuse to talk with you, Sarala."

She only stopped because he didn't move after her and didn't try to grab hold of her. "About what?"

With a grimace he sat on a partly rusted metal garden chair. "I wanted you to know that you don't have anything to fear from me."

"I don't fear anything from you, John," she returned, pleased by her own calm, matter-of-fact tone. The six years she'd spent helping negotiate prices for her father's business had definitely stood her in good stead.

"I mean, I think it's grand that you've caught the interest

of a Griffin. You couldn't aim higher than that if you tried. Well done."

"I wasn't hunting or fishing or whatever it is you're metaphorizing. It happened, and I'm very happy." Or she would be, if she could convince herself that Shay wanted to marry her because he wanted to marry her, and that he wasn't merely doing his gentlemanly duty or working to come out the victor in their very personal negotiation.

"And that's why I'm glad for you. And that's why I wanted to assure you that I won't do anything to put a brick in your road."

Sarala didn't move, despite the sudden hard pounding of her heart. "Considering that you've twice mentioned how you won't make trouble, I assume you mean to. What do you want, John?"

He put a hand to his chest. "That's rather unpleasant, Sarala. We're simply old friends, and as such I know one or two . . . personal things about you. Things I would never relate to anyone. I just want to assure you of my discretion. Please don't push me out of your life *because* we're old friends."

"Have I indicated any such thing? I would like us to keep the same relationship we've had for the past two years—not seeing one another." She turned around again and walked back toward the house.

Halfway there DeLayne *did* grab her shoulder. "Don't be difficult," he said, pulling her around. "You know what I meant. You now have a very interesting circle of friends. I only want to be included among them, as I used to be."

She pulled her arm free. "Continue following my father about as you have been, and you shouldn't have a problem meeting a fair number of peers."

The viscount shook his head. "Not good enough."

Her uncertainty began to spin into anger. "Make do, John. I don't want to see you every time I turn around."

"Friends help friends. And now you've become acquainted with the bluest-blooded nobles in London. Without your guidance, I might well end up knowing only the Duke of Melbourne and Charlemagne Griffin, for example. I'd hate to have to spend all my time chatting with them and no one else."

Black panic clawed at her. That was what DeLayne wanted, of course. That was how he did things—charm, and if that didn't work, veiled threats. "Chat with Charlemagne about whatever you choose," she said stiffly. "My only suggestion is that you stand well away from him when you do so. I've seen him box."

DeLayne gazed at her for a long moment. "I suppose we could discuss where we've traveled in our lives, and who has been where. I believe I've been some places well before anyone else, for instance. Whether anyone else has been there after me or not, I don't know."

Sarala struggled to keep breathing evenly. "As I said before, do as you will. Good day." Jaw clenched, she backed away from him.

"He's a Griffin, my love. Do you think he would ever settle for a bundle of used goods? Especially if the rest of London were to discover such a thing?"

That would destroy her relationship with Shay. However staunchly he might wish to stand with her, the rumors would hurt him, and the Griffins. From his heated questions about who her lover had been, she had no idea what he might do in return. Regardless, even the thought of it made her simply want to curl up and die.

"All I ask," DeLayne continued in the same easy tone, as though he hadn't just been threatening to destroy her life, "is that you include me in your next family gathering. And that the next business venture in which the Griffins participate includes me."

Sarala opened her mouth to retort, then closed it again. She wanted to hit him, to tell him to go to the devil. At the very worst she'd thought her poor judgment five years ago might ruin her chances at a marriage her mother could rejoice over. With Shay, she'd found someone whose capacity for reason and logic ran as deeply as his passion and his compassion. She'd been very lucky, very fortunate, and she knew it. Her future was so delicately balanced that a word from either DeLayne or Shay could send her tumbling past all hope.

"Very well," she snapped, turning her back on him so he wouldn't see the tears in her eyes. "I will see what I can arrange."

"And that is all I ask," his smooth voice came. "Please give your father my regrets; tell him I had a tailor's appointment or something."

She walked back to the house numbly, barely pausing to wait for Blankman to open the door for her. Oh, she'd done nothing but make trouble for herself and for everyone around her since she'd stepped off the ship and onto English soil. The most useful thing for her to do would be to vanish, take up life somewhere in the north country as a governess or something. Surely some family would be willing to hire her despite her accent; her dark skin would pale in time.

The door rattled as she stood there in the foyer. Sarala jumped.

"I'll see to it, my lady," Blankman said, pulling the door open yet again.

Charlemagne stood in the doorway, a huge bouquet of red and white roses in his hand.

"Hello," she said.

He smiled, the expression warming the gray of his eyes. "Hello. Are you in?"

"I seem to be." She drew in a hard breath, wishing that she'd had just a little more time to think, and ultimately a little more time to feel happiness and joy before DeLayne ruined everything for her. "Do come in."

"I wanted to apologize for being abrupt this morning," Shay said, handing her the bouquet as Blankman sent for Jenny. Odd, that she still needed a chaperone after all this.

He followed her into the morning room. "You weren't abrupt," she said, trying to regain her usual sense of logic. "We both have several things to cope with at the moment. I do understand." As she took the roses their fingers brushed, and she shivered. "Jenny, will you fetch a vase and some water?"

The maid hesitated in the doorway, then gave a nod and dashed off. Immediately Charlemagne closed the short distance between them to kiss her, deep and slow. She closed her eyes, relishing the perfection of his scent and his touch.

"I feel much better now," he said, stroking the rim of her right ear with his fingers.

"I need to talk to you," Sarala blurted, pushing backward and walking with shaking muscles to the nearest chair.

He stayed where he was. "I'm listening."

She cradled the roses, breathing deeply of their faintly spiced perfume. "I'm changing my mind," she said, lifting her chin. "I won't marry you."

Jenny skidded back to the door just as Shay reached it and closed it in her face. He didn't slam it, of course; being a Griffin, he wouldn't. He did latch it, however, before he strode back to stand in front of her.

"Why not?" he demanded.

Wishing she could at least sound as calm and relaxed as

she had when talking with DeLayne, she set the flowers aside. "Can't you simply be a gentleman and accede to my request?"

Trying for a moment to look beyond his own abrupt hurt and frustration and anger, Charlemagne studied her face, her expression, looking for any clue to what might have happened. Her color was high, her gaze darting everywhere but to meet his, and her hands had clenched the rose stems hard enough to draw blood on the thorns. And yet from that kiss a moment ago he'd thought her finally reconciled to all of this.

"Humor me if you would," he said in a low voice, the best he could manage and still sound in control of himself, "and tell me why you won't marry me."

She cleared her throat. "I've had time now to think about things, and you and I simply do not match well together."

"I can scarcely think of anyone who matches me better, Sarala."

"Well, that's your thinking. Not mine."

God, he wanted a drink. A very strong one. He felt as blindsided as if someone had struck him with a club. But getting drunk would have to wait—he needed all his faculties to figure this out before it was too late. And he thought he knew where to begin. "Did Melbourne say something to you?"

"No! No, of course not."

"Then I don't under . . ." His voice caught. He covered it by pacing to the door and back. "Did *I* say something? Because I certainly didn't intend to injure you in any way, Sar—"

"No! I just don't want to marry you. Now go home."

He caught the shine of tears in her eyes. Moving closer again, he took the seat opposite her. He damned well wouldn't beg, but something was very, very wrong. And he had no intention of leaving without knowing what it might be. "No."

Those same eyes widened. "Shay, you can't do that! If someone says they don't want to get married, the other person has to honor that re—"

"I don't have to do any such thing." Charlemagne folded his arms. If nothing else, maybe he could goad her into a confession. "I'm a Griffin."

"Aha!" She jabbed a finger at him. "That—*that*—is the problem. You think that by virtue of your bloodline you're indestructible, immune to any and all threats and dangers. And that is simply not true."

He felt like giving a triumphant yell, himself. "Which threat am I not immune to?" he asked more quietly.

"Me. Do you have any idea how much damage I could do to you and your family?"

"Yes, I do. None."

"Well, you are very, *very* wrong."

A tear ran down her cheek, but Charlemagne held his muscles rigid to keep from rising to brush it away. He needed an answer to this before . . . before he fell into the chasm inside his chest that her words were ripping open.

"Why don't you explain how that is?"

"Don't make me call for my father, Shay," she shot back, another tear joining the first, "to have you shown out."

"I think you *should* call for him. Or shall I?" He rose, walking as evenly as he could make himself to the door.

"Stop!"

At the absolute misery in that single word he did stop, and turned around to kneel in front of her. "Then tell me what's wrong."

She drew a ragged breath. "But you'll hate me," she whispered.

"Impossible."

"Shay, it isn't—"

He took her hands. For someone with as much common sense as she had, for her to be so upset was unnerving. "Just tell me. If it's as bad as you think, at least it won't be your secret alone."

For several hard heartbeats she stayed silent, but finally she let out a shuddering breath. "What would happen," she said slowly, seeming to have to pull every word from her chest, "if someone who knew something . . . scandalous about me told everyone? And I do mean *everyone*."

"The Griffin name would protect you," he answered. "I would protect you."

"You don't understand. It's not as easy as that. The man with whom I had a very brief . . . affair is in London, and if I don't make introductions between him and the Griffins, if I don't assure that he will be allowed to join in your business and enjoy a share of your profits, then he will tell everyone that you were tricked into marriage with a whore."

He went cold all the way down to his bones. Her eyes, desperate and miserable, watched his, waiting to see what he would say, whether he would look away or frown or simply stand up and leave. "Is . . . does he have any proof that he took your virginity?"

Hope crossed her features so briefly that it might not have been there at all. "Does he need to have proof?"

"Not if he's a believable, honorable-seeming gentleman, which I don't see how he could be if he would threaten you like this."

"He *seems* like a very charming, believable gentleman. That's why I . . . was with him in the first place."

"How old were you?" he asked, running fingers over the back of the tense muscles of her hands.

"Seventeen. It's not entirely his fault, you know. He was older, yes, but he said things I wanted to hear, and I thought I knew everything. And what I didn't know, I wanted him to show me."

"You said you loved him."

"I thought I did. I was very stupid. He wanted what a connection with my father would guarantee him. When I realized that, I told him to go away. He did, but was obviously intelligent enough to keep up the pretense of friendship with everyone involved. And now—"

"DeLayne," Charlemagne ground out.

Her hands jumped. He didn't need any other confirmation but that. The viscount hadn't particularly impressed him, but he supposed to a young English girl living in India, he must have seemed exotic—not a soldier, not employed by the East India Company, but a landowner and a nobleman.

"His identity doesn't matter, Shay. What matters is that if he doesn't get what he wants, he *will* do as he threatens. So the choices are for the Griffins to make him wealthy and important, or for me to distance myself from you before he can do any damage to your family in addition to mine."

"And what would you do once you'd distanced yourself from me?" If he'd been completely mercenary and without any conscience at all, her suggestion would make the most sense as far as the Griffin name was concerned. God, if Melbourne found out, was that what his brother would recommend, too?

"I'd be ruined. If my parents and I returned to India at once, though, Father could hopefully renew some of his business dealings before the news reached Delhi." She gave a grim smile; obviously she'd been thinking this through in her usual logical, intelligent manner. "If you weren't a Griffin, I doubt the news would even travel that far. You're so famous, however, that even *I* had heard of your family before I arrived in London."

This was not going to happen. Not like this, and not for this reason. "You did leave out one alternative," he said in a low voice.

"And what might that be?"

"Dead men can't gossip." He stood, releasing her hands in the same motion. "Any idea where the bastard is staying?"

"Shay! No, this is—you can't be serious! Stop!"

"Don't trouble yourself," he muttered, ignoring her protests, his mind already plotting the deed as he strode to the front door and outside to Jaunty. "I'll be able to find him easily enough." No one threatened his loved ones. Ever. DeLayne was a dead man.

Chapter 18

And Sarala had thought things couldn't get any worse. "Shay!" she yelled, but he and his chestnut horse galloped down the drive without giving any indication that he'd even heard her.

"My lady?" Jenny asked from behind her in the foyer, a vase in her hands and her expression bewildered.

"Jenny. Come with me at once," she said, running down the front steps toward the stables.

"My lady!" Blankman called after her. "What shall I tell—"

"Tell my parents I've gone to dinner with Lady Deverill!" she yelled back, not slowing. "Horton," she continued as she reached the stable, Jenny behind her, "I need a carriage. Now."

The head groom took one look at her face and charged back into the wide open doors of the stable, shouting at his groomsmen to harness up the coach. She would have preferred a curricle or phaeton or something she could drive herself, but as poor as her knowledge of London streets was, that made no sense.

"Where are we going, my lady?" Jenny panted, the vase still clutched to her breast.

Sarala took it, handing it to a passing gardener. "Return this to Blankman," she instructed, and looked back at her maid. Where were they going? She could hunt Shay down, but even if she could find him, she doubted she could convince him of anything now any more effectively than she'd done five minutes earlier. "We're going to Griffin House," she decided. Her own life, her own reputation—none of it would matter if something happened to Charlemagne.

"But Lady Sarala, you're wearing a morning dress. You can't go to Griffin House looking like that."

"Fashion will have to wait." The horses and coach thundered into the yard, Horton himself on the driver's perch. "To Griffin House, at once," Sarala ordered, allowing another of the grooms to hand her and then Jenny into the carriage.

Halfway to Grosvenor Square two additional difficulties occurred to her: first, that the Duke of Melbourne might be elsewhere on a late Monday afternoon; and second, that during the course of one of their brief conversations, DeLayne had given out his address in London to Charlemagne.

"Hurry, hurry," she muttered, leaning forward to look out the window. She couldn't sit by while Shay committed murder on her behalf.

As soon as the coach stopped in front of Griffin House she flung open the door and jumped to the ground. "Please," she said, hurrying up the steps to where the tall, white-haired butler pulled open the front door, "is the duke in? I need to see him immediately."

"If you'll wait in the blue room, my lady, I shall inquire."

She allowed herself and Jenny to be herded into the pretty blue room off the foyer. "At least tell me if he's here," she said, turning in the doorway. "It's very important."

"I shall inquire," he repeated in the same tone, backing out of the room and closing the door behind him.

"Damnation. Idiotic pride and propriety. Don't they know what could be happening right now? Shay could . . ." She couldn't finish the sentence, or the thought. DeLayne had hunted tigers with her father. If he saw Charlemagne coming, she had no idea which of them might end up injured or dead. Her breath choked in her throat. "I can't wait here."

"But my lady, you—"

Sarala strode to the door. "I am not going to sit about and be polite when—"

The door opened just as she reached it. "When what?" the Duke of Melbourne asked.

Thank goodness. She seized his arm. "Your Grace, I need to speak to you in private. At once."

He nodded, sending a glance over her head at Jenny. "Wait here."

Sarala followed him down the long hallway to a large office dominated by an exquisite mahogany desk. Once inside the room, he gestured her to a chair.

"May I offer you some tea?" he asked, leaning back against the front edge of the desk.

Tea? "No, thank you," she said, declining the seat. They didn't have time to chat. "I'm here because I didn't know what else to do. Shay—"

"If you're here with some complaint that you think will cause me to settle more money on your family, I'm afraid you're going to be disappointed. And you can't know already if you're with child."

Sarala blinked, stunned. "What?"

"Shay didn't drag you off unwilling last night. And I won't allow him to be blackmailed or cajoled into—"

"No!" Sarala strode up to him, anger and indignation and embarrassment warring with her growing worry over Shay. Obviously she needed to tell Melbourne what was going on, or he would never surrender his own opinion of her reason for calling on him. "I was indiscreet five years ago," she said bluntly. "With Lord DeLayne. He has now threatened to tell everyone in London and ruin both of our families in the process, unless I guarantee him an inclusion in and profits from your business."

The duke stood, and she had to adjust her stance to look up at him. "And?" he prompted, his eyes ice cold. "I presume this isn't merely for my edification."

"No, it isn't. I told Shay that I wanted to break off our engagement, and advised that he distance himself from me before any of the rumors could begin." She clenched her jaw. "I have no more love for blackmail than you do, nor do I intend to give in to it. Shay guessed that it was DeLayne making the threats, though, and he's gone to find him. He said that a dead man can't gossip." Gulping air, frantic now to get the tale told, Sarala continued before the duke could interrupt. "I won't have Charlemagne pay the price for my mistake. You have to stop him."

Melbourne uttered a single, low curse. "You brought your coach?" he asked, moving around behind the desk and pulling open a drawer. He withdrew a pistol, dropping it into his coat pocket as he strode past her to the door and yanked it open.

Obviously he understood. "Yes."

"Good. It'll attract less attention than mine. Stanton, I'm

going out." As he passed the blue room he leaned inside. "You. Come along."

With a squeak Jenny emerged into the foyer as though propelled by a kick. "My lady, what—"

"You're chaperoning His Grace and me," Sarala said brusquely, following the duke out to her waiting coach.

"Do you know where he's gone?" he asked as he motioned the footman back and pulled the door open himself.

She shook her head. "I don't think he knows where DeLayne is staying. All *I* know is that John is residing with his cousin William Adamsen somewhere in Knightsbridge."

"Adamsen in Knightsbridge. I've met him. He has a minor cabinet posting under Lord Beasley. Get in."

Not taking the time yet to wonder why he wanted her along, Sarala climbed into the coach, half pulling Jenny up behind her. The duke barked an address at Horton and stepped up after them.

"My father probably has DeLayne's address," she offered after a moment. "I didn't think to ask him before I left."

Melbourne nodded from the seat facing hers. "If Beasley doesn't have it, we'll go to your father. At the moment I prefer to keep him away from this, if possible."

"He won't gossip if you ask him not to," she blurted, remembering the Griffins'—and her—previous reaction to his conversation with DeLayne. "It's just that he's been away from England for so long, and he never thought to end up as a marquis. He knows business, not political intrigue."

Gray eyes studied her for a moment. "Your father is friends with DeLayne. If he should hear all of the facts behind this outing, I don't want to have to pull two men off the viscount. Shay will be difficult enough. *That's* why I don't want him included, Lady Sarala."

"Oh." *Stupid, stupid.*

"A few moments ago," Melbourne continued, "you said that Shay 'guessed' that DeLayne was involved. Would you care to elaborate?"

"I'm not sure how many of the details you need to know, Your Grace." Though he'd already guessed a few of them, obviously. The man opposite her was clearly as much a master of intrigue and calculation as Shay. "If you're implying that I invented DeLayne's threats to encourage Shay to take care of my problems, I assure you that that is not the case. Your brother is very stubborn, and when I told him that I'd changed my mind and didn't want to marry him, he refused to simply take me at my word."

"He can be rather single-minded," the duke conceded, a breath of humor touching his voice.

"I told him I would go back to India, and that he could blame any rumors on me. He knew that any scandal would follow me, rather than him and his—your—family. He wouldn't agree, even though we both knew it was the logical course of action to take. I don't need someone else to save me from my own errors." It had been so indescribably . . . nice, though, that he'd offered—insisted really, that he would stand beside her.

"If I may be blunt," the duke said, interrupting her thoughts, "I assume under the circumstances that Charlemagne knows of your . . . indiscretion, as you put it."

Sarala lifted her chin. Soon everyone in London was likely to know about it. She'd best get used to hearing it spoken of. "He knows. He didn't know . . . who, until today. I think that was another reason he was so angry."

"Five years ago. You were what, sixteen?"

"Just seventeen. But DeLayne didn't . . . That is—I knew what I was doing." Honesty made her continue. "I thought

I did." She cleared her throat, knowing she must be scarlet. "That is not what's important, now. I won't have Shay hurt, physically or socially, because I was a stupid girl."

The coach rocked to a stop. Melbourne glanced out the window, then stood. "Beasley's house. Wait here," he said, pushing open the door. "I'll be back in a moment."

Logically Sarala knew that they were proceeding speedily and efficiently. She also knew that Charlemagne would at least have to begin his search for DeLayne randomly, and that she and Melbourne were more than likely closer to finding the viscount than he was. Unless Shay had gone to her father for an address, of course.

"Blast." He wouldn't go to her father; he was too angry, and not thinking logically—or at least not logically for him. Undoubtedly to anyone else involved he would appear to be ruthless efficiency personified.

The duke outside said something to Horton, then opened the door and stepped back up into the coach. "According to Beasley we're less than a mile from Adamsen's residence," he said, knocking on the ceiling as he sat.

The coach lurched into motion again.

Sarala shut her eyes for a moment. *Thank goodness.* Charlemagne had left her house only half an hour ago. Surely he couldn't arrive before they did. Could he? "What do we do if Shay arrives there first?" she asked, opening her eyes again.

Melbourne was gazing at her again. "I don't know. And we have another dilemma."

"You mean DeLayne might not be home."

"That's one possible complication."

"You're right," she muttered, turning her gaze out the window at the rows of passing houses. "If Shay *isn't* there, how long do we wait for him? And can we risk going to look for *him,* when at any moment he might arrive to kill DeLayne?"

"We might remove DeLayne from his residence and return him with us to Griffin House," the duke suggested.

Sarala frowned. "Considering what the viscount seems to do with the information he acquires, I don't think informing him of Shay's intentions would be very wise."

"That's not precisely what I meant."

Gasping, Sarala looked down to the pocket of the duke's coat, where his pistol rested. "I won't allow you to kill DeLayne, either."

"You would protect him, then?"

"I would protect *you.*"

He lifted an eyebrow. "I hardly think that's necessary."

It seemed arrogance and obstinance ran deep in Griffin veins. "Men," she sputtered. "If you think for one minute that I would allow anything to happen to Shay or to the people he cares about because of me, you are *very* much mistaken, Your Grace."

"Oh, dear," Jenny whispered, pressing as far into the corner of the coach as she could manage.

"For the moment I'll refrain from asking how you would prevent me from taking action," Melbourne said, crossing his arms. "What I had in mind, however, wouldn't involve murder or kidnapping as much as it would involve cooperation."

She looked at him. "You . . . you can't be saying you would give in to DeLayne's threats."

"I'm saying I would appear to do so, at least for the moment. But I will need your assistance."

If DeLayne believed they would all fall into line with so little resistance, it would certainly give them time to develop a plan. "To gain myself some time to think earlier," she said slowly, "I told him I would do what I could to gain him access to your wealth."

"That's handy." The coach stopped again. "I doubt he would risk joining us in here, however, whether he believed you or not."

"If Jenny went to see him with a message, though," Sarala took up, "I imagine he wouldn't waste any time getting himself to Griffin House." She stopped. "If you're certain you want to do this, Your Grace. I have been reminded several times of your abhorrence for scandal of any kind."

"Have you, now?" he asked dryly.

"I could just as easily walk in to see DeLayne myself and tell him I've called off the wedding and am returning to India with or without my parents." She meant it, too, and hoped the duke realized that. She willed him to understand that she was serious. Whatever happened, she wouldn't allow the Griffins to suffer for her mistake.

"I believe that action would cost me a brother," he said crisply, and faced Jenny. "Your mistress has sent you to see Lord DeLayne and inform him that she's spoken with the Duke of Melbourne. Rather than allow a scandal," he went on, glancing at Sarala, "the duke is willing to come to terms—but only if the viscount comes to Griffin House immediately to meet with him. Can you tell him that?"

To her credit, Jenny didn't hesitate before she nodded. "What if he should ask me what the terms are, Your Grace?"

"You don't know what they are, but you do know that I'm not very happy."

Jenny's shoulders heaved. "I can do that, Your Grace."

"Then do so at once. We may not have much time. Shay's a resourceful fellow. We'll wait for you there," he continued, pointing, "around the corner."

The maid stood as Melbourne opened the coach door for

her. "Oh, dear. What if Lord Charlemagne should arrive while I'm there?"

"Duck."

Damned DeLayne hid himself as well as a rat in a sewer. Charlemagne didn't mind the hunt; with each passing minute his anger deepened into a thick, simmering miasma just under his skin. Not only had DeLayne taken advantage of Sarala's naivete five years ago, he was trying to use her own sense of honor against her now. The bastard had nearly taken her away—and that could not be allowed to happen.

After an hour of searching, he turned up at Adamsen's house and spoke to a maid who was all too happy to inform him that her master's cousin had been summoned to Griffin House. Whatever the devil was going on, Melbourne would not be allowed to step into the middle of this.

As he reached Griffin House, he spotted both DeLayne's curricle and the Carlisle coach. Had Melbourne summoned Sarala, as well? Had DeLayne said something about her? His heart pounding, Charlemagne handed Jaunty over to Timmons and strode up the shallow front steps.

The door opened as he reached it. "My lord," Stanton said, stepping aside.

"Where's DeLayne?" he asked, yanking off his coat and hat and throwing them aside.

"In the blue room, my lord."

"Good. Leave us be." He walked to the door and stepped inside. "De—"

Someone shoved him hard from behind. As he stumbled, the door slammed and the key turned in the lock behind him. "Stanton!" he roared, charging the door and hitting it with all his weight. It groaned, and he heard something crash to the floor out in the hallway. *Good.*

The door at the other end of the room was locked as well. Well, that wouldn't stop him. Not when he was this close to killing that devil. Charlemagne picked up the writing desk chair and headed for the largest of the front windows. As he raised the chair over his shoulder, the door rattled and opened again.

"Shay! Put that down."

He did, none too gently. "I know you're not stepping into the middle of my business, Melbourne," he snarled, heading straight for his brother and the open door beyond him.

The duke put out his hand. "No, I'm not. But you need to listen for a moment."

"I've listened all I intend to today. Get out of my damned way."

"Don't you want to know why he's here?"

For a second he allowed himself to wonder, then pushed the question away again. "Get out of the way, Melbourne. I'm not going to say it again."

His brother stepped aside. Eyes narrowed and his breath hard and fast, Charlemagne pushed past him—and stopped. Just beyond the duke, Sarala stood, her eyes wide and worried.

"What—"

She moved up to him, grabbing his clenched hand and pulling him back into the blue room. "I'll tell him," she said over her shoulder, her gaze not leaving his face.

With a nod Sebastian closed the door again, leaving them alone in the room. Charlemagne pulled his hand free. "Tell me what?" he snapped.

"You have to stop and listen to me," she returned, her own voice clipped.

"I'm already rather angry," he said in a low voice, still pacing. "I'm not certain I want to know what you've done."

"Listen anyway," she countered. "When you left my home, I came to see your brother."

"And why is that, pray tell?"

"Because I didn't want you to kill DeLayne."

That was exactly what he *didn't* want to hear—that Sarala had a reason, any reason, for wanting to protect that bastard. "What did you think would happen after what you told me?"

"I thought you would let me go, idiot."

That shook him a little. "That's the second time you've called me an idiot," he ground out. "Explain."

"If you kill DeLayne, you could be sent to prison, or hanged, or transported. I won't let that happen to you."

"I'm not letting you go back to India for *any* damned reason. So I think we're at an impasse."

"No, we're not. As I said, I talked to your brother. I told him everything."

" 'Everything.' " Hot anger began turning to cold dread. Melbourne knew about a threat of scandal. A threat through Sarala, for whom he didn't feel any particular affection. Charlemagne would not let her be sent away, whatever his bloody brother decided. At worst, he would go with her. "And what was Melbourne's suggestion?" he asked, his voice shaking.

"We're still working on that. At the moment, the plan is to pretend cooperation with DeLayne until we can determine just how greedy he is, and how much risk he might be willing to take to get what he wants."

His breath left him with a rush. Charlemagne sat in the chair he'd nearly smashed. "I don't understand."

Sarala walked carefully closer. "What don't you understand?"

"Sebastian wouldn't do this."

"But he is. It was his idea, in fact. And if you can assist us, we could certainly use your help."

"How can you stand to be in the same room with him?" he asked, looking up and meeting her gaze for the first time since she'd surprised him in the doorway.

"Because I don't want to have to leave London," she whispered, and a tear ran down her cheek.

His heart thudded in his chest. That did it. Slowly, working to rein in his rampaging temper, jamming his anger and his surprise back down to where he could control it, Charlemagne stood. "What do you need me to do?" he asked.

She swept forward and wrapped her arms around his shoulders. "I don't know," she said, her voice muffled against his neck. "We've been trying to get him to drink and not punch him while we waited for you."

For a long moment he stood with his arms around her, breathing in the cinnamon scent of her hair, before he slowly extricated himself. "Let's go plan something, then," he murmured, shifting his grip to her hand.

"You won't kill him?" she whispered.

"I won't kill him *right now*."

Chapter 19

John DeLayne set aside his glass and stood as Charlemagne entered the Griffin House drawing room with Sarala. Shay saw the viscount dart his eyes toward the poker resting in the fire as they approached.

The bastard would be dead before he ever reached it. Charlemagne half wished he would make the attempt, but after waiting a second for something to happen, he nodded and gestured the viscount back to his chair.

"What have you been chatting about?" he asked, glancing across the room at his brother as he walked to the liquor cabinet and poured himself a generous drink.

"Business," Melbourne answered from his position by the window.

"Any in particular? What do you fancy, DeLayne?"

The viscount cleared his throat, pushing forward in his chair. "I'm glad you asked that, Lord Charlemagne. The—"

"Call me Shay," Charlemagne broke in.

"Shay, then. The Marquis of Hanover happened to mention that you've entered into some sort of dealings with the emperor of China. That you even have Prinny and Liverpool involved. This is exactly the kind of trade I'm looking to be involved in. High-profile, prestigious, and clearly lucrative."

"That's not—"

"Interesting that you should choose that one," Charlemagne said, cutting his brother off. It was a pity he hadn't had more time to develop a relationship with Yun and the other soldiers—if he could convince them that DeLayne had been behind the theft rather than Blink, he would consider that a good day's work. Still, there were several possibilities, and some very sharp-looking weapons. "We're meeting with the Chinese buyers tomorrow."

"That's what Hanover said. I think I'll join you."

"Very well."

Charlemagne wanted so badly to put a fist into DeLayne's face that passing by him without doing so was actually painful. He stopped by Sarala, brushing her elbow with his hand, seeking control from her appearance of calm. "Our meeting will be at noon tomorrow, just west of the pond in St. James's Park. Don't be late, DeLayne. They place a very high importance on promptness."

The viscount nodded. "And what will my role be? I don't relish standing in the background and going unnoticed."

"I'll make certain they know you're our partner," Charlemagne assured him. "And dress well—they admire wealth and ostentation."

"That sounds simple enough. What about profit?"

"We haven't agreed on all the details yet," Melbourne put in, walking to the drawing room door and pulling it open, "but as you said, it looks to be very lucrative. For all of us, of course."

DeLayne, unmoving, sipped his claret. "Of course."

"And in return, we will have your silence, yes?" the duke continued.

"Yes. Why would I wish to harm my business partners?"

Beside Charlemagne, Sarala began shaking. "I'm going to kick him," she breathed, starting forward.

He put out a hand, gripping her wrist above her tightly clenched fist. At least he wasn't the only one beyond fury at both DeLayne's arrogance and his pomposity. "If you'll excuse us," he said, facing the viscount again, "we have a few things to attend to. We're planning a wedding, you know."

DeLayne stood. "I understand. But don't attempt to cross me, or to cut me out of this, or you will regret it."

Beside the open door, Melbourne stiffened. "I am a man of my word," he drawled. "Stanton, will you see Lord DeLayne to his carriage?"

The butler appeared in the doorway. "Right away, Your Grace."

"And I'll see you tomorrow at noon." DeLayne nodded at Sarala. "My thanks, my dear. I knew you would be profitable."

Charlemagne charged the door, but Melbourne closed it just before he reached it. "If this is going to succeed," the duke said, "you are going to have to control your temper."

"I am controlling my temper," Shay snarled.

"So your plan is to make DeLayne overdress for the Chinese, and have him appear an hour late?"

"Yes, that's exactly my plan, since you seem to have an objection to my killing him." Charlemagne took a deep breath. "Since I, for one, can't think of anything more absurd-sounding than a trio of Chinese swordsmen descending on London, and since we will have to discredit DeLayne if I *can't* gut him and toss him into the Thames, the best I could come up with in two minutes is to combine the two."

For a long moment Sebastian looked at him. "I think it's fortunate that we're brothers," he finally said, "because I shudder at the thought of ever going up against you in a fight."

"I'd still rather kill him," Shay said, meaning it.

"There's always time for that if your plan doesn't work." As they heard the front door open and close again downstairs, Sebastian pulled open the drawing room door once more. "We still don't have much time. I'm going to summon some reinforcements. I hope you'll be staying for dinner, Sarala."

Sarala looked from one Griffin to the other. Her head was spinning, the circumstances were changing so quickly. "I'll have to send a note to my parents," she said, "but I doubt they'll object."

"Hold off on that for a bit," the duke returned. "We may wish to have them here, as well."

With a nod he left the room. She looked at Shay, who was gazing at her intently. "What is it?" she asked.

"You went to Melbourne."

"I told you that I had."

He closed the door with one foot while he yanked her up against him and lowered his mouth over hers. Sarala closed her eyes as heat washed over her. She'd nearly lost all this today, before she'd figured out exactly how much it—he—was coming to mean to her.

"You risked our betrothal," he continued, turning them so she was pressed between him and the door. His hands twisted into her skirt and lifted the material above her knees and past her thighs, bunching it at her waist.

"Because that was better than risking you," she returned unsteadily, kissing him hungrily, reaching down to unfasten his breeches and fumbling to pull his shirt free.

"But I won't risk losing you," he breathed, shoving his trousers down. He lifted her up, guiding her legs around his hips. Slowly he pushed forward, impaling her with his hard, engorged manhood.

Pinned between him and the door, Sarala could do nothing but hold on to his shoulders, moaning as he thrust into her, filling her again and again. She could feel the remnants of anger in him, feel as they slid into fire that seared her heart. That had been his one and only worry, that he would lose her.

With a gasp she shattered, clinging to him as he continued to ravage her. "Shay, Shay," she murmured, no breath left in her body.

A low, guttural growl burst from his chest as he gave a last, deep thrust and held her to the door. She felt his shudder all the way through to her bones. They had to do something. This man aroused her mind and her body like no one ever had and ever would. Whatever hesitation she'd felt about joining with him was gone. If after all this they had any choice in the matter at all, she was not going to give him up. Ever.

Melbourne's reinforcements began to arrive within the hour. Charlemagne watched from the window of the billiards room as first Zachary and Caroline, closely followed by Deverill and Nell, emerged from coaches and hurried into the house. To the outside world it would look like another of the frequent Griffin family gatherings; only those inside knew that there was nothing typical about it.

"Are you hiding?" Sarala asked, stopping at his shoulder.

He shook himself. "No. I'll let Melbourne give them the

background information. I'm still trying to decide how best to handle DeLayne." And he didn't want to hear whatever comments the rest of his family would be making about Sarala and her poor judgment, and then him and *his* poor judgment in compromising her.

"You're hiding me, then. I'm not a fool, you know. I haven't been for several years."

"That's not it. They will probably want to know the reason we have to take DeLayne's threats seriously, though. Melbourne can tell them that story."

"You know, back then my eyes were clouded with flattery and promises of things I don't even remember any longer. Now my eyes see quite clearly what I'm doing. And what I'm willing to do to make amends."

"Sarala, you frighten me a little, do you know that?"

With a nod she leaned over the billiards table and made another shot, sinking two balls. "I like this game," she said with a slight grin. Her eyes remained serious, though. They both knew what was at stake here.

"Are you certain you've never played before?" he asked, moving around to the far side of the table to watch her line up her next shot. Who would have guessed: Sarala Carlisle was a billiards fiend.

"I've watched, but I hadn't realized how mathematical it all is. Fascinating." She made another proficient shot, then straightened. "Jenny and I will be fine in here," she said, indicating her maid sitting in the corner. "Go talk to your family."

Still thankful that Melbourne had banished Jenny to the kitchen during their negotiation with DeLayne, Charlemagne reluctantly set his billiards cue back into the rack. He walked up to Sarala and kissed her deeply, ignoring the maid's gasp and drawing strength from her boundless spirit.

"The library's right next door, and you can ring for Stan—"

"I won't flee," she interrupted. "But don't think I'll sit by while the lot of you decide what to do about John without my participation, either. I'm staying in here for your benefit."

"I've learned the wisdom of not trying to exclude you from a plan, princess."

She sighed. "I don't feel as much like a princess today as I do a rampaging elephant in a house made of glass."

Charlemagne chuckled as he pulled open the door. "You're *my* princess."

Downstairs he could hear muffled conversation emanating from behind the morning room door. With a wary glance at Stanton to make certain he wasn't going to be tackled and thrown into the pantry, he knocked and pushed open the door.

"How far along are we?" he asked.

Five pairs of eyes looked at him, three gray, and the other two dark green. Interesting that the Griffins seemed to favor green-eyed mates. His own green-eyed, exotic princess had become an obsession; he would risk losing everyone in this room for her.

Eleanor rose from her seat and walked up to kiss him on the cheek. Surprised and relieved, he hesitated only a second before he returned the gesture. "That's not quite the greeting I expected," he conceded as she released him.

"I knew I didn't like DeLayne," she said, scowling as she said the name. "And now I know why."

"What's the plan, then?" Zachary took up, standing himself and offering Shay a deep bow.

"That's enough of that, you muggins."

"Mm-hm. Insult me all you like, big brother; I'm not the one with a blackmailer chasing me about."

"That's the thing," Melbourne interrupted from his chair

closest to the fireplace. "We all have a blackmailer. DeLayne's threatened all of us. And while the damage to us would probably be negligible, that wouldn't be so for Shay, and especially for the Carlisle family—and it would be worse for them *because* of their connection to us."

Charlemagne's jaw tightened. "I'm sorry for the tangled web," he said stiffly, "but I'm not going to separate myself from Sarala because of it."

"I didn't expect that you would," the duke returned, gesturing for him to take a seat. "But I do want to make clear precisely what the situation is. That being said, perhaps you'd care to elaborate on your plan to put that frig pig out of our misery?"

"*Sebastian,*" Eleanor exclaimed.

The duke raised an eyebrow. "You think I can't be vulgar simply because I generally choose not to be?"

"I think a bit of vulgarity is rather called for," Deverill said, speaking for the first time since Charlemagne had entered the room. "Seb said the royster wants to be part of your Chinese dealings. Do you think you can convince them to lop off his head?"

"I have a few ideas," Charlemagne said, "but first I have to say that I'm a little . . . surprised that you want anything to do with this. You especially, Sebastian. I mean, it's not as if DeLayne would be lying."

"What the devil makes you think we wouldn't wish to help you if and when you found yourself in trouble?" Melbourne retorted. "We don't abandon Zachary when he gets into some difficulty."

"Yes, but Zach's always blundering about."

"I say!" Zachary put in mildly. "That's all very nice, isn't it? I think the point, Shay, is that, yes, you generally toe the line. You're the steady one, the smart one. But I for one am a bit relieved to see that you're not an abacus. I like your Sarala, and she shouldn't have to pay now because some shocking bad hat tricked her when she was a girl."

From the nods of the others, Zachary had merely spoken aloud the sentiments they all felt. For a moment Charlemagne stood there, unable to speak. He knew how supportive his family was, how close they all were, but it warmed his heart deeply to see how staunchly they were willing to stand with him in the face of a possible scandal, and even after he'd practically forced them to admit Sarala into the family. "Thank you," he said finally.

"Well, get on with the plan, then," Deverill drawled. "I want to do something nefarious. It's been at least a fortnight for me."

"I'll get Sarala, then," Charlemagne said. "She's got a few ideas, herself."

"Why didn't you bring her in here in the first place?" his sister asked.

"She wanted all of you to be able to speak your minds."

"You stay here," Nell countered, pulling Caroline to her feet. "We'll fetch her. She should know that we're here to help."

"She's in the billiards room," he said over his shoulder as the two women left the morning room.

"So what about killing the bastard?" Deverill asked as the door closed. "We're not overlooking that option, are we?"

"Someone would have to take the blame," Melbourne returned smoothly, "and I prefer that none of the suspicion fall on us. With Shay's plan there will be some gossip, but it should for the most part be in our favor and otherwise harmless to everyone concerned—except for DeLayne."

"There is the possibility that whatever we plan won't work. If it doesn't, everyone connected with me will feel the sting." With the scheme they were about to embark on, the family needed to realize how possible a negative outcome would be.

Melbourne held his gaze for a moment. "Then we'll find butter to soothe the burns," the duke finally said. "I had a rather long chat with Sarala while we were hunting down DeLayne. She may be an outsider, but I can easily see her as a Griffin." He cleared his throat. "I'd be happy to see her as one, Shay."

Today had been full of surprises. He'd known Sebastian for all of his own twenty-eight years. It didn't seem possible that he could be learning something new about him after all this time, but that was precisely what had happened.

Sarala glided into the room, Nell and Caroline with her. Her green gaze met his, and he smiled, offering his hand. "I almost pity DeLayne," he said, drawing her close. "He doesn't stand a chance."

Charlemagne watched Sarala trying not to pace. The population of St. James's Park at eleven o'clock on a Tuesday morning consisted mainly of governesses with their charges, and a bevy of gardeners. He'd selected the park for its fairly sparse population, and because it would be difficult for anyone to approach unseen. It looked as though he'd chosen well.

"You look worried," Sarala said from beside him.

"I am worried. Do you know how much of my plan relies on gaining the cooperation of three men who've threatened to drag me off to China in chains? Or worse?"

"Hence *my* worry. This is such a bad idea, Shay."

"You contributed your share of ideas to it," he said, eyes on the area around the pond. He took a moment to look over at her. "And given the alternative, I'm willing to accept the risk that things might go wrong." He put an arm across her shoulders, wishing he could protect her from DeLayne as easily as he could from the cool breeze. "Besides, you wanted to be here today, and here you are." His muscles tightened as he glanced toward the pathway again. "And here *they* are."

The three Chinese soldiers appeared from around a stand of drooping willow trees. "Shay, we could escape together to India," she whispered abruptly.

"Sarala, I—"

"I know, I know. You could never leave your family or your business."

"I wouldn't give DeLayne the satisfaction of besting me without a fight. Now wait here for a minute," Charlemagne said, releasing her. "If everything goes well, I'll nod, and you come forward. If it doesn't go well, then—"

"Then you'll cross your arms, and I'm supposed to run. I remember the signals, though I doubt I could outrun those men in this dress."

"Don't forget that Zach and Valentine and their muskets are in the trees behind us. Run in that direction."

"I will." Sarala took his hand and squeezed his fingers. "Just make certain everything goes well," she whispered.

"I will," he repeated, and strolled over to the pond to meet Yun and his two companions.

"Griffin," Yun said, bowing.

"Yun. Have you discussed with your companions how we should proceed?"

"We have. And we are all very distressed by the gravity of the crime committed against our emperor."

"As am I. What are your recommendations?"

"A personal apology from your Regent would do much to calm His Eminence's wrath. And a gift of respect might enable our two nations to remain friends."

Charlemagne nodded. He'd expected as much. "I believe

I can arrange for both of these. And of course for the return of the silks."

"Our ship leaves for China in ten days," Yun continued. "All must be accomplished by then."

"And what of Captain Blink?"

"He remains a thief, and will pay the penalty for being one."

Damn. Their refusal to make a concession about Blink didn't bode well for what he needed to ask of them next, but he had to give it a try, nevertheless. "I understand."

"And what are your demands, then?"

"Demands? There was a theft, and I'm in the position to return the items and recompense the owner for the inconvenience. I have no demands." He pulled a piece of paper from his pocket and handed it over. "There's the address of the warehouse. My men are guarding it to be certain the silks remain safe."

The soldier looked at him. "I may have been mistaken in my estimation of the English."

Not all of them. "Yun, I do have a *request* to make of you and your companions."

Yun cocked his head. "What kind of a request?"

"I have no right to ask it, and I would consider anything you could do to be a personal favor to me."

"And if I decline?"

"Nothing. I've given you my word about the return of the silks and the gesture from Prince George. That won't change, regardless."

"Then what is this request?"

Charlemagne cleared his throat, his hesitation only partially feigned. "There is a man, a lord, who has threatened to tell certain tales about my family. These stories are true, but they are private, and of no one's concern but ours. Nevertheless, they could be very damaging—to one young lady in particular."

"We are not assassins for another man's cause, Griffin."

"I know that. What I need to do is discredit this man, so that no one will listen to the tales he tells. You are in a perfect position at the moment to assist me with that."

To his surprise, Yun grinned. "That is the lady, yes?" he asked, gesturing at Sarala.

"Yes."

"She is ready to come rescue you now if we should attack?"

Charlemagne smiled. "Most likely."

"This man, he stole from her?"

"He dishonored her."

Yun turned and said something in Chinese to his companions. After a moment of conversation, he faced Charlemagne again. "What is your plan?"

Thank God. Charlemagne faced Sarala and nodded. With a visible lowering of her shoulders she approached. "First of all," he said, "this man, John, Lord DeLayne, will be here in approximately thirty minutes. He is using the threats of these stories to tangle himself into my business. Into *our* business, with no regard as to how important it is to both our countries. He wants profit, and he wants recognition."

"I think I understand," Yun returned, sending Sarala an intent look as she reached them. "You wish to catch him in his own web."

"Exactly. Lady Sarala, this is Yun. Yun, my wife-to-be, Lady Sarala."

"Ah. Now I see all."

Sarala bowed much as Yun had when the soldiers had arrived. "Thank you so much for helping us. I don't think anyone else in England could do it."

"What do you require, my lady?"

"We need you to offer us some porcelain vases in exchange for the silks," she said, beginning the plan they'd outlined last night. "Vases that we will provide, of course. And a large ribbon of honor for Lord DeLayne to wear in exchange for his assistance in this highly important matter."

"And ultimately," Charlemagne put in, "we will need you to cut off my head."

Chapter 20

John DeLayne arrived at St. James's Park in his cousin's coach. Sarala narrowed her eyes as he came down the carriage steps and approached them. He'd done as Charlemagne requested and arrived both promptly at noon and attired in his very best evening wear.

"Remember," Shay said in a low voice, "we're not happy to have him here sharing the profits, and especially not taking the lion's share of the glory."

"I don't have to pretend being unhappy about him," Sarala answered, settling for a mild glare at John.

"Are your Chinese swordsmen not here yet?" the viscount asked as he reached them. "I thought they valued timeliness."

"They do," Shay said, keeping his voice low. "If I'm not mistaken, they're in those trees watching us." He indicated the stand of trees where Zachary and Lord Deverill continued to hide, though Sarala imagined their firearms were now pointed at DeLayne rather than anyone else.

"How many of them are there?" the viscount asked, taking a step to put Sarala between the trees and himself. "Hanover said three."

"I reckon at least a dozen," Charlemagne returned, from the clench of his jaw noting just where DeLayne had moved and why. "Keep your eyes open. They're suspicious devils, and I cannot figure out how to gain their respect."

The Duke of Melbourne, who'd been standing closer along the pathway some distance away from them, came forward. "They're on their way. I still think this is a mistake, Shay. If they don't like your price or your conditions, they may just take your head off."

"Yes, but if they *do* like conducting business with the Griffins, we'll make a fortune. You saw that vase the one with the scar showed us. Lord Yun."

"It would be easier," the duke put in, "if they weren't convinced that the lot of us stole those silks. Getting them to pay for their return—that's a risk I'm still not convinced we should take."

While DeLayne followed the brothers' conversation intently, Sarala took a moment to study him. Last night Lord Deverill, especially, had seemed to have a grasp on what to look for as evidence that the viscount was becoming "entangled," as he'd put it. And she saw all the signs already this morning—the way his gaze darted from one Griffin to the other, the repeated licking of his lips as though he could already taste the spoils of success.

"You're always sure of yourself," Melbourne was saying. "I just hope you realize the ramifications of failure."

"Shh," Sarala interrupted, "They'll hear you."

An open wagon, a tarp thrown over the back, stopped parallel to them on the riding path. The one Shay had introduced to her jumped to the ground, his sword flashing in the sunlight as he sheathed it at his waist. The other two waited with the cart, their unconcerned gazes on the proceedings, as if they truly did have a dozen men hidden in the undergrowth.

"Lord Yun," Charlemagne said, bowing reverently.

"I have no time for pleasantries, thief," Yun growled. "Where are Emperor Jiaqing's silks?"

"They're safe. Do you have our payment?"

"Payment, ha. You should call it a ransom. This will mean war between our nations, you know. And you will be the first to die."

Heavens. Yun could give Edmund Kean a lesson or two in acting. No wonder DeLayne looked rather taken aback; Sarala was half ready to run for help, herself.

"Look, Yun," Shay snapped back, "we don't have to give you the bloody silks at all. I could have them cut into rags or saddle blankets."

Yun drew his sword. "Infidel!"

"Do something," Melbourne whispered urgently at DeLayne, nudging him forward. Charlemagne gave Sarala a quick wink as the viscount stumbled into the forefront.

"Gentlemen!" John squeaked, his voice wobbling. "If there's bloodshed, no one will get what they want!"

"Who are you?" Yun demanded, pausing in his attack.

"I am John, Viscount DeLayne. I'm here to see that everything proceeds smoothly and fairly."

The soldier took in the viscount's over-elegant attire. "Did your Regent send you to negotiate?" he asked.

"Tell him yes," Shay whispered, dodging behind John and away from Yun's sharp sword.

DeLayne threw him a contemptuous glance. "No, he did not. I very much doubt that His Highness has any idea what these men are up to."

Yun lowered his sword an inch or so. "Then why are you here, and dressed so fancily?"

"I believe these men meant to make a fool of me, or of you by convincing you that I *do* represent His Majesty," the viscount returned. "I don't think they have much liking for either of us. You would prevent them from selling the silks, while certain of their family have behaved dishonorably, and I have knowledge of it."

"Then I will conduct Emperor Jiaqing's business with you," Yun stated, sheathing his weapon.

"For a fair recompense, of course," John said, displaying his smooth, charming smile.

Yun inclined his head. "Of course."

"Wait a damned minute," Shay burst out. "*I'm* the one who arranged this meeting."

"And if it goes ill, *you* will pay the price." The Chinese soldier kept his hand on his sword hilt to emphasize the threat. "Where are the silks?"

The viscount faced Charlemagne. "I suggest you tell him, Shay. This man doesn't care about your pedigree."

With a curse, Shay gave the address. "A warehouse. Number nine, Half Moon Street."

Yun called out something in Chinese to his companions by the wagon, and they cheered. "Finally, an Englishman who is a gentleman," he continued, facing DeLayne again.

"And now where is our porcelain?" Charlemagne demanded from his place safely behind John.

The soldier motioned toward the wagon. The younger of his two companions reached under the tarp and pulled out an exquisite-looking vase in blue and yellow and green. He brought it to Yun, who hefted it in his hands and then passed it to the viscount.

"Just a damned minute, you bloody savage," Shay sputtered.

"There are two dozen vases of the same quality inside the wagon," Yun said, ignoring the outburst. "We will leave a like amount at the warehouse in trade for the silks at eight o'clock tonight. They are all yours, Lord DeLayne. Do with them what you will."

DeLayne bowed. "My thanks, Lord Yun. I'm glad I could see justice done."

Moving with lightning speed, Yun reached around the viscount and grabbed Charlemagne by the lapels, dragging him forward. "You and I, Griffin, had best not meet again. If there is one bolt of silk missing, I will take your head back to the emperor as compensation." Releasing Shay, he took a step back to stand eye to eye with DeLayne. "This is for you, Lord DeLayne, by order of the Blessed One, Emperor Jiaqing."

From the loose folds of his silk shirt he produced a wide red and silver ribbon garnished with a huge ruffle of yellow silk in the shape of a rose. With great ceremony he placed it over the viscount's head and under one arm.

"All who see will know that you are a revered member of Emperor Jiaqing's personal Dragon Guard," Yun said reverentially, "the first Englishman ever so honored."

"Thank you, Lord Yun. I *am* most honored."

Sending a last hard glare at Charlemagne, Yun and his men departed, leaving the laden wagon behind. Once they were out of sight, Shay lunged at DeLayne, only to be pulled bodily back by his older brother.

"Enough, Shay. He very likely saved your life."

"And don't you forget that," DeLayne said, practically preening as he looked down at his ribbon. Caroline and Eleanor had outdone themselves with its manufacture.

"What about our profits?" Charlemagne asked, shrugging free of his brother's grip. "Yun just gave everything to our glib friend, here."

With a smile, DeLayne handed the duke the vase he still held. "Have this one. The rest are mine. What did you say they were worth?"

"About eighty or ninety guineas each. That's not what we agreed on for any of th—"

"Then that's my price today for keeping quiet about Sarala's . . . indiscretion." He walked to the wagon, pulling back the tarp to reveal twenty-three additional vases. "And I'll collect the rest tomorrow morning from the warehouse."

"At least we won't have to see him tonight at the Ellis soiree," Sarala said, just loudly enough for him to hear. "As if we want him parading his honors about in front of everyone."

"Shh," Shay cautioned.

DeLayne turned around. "By the by, I think we should all celebrate the return of the silks to China. I'll join you at the—what was it, Sarala—the Ellis soiree? Please inform Lady Ellis that I am your guest."

Melbourne stepped forward. "Just remember, DeLayne, that the deal's not finished yet. If it goes ill, the Chinese may blame Charlemagne. I, however, will turn my attention elsewhere. And you don't want to be the object of that attention."

The viscount had the intelligence to pale. "You should be nicer to me, Your Grace," he said, though, his voice fairly steady. "This is only the beginning of our partnership. I hope it continues to be as lucrative."

Without waiting for an answer, he climbed onto the

wagon's seat and clucked at the gray mare harnessed to it. His cousin's coach fell in behind, and he rolled back in the direction of his residence.

"Buffoon," Melbourne muttered at the viscount's vanishing backside.

"Oh, my goodness," Sarala breathed, her heart still racing, "that was marvelous to behold." Before she could think better of it, she flung her arms around Charlemagne's neck.

He lifted her in his arms, kissing her fiercely. "I almost pity that idiot."

"Shay, decorum," Melbourne said mildly, turning to wave a hand toward the nearest stand of trees.

Zachary, then Deverill with slightly more grace, dropped to the ground and came forward. "It went well, I assume?" the youngest Griffin brother asked.

"Better even than we'd thought." The duke eyed Charlemagne. "That was a bit of a risk, wasn't it, calling Yun a bloody savage?"

"He nearly took my head off with that damned sword," he returned, putting a finger just beneath his chin and then looking at it. A drop of blood shone red on the pad of his finger. "I thought it was fair payment." He pulled out his pocket watch. "We'd best get to the warehouse and help Yun load up the silks."

"How much are those vases actually worth?" Sarala asked, transferring her grip to Shay's arm as they headed toward their waiting carriages. She craned her head to look under his chin. It was a small scratch, but considering the speed at which Yun had gone after him, she had a whole new respect for both the swordsman's skill and Shay's nerves.

"This?" With his free hand Charlemagne took the one remaining vase from the duke's grip. "About a shilling, isn't it, Sebastian?"

"Yes, but don't break it. Two dozen of them nearly cleared out the pottery shop. If we need another lot for the warehouse, we may have to ask Caroline to paint them for us."

"You chose nice ones, anyway."

"You had him studying your damned antiquities of China book all night," Zachary broke in, grinning. "What do you expect?"

"Children," Melbourne said, drawing to a halt beside his coach. "As well as it went, please keep in mind that this isn't a game. We have more to do to prepare for tonight, and we cannot afford to make a mistake. It's not only our honor at stake, now. Yun is doing us a great favor. If he's humiliated, then we can assume Emperor Jiaqing has been humiliated, as well."

"Then we have to make certain nothing goes wrong," Charlemagne said in a somber voice. "Yun's not the only one doing me a favor. I owe all of you."

"Nonsense," the duke returned. "Just don't tell Peep we've taken up acting. I am not going to encourage her in that direction." He stepped up into his coach. "I'm off to see Prinny. Let Master Yun know that I'll hopefully have a schedule for him this evening."

Once Sebastian had gone, Zachary and Deverill headed off toward Half Moon Street to help coordinate the removal of the silks from the warehouse. Charlemagne looked down at Sarala. "How are you?" he asked, handing her into the second Griffin coach.

Her maid sat in the corner, half asleep. She could stay that way, as far as Charlemagne was concerned. Once they were married, he and Sarala were going everywhere unchaperoned.

"I think my heart might burst right through my chest,"

she said, her voice a little ragged. "I can't believe everyone is willing to go through this for m—"

"For *us,*" he corrected before she could finish. "I've been thinking."

"About what?"

"I told you that Sebastian wants us to name a wedding date so he can announce it next week."

Green eyes watched him, immediately wary. "Yes. And?"

"And so I think we should set a date. Perhaps the Saturday after."

"Shay! For one thing you told me we could remain betrothed until I decided marriage was what I wanted. For another, that's less than a fortnight from now."

He took her hand, wishing he could simply kiss her until all of her concerns melted away, and hoping it wasn't only his imagination that heard more surprise than reluctance in her voice. "Then the Saturday after that. The point being, Sarala, that I want to marry you. And nothing that happens with DeLayne will change that."

"You shouldn't speak so soon."

He drew her across the coach and onto his lap. "Come now, princess. I'm getting my head chopped off tonight. Show me a little charity, will you?"

She chuckled, running her fingers through his hair and kissing him feather-light on the corner of his mouth. *Good God.* He went hard, and knew from her playful wriggling on his lap that she was quite aware of his state. "A very little charity," she whispered.

"The devil you say." He cupped her cheeks in his hands and kissed her until neither of them could breathe. The maid was mumbling something about propriety and getting sacked, but he ignored it.

"I surrender," Sarala finally gasped, lowering her head to his neck. "You have a great deal of charity."

"Much better." A thought abruptly occurred to him, and he sat straighter. "Do you think DeLayne would go brag to your father about what's happened?"

She lifted her head. "My—I don't—I don't know. He might. Oh, dear. Papa doesn't know anything, but he could still—"

"We'd best go speak with your parents, especially since you're attending the soiree with them tonight."

"Do we have to tell them?" she whispered, her arms tightening around his shoulders. "Papa will be so disappointed in me. And he truly thought John DeLayne was a good friend."

"All the more reason we should tell him the truth." He kissed her cheek. "I would say they don't need to know everything, but if this goes awry, I don't want them hearing the stories for the first time from DeLayne—or from whomever he gossips to about it."

"No. You're right. *I'll* tell them, though. You wait somewhere close by in case I need to flee."

He smiled, feeling the tension in her shoulders. "Agreed," he said. "I won't ever abandon you, you know. Not even if you wear that hideous brown bonnet again."

Sarala chuckled, as he'd intended. It seemed odd that with so much still hanging in the balance, so much could feel right with the world. All he needed, apparently, was to have Sarala in his arms to forget for the moment that he still had several dragons to slay. Of course that was all a part of the plan, according to Peep.

Chapter 21

Charlemagne paced in the Carlisle morning room. They'd arranged everything as well as they could, and all that remained was to wait for the Ellis soiree to begin. Muted shouting from the room across the hall drew his attention once more, and he frowned. Not everything was arranged to his satisfaction.

Every fiber of him bellowed that he shouldn't be waiting elsewhere while Sarala told her parents both that she'd thrown away her virginity five years earlier, and that two families were now being threatened with blackmail because of it. She'd made him promise, though, that he would stay out of the argument. He still didn't like it one damned bit.

After another two minutes, he couldn't stand it any longer. With a curse he shoved open the door, strode past the surprised butler, and barged into the opposite room.

"Lord Hanover, Lady Hanover," he said, taking in their

angry, startled expressions and Sarala's miserable, defiant tears. His heart wrenched. For the devil's sake, two hours ago he'd promised that he would never abandon her.

"I beg your pardon, Shay, but this is a private family matter," the marquis returned stiffly.

"Yes, I know. I wanted to make clear, though, that neither my family nor I have found any fault with Sarala," he said, facing her, looking hard into her eyes. "Just the opposite. She is a remarkable woman," he went on, knowing that he was blathering and afraid that if he stopped, the overbearing, logical part of his mind would point out that he shouldn't even be in the room, much less talking. "She is intelligent and strong and stunningly beautiful, and if she doesn't fit the mold of a perfect London miss I thank God for it. Every day since I met her."

The rest of the room, her parents, seemed to melt away as he held her gaze. She stood halfway across the room from him, but he almost felt as though they were touching.

"She . . . she and I complement one another," he continued more slowly, not having any idea what he was going to say until he heard himself speaking. "We're both logical, and trust our intellect over our imaginations or our hearts. But I'm coming to realize something."

"What might that be?" she asked quietly.

"That love is illogical. It has nothing to do with intelligence or common sense. And I have realized that I would rather love you and have your love than . . . all the silks and all the tea in China. I love you, Sarala. With every ounce of my ignored, undervalued heart."

She walked forward, not stopping until she'd walked into the circle of his arms. "That was a very fine argument," she whispered, lifting her face to look up at him. "I love you."

His blood humming, he kissed her. This was it. This was what he hadn't been able to figure out. And it was so stupidly simple. He loved her, and he didn't need to prove a hypothesis or solve an equation in order to feel that way. Sarala tangled her hands into his lapels, pulling him down to her mouth.

"Ahem," the marquis's low voice came.

Bloody hell. Genuinely startled, Charlemagne lifted his head. "We . . ." He cleared his throat.

"Yes, you're getting married. And it would seem to be a damned good thing, considering that display."

"Oh, be quiet, Howard," the marchioness said, dabbing at her eyes. "That was lovely."

Keeping Sarala close in his arms, Charlemagne took a breath. "I don't know how far you got with the story, but the most important component will take place tonight. DeLayne will be attending the Ellis soiree."

"So will my pistol be, then," Hanover growled, real anger in his voice.

"Sarala has decreed that no one is to be killed," Charlemagne countered. "Unless there is no viable alternative, I'll abide by that."

"What are we to do, then, smile at the bastard?"

"By no means. By now he can't be certain whether you know all that's transpired or not. I'll let you decide how you wish to play that hand. However, what *is* important is that none of us discuss the Chinese or the silks where anyone else can overhear. If directly asked about something by DeLayne in someone else's hearing, humor him. And make it clear that you are humoring him, nothing more."

Hanover nodded. "I understand. I can't believe he would abuse my trust in him like that. I had considered him a close friend." He looked over at his daughter. "I would have treated him with far less . . . tolerance if I'd known all of the facts."

"What's done is done. All that concerns me is making certain that no one believes the stories he tells—or that he's afraid to tell any story at all."

"That blackguard," the marchioness said, picking up her embroidery and roughly putting it aside again. "To seduce a young girl, to pretend to be our friend, to eat our food, and to have no intention but to serve himself no matter the cost to others. I shall never forgive him."

"Nor shall I," Sarala said.

"I think altogether we are an unstoppable force," Charlemagne commented with more enthusiasm than he felt. So many things could still go wrong. "I have a few more things to tend to. I'll see you at seven o'clock, yes?"

Sarala raised up on her toes and kissed him again. "We'll be there."

"And then the game shall begin in earnest."

Sarala practically floated on air as she walked into the Ellis ballroom on her father's arm. All day she'd feared disaster, and then Charlemagne had declared in rather dramatic fashion that he loved her. Even her usually critical mother had said some quite flattering things about Shay's gentlemanly behavior and stunningly handsome appearance. Her father simply shook his head at them, but managed to look grateful that things weren't as bad as they obviously might have been.

Underlying even her surprising happiness, though, was worry; worry that DeLayne would realize what they were up to, worry that Charlemagne would be hurt—or worse—in the course of the evening. It was so strange. Two weeks ago she'd wanted nothing more than to return to a familiar life in India. Now, however, the idea of being anywhere without Shay left her cold and empty.

A warm breeze seemed to lift the hairs on her arms, and she knew he'd arrived before she'd even set eyes on him. Sarala turned to see Shay standing just inside the doorway, where he and Melbourne chatted with Earl and Countess Ellis and their trio of marriageable daughters.

In a moment his gaze found hers, and a soft smile curved his sensuous mouth. The rest of the world might think him calculating and cold and logical, but she certainly knew better.

"He's here," her father said from beside her.

Her own smile deepened. "Yes, I know."

"Not him, goose. *Him.*"

Sarala's expression froze as she looked toward the back of the room. John DeLayne stood behind a pair of footmen, and she couldn't see anything below his head. She held her breath until the servants wandered away. He'd worn it—the red and silver bandolier with its gaudy yellow flower. *Thank God.* Everyone would notice him now; and everyone would want to know the story behind that singular decoration.

"Good evening," a low drawl came from behind her, and her heart flip-flopped.

"Shay," her father said, shaking Charlemagne's hand as she faced him.

"We've arrived just in time to see the show, it seems," he commented, glancing beyond her in DeLayne's direction. "Our tale tonight is that Sebastian had to ask Ellis's indulgence when the viscount appeared; apparently the idiot sent a note begging to be included with our party. Seb turned him down, but there he is, anyway."

"I'm glad you lot have turned out to be our friends rather than our enemies," her father said feelingly.

Shay's gaze returned to Sarala. "So am I. Deverill's wandering over to listen in on DeLayne's conversation. I, for one, am quite interested to know what tale our rat will carry through the assembly." Anger deepened his voice, despite the light words. Whether he referred to all of this as a game or not, he obviously took it very, very seriously.

"All you lack is the actual shining armor, you know," she commented.

Shay visibly shook himself. "There's a suit of it in one of the upstairs sitting rooms at home. Great-great-grandfather Harold Griffin's. Apparently he bashed several deserving people with a mace. I should have worn the lot of it."

"No need. I see it in place, just looking at you."

He took her hand, bringing it slowly to his lips. "It seems, princess, that I shall have to dance with you. You make a fellow feel very heroic."

And he made *her* feel safe, and excited, and loved—as if her life and her reputation didn't still rest in the hands of a scoundrel. When she thought about what DeLayne had nearly destroyed—could still destroy—all for the sake of gaining himself money and admiration, it—

"Don't glare at him like that," Shay cautioned her quietly. "You'll burn a hole through him before I get my chance to shove a hook in his over-large mouth."

"His over-large mouth is very busy at the moment." Lord Deverill and Eleanor joined them, the rest of the family approaching from various places about the room. And there she was, directly in the middle of a Griffin family gathering.

"What's he saying, Valentine?" Melbourne asked.

"Apparently he is responsible both for saving Shay's life and for curtailing an outbreak of hostilities between China and England. The ribbon is an honor from Emperor Jiaqing, making him lord of the Dragon Guard."

"Well, that's better than what we came up with," Zachary muttered.

"But does anyone believe it?" the duke pursued.

"The room's about split down the middle, I think," Deverill continued. "The consensus seems to be that only a madman or an actual participant would wear that ribbon."

"Good," Shay said very quietly.

"Barbara Howsen already approached me to confirm the story," Eleanor said. "I told her that DeLayne met the Carlisle family in India, and has apparently become fixated with making a grand impression in London now that the Carlisles are allied with the Griffins. I implied that he couldn't abide being in an inferior position."

Charlemagne kissed his sister on the cheek. "Brilliant. And nary a lie in the mix."

The duke nodded, pulling out his pocket watch. "Let's continue as we have, then. In . . . forty minutes, Shay will go out onto the balcony for a cigar, and then the rest of us will wait."

With murmurs of good luck the family drifted into the crowd, and Charlemagne slipped an arm about Sarala's waist just as a waltz began to play.

They danced in silence, Sarala enjoying the sensation of being in his arms again and half wishing she hadn't rejected his outlandish suggestion that they marry next Saturday. The idea of waking in his arms every morning intoxicated her—her, who until a few weeks ago had thought a good business agreement the best thing she'd ever known.

"Shay?" she murmured.

"Yes?"

"The first Saturday in July."

His brow furrowed. "What's the first Saturday in July?"

"Besides being four weeks from now, it's our wedding date. You said Melbourne wanted to ann—"

Charlemagne let out a deep, resounding whoop. The sound caused two collisions on the dance floor, and nearly sent Lady Grodin onto her backside. "Apologies," he drawled with a grin as Sarala chuckled. "I seem to be in love."

John DeLayne surreptitiously fluffed the yellow silk rose he wore. Those Chinese fellows were brilliant. Not only had they given him a flattering tale to tell, they'd provided him with the ribbon as proof that he spoke the truth. It was a bit gaudy, but it more than made up for that by catching everyone's attention.

His cousin had actually tried to warn him not to make the Griffins look foolish, but William had no idea just how powerless the Griffins were where he was concerned. Of course he supposed they could have murdered him when he first proposed the partnership, but not any longer—now if anything dire happened to him, everyone would know precisely whom to blame. And he'd made that part of his plan tonight, too; by emphasizing the bit about saving Charlemagne's life he'd made it clear to all and sundry that he'd placed the almighty Griffins in his debt. *His.*

This was much better than marrying that outlandish Sarala, pretty as she was. Let Charlemagne Griffin have her. *He* would now reap the benefits of fucking her long past the time when he would have grown tired of her incessant know-it-all-ness.

He watched as Shay went out to the balcony, without his precious lady. The family had been avoiding him all evening, and he could hardly blame them for that. Still, it couldn't hurt to remind Charlemagne that any injury or alteration of their relationship was now a very poor idea.

Taking a glance first to be certain none of the other Griffins would notice and rush out to outnumber him, he slipped through the open full-length window and out to the balcony. "Good evening, Shay," he said, seeing the middle Griffin brother leaning over the balcony, a cigar between his teeth.

"What do you want?" Charlemagne asked, not bothering even to look at him.

"Just to thank you again for including me in your negotiations. The Chinese should have collected their silks by now."

"I know. That's what worries me."

John frowned. "What worries you?"

"The silks. I might have . . . borrowed a bolt or two. My sisters and Sarala wanted some dress material." He straightened, tapping the cigar out on the stone railing. "Still, I doubt those savages can count to five hundred. I hardly think they'll notice if—"

A shadow streaked out of the darkness behind them to grab Charlemagne around the throat. John stood frozen as a gleaming silver blade pressed into the skin above Griffin's snow white cravat.

"We noticed," Lord Yun's near-silent hiss came.

"John, help me!" Charlemagne wheezed, his air clearly choked off by Yun's bent elbow. His lifted his hands, fingers digging into the swordsman's silk-covered arm.

DeLayne gulped. "Lord Yun, surely there's something that can be done to resolve this little—"

Yun muttered something in Chinese, and the other two he'd seen that morning appeared from the far, dark end of the balcony, swords bare and pointed at him. "Do not interfere, Lord DeLayne. You are fortunate that we heard this thief confess to you. Only your innocence has saved you from suffering the same fate as him."

"For God's sake, John!" Charlemagne rasped. "This isn't—"

The sword flashed. Red spurted into the air. With a choked sigh Charlemagne arched his back, then crumpled forward. Unceremoniously Lord Yun shoved him over the railing and into the dark garden below.

"You—you *killed* him," John stammered, feeling his own blood draining from his face.

"He thought his family name would protect him, the fool." Yun wiped his red-covered blade on a silk handkerchief and sheathed it in his belt again. "Your payment is waiting in the warehouse." He gestured with the bloody cloth, and one of the others backed away, bent down, and reappeared with a vase. "We were going to leave this by your body, but you have again proven yourself an honorable gentleman."

His fingers numb, DeLayne took the vase. "But—"

"Go and tell his family. I want to see his lady weep when she sees his bloody corpse."

"Oh, good *God*," John burst out, and with a shriek turned to run back inside.

Sarala danced with the Duke of Melbourne. She'd never seen him dance at all, much less waltz, but he was quite good at it, if a little rusty.

"DeLayne's gone out," he murmured, his gaze over her head.

Her heart pounded even harder. "How did you know he would?"

"Shay did. He has a rather remarkable ability to understand people and what they will do under given circumstances and in given situations." His gray eyes returned to her. "Which is why I should have trusted his judgment in the first place. I owe you an apology, Sarala."

"For what? For thinking that a girl fresh from India might try to trap a handsome, wealthy young man into marriage?"

"For thinking only that. I am generally more circumspect."

She smiled. "Whatever your first impression, considering all that you've done for me over the past few days, you don't owe me any sort of apology." With a glance at the empty balcony window, she lowered her lashes. "If it makes you feel any better, my mother initially thought I should marry *you*."

He chuckled, another thing she hadn't seen him do very often. "Best laid plans," he said, then stiffened. "Get ready."

A high-pitched shriek came from the direction of the balcony.

Sarala whipped around as John DeLayne ran back into the room, his face gray, and a blue and yellow vase clutched in his hands. For a heartbeat she allowed herself to feel sorry for him, but she quickly overcame that. He'd done it to himself; the Griffins had simply pointed that fact out to him.

"Melbourne!" the viscount yelled, staggering forward as the other guests got out of his way. "For Christ's sake, Melbourne!"

"What is it?" the duke snapped, releasing Sarala to stride forward. "Get hold of yourself, man."

"He's dead!"

Melbourne frowned. "Who's dead? And stop waving that thing about."

"That's my vase!" Lady Ellis cried, sweeping forward to snatch it from the viscount. "It came from my grandmother!"

"It's my vase! They gave it to me!"

"You idiot," Lord Ellis muttered. "Garvey, take the vase somewhere safe."

A footman stepped forward, taking possession of the beautiful porcelain creation. "Yes, my lord."

"No, it's mine!" DeLayne sputtered again. "They were going to kill me, but they killed Charlemagne instead!"

"*What?*" the duke roared, grabbing DeLayne's shoulder and keeping him from tackling the servant.

Sarala shook herself. The play was so engrossing, she'd nearly forgotten it was her turn to step in. "What are you talking about, John?" she asked, hands over her chest.

"The Chinese swordsmen," he gasped, gesturing frantically toward the balcony. "They're out there. They cut his throat, and threw him down into the garden!"

Hopefully not on his head. "My God," she whispered, and sank into a faint.

With splendid timing Zachary caught her under the arms and lifted her upright again. "Steady, Sarala," he soothed, his eyes dancing. "We'll go have a look. I think your friend may be having a bit of fun with us."

"This is not my idea of fun," she snapped, holding her head as Eleanor and Caroline came to her aid. "I've humored you with your little parades and imaginings and claims of heroics, John, but now you're inflicting them on innocent people."

"Ha! You're trying to make me into a fool," he returned, "but I am not a fool! Charlemagne Griffin is lying out in the garden with his throat cut! And those swordsmen are out on the balcony, waiting for us!"

"I've had enough of this," Melbourne growled, and headed for the balcony. Half the ballroom fell in behind him.

Sarala stopped in the window. "There's no one out here, John," she declared. "This is beyond anything. Shameful."

"I am not . . ." Still unsteady on his feet, DeLayne stalked out to the balcony. With almost comic exaggeration he looked around the empty space. "They've gone. No doubt they didn't want to be arrested for murder. But Charlemagne is right down there." He pointed, though he stood well away from the railing.

Melbourne leaned over it, looking down. "There's nothing down there but flowers and shrubbery." He rounded on DeLayne. "You have a great deal to answer for, sir."

The viscount charged the railing, leaning out so far that for a moment Sarala thought he might go over. "But I saw— The blood! There must be blood!"

Someone brought a candelabra out to the balcony, but the stone floor was clean except for a few scattered leaves. By now people had begun whispering and giggling, and the story Eleanor had suggested was spreading faster than ever.

"Let's return inside, shall we?" Melbourne suggested, taking the viscount bodily by the arm. "And I think we've all tolerated enough from you."

DeLayne shrugged free. "If I'm lying, then where is Charlemagne? Where is Lord Charlemagne? You see, he's dead! They must have dragged his body off somewhere!"

Everyone began looking about, muttering. "There he is!" someone shouted.

The crowd surged toward the gaming room door, where Shay emerged, a half-empty glass of claret in his hand. "What the devil is going on?" he asked.

"Shay," Sarala shrieked, and threw herself on him. "Oh, thank goodness. John said some Chinese people had killed you!" As she grabbed his lapel she felt a leaf, and swiftly clenched it in her fist.

"Some what?"

"The—but—I saw—" DeLayne appeared frantic, his eyes wide and darting about.

"I went to find a bottle of champagne," Charlemagne explained, his voice still quizzical. Right on cue, a footman appeared with a bottle. "Ah, there it is. It seems my betrothed has named our wedding date. I wanted to celebrate."

"Oh, Shay," she breathed, not having to pretend her tight hug. "I was so frightened."

Charlemagne faced DeLayne. "Whatever it is you're playing at, it wasn't amusing. I think you owe Lady Sarala, and everyone else here, an apology."

"I will not," the viscount returned, backing away. "I know what you've done. I see it now. It's because you don't want anyone to believe me. Well, I know, and you can't fool me, now." He gestured from himself to Sarala. "I took her to bed, and they don't want anyone to know."

Taking a single step forward, Shay punched him in the jaw. DeLayne dropped like a stone. "Your weak-mindedness is one thing," Shay growled, as the viscount reeled to a sitting position, "but I will not tolerate you insulting Sarala simply because you want attention or admiration or whatever the devil it is you're after. If you mention her name in that tone again, I will kill you."

"Shay," Melbourne said, stepping in front of his brother, and from his expression not quite certain whether Charlemagne was playing or not, "that's enough excitement. We can't fault someone for being weak-minded. We can only pity him."

Lord Ellis and his butler yanked DeLayne to his feet. "You need to go home, Lord DeLayne," their host stated. "And please do not return. This is the most shameful display of self-indulgence I have ever seen."

Lady Ellis batted at the viscount with her reticule. "For shame! You, orchestra! Play another waltz, if you please. Dance, everyone, and we'll simply pretend this never happened."

The rest of them could pretend that if they wanted, but Sarala didn't ever want to forget it. "He said Yun threw you over the balcony," she whispered, wrapping her hand around Shay's sleeve.

"I landed about an inch from a blasted rose bush," he returned in the same low tone, "even with the rope. And then I had chicken blood all over my cravat, and I had to change it. Yun's starting to enjoy this just a little too much—he nearly broke my neck." He gestured at the footman still standing close by. "I think we deserve a bit of champagne now, don't you?"

"Absolutely," she said, smiling at him.

Chapter 22

Charlemagne stood to one side of the splendid white stateroom, Sarala beside him. Closer to the middle of the room Melbourne and Lord Hanover waited at Prince George's side as the Regent chatted with Yun and his companions.

Prinny had been only too happy to sign a proclamation declaring Britain and China friends and allies. Charlemagne wasn't surprised; the Regent was mad for anything in the Oriental style.

"How is your neck?" Yun asked a few minutes later, strolling up to them.

"Better than if you'd actually cut my throat," he returned. "I owe you a great deal, Yun."

The soldier glanced behind him. "When Emperor Jiaqing hears of your Regent's enthusiasm for trade, I believe I shall find myself in a favorable position."

"Good." Charlemagne offered his hand. "If you find yourself in England again, our home is yours."

"And if you ever come to China, I will introduce you to my world." He flashed a grin. "If you are able to keep your head long enough to see."

"I'll do my best."

Sarala stepped forward and kissed the soldier's cheek. "Thank you, Yun."

Melbourne with Hanover joined them to watch Yun and the other two soldiers out the door. "That went well," Sebastian said, clapping Charlemagne on the shoulder. "Prinny's sending a sixty-piece Wedgwood dinner setting back to the emperor as a gesture of friendship."

"And what about Captain Blink?"

"He's to face charges of theft here. A detachment of soldiers was dispatched to collect him from the warehouse where Yun had him stashed. He should be at the Old Bailey by now."

Charlemagne nodded, relieved. "He caused a fair amount of trouble for us, but under the circumstances I'm inclined to forgive him. He gave them my name rather than Sarala's."

"Shay!"

He turned to face Prinny in the far doorway. "Yes, Your Majesty?"

"Invite me to the wedding."

"With pleasure."

"That settles that," Melbourne said, as they all left Carlton House. "There's no chance of elopement for you now."

"Are you certain you want to see us at Westminster Abbey?" Sarala asked, putting a hand on the duke's arm.

He covered her hand with his. "I am certain. Hanover and I are going to White's for luncheon. Where are you off to?"

Charlemagne looked down at Sarala, warmth coursing

through him. "I thought I'd take her about for a bit more sightseeing. And I want a word with Captain Blink, if I can get in to see him."

"Don't be too grateful to him," his brother returned. "He began this mess."

"It ended well enough." Shay lifted Sarala's fingers and kissed them.

She smiled. The sight she most wanted to see was Shay naked again, but she would do her best to be patient. Four more weeks.

Jenny waited for them, and Shay handed them into his coach. "Where are we going, then?" Sarala asked as the coach rolled into the street.

"Since you were only able to view the Egyptian room at the British Museum, I thought you might enjoy seeing the Roman collection there."

"Yes, please," she said with a smile. "But first tell me this: Have you heard anything about DeLayne?"

"Melbourne heard through his cousin that he's making plans to return to India." Gray eyes gazed at her. "You're not sorry for him, are you?"

"No. I just keep thinking that he went from believing he owned the world to being the laughingstock of all of his peers."

"He would have done the same to you."

She sighed. "I know. In a sense, though, it's hardly fair that he gets India."

"And you only get me?"

The wooden panel at Shay's shoulder exploded inward. Sarala shrieked as he tumbled sideways. "Shay!"

He clawed to his feet, kicking the door opened as he straightened. "Wait here," he growled, and launched outside.

She was blasted well not waiting there. Sarala jumped to the ground to the sight of absolute chaos. The coach was stopped in the middle of the street, pedestrians running and yelling and mostly rushing forward to see the tangle of dark suits and greatcoats smashing into one another in front of the bakery. *John DeLayne.*

Charlemagne heaved the viscount to his feet and swung a fist at him. DeLayne blocked the blow, grabbing the lapel of Shay's coat and hurling the two of them through the bakery window. In the confusion of feet as everyone swept forward to get a better view, Sarala saw a pistol. Pushing hard, she made it through the crowd and crouched to grab it. The muzzle was still hot.

DeLayne had actually tried to kill one or both of them. He probably didn't care which. Shaking, she clutched the pistol, lifting it. "Move aside!" she yelled.

More screams erupted as she waved the weapon, but the spectators moved. She pushed the bakery door open with her shoulder and stalked inside. A knife in one hand, John slashed toward Shay. Shay ducked, striking out with a lightning punch that sent DeLayne reeling backward.

"Stop!" Sarala moved closer, aiming the pistol at John. "Don't make me shoot you!"

"You'll have to shoot me!" the viscount sputtered, staggering back to his feet. "You've already ruined me!"

He took a step toward her, and Shay tackled him in the chest, sending the two of them through the wooden counter. With a wrench he grabbed the knife away from the viscount and tossed it aside. "Don't shoot him," he panted, blood streaking down one cheek. "I've been wanting to do this for days."

"I am not going to allow you to beat him to death, Shay," she snapped, worried both by the blood and by the ferocious light in his eyes. For the first time she realized just how tightly he'd been holding himself in check, and how serious Melbourne's warnings for him to mind his temper had been.

"Then what's to keep him from shooting through windows at us again?" Shay demanded, hitting the viscount again. DeLayne sank to his knees, his eyes rolling back in his head.

"What's all this?" A bevy of men in the garb of Bow Street Runners shoved past the bystanders and into the small bakery.

"Thank goodness," she breathed, releasing the spent weapon as one of them grabbed it from her. "That man," she stated, jabbing a finger at the reeling DeLayne, "just tried to kill us."

"I did not!" the viscount mumbled through bloody teeth. "He attacked me!"

"There's a hole in my carriage, and one in my shoulder," Shay retorted, taking a step back only when two men grabbed his arms and hauled him that way. "He's been running mad for days. Last night at a soiree he was practically frothing at the mouth. I want him arrested."

"And who are you, sir?"

"Charlemagne Griffin," he answered promptly. "That's Viscount DeLayne."

"The one with the Chinese swordsmen story?" someone from outside the shop called. "I heard he'd been sent to Bedlam."

The Runners released Shay as soon as he said his name. "We'll take him to the Old Bailey, my lord," their captain said. "I take it you're willing to press charges?"

"Absolutely."

With DeLayne still shouting his innocence, the Bow

Street Runners dragged him out of the shop. As soon as the way to him was clear, Sarala rushed Shay. "You were shot? Why didn't you say anything?" She yanked him around, searching his shoulder. "You might have been killed!"

"So might you have been," he returned, wincing. "It's just a graze. But we'll settle this in a moment." Shaking her off, he walked to the corner of the shop where she finally noticed the poor baker still cowering, a sack of flour in his arms. "Will twenty quid pay for the damage?" he asked, still breathing hard.

"Y . . . yes, my lord."

Nodding, Shay counted out the money and set it on the counter. "My apologies, sir. And my thanks for helping to catch an attempted murderer."

Shay took Sarala's hand as they picked their way through the wreckage at the front of the shop. He staggered a little, and her heart stopped. Good heavens, how badly had he been hurt? "We have to get you to a physician," she said, helping him to the coach.

"I'll be fine."

"You can barely stand."

"He kicked me in my damned knee. No physicians."

"Shay, you can't—"

"My home is right around the corner. Oswald can patch me up."

She half shoved him into the coach, and followed behind him. "To Gaston House," she ordered the driver, pulling the door closed. "Now take off your coat. Jenny, help us."

The maid scooted forward to help Shay shrug out of his dirty, torn coat. His left shoulder was bloody, and she gasped. "Shay, why didn't you—"

"He might have shot you instead of me," Charlemagne

growled, pulling her forward and kissing her fiercely. "You should have let me kill him."

"I just didn't want you to be hurt," she said, a tear running down her face.

"Losing you would hurt much more than this." He backed off a little, running a finger along her cheek. "Melbourne's not going to be happy, though. I wrecked a bakery."

A laugh escaped her throat despite herself. "You paid for the damage." She pulled out her handkerchief and wrapped it tightly around his upper arm. "But how will you testify against DeLayne? What if someone asks you about the Chinese soldiers? They were real, you know."

"I don't think it'll come to that," he returned, wiping blood from his cheek with the back of his hand. "I wanted him locked away from us, but I think if I offer him the choice between prison and a permanent residence in India, he'll take the latter. I'm even willing to sweeten the pot, if necessary, to keep him away from us."

"That's probably what he wanted."

"Then he's lucky you stopped me from killing him." He said it lightly, but she heard the steel in his voice. He would have killed DeLayne. She wondered if the viscount had any idea just how lucky he *had* been.

Sooner than she expected, the coach rolled to a stop. "Jenny, fetch Mr. Oswald," she instructed, unwilling to leave Charlemagne's side.

Jenny bolted out the door, and a moment later a large, broad butler in livery appeared in the coach doorway. "You've taken hurt, my lord?" he rumbled.

"A scratch. But I've learned never to dissuade a woman who wants to coddle me."

Despite the words, he staggered a little as she and Oswald

helped him to the ground and up to the door. For a brief moment Sarala stopped on the front steps, looking up. Gaston House resembled most of the wealthier town houses, fairly narrow but at least three stories tall, two dozen windows overlooking Piccadilly and the park beyond, the front a freshly painted white.

"Where's your bedchamber?" she asked as they continued inside, pulling his wounded arm over her shoulder.

He hesitated. "The morning room's fine," he said, angling them toward the nearest doorway.

"No. You need to lie down."

"It's upstairs, first door on the right, my lady," Oswald contributed.

"Very good. Will you fetch some water and bandages?"

"Right away, my lady."

On the landing, Charlemagne pulled her into a close embrace. "You're rather wonderful, you know?" he murmured, kissing her softly. "Jenny, wait downstairs."

The maid dipped a curtsy. "Very good, my lord."

As they climbed to the first floor, Sarala looked about them. Scattered on the walls and on the tables along the upstairs hall she saw a sampling of some of Charlemagne's antiques and artifacts. He had exquisite taste; she looked forward to exploring.

The door Oswald had indicated was closed. She reached out to push the latch, but Shay blocked her arm. "It's not ready," he said abruptly.

"What? I don't care if your bed's unmade, Shay."

"No, it's not—"

She pushed open the door and walked inside. And stopped dead.

Yellow and gold silk curtained the windows and great swaths of the walls, with pillows and throws draped across the bed and the floor. The bed itself was deep green and gold silk shimmering with gold threads. All the furniture was deep red-brown burnished mahogany, rich and gold-tinged with age and care.

"Oh, Shay," she breathed.

"I still need a few more pieces. I wanted to surprise you."

"I'm surprised," she said shakily. "It's lovely. You did this for me?"

"Of course I did. I know you miss India, and I thought—"

She grabbed his waistcoat and yanked him forward, covering his mouth with hot, deep kisses. "I love you," she murmured.

"I love you," he returned, reaching back behind him to close the door. "I want you to be happy here."

Oswald scratched at the door. "My lord? The—"

Reluctantly Sarala broke free and opened the door, taking the water bowl and cloths and then closing it again before she set the things aside. Apparently she would see Shay naked again sooner than she'd expected. Slowly she approached him and pulled his shirt free from his breeches.

"*Mai khush hu. Mai tum pyar karne*," she said unsteadily, as his hands slid around her waist and his mouth dipped to her throat. "I am happy. I love you."